To Sakara

with love

My Sister's Pain

My Sister's Pain

Emeka Egbuonu

Knowledge Bidders

© Copyright 2017 by Emeka Egbuonu

Emeka Egbuonu asserts the moral right to be identified as the author of this work. A catalogue record for this boo is available from the British Library.

Cover Art – Azaria & Zalika Ledeatte-Williams – *www.aminajohn.com*
Cover Design – Mike Keeling-Smith Artillery Design Company
Book Design – James Robinson – *www.wordzworth.com*

ISBN: 978-0-9569810-4-2

For information contact; address *www.emekaegbuonu.com*

This book is dedicated to
Nnenna, Onyinye, Summer & Chinenye
And to all my Sisters out there
Stand Strong – Stand Together

Contents

Chapter One

HIGH-PITCHED SHOUTING PENETRATED the walls of a beautiful semi-detached house and came tumbling out onto the unexpectant street. Pedestrians, arrested by the noise, were momen-tarily paralysed, ears pricked in intrigue; but since attempts to decipher the source of anguish were futile, they moved on with their journeys. An elderly local resident, clutching her dog's lead, looked intently at the window while her small brown Yorkshire terrier impatiently hovered about her ankles. She was jolted out of her curiosity by shrill barks and a pull on her wrist. Smiling at her companion, she continued their routine daily walk.

The house stood in a perfect row of well-kept houses in beautifully landscaped front gardens with driveways boasting the latest-model cars. Although usually a genteel and tranquil neighbourhood, this incident had all the neighbours twitching their curtains and calling their spouses as they attempted to play detective. Shock was the general response, especially when they realised that the noise was coming from number 22. The Edozie family had a well-known reputation for being polite and private, so this change in behaviour – the airing of dirty laundry – was unheard of.

The echo of slamming doors vibrated over the tightly-curled kinks of Adaora's afro as she stomped out of the house, fuming. Her usually smooth skin was creased into a frown, and she breathed heavily. Her feet purposefully pounded in the direction of her car.

She barely heard her name being called by the man next door as he raised himself from sloshing soapy water over his Mercedes alloys.

An echo chased her: 'ADA!' but she refused to turn, recognising the sound of her sister's voice. Rummaging in her jeans pockets for her car keys, she had scarcely opened the driver's door before Nkechi was behind her, concerned and slightly out of breath.

'Ada, please do not let it get to you.'

A sigh filled the space between them as Adaora looked into her sister's eyes, noticing the worry across her forehead.

'I don't want to talk about it!'

'But…'

'NO! Honestly, standing here discussing it will not change a thing. I've let it go,' Adaora replied firmly.

Nkechi knew there would be no budging her now. Placing her arm around her sister's waist, she squeezed her gently. 'Ok. I'm sorry. Let's forget I said anything. Are you still coming tonight?'

'Perhaps. I haven't made my mind up yet. I need to go home first.'

'Oh, come on, sis! When's the last time you did something fun?'

Adaora rolled her eyes. 'I do have a social life you know!'

'Yeah, yeah, yeah,' Nkechi teased. 'It'll be a new experience. Who knows? You might even like it!'

Adaora was still far from convinced. Nkechi saw the look and continued her persuasion. 'You don't even need to pay. I put you down on the guest list and I'll be there as well. If you hate it, we'll cut our losses and leave – go see that film you wanted?'

Her sister was persistent and Adaora knew it. 'OK, ok. I'll go.'

'Not like that, I hope?' she laughed, her beautiful dimples evident.

'Look, you! Cheeky! I was intending to go home and change!' she retorted, a smile blossoming on her cheeks.

'Perfect. I'll come with you, help you choose an outfit. Wait for me. I need to grab my bag.'

Adaora, reflecting on their relationship, watched Nkechi's 5ft 9 frame effortlessly glide back to the house. From a young age, they'd had such a close bond that people often asked them if they were twins. Telepathic, she always knew when Nkechi was in pain and she knew the feeling was mutual. She appreciated their close relationship. Especially today. Without her sister racing after her and calming her down, who knew what she would be thinking or feeling?

As Nkechi bounded out of the front door for the second time, bag hanging from her arm, she saw her neighbour waxing the bonnet of his car and smiled at him. He called her over.

'Is everything okay, dear? I heard shouting. Tried to ask your sister but I don't think she heard me,' he began.

'Oh, did we disturb you? I'm sorry. Everything is fine, thank you for asking. The car looks gorgeous!'

'My pride and joy,' he replied, smiling, as Nkechi hot-footed to her sister's car.

Sitting back in the passenger seat, Nkechi laughed with her sister as they journeyed to Chadwell Heath. Messing about with

3

the radio and doing her best karaoke impressions, Nkechi filled the car with joy and music. Thirty minutes of Nkechi solos later, they pulled up at Adaora's one bedroom flat. Corporate-looking, it stood in direct contrast to local architecture, an imposing new-build with polished lines and fresh paint. Various plants and animal art were dotted along their walk to the elevator; it resembled a high-end doctor's waiting room. The staidness of the public decor had prompted Adaora to infuse her rooms with bold colours and prints.

Prising the apartment door open, they were hit by a wave of humidity that had been trapped inside. Running to the thermostat, Adaora switched off the heating, while Nkechi stripped off her jacket and made herself at home. She adored her sister's flat: the quaintness of the rooms with snapshots of their childhood and adult achievements proudly framed on the lilac-painted wall. The pictures flooded Nkechi with nostalgia as she wandered around reminiscing, smiling, shaking her head in amusement. Adaora was such a keeper of memories. As a child, she had made a scrapbook, filling it with keepsakes, ticket stubs and photos; her camera permanently swinging from her neck. Nkechi had been her prime model, while she practised her angles and techniques. The result was a glorious testament to their life. Above the sofa, four pictures of Adaora confidently hung: graduation pictures - her smiling image encased by a cap and gown, her hands clutching her reward.

Nkechi poked her head around the corner and shouted, 'Look how young Chidi looked at your first graduation! He looks too cute.'

'I know! Can you believe it was almost a decade ago?'

'Now he thinks he is Mr know-it-all! He must have been, like, nine in this picture.'

Adaora came out of her bedroom, wearing a tight pair of denim jeans that hugged her thighs and a loose cream top with one side hanging off her shoulder.

'Oooh! I love that top!' Nkechi said excitedly. 'It brings out your complexion.'

'Yes, I know you love it!' Adaora laughed. 'I'm sure I caught you trying to sneak it out of my wardrobe, the other day.'

'Younger sister's privileges,' Nkechi replied. 'Where's that blue and cream necklace you have? It'll go well with that.'

Adaora disappeared into her bedroom, scanning the room for her jewellery case. She returned, holding the necklace. 'This one?'

'Yeah.' Nkechi took it from her sister and began to place it around her neck.

Ada was slightly shorter than her sister, at five foot seven, with a slim frame and pale brown complexion, lighter than Nkechi. She had more of her mum's genes, whereas Nkechi took after their dad, who was a darker shade of brown. Not many would assume that they were sisters.

'How is my hair? Is this too much?'

'Relax, sis, you look gorgeous! I'm loving this afro look you have going on. It really suits you.'

Adaora picked up her jacket and keys, managing to get one more glance in the mirror before they left. Plumping her lips and raising her eyebrows, she caught her sister's eyes in the glass. 'I can't believe I let you talk me into this.'

Nkechi smiled at her. 'Look, it will be fine. Don't think about it too much. I just want you to go out and have a bit of fun. Speed-dating is something different. You've never done it before.'

'I guess I would have been more comfortable if you were doing it as well, but I don't think Patrick would be too happy with that.'

Nkechi laughed. 'Yeah. I don't think Patrick would be impressed at all, but I'll still be there. *Trust me!* It will be fine. My friend, Gloria, is one of the organisers, and it will be only professional people, getting together and having fun.'

Parking had been an issue: the joys of central London events. After circling the area for ten minutes, Ada was sure the universe was instructing her to go home. Just as she had decided to give up, a white van pulled out of a space and Nkechi breathed a sigh of relief. Walking towards the venue, Adaora's stomach began to churn, her palms clammy and knees wobbling slightly. Her conversational skills dried up and Nkechi stepped in quickly to reassure her.

'Mint Leaf Lounge,' the swanky sign vaunted. As they approached the door, two muscular men dressed in expensive suits greeted them and Adaora's nerves began to settle. The room was perfectly symmetrical and she was impressed by the floor-to-wall mirrors, shimmering chandeliers, leather furniture and luxurious wallpaper. Mood lighting and soft jazz instrumentals complemented the room; wine glasses and roses lay on each table. Ada assumed the interior designer was a woman. As she inhaled the ambience, Nkechi grabbed one of the event organisers.

'Mark, this is my sister Ada. I told you I would bring someone with me.'

Mark leaned over and gave Adaora a kiss on the cheek, all charm and aftershave. 'Nice to meet you,' he whispered into her skin.

'Likewise. This venue is beautiful.'

'Yeah, we struck gold with this one. Definitely one of the best in London. Glad you approve.' He smiled, showing off perfectly white teeth.

'My sister tried her best to explain how tonight will work, but could you please fill me in, if you don't mind?' she asked sweetly.

'That is fine. Well, it's pretty simple, really. We have twenty women and twenty men signed up. Each woman will be allocated her own table with a number, while the men will move around the room. Three minutes is all you have, to make an impression before the next suitor arrives. Make a note of the guys who get your attention. There'll be a break halfway through, and at the end, you can exchange numbers with the guy you like, if any. That's it.'

Nkechi shook her head. 'Ada, that is pretty much the same thing I told you.'

'Mark was much clearer in his description.'

Nkechi rolled her eyes.

'Well, I hope you enjoy the event and I look forward to your feedback,' Mark said, before he walked away.

The room soon blossomed with the anxious beauty of excited women, each table occupied in anticipation, the walls throbbing with expectancy. It was about to start. Adaora took in the atmosphere, eyes darting around, absorbing her surroundings and assessing her rivals. They were all gorgeous: dressed with class, oozing sex appeal; from a variety of cultural backgrounds, although she witnessed more magical melanin glowing in the dim light. Tingles, goose-pimples and butterflies were present as the doors swung open and the men, who had been locked away up to this point, were ushered to the women's tables. An army in smart suits with fresh trims marched with purpose, leaving trails of cologne as they took their seats.

Checking her afro with her right hand, Adaora held her breath. Fondling her wine glass but attempting to keep her fidget to a minimum, she raised the glass to her lips and sipped carefully.

She felt his presence, smiling. Her gaze met his greyish-blue eyes, after skimming over his tanned skin and clean-shaven face as she stood to greet him. His lips connected with her cheek and he tucked her chair in for her, before sliding in the seat opposite. Moments passed between them, the silence yawning into awkwardness. Adaora's fingers returned to her wine glass as she waited impatiently for him to say something; anything. Picking up on her body language, he smiled.

'I'm so sorry. I am being rude, but I am frankly struck by your beauty,' he started, his eyes penetrating.

She shuffled uncomfortably. 'Thank you,' she began. 'But I didn't even get your name yet.'

'Apologies. My name is Francis.'

'Hi Francis. I'm Adaora.'

'That is a very beautiful name. Where is it from?'

'It's a Nigerian name. It means daughter of all.'

'That's really nice: a name with a meaning. Well, Francis is just Francis, I think. Nothing special, there.'

Adaora smiled at him and shook her head.

Francis saw her expression through the glass of brandy and ice he was drinking. 'What?'

'I think I know more about your name than you do!'

'Oh, do you, now? Please enlighten me.'

'Well, it's a form of the late Latin name, "Franciscus", which meant "Frenchman". This name was borne by the 13th-century *saint*, Francis of Assisi, who was originally named Giovanni but was given the nickname "Francesco" by his father, an admirer of the French. Francis went on to renounce his father's wealth and devote his life to the poor, founding the Franciscan order of friars.'

Eyes wide, mouth open, Francis collected all the information spilling from Ada's lips. 'How the hell do you know all that?'

'You didn't let me finish!' she scolded, before continuing. 'Due to the renown of the saint, this name became widespread in Western Europe during the Middle Ages. However, it was not regularly used in Britain until the 16th century.'

'Ok. Now you are just showing off! Seriously, how do you even know that?'

'I have a love for knowledge. History, especially. There is so much to be learnt about our present state, from understanding what has gone before. My nose is always buried in a book. I get lost in words. I guess I just have a fountain of information and your name happened to be amongst that.'

'Well, thank you! I have no excuse to not know the meaning of my name after that lesson,' he laughed. 'I'm almost embarrassed.'

'Don't be. It's just the geek in me. I don't think you will be getting that from any of the other ladies in here.' She glanced over at the clock in the corner. 'We probably do not have much time left, so tell me more about you.'

After a rocky start, Adaora started to relax and used the three minutes to her advantage. In between sips of wine, general knowledge questions and laughter, Adaora began to loosen up and enjoy herself. There was no need to fear. The men who sat at her table were in awe of her beauty and intelligence as she kept them on their toes with her witty responses. She had grasped the attention of the whole room, her smile shimmering, her laugh endearing.

Women at other tables noticed their partners' eyes often wandered in Adaora's direction, especially when she stood; captivated by her curvaceous body's delightful assets.

Before she knew, it was time for the interval. The men were quickly separated, to prevent further interaction and the room buzzed with conversation and soft jazz. Adaora scanned the room looking for Nkechi. After weaving in and out of the crowd, she eventually found her at the main entrance, talking to a handsome young man, no older than 21. She was letting him down gently. Adaora laughed at his audaciousness.

'Could you believe that small boy was trying to ask for my number?' she asked and then gave Ada a hopeful look. 'Anyway, how are you finding it?'

Unable to conceal her excitement, Adaora burst into a wide grin. 'I'm actually having a great time, sis! Way better than I expected.'

'YES!' Nkechi squealed triumphantly. 'I told you! Didn't I tell you? Soooo – tell me! Who's taking your fancy?'

Before she could respond, they were interrupted by a loud announcement on the tannoy instructing all the women to return to their seats for the second half of the event.

'Look, I'd better get back. I'll fill you in later.'

Sitting back in her seat, Adaora watched as the men came filing through the room once more. She took notice this time, checking off the men she had already spoken to, wondering what was in store for the second half. As she went to fill her wine glass, she realised that the bottle was empty. Ready to signal a host, she noticed ushers already replacing bottles on tables and relaxed. Nkechi would have to drive home, she thought, daydreaming about her level of intoxication and giggling to herself.

The vision of a man approaching snapped her out of her thoughts and slammed her back into reality. His athletic build, toned arms and washboard abs were bursting to be noticed through his fitted, grey V-neck jumper. She subconsciously licked her lips before standing, seductively.

Smiling, she kissed his cheek, lingering ever so slightly while noting that he passed her height requirement, too. Taller than her, even with her six-inch heels. Their eyes locked across the table.

'My name is Henry Ofori – and you are?'

'Adaora Edozie'

'Nigerian, I take it.'

'Yes. I take it you are from Ghana?'

'Yeah!" His frank, smiling face looked surprised. 'How could you tell?'

'Your surname.'

'Oh, I see,' he chuckled. 'It does give it away, doesn't it?'

Adaora looked steadily at Henry before offering him some of her wine.

He kindly declined and ordered a beer instead, continuing: 'So, tell me more about yourself…'

'Well, I am a Psychotherapist and have just received my doctorate in Clinical Psychology.'

Henry's eyes widened in apparent delight. 'That is impressive! I do *love* my sisters who are well educated. What type of therapy do you specialise in?'

'I am a CBT therapist at the moment.'

'CBT? What does that stand for?'

'Cognitive-behavioural therapy.' He still looked blank, so she continued. 'It is all about changing the negative thought processes we all have. It's a mainly therapeutic modality, with particular strengths in family therapy, mindfulness-based interventions, neuropsychology and clinical health psychology.'

'Impressive, I must say. Wow! Congratulations on becoming a doctor! All that hard work must have paid off.' He glanced at her quizzically. 'You look so young! How old are you? If you don't mind me asking…'

Adaora chuckled. 'Seriously, Henry, didn't anyone ever tell you never to ask a lady her age?'

'Well, I knew that was coming!' he laughed. 'Can't blame me for trying.'

'I'm only messing with you. I'm 29. I'll be thirty this year.'

'That's amazing. Such great achievements – and before you are 30!'

'Thank you,' Ada felt herself almost blush. 'But that's enough about me. What do you do?'

'I am a businessman. I own my own cleaning company. My day to day is all about securing new clients and making sure that my employees are happy.'

'Mr Entrepreneur!'

'Yeah, that's me. I've always wanted to run my own business and I'm loving every minute of it.' He grinned, his eyes twinkling.

The three minutes weren't long enough. They had only momentarily whetted their appetite for each other. While they spoke, the room disappeared, and Adaora's attention was solely on Henry, her cheeks aching in a constant smile.

She met other men; she talked and engaged with them, but her mind was elsewhere. Henry moved from table to table, his eyes always returning to number 12, watching and admiring her from across the room. At the end of the event, they were only interested in each other. Disappointment ricocheted through the egos of many handsome bachelors who had waited hopefully for Adaora's contact.

As Henry and Adaora exchanged numbers, knowing that they each felt the same way, the chemistry between them sizzled and Adaora's joy increased. She knew she had chosen well and was excited about what the future held.

The venue emptied and Adaora waited as Nkechi helped to clean up. Finally, they were alone and could indulge in sisterly chat.

'Your smile has been getting bigger and bigger all night, sis,' Nkechi teased.

'I know. It's just… there was something different about him.'

'Well, I hate to boast… but when I'm right, I'm right, eh?'

'Yeah, yeah, Chi. I'm not going to lie; it was a great evening and I'm so glad I came.'

'Seems like you disappointed a lot of brothers tonight, as well, Ada. My sister: the catch!'

They both burst out laughing, as Adaora navigated the London streets to drop Nkechi home.

'He just checked a lot of boxes you know?'

'And you have plenty, plenty, boxes Ada – so he must be doing something right!'

'One thing: I didn't feel like he was intimidated by my job or my education and that's hard to find, these days.'

Nkechi smiled and planted a big kiss on her sister's cheek as she released her seatbelt and rummaged for her keys. 'You deserve to be happy sis. Keep me updated!'

'I will. Love you!'

The morning broke, wretchedly. Mondays – the beginning of a working week and the start of the dreaded commute. Yawning and flinging the curtains open, Nkechi grimaced at the unimpressed sky. She was late. Her outfit was hanging outside her wardrobe, freshly pressed and ready as she dragged herself into the shower.

Submerged in the steaming heat of the water, Nkechi began her karaoke routine, holding the shower gel like a personal microphone. Enjoying herself, she returned to the bedroom, turning up the music on her stereo as she primped herself in front of the floor-length mirror. Shoving her feet into heels, she had a few mouthfuls of toast and tea before leaving the house. Nothing had changed. The streets were dressed in a landscape of déjà vu: familiar and predictable.

She turned to see Exhibit One – Ms Pritchard from number 28, dog lead in one hand, cigarette in the other, taking her morning stroll. At the bus stop, Exhibit Two – the twin brothers who reminded her of Chuckie Finster from the Rugrats: all ginger tousled hair and freckled faces, poorly fitting clothes and misshapen shoes. Although they looked unkempt, they were always smiling. Today, their dirty fingernails gripped copies of 'Of Mice and Men'. A classic, Nkechi thought, as they piled on the screeching bus.

Her favourite seat was free. She sat five rows back, on the right, against the window, sightseeing. The skyline boasted change: skyscrapers, cranes and scaffolding. New builds meant new residents, while current residents watched regeneration infiltrate their communities. Even Premier Inn had wormed its way into Dalston Junction. Nkechi shook her head in disbelief.

Sashaying from the bus, Nkechi made her way through the staff entrance of Cardinal Pole Secondary school. Already, the street was packed with charcoal grey blazers with faint red stripes, neatly knotted grey ties decorated with the repetitive pattern of red crosses: it was a Catholic school, after all. And most were wearing the favourite footwear of this generation: black Kickers.

This had been Nkechi's home for the last two years. Twice, she had watched the youngest pupils grow and mature while new, anxious Year 6s took their places each September. It was a place of transition and change. They had just moved into new premises and Nkechi relished the opportunity to decorate her new classroom. Sidestepping the staffroom, she waltzed into her office, with barely enough time to check her emails before the bell went for first period.

A favourite amongst the students, she stopped a few times before reaching her classroom, greeting youngsters. Her class was lined up neatly outside her room; they knew the drill by now – respect was mandatory, and Nkechi did not tolerate rudeness or insubordination. She ushered them in quickly, preparing her table and placing the lesson plan aside while they took off their coats and got seated.

'Good morning, class.'

'Good Morning, Miss Edozie!' the unanimous chorus replied.

'It's good to see you all, fresh faced and ready to learn. I trust you all had a good break. Now, we have a short 5-week term before the Easter break, so we have a lot of work to do…'

Creaking open, the door revealed an untidy student creeping in, eyes fixed on the floor. No blazer: he was in his shirt-sleeves, and his tie was hanging loose and untied around his open collar.

'Sorry I'm late, Miss,' he said.

'Alex! Why are you late, and where is the rest of your uniform?'

'Come on Miss… Why are you always getting onto me?' he grumbled, his eyes twinkling to show that he wasn't serious. 'It's Monday morning and I'm tired.'

'You've had a whole week off! You should be raring to go. So, see me after this lesson. Hurry up and sit down. Thank you.'

Alex sat down, tucking his crumpled shirt into his trousers and knotting his tie, a cheeky smile plastered across his face. 'Miss, I like your new hairstyle by the way. The twists look good on you. It brings out the dimples on your face even more. Very nice!'

The whole class erupted in laughter. Typical Alex – always the charmer. Even Nkechi chuckled.

'Listen to me, Mr Smooth Charmer. Your lyrics won't work on me. You still have detention. So, I will see you afterwards.' She turned back to the class. 'As I was saying, before Alex came in and distracted us all, we have a lot of work to do for the next few modules. Please bring out your Business Studies book, the Edexcel 2011 edition by Rob Jones.'

The day proved to be long and tiring for Nkechi: back-to-back lessons, books to mark, staff meetings, plus covering detention. By the end of the day she was completely exhausted. As was her bad habit, she hadn't taken a proper lunch break and her stomach was communicating multilingual complaints.

Once she reached her house, the waft of generational perfection hijacked her senses: herbs and spices, secret recipes, tantalising flavours – mum was cooking and Nkechi's body rejoiced at the prospect of digesting the finest food of her heritage. The benefits of living with your parents: heaven on a plate.

'Nkechi?' Her mum yelled '*ọ bụ gi?*'

'Yes, mum, it's me. I'm back. What are you cooking?'

16

Nkechi's mum appeared from the kitchen, wiping the steam from her glasses, her arms outstretched in greeting. 'My dear, I am making fried yam and egg stew with plantain.'

Nkechi collapsed into her mother's arms, exhaling in pleasure. 'See mummy, this is why I love you. I don't think I will ever want to move out. I know Adaora is suffering when it comes to cooking.'

'*Cheregodi*? Excuse me?' Her mum gave her a stern look. 'You will move out one day, when your husband comes knocking in Jesus' name.'

Nkechi laughed. 'Amen.'

Nkechi's mum removed her colourful printed headscarf, wiping her brow before heading back into the kitchen. She had left the styles she used to sport in the past: long braids, weaves and wigs. She now embraced her natural curl, sporting a low maintenance cut, speckled with whispers of grey. It was beautiful, and she felt liberated.

'So, my dear, how was work today?'

'Mum, to be honest, I am so tired. These students can really tire you out. The first day back is always intense. What makes is worse is that I've already received notification of my lesson observation.'

'They do not waste any time at your school, do they? Observations again! Didn't you have one before Christmas?'

'Yes, I did, but the school is outstanding, so they want to ensure that we maintain that standard,' Nkechi shook her head. 'The reason I am so tired is because I have started planning my lessons already.'

'It is always good to plan ahead, my dear,' Mrs Edozie said, stirring one of the pots. She saw Nkechi peering into it, curiously. 'Don't worry. The food will soon be ready. So, what have you prepared so far?'

'My scheme of work is already done. I just need to do a few different lesson plans, to make sure there is differentiation in all the lessons. Then make sure I can show student progress, through formative and summative assessments.'

'So much to do. Although you know what you signed up for when you became a teacher.' Mrs Edozie shrugged. 'They do not rank second in the stress league table for no reason, my dear.'

'Yes, I know, mum. I am not complaining. I love the classroom part of my job, interacting with the young people and making a difference that way. It's just all the tedious paperwork that I can't stand,' she murmured, clearing the dining table.

The dining area was the heartbeat of the house: full of life and passion, with love dished out for the whole family. Her mum loved to host, to cook and to enjoy the social togetherness of breaking bread.

After refuelling her soul, Nkechi retreated to her room; lying on her queen-size bed amongst a pile of pillows, cushions and paperwork. During the middle of her focus on marking, her phone rang.

'Hi, beautiful!' It was her long-term boyfriend, Patrick.

'Hi, Pat. How are you?'

'I'm good. Just thinking about you. How was work?'

'Same old. Work, work and more work! I'm just in the middle of marking, actually.' She shifted her position, setting her red pen down on the open exercise book.

'You work so hard, babe. Sometimes you need to relax!'

Nkechi snorted. 'You can talk, Mr Lawyer! You work harder than me!' She paused, then added, 'It's one of the things I love about you – your work ethic. It inspires me.'

'Ok. You got me! I always had to work hard, though. I didn't want to be in debt. So, all those hours at Sainsbury's, dealing with annoying customers to pay off my Uni fees – it's all worth it now.'

'Yeah. My mum loves you. She can boast to all her friends about her daughter with the lawyer boyfriend.' Nkechi grinned to herself.

'Hahaha. Got to keep Aunty sweet. Well, I don't want to distract you babe; I'm just calling you to tell you to keep Saturday evening free. I've got a surprise for you.'

Nkechi sat up, alert. 'What is it?'

'Come on Chi. You're a teacher now… you know what 'surprise' means!'

Nkechi laughed. 'Ok, Maestro. At least tell me what I need to wear!'

'Just look your usual sexy self. I'll call you tomorrow.'

'Ok, babe. Love you.'

The week was repetitive but Nkechi was holding out for the weekend and the surprise that awaited her. They had been dating for five years now and Patrick wasn't always the romantic type; although he could pull out the stops when he wanted to. So, this had Nkechi even more intrigued.

On Saturday evening she beautified herself, slipping into a sexy, red figure-hugging dress and pulling her twists up into a high bun. A dash of red lipstick and a spray of perfume and she was ready.

Patrick arrived outside Nkechi's house dressed up in blue chinos, brown boots, a thin beige jumper and a grey trench-coat. He checked his reflection in the window before climbing the steps and ringing the bell. As the door swung open and he saw his girlfriend, he gasped and almost lost his footing. There was a brief moment of silence as he stared at her before he shook his head in disbelief.

'Babe, your beauty always catches me by surprise! The way the light reflects off each curve, your eyes sparkle in the moonlight. Aiiiiiii! It's like you age with more beauty.'

'Awww, baby!' she blushed. 'Thanks. You look good.'

'Is that all I get? I pretty much just gave you a poem that would give William Blake a run for his money!'

'I'm just joking, babe,' she laughed. 'You look handsome. I love it when you get that low cut. Your moustache and goatee look sharp, as well.'

'Not exactly poetry, but I'll take it.'

They laughed as Nkechi stepped forward into his arms and kissed him. She walked in front of him to the car, while he watched her body and tried to keep himself from rising to the occasion.

They drove to a small Thai restaurant, next to a pier by London Bridge.

'Oh, Pat!' Nkechi gasped, in recognition.

It was atmospheric, as if they had stepped into another world: the decor, the ambience, the aromas, complemented by the sweet sound of bells and strings. A petite female staff member greeted them, placing her palms together before her chest and bowing, before showing them to their seats at a candlelit table in the corner of the restaurant. Patrick stood behind Nkechi, taking her coat and pulling out her chair.

'I can't believe this place hasn't changed at all!' Nkechi held Patrick's hand across the table.

'No, it hasn't,' Patrick replied, looking at the artwork of the red dragon on the wall next to them. Nkechi's gaze followed his as they both looked at the art, soft Thai instrumental music playing the background.

'You brought me here on our first date! We used to come here all the time.'

'Yes, it's been three years since we were last here. I just thought it would be nice to come back to where it all started.'

'Yes, it is. I am just getting flashbacks of our time here.' Nkechi squeezed his hand.

'Likewise. I guess we should order. Let's get our usual.'

Nkechi nodded and smiled at him. Patrick raised his hand to get the attention of the waitress. She came over and took their order.

The portions of food served were enough for four people; bright and colourful dishes were presented to them. Midway through their dinner, the background music stopped, and two elderly men approached Patrick and Nkechi's table, both with green round lanterns on their heads. One had a small flute with him, and the other had a three-stringed fiddle. They each stood on either side of Nkechi and started playing their instruments. Patrick took a hold of Nkechi's hand. Her eyes lit up and she played with her hair; the more she smiled, the bigger her dimples became.

Patrick looked her dead in the eye. 'Chi, I just wanted you to know how much I love you. Some days, I look back and think about the course of actions that led to me meeting you, and I always thank God for making me late to work that day. It has to be the best day of my life, because since you came into my life, an unresolved equation was finally solved. This night is just to remind you that I love you.'

The music stopped and the two men walked away, Patrick leaned over to kiss her.

'I love you, too,' Nkechi said.

They continued their dinner, but Nkechi did not speak much after the romantic gesture. Patrick could sense that her attitude had changed, but he was unsure why. He kept looking over at her but she seemed distracted, unable to hold his gaze, almost tearful. Maybe she was just overwhelmed. After dinner, they took a romantic walk along the pier, watching the beautiful view of London lit up against the darkness.

The following day, Adaora and Nkechi were out shopping for clothes at an outlet store in Kent. Shopping was a cure for when Nkechi felt low and she would always drag her sister along.

'You have been fidgeting all day. What is wrong?' Adaora asked.

'Remember I told you that Patrick was going to take me out yesterday? Well, he did and it was the most romantic evening. He came to the house with a rose, then dinner at the restaurant we went to on our first date…'

'So, what is the problem?' Adaora interrupted.

'The problem is… it was the perfect opportunity for him to propose. He even made these two elderly Thai men play very romantic sensual instruments, as he gave a loving speech…'

'Awww, that sounds really romantic. Chi, look – when the time is right, he will propose.'

'I know,' Nkechi sighed, fingering the fabric of a dress without any awareness of it. 'I guess I just built up my expectations as the night progressed. At one stage, we were on the pier, right by London Bridge. The night was beautiful and London was lit up with the light from the buildings reflected on the river Thames…'

'Just be patient and try not to think about it.'

'Mmmm. I suppose…' Nkechi smiled uncertainly. 'Anyway, how are things with you and Henry from the speed dating event?'

'Well, we have been texting,' Ada grinned. 'And… we went out on a date yesterday, actually. He seems very narcissistic, though. Most of the conversations were about him and his business. He is a nice guy. I did enjoy the date, but I am wary of him – since he invited me back to his place and that is a red flag – especially on the first date.'

'Well, let me know how that pans out. All I know is… he was very handsome.'

Adaora smirked at Nkechi and shook her head. 'Are we done yet?'

'Yes, I'm done. Time to get home and prepare for work. I have so many lesson plans to do.'

Monday evening, Patrick was waiting for Nkechi outside her school. She came out with two bags, struggling, and Patrick rushed to help her.

'Hey, babe,' she said after giving him a kiss. 'Are you going to tell me where we are going?'

He smiled. 'Nope.'

They drove east towards Essex, along the A12. Patrick didn't say much on the journey. Nkechi thought he was taking her to his apartment, since this was en route, but that was clearly not the case, when he drove past his house. They finally arrived on a suburban street filled with detached houses and high-spec cars. To Nkechi's bewilderment, they parked on a driveway where there was another car also parked.

'Stay here a second, babe,' he said and walked over to the adjoining car.

A tall black woman exited the car, handing Patrick a set of keys. Smiling, he signalled to Nkechi to come over. Slowly getting out of the car, Nkechi stared in shock at the area: such a beautiful street, lined with trees and well-kept gardens. Holding her hand, Patrick opened the front door and led her inside. Her eyes widened in amazement as she took in the enormous house. Void of furniture, the hallway stretched out into a large, open-plan kitchen with classy, streamlined white cupboards and marble floors, looking out onto a vast garden edged by roses.

She looked at Patrick, one eyebrow raised. 'Why are we here?'

He kept quiet, took her hand and led her upstairs, moving from room to room.

She walked from the bathroom, and two double sized bedrooms: empty except for new carpet and cream-painted walls. Finally, she turned into the master bedroom, which was full of light with a king-size bed, huge windows and an en-suite bathroom. Her hands covered her mouth when Patrick pointed to a little black box resting on the bed. As she opened it, tears began to freely fall from her eyes.

She turned and found Patrick down on one knee. 'You are the only woman for me. I love you with all my heart. Will you marry me?'

Nkechi could not find the words but was nodding her head up and down.

Patrick stood up, took the box off her and placed the ring on her finger, grinning. He kissed her softly, then asked: 'Do you like this house?'

'Yes.'

'Do you want this house?'

'Yes.'

'Then, this is the house we will live in as man and wife.'

Chapter Two

S UNDAY DINNER WAS A GIVEN IN THE EDOZIE HOUSEHOLD. It was part of the fabric of their existence. As far back as their memories could stretch, Adaora and Nkechi could picture sitting, legs swinging, at the table spread with the various cultural delicacies made by their mother's hand. This privilege was only for a time; as soon as they were old enough, they were initiated into the family tradition. Under their mother's tutelage, they learnt their way around the spice cupboard, understanding how long to allow meat to soak up the seasonings and which combination of herbs was attributed to which dish. It was a rite of passage; not even Chidi, their younger brother, could escape it. Mrs Edozie would never have any person reprimand her daughters or her son for being unskilled in the kitchen. Her passion and pride lay in the cultural dishes she passed down. Her children would not become so British that they could not produce the food of their heritage.

At University, Chidi had already put into use the lessons he had learnt. He watched in dismay as the other young men in his year lived off Pot Noodles, dry bread and cereal, or tried to charm the women to cook for them. He laughed at their lack of knowledge while he whipped up stew and rice on a regular basis. Some of his friends had taken to 'popping around' unexpectedly at dinner time, their hands and stomachs empty. He loved showing his Mum that her lessons had not gone to waste, although her cooking was undoubtedly the best. The last sibling and the only boy, Chidi often felt like the baby of the family despite his height, broad shoulders and husky voice. Although he was the youngest, he felt a responsibility to protect his sisters and would do so, any chance he got.

Laying the knives and forks on the tablemats, Chidi heard the key in the lock: it must be Adaora. Now an independent lady, she rarely made it home for the cooking preparations; conveniently turning up as the dinner was about to be served. Adaora walked into the sitting room where her dad was zoned out to his highlife music; his head rocking in time with the gentle drum beats and percussions.

She tapped him on his shoulder. 'Daddy, good evening.'

He snapped out of his daze, took off his glasses and turned around to acknowledge her arrival. 'Ada, *nnöö.*'

He welcomed her with a hug. She loved her dad: a traditional cultural Igbo man who lectured in Business at East London University. His belief about the importance of education had not fallen on deaf ears, since he was the proud father of three high-achieving children. Whilst all his children carried a love for learning, Chidi carried his genetic make-up – he was a carbon copy of him in a taller model. Now, Chijoke's hairline was slightly receding but his moustache was thick and alive. His face carried two small tribal marks, one under each eye – reminders of the Nigerian war. Battle scars. Walking over to the CD player, he turned the music down and shouted: 'Mama Ada! Mama Ada, *aguu na-agu m?* Is the food ready?'

'My dear, it is almost ready,' came the soft reply.

Oluchi Edozie, also known as Mama Ada to her husband and close friends, was the anchor of the family. She stood victoriously in her kingdom, amongst the pots and pans; shouting instructions, giving orders, being obeyed. This was her domain and she relished her role when all her family were together. Food was a necessity that bound them; kept her children returning. Her food was renowned for its taste, its authenticity and its quality. Her long, home-made Ankara skirt, as colourful as her personality, swept the floor. She was a walking advertisement for her new profession as a full-time dressmaker. The days of stressful working for local councils as a social worker were over. The constant burden of overwork, with an unattainable caseload and uncaring management, had taken their toll and she left after ten years in the profession. She had told them: 'This job will not kill me' and left to pursue her passion for fashion, of which she was queen. She always dressed elegantly in her traditional attire. Everything she wore, she had made; it was her uniqueness.

Finally ready, the dinner dishes were lovingly spread across the red tablecloth. Jollof rice, fried plantain, salad and grilled fish awaited them. The family found their familiar seats, Mr Edozie's stomach playing all kinds of erratic musical notes in expectation. Licking his lips and smiling at the spread, he took his seat at the head of the table whilst unbuttoning his trousers. The button would not become an enemy of progress.

As was customary, Chidi was required to bless the table and, as eyes closed around him, he became nervous. His forefinger and thumb caressed the stubble on his chin. Nkechi saw and smiled, waiting for the thanks to God to echo with a unanimous 'Amen'.

It was not long before the neatly-arranged serving dishes had fulfilled their purpose and lay empty before them. After a second double helping of Jollof rice and plantain, Chidi reclined in his chair, releasing his gut from constriction by following his father's lead and undoing his jeans button.

Nkechi was observing the dynamics of her family keenly, looking for a suitable time to interject and make her announcement. It hadn't seemed right when everyone's mouths were full, but now they were settled, she raised her glass and sipped the ice-cold water before clearing her throat. Removing a little black box from her pocket and placing it on the table, she gathered her family's attention. A suspicious hush filled the room.

'I have some news,' she said, her eyes twinkling.

'Is that what I think it is?' Adaora gasped, watching her sister's grin grow wider.

Without missing a beat, Mrs Edozie leapt out of her chair and began to dance; the joy in her heart a melodious rhythm for her feet. Nkechi laughed.

'Oluchi, *ndidi,* my dear, be patient!' Mr Edozie retorted. 'Nkechi, go ahead.'

Mrs Edozie sat back down, beaming, her body leant towards her daughter.

'Patrick proposed to me last night – and this is the ring,' Nkechi said, as she opened the black box.

Reaching across the table, Adaora grabbed the box before her mum could get it. 'Congratulations, sis! See, didn't I tell you to just be patient?' She winked. 'Patrick is an intelligent man. He wouldn't let you get away! Oh, it's beautiful sis! I am so happy for you both.'

'I know, right? All that distress for nothing! Thank you. It's gorgeous, right? I am so happy, I can't stop smiling.'

'So, tell me – after your disappointment – how did he propose?' Adaora enquired eagerly.

'I'll tell you later.'

Chidi stood up and gave Nkechi a hug. 'It's about time, sis. 5 years, I was wondering what he was playing at!' They both laughed. 'No, but seriously, this is great news. I am so happy for you!'

Mrs Edozie was dancing again. '*Nne*, this is the best news I have had in a long time.' She hugged her daughter. 'Chidi, go and find that Princess Njideka Okeke praise and worship CD for me, please. It is time to sing, dance and praise God.'

Nkechi put the ring on and looked up to see her dad smiling at her.

'*Obi na atọ m ụtọ*. My daughter, my heart is filled with joy and happiness!' Mr Edozie beamed.

Nkechi walked over to her dad, bowed down in front him and laid her head on his chest. He covered her face with his hands, and kissed her on the forehead.

'I knew that he was going to propose to you soon, as he came to me to ask for my blessing. I told him to go ahead, because we have known him for quite some time now. I also told him that things will need to be done the proper way for us to move forward.'

Nkechi sat back up and looked at her dad. 'What do you mean, 'proper way'?' she asked.

'He must come here officially with his elders to begin the traditional process.'

'Ok. I see,' Nkechi said, uncertainly.

'So, I believe that they will be here next week.'

'Okay, dad. You need to refresh my memory on all this cultural stuff.'

'*O di nkpa*, it is very important to know our culture and embrace it.

'Yes daddy, I know that. You remind us all the time.'

'Let me see that ring again,' Adaora interrupted.

Nkechi flashed her left hand in front of Adaora's face and gave her cheeky smile before following the sound of the music.

In the living room, Mrs Edozie was in full dancing mode, bent over at a 90-degree angle, her hands swaying along with her hips, in time with the energetic gospel lyrics over African beats. Turning to see her daughter, Mrs Edozie pulled her onto the newly-acclaimed dance-floor and motioned for her to copy her steps. Throwing her head back in amusement, Nkechi emulated the whirlwind choreography of her ancestors, her hips finding their groove, her feet following suit. Adaora stood by the door, observing the pure joy generating from her sister. It was a gorgeous sight: she was moving at liberty – a manifestation of perfect bliss. Leaving the women to celebrate, Chidi and his father got to work clearing the table and cleaning the kitchen.

After a full high-energy work-out, Nkechi and her mum collapsed onto the leather sofa next to Adaora, their skin glowing in proof of their exercise.

The atmosphere shifted slightly and Nkechi became aware of the tension between Ada and her mother. There was no eye contact between them and thinking back, even Adaora's earlier greeting to her mum had seemed strained and forced. She hoped that her engagement news would ease the pressure between them.

Nkechi broke the silence, turning to face her sister. 'Ada I want *you* to be my maid of honour.'

Adaora coughed twice, blinked hard and peered at her sister. 'Me? Are you sure? What about Gloria?'

'Well, she is *like* a sister to me, but you – you *are* my sister AND my friend. I want you beside me on my special day. So, that's decided. Don't worry about Gloria – she'll understand.'

Adaora was notably thrilled. She shuffled closer to her sister, grabbing her around the waist and squeezing her tightly. 'I would be honoured to be your maid of honour.'

'Adaora, this is your second time of being maid of honour. When will it be your turn to be a bride?' Mrs Edozie asked.

Adaora sat back on the sofa, covering her forehead with her palm. 'Mum, please. Not today. It is not about me! This is about Nkechi.'

'My dear, I am just stating the facts, and asking a simple question.'

'Well, when the time is right, it will happen!' Adaora huffed, getting up from her seat. She stood awkwardly by the door as her mother continued.

'*Oge adighi eche mmadu.* My dear, time waits for nobody. You are well educated and have received the highest honour in education. But these things alone are not the main factors in you finding a husband. It is the way you live and your mentality that is stopping your progression.'

Once Mrs Edozie got into a lecture mode, she was relentless. Adaora remained paralysed by the door. She wanted to escape the claws of her mother's disapproval but had been raised better than to be disrespectful. Nkechi watched her sister's face fall and felt the ache in her heart as their mum continued to bombard her. She

31

came to feel uncomfortable for her sister, crossing her legs with her head in her hands. This evening was supposed to be full of love and laughter. *Why does it have to end like this?* she pondered.

'Mum, please. That's enough,' Nkechi pleaded.

'I think I am just going to leave, now, to be honest,' Adaora stated, thankful for the interruption. She opened the cupboard underneath the stairs and took out her black leather jacket.

'You should be ashamed of yourself! Look how your younger sister will be getting married before you!' Mrs Edozie shouted.

Nkechi was frozen in horror, helpless to stop the inevitable.

'Mum, I don't understand why you are shouting,' Adaora was struggling to remain composed. 'Plus, for your information, I have no reason to be ashamed. It doesn't matter who gets married first. I am happy for my sister. That is it.'

'You are correct. It is not about who gets married first,' Mrs Edozie admitted. 'But it is your mentality that is your biggest barrier.'

'My mentality is fine,' Adaora snapped.

Mrs Edozie got up and blocked Adaora's path, squaring up to her, staring directly at her. Without warning, she flew into a rage. 'How dare you say your mentality is fine! What type of woman does not want children?' she yelled. 'Are you my child, saying such things? Did I raise you to perpetuate this madness? NO! You are a clinical psychologist! You need to look at yourself and overcome that mind-set, because no man would want a woman who wants to bear no children.'

Hearing the noise, Mr Edozie stormed out of the kitchen.

'*O bu gini?* What is the matter now?'

'Papa Ada, talk to your daughter!'

32

The front door slammed shut behind Adaora.

'Mum, why must you always make her leave the house like this?' Nkechi complained. 'Last Sunday, it was the same thing. You need to accept the choices she makes as a woman.' Tired of the commotion, Nkechi retired to her room.

Mrs Edozie sat back on the sofa, fuming, and the men returned to their cleaning duties.

Arms outstretched, fingers pointing to the heavens, limbs yawning, Adaora sat up. Rolling her shoulders anti-clockwise a few times while checking the time on the clock, she decided to get out of bed. Avoiding the piles of paperwork littered by her bed, she made her way to the bathroom. Her snooze alarm shattered her senses as she brushed her teeth and glanced into the mirror, shaking her head at the bags under her eyes. She was exhausted; the late night had affected her but there was no time to wallow; she had work to do. Emerging from the steam and wrapping her nakedness in a luxurious black bathrobe, she viewed the multiple potential outfits, organised by colour palette, in her walk-in wardrobe. Particular about her choices, Adaora contemplated which clients she had appointments with. Certain colours could be triggers for behaviour and emotions, hence her deliberate and conscious decisions on clothing. She dressed in her favourite grey trouser suit with fitted blazer, matching it with a cream blouse and comfortable low wedge heels.

Applying a light coat of foundation, lip gloss and two sprays of Chanel No. 5, she quickly left the house. There was no time for breakfast, much to the disappointment of her stomach; she tried to ignore its groans as she made her way to the GP surgery. As a child, Adaora had loved dressing up as a doctor and playing with the kit she had received for her eighth birthday. Nkechi was always a willing patient and they had spent hours in dress-up and imaginative play. A helper by nature, Adaora loved that her career had been a life-long dream – and she was now a fully qualified doctor.

The surgery was purposefully a lighthouse in the community: two floors high, constructed in sunset brick, its name was blazoned in large silver letters: 'Chadwell Heath Surgery'. This was Adaora's second home; it utilised most of her time and she was accustomed to its atmosphere, sounds and smells. She walked through the large, glass double doors, pausing momentarily to greet the always friendly and welcoming receptionists, before making her way down the hall to her office. Upon opening the door, the opposite wall screamed beauty: a giant sunset landscape in Kenya hung centrally above her desk. It was a conversation starter. Adaora had chosen it to liven up the whitewashed walls and prevent a hospital feel. She wanted her patients to feel warm and that painting did a wonderful job. Mahogany frames dressed her medical certificates and achievement awards, co-ordinating with her desk – barely noticeable under the paperwork and computer. Two leather armchairs sat facing each other, their padding like quicksand taking the weight of the patients' burdens while they relaxed. Sitting in her reclining chair, Adaora scanned her tasks and quickly began organising her paperwork. There was an only an hour before her first patient was due to arrive. She focused intently on sorting through it efficiently and reading the notes for her next clients. Before she noticed, time had flown and it was ten minutes into the appointment. Her client had not turned up. As she was about to pick up the phone, the receptionist rang, letting her know he had just arrived.

A sunken teenaged figure skulked into the office, under a cloud of misery. Without acknowledging Adaora, Kevin plonked unto the nearest armchair, eyes firmly downward. Adaora moved to the adjoining armchair.

'How are you today, Kevin?'

The question lingered in the air between them. Biting his bottom lip, Kevin continued to melt into the floor. In the silence, Adaora assessed her client. His skin was burnt sienna, exuding a musky odour. Moments passed.

Adaora repeated her question, smiling. 'How are you today, Kevin?'

A flicker of recognition. Kevin looked in her direction. 'Do you have any water, please?'

Adaora went to the mini fridge by her desk, pulled out a bottle of water and handed it over to him.

'Thanks,' he said, offering a glint of a smile back towards her.

'So, tell me how you are today, and how you have been since our last session.'

Kevin took one more sip of the water before putting it down. 'Well, things are not getting any better at home, to be honest. I am always fucking pissed off. Every little thing gets to me. I just need to get out of that house.'

'I see. Before we move on, did you bring the journal I gave you to help to monitor your moods?'

Kevin took out the small book from his back pocket and handed it Adaora. She had a quick glimpse at the entries he had scrawled in barely legible handwriting. Aware of the potential for triggers, Adaora adjusted her presentation appropriately: open body language, soft speech. She turned to a particular page and looked up.

35

'You mentioned here that "every little thing" gets you angry. Tell me more about those things that get you so worked up.'

'At home, my step mum is always blaming me for things I didn't even do. I swear she likes to push my buttons. Does it on purpose to wind me up. And my dad? Well, you would've thought he would take my side. But no. He believes everything she says without question. On my case, the both of them. And I can't even get anything right at college, either. I'm frustrated all the time; can't do simple things. I'm so stupid,' he sighed. 'I'm worried one day my anger will get me into a lot of trouble.'

'From what you have told me, it sounds like you are worried about where this anger and the actions of that anger could take you.' She paused. 'Can you tell me what type of thoughts run through your head when you cannot do a simple task?'

Kevin kept his eyes on the painting as he spoke. 'I don't know what it is, exactly. I'll be in class at college and if I can't structure a sentence together, the first thing I think is that I am stupid. At that point, I just want to smash things around.'

'Ok. There are quite a few things I would like us to cover in this session, based on what you have told me. Most of it is addressing negative emotions and thinking processes, which we will need to change. I see you did not mention any positive things that happened to you – either in your mood journal or just now. I also want to focus on that. At the end of the session, I will give you your journal back and ask you how the session went, as usual.'

Adaora felt that CBT would be beneficial to Kevin, as a young person. He was a new referral from the GP, with signs of depression and serious anger issues. Although they had only had a few sessions, Adaora was confident in the methods and techniques she was using.

Kevin didn't engage much during the first session, but building rapport was helping them to make progress.

She saw a variety of patients that day and once finished, she felt slightly drained from the negative energy they had left behind. A glass of wine, her bed and a good book was the perfect combination for unwinding after a hard day. Adaora curled up in bed, attempting to read, but her eyes had other plans. They dropped and drooped and before long, she was riding a wave of unconsciousness. Vibrations across her cheek roused her and reaching out, she tossed and turned before getting to her phone. Henry's name was displayed.

'Hi, Henry.' Her voice was groggy.

'Just calling to check in with you. How have you been?'

'I'm good,' she replied, sitting up and propping her back with pillows. 'I have just been consumed by work. Sorry I haven't been in touch. How are you doing?'

'It's fine, trust me. I can only imagine how demanding and exhausting your job must be. Me? I'm fine.'

Adaora yawned.

'Am I boring you already?' Henry laughed.

'I am so sorry. I do not normally sound like this at eight o'clock in the evening.'

'It's fine. I totally understand. You should really get your rest and call me tomorrow.'

'Thanks for understanding. I really appreciate that. I will definitely call you tomorrow.'

'Alright. Goodnight,' he said gently.

There was a buzz at Cardinal Pole school and Nkechi's name was at the centre of it. Rumours had spread like wildfire and whispers were contagious in the hallways of the school. Nkechi felt somewhat like a celebrity as she smiled, thanked and showed her engagement ring to students and teachers congratulating her. By lunchtime, her cheeks were burning from all the exercise and she needed a moment's peace. She had Gloria to thank for the fanfare. Her best friend and fellow teacher was unable to contain her excitement about the news. Hence the ambush.

Nkechi was desperate for peace and quiet, so slyly made her way to the roof deck to have her lunch. Although March had just shown its face, the sun was bursting with heat from a clear blue sky and Nkechi enjoyed the sun and her sandwiches alongside a few sixth formers. The skyline bragged about brand new, swanky builders: more skyscrapers. Nkechi contemplated the changes in the borough. The 2012 Olympic bid had transformed the culture and perception of the area, with redevelopers trampling over each other for a piece of the action. It was relentless. In with the new, and out with the old. Residents of Hackney were being priced out of all they had ever known; relocated to the outskirts of London and even as far as north of the country – away from generational memories. It was a shame, she surmised to herself. Change was inevitable, but this was drastic. In her teenage years, Hackney schools had been treated as if they were plague-ridden. Parents went out of their way to avoid them, preferring their children to travel long distances in unfamiliar uniforms because 'out of borough' was associated with success. Now, even waiting lists were full and overflowing. Parents were desperate to secure their children places in Hackney schools, partly due to academies taking over and rebranding.

Hearing the bell ring, Nkechi left her thoughts and rushed to her classroom.

That evening, Nkechi arrived excitedly at her sister's house. They had planned a film night – featuring sweet popcorn and red wine. Both avid film addicts, watching films together was a favourite pastime that always ignited fierce discussion and critique afterwards.

'Finally!' Dressed in her silky red pyjamas, Adaora ushered her sister inside.

'Sorry, Ada. Work – you know how it is!' Nkechi hung her coat on the banister and peeled off her ankle boots, releasing her poor toes from the crushing they had suffered all day. Clutching a glass, she topped it up and searched for the popcorn bowl.

Throwing her head back she laughed loudly. 'Ada! Is this all that's left?'

Ada smiled, her mouth full of popcorn. 'Latecomers shouldn't complain. I had to do something while I was waiting. Plus – Ms Engaged, I'm sure you need to watch your figure, now!'

'Popcorn is pleasantly low in calories, I'll have you know!'

'There's more in the cupboard – grab another pack.'

Nkechi disappeared into the kitchen.

'While you're in there could you get the Ben and Jerry's for me too please?'

'Oooooh! My friends, Ben and Jerry! What flavours do you have? ... Never mind. I see it.'

Nkechi returned, arms full of treats and collapsed on the sofa next to her sister, who was waiting, film paused, remote in hand.

'OK. Let's do this.'

'Turn the lights off.'

As the credits rolled across the flat screen TV, a sombre silence filled the living room. The heaviness of the atmosphere caused tears that Nkechi wiped with her shirt sleeve.

'So, what did you think of the film?' Adaora asked.

'Hmmm. Where do I start?' Nkechi replied quietly. 'It was very emotional. You know I'm not really a crier with films, but this one… it got me. There were moments that were really hard to watch. I felt the pain…'

'Yeah, it was emotional. I had a few tears myself. Cinematically, I guess what I liked was the absence of time. It didn't feel like twelve years went by.' Adaora scooped melted cookie dough ice-cream into her mouth. 'I was a bit sceptical at first. My thoughts were, like, how many slave movies do we need? That part of the black story has been emphasised many times over. We need stories of how things were, before that.'

Nkechi nodded her head in agreement. 'Not just before it, but stories after, as well. I was impressed with Chiwetel's performance, though. He was incredible.'

'He really was. I find it painful to watch, though. Even though I know it happened, I've read about it, been taught about it – but the visuals… they reach a different place. The hardest part for me, watching that, was when the mother's children were auctioned and sold to a different plantation owner. No mother should have to go through that. And to think millions had to endure that torture!'

'I really think that knowing our history and heritage before slavery is also vitally important. It's easy to get wrapped up in this narrative, as if that's our whole contribution – enslavement. But knowing where we come from changes how you view yourself. Even me. There's so much about Igbo culture that I'm learning. I was even going to ask you… When dad mentioned doing things properly with Patrick and I, does he mean the knocking tradition?'

'Yeah, that's the one.'

'Please refresh my memory. You know you are more cultured than me.'

Adaora chuckled, grabbing her headscarf and sitting up from the sofa. 'The only reason I know more than you, is because, when daddy use to tell his stories, you would always disappear. I was genuinely interested.'

'I know you were, daddy's little girl. You had more patience than me. I didn't want to sit around listening to stories about things I couldn't understand. Me… I wanted to parrr-taaay!' Nkechi gestured a dance move with her hands. 'But anyway, fountain of knowledge, what is the process?'

'Well the *Iku-aka*, which you call 'knocking' is the formal introductory meeting of both families. So, Patrick will come with his kinsmen to officially greet daddy and our uncles and officially show their intention of marriage.'

'So, what you're saying is, even though I have an engagement ring, in our culture it doesn't show intention.'

'Not at all.'

'Well, the carats on this thing say otherwise! Shows real intention, in my eyes. But don't look directly at it,' Nkechi bragged. 'You will be blinded!'

'You are so silly.' Adaora rolled her eyes.

Nkechi sighed. 'I can't be bothered to go home, sis. Let's have a sleepover! It'll be like when we use to stay at Auntie's and shared a bed…'

'Yeah, with you kicking me and stealing all the covers!'

'I'm good, now. I promise to share.'

Adaora laughed. 'I better enjoy your company before you get married and forget about me.'

'Oh, please! You know I'll be here stealing your shoes for many years to come!' Nkechi winked.

Even the sun knew that it was a special day – pouring light in delightful streams into the Edozie household; although outside, it was accompanied by unexpected blustery winds. Adaora was at her parents' house for the occasion. The awkwardness between herself and her mother had not subsided and they strategically avoided each other. A palpable, unspoken bitterness festered beneath the surface.

Standing in the living room, Adaora flung the curtains open, shifting the shadows and brightening the room. The light showed the dust that had collected on the glass TV stand that housed Mr Edozie's pride – a 61-inch flat-screen purchased to watch sports in High Definition, and Mr Edozie was often to be found cheering in front of it.

They were to have visitors, and dust was not a welcome guest. Without hesitation, Adaora picked up a cloth and began to work her way around the room, exterminating all traces of dust. Nkechi was nervously stirring a pot of stew in the kitchen, her mind cast back to the last run-in between her mother and Adaora. Between the two of them, they had ruined her engagement announcement, and today – today was more important. As she stirred, she lifted her eyes and silently prayed for peace to reign in the household.

Mrs Edozie took the spoon from her. 'My dear, go upstairs and get ready. I will finish here.'

'Thanks, mum.'

The anticipated knock on the door came. Adaora was nearest and went to open it.

'Ndewo!' *Good afternoon*, she greeted: it was one of the few things Adaora could say in her native tongue. She was frustrated that her parents had not spoken to her in Igbo more often as a child. Although Adaora was better at trying to speak Igbo than Nkechi, who was utterly hopeless.

At the door, Patrick looked prestigious, in a fitted blue suit and crisp white shirt. He had arrived with a small entourage of people. Behind him, his father, Mr Eze, and three uncles were adorned in traditional Igbo attire. The elders wore long black shirts decorated with tusks and embroidery patterns, with round red hats on their heads to complete the look. His mother and two good friends, Kola and Iyke, were also in attendance. Iyke was a mutual friend of both families.

Mrs Edozie immediately took care of her guests and ushered them warmly into the living room, where Mr Edozie's two brothers and sister were already sitting. It was a tight squeeze, and Mr Edozie brought a few chairs from the dining table to cater for everyone. With all the guests seated, Mr Edozie poured drinks and welcomed each guest individually. The room was full of colour and language as the elders communicated in their native tongue. Patrick stood nervously against the wall, sweating and checking his collar in various increments. Although he had already proposed, this occasion seemed more serious, more formal and he didn't quite know how to stand or where to look.

As the families sat facing each other, the custom began. Patrick's family presented gifts to Mr Edozie and his family. Two full bottles of palm wine, some kola nuts and a bottle of Remy Martin were exchanged.

'*Da alü. Well done!* You have tried,' Mr Edozie said.

It was customary for a prayer to be conducted whenever there was a gathering of this nature. Mr Edozie handed the kola nuts to his elder brother, since it was traditional for the eldest man to acknowledge that he had seen the kola nuts. Then he handed it back to Mr Edozie, who took one of the kola nuts and handed it back to Mr Eze. It was a choreographed dance, and they all knew the steps.

"*Ọ̀jị̀ luo ünö okwuo ebe osi bia.* Take this one back, so that they will know that you have visited us here today,' Mr Ezodie said. He floated from Igbo into English; feeling that translation was appropriate and more inclusive. He took a knife and broke the kola nut, while saying a toast.

'For the benefit of our children, I will speak in English,' Mr Eze began. 'Our coming here today is one of utmost importance. There is a beautiful rose in your garden we have seen, and as a family, we are here to pluck that rose and give it a new home.'

Beside him, Patrick's family nodded their heads in unison; a silent agreement.

'Okay, we have heard what you have to say,' Mr Edozie replied, smiling. 'You see that I have more than one rose blossoming in this house.' He looked in the direction of his wife. 'Mama Ada, call Adaora and Nkechi for me, please.'

Listening keenly from the kitchen, Adaora and Nkechi stood up simultaneously, as their names were called. Gripping Adaora's hand, Nkechi held her breath as they walked into the living room. They stood side by side in the door frame.

Nkechi caught Patrick staring intently at her and smiled, blushing slightly.

'So, Patrick, can you identify the daughter you came here enquiring about?' Mr Edozie asked.

44

Patrick opened his palm and pointed it straight at Nkechi.

Mr Edozie looked at Nkechi. 'Do you recognise this man that has come here to enquire about you being his wife?'

'Yes, I do,' she replied.

Adaora leaned over towards Nkechi's ear, whispering, 'Go over to Patrick and kneel before him.'

Nkechi followed the instructions of her sister, then Patrick held her hand as she got up to sit next to him.

The fellowshipping between the two families continued for a few hours. Mrs Edozie served food and all stomachs were satisfied. As they broke bread together, jokes were told and laughs were shared between them.

'As the old saying goes, a man without a wife is like a vase without flowers.' Mr Edozie said. He turned to Patrick's father and uncles. 'My people, we appreciate your visit and we have heard all you have had to say and we will get back to you in due course.'

Nkechi's head whipped around in surprise. *What?* Was she still not engaged? Adaora patted her hand, smiling reassuringly.

'Thank you for your hospitality.' Mr Eze replied, standing from his chair. With that, Patrick and his kinsmen left the Edozie house.

The following day, Nkechi skipped the customary Sunday dinner at home. It would not have been the same – Adaora wasn't coming, due to the issues between her and her mother, and Chidi was back on campus. Leaving her mum and dad to have a quiet dinner, Nkechi chose to spend some quality time with her fiancé.

The universe was at odds with her plans. TFL, especially, wanted to ruin her Sunday – cancellations, engineering work and replacement bus services plagued her journey. With each change and delay, Nkechi became more irritated, unable to settle into her book.

When she arrived, Patrick embraced her passionately, enveloping her in the delicious fragrance of love and baked sweet potato. Finally, in the arms of the man who loved her unconditionally, she felt safe.

'Babe, have a seat and relax. Dinner is almost ready.'

Walking into the living room, Nkechi was stunned by the room, drenched in romance. Rose petals were under her feet and scattered all over the table and sofa, and it was candlelit – two red candles dripped seductively, releasing sweet aromas of spring flowers. She was in utter awe and wonder.

Removing her jumper, Nkechi sank into the sofa and let her fiancé treat her like a princess.

Patrick walked in, holding two steaming plates. 'Dinner is served.'

'Wow, it all looks great. Sweet potato… Babe, that lamb looks delicious.'

'It tastes even better,' he boasted.

'I'm sure it does,' she agreed, as she picked up her knife and fork and put a piece of the lamb in the mouth. Patrick watched her eat it, patiently waiting for the verdict as she chewed. She nodded. 'You were right, babe. It is delicious. I love the blend of flavours and it's just spicy enough to enjoy.'

After dinner, they both retired on the sofa, still littered with rose petals. Patrick sat upright, his foot up on the recliner. Nkechi lay her head on his lap.

'How do you think the yesterday went?' Patrick asked, running his hand gently over her naked shoulder. She flinched, ticklish.

'I think it was beautiful, seeing both our families together. I'm just getting to grips with the cultural aspects of marriage.'

'Do you know what would have been a laugh? When your dad said "identify the women you came here for", imagine if I picked Ada.'

'You are so silly!' Nkechi sat up, and snapped: 'That would have been so embarrassing and not funny at all!'

'Hmm, I guess you're right,' Patrick admitted. 'I don't think our parents would find it funny.'

'So, now that the *iku...aka* is done, what happens next?'

'Well,' Patrick stroked her hand, thoughtfully. 'Your family will probably be carrying out an investigation into my family to see what type of people we are... if we have a history of disease, cults, suicide, et cetera. Once they are happy, your family will contact my family and give a response, with a list of things we must provide during the traditional ceremony.'

'Imagine, after all this, if they said no!' Nkechi joked.

'That certainly wouldn't be a laughing matter.'

'Well... on a serious note, we need to discuss when the date for wedding will be.'

Patrick sat there in deep thought. 'Well, 2016 – Spring. Basically, this time next year. Before we do that, we have to do the traditional marriage this year.'

Nkechi covered her face with her hands. 'There is just so much to do!' she moaned.

'Don't worry, we'll get there. Are you still up for doing the traditional back in Nigeria?' he asked her, moving her hands from her face.

'Yes, definitely. If we are going to do a traditional, we might as well do it properly, and the only way to do that is back on my father's land.'

'Good. Well, when your family officially responds, we can start planning that for some time in August.' Nkechi nodded in agreement, and Patrick went on: 'Are you still going to Nigeria with your dad in April?'

'Yes, he confirmed the tickets yesterday. So, as soon as this term is done, I'll be there for two weeks. It will be good for me to go back and visit before the traditional, so I can get use to the surroundings.'

Nkechi was excited about her trip with her dad, back for the first time in almost a decade. Adaora had been back since then, but Nkechi never had the chance then, because of the timing of her postgraduate course. Her culture had never been a priority, but since becoming serious with Patrick, Nkechi yearned to understand her heritage. This trip was an excellent opportunity.

'You will love it out there. Will you also be going to Nnewi?' Patrick asked, referring to the second largest city in Anambra State.

'Yes, my dad has some unfinished business to do there and plus, it gives me an opportunity to see your village.'

'They will welcome you with open arms.'

'How far is Nnewi to your village?' Nkechi queried. 'I never know how to pronounce it.'

Patrick shook his head in disappointment. 'You *are* a teacher, right? Break it down with phonics... *Aron-di-zu-ogu.*'

Nkechi attempted it, struggling slightly: 'Arondizu-ogu.'

'See? You got it. It's about an hour's drive from Nnewi, with no traffic. Anambra and Imo are neighbouring states.'

'I can't wait. It will also give me the opportunity to see what business opportunities are out there.'

Sitting in the back of the cab after a romantic night with Patrick, Nkechi was glowing, a permanent smile on her face. Even the driver had commented on it. Lost in thought about her future as Mrs Eze, she felt her phone vibrating. It was Adaora.

'H-hello…' uttered a trembling voice.

'Ada? Are you okay? What is the matter?' a concerned Nkechi asked.

Adaora's voice was soft and brittle. 'Ummm… yeah, I guess. I needed to talk to you. I just finished my date with Henry.' She paused.

'Ada? Are you there?'

'…Yes, it's just…' She sighed deeply. 'Maybe mum was right all along. Maybe there is no man out there who is willing to be with a woman who doesn't want children.'

'Oh, sis! What happened? What did he say?'

'Well, we went out to eat, and it was going well, to begin with. You know that Chinese restaurant we like? Yeah, we were there. Remember I told you he was slightly narcissistic? Well he is, but it's bearable. Just. So, we're eating, having a good time, laughing, joking, and he's giving me compliments… and then, it happened. Mood change. Middle of dinner, he starts talking about family and children etc. I didn't really want to get into it. I mean, it's early days, but he was really pushing the subject… So, honesty is best, right? I told him. And he switched on me.' Ada's voice quavered. 'Told me he was adamant about wanting four children, passing down his legacy – blah blah blah. I told him I wasn't budging – and the night died in that instant. Sudden death. So, we just went our separate ways.' Ada gulped. 'What am I going to do? Am I cursed to be single forever?'

'Oh, hun, I'm sorry he didn't take it well. I know it hurts, but at least you were honest. It would have been harder if you'd invested feelings in him. It will be difficult – especially at our age – many men are trying to build for the future. But don't worry. There are plenty of men who don't want children. Henry just isn't one of them.'

'That is true,' Ada sniffed. 'Well, it is what it is. If it was meant to be, it will be. Sorry to call you in such a state, I just needed to get it out of my system.'

'Of course, sis. I'm here for you, no matter what. I love you.'

'I love you too, sis,' Adaora replied.

Chapter Three

THE BED WAS A MESS: A COLLAGE OF FABRICS STREWN OVER THE MATTRESS – a jumbled heap, representing a confused mind. She clutched hangers of different clothes against her slim frame while she stared into the floor-length mirror, waiting for a sense of peace. Nothing. Tossing the outfit onto the pile, Adaora sighed. She never usually had this problem: work suits were always similar – dark trousers with a matching blazer. Today, inspiration was ignoring her pleas and the possibilities were exhausting.

Collapsing onto the bed, Adaora picked up the flyer for the event she was attending. A conference at her former college. This wouldn't normally be an issue, but as keynote speaker, hundreds of fashionable teenage eyes would be watching her every move and she wanted to make the right impression. As an alumnus, she had been excited to receive the call inviting her to speak. She had fond memories of City and Islington College as the place she had matured, the catalyst for her academic success. Scanning the remaining dresses in her half-empty wardrobe, her eyes found a fitted, white shift dress, and lit up. She put it on, finding that it still fitted. Fumbling through her bottom drawer of accessories, she located a white scarf with blue polka dots and used it to decorate her beautifully-shaped afro. Admiring herself in the mirror, she saw that the white dress shaped her perfectly, so she added a royal blue blazer and grinned at her reflection. Feeling elegant, stylish and confident, she glided out of the house.

En route, Adaora stopped at a nearby coffee shop to wait for her best friend, Temi. Checking her phone, she saw a message from her, saying that she was a few minutes away. Adaora smiled to herself, knowing that 'a few minutes' for Temi usually meant that she had only just left home. This time, however, Temi proved her wrong – she was striding up the road – her supermodel appearance grabbing the attention of all men and women around. Seeing her, Adaora immediately felt at ease – in a friendship that had started in nursery and blossomed over the last twenty-five years, Temi had always been at her right hand, and her moral support was welcome. In the early years of their friendship, they had often been the talk of local boys, trying their luck to secure a date with either one of them. Most people assumed that Temi would become a model, but her passions had led her into interior design. As a happily married woman, she had no interest in shooting pictures for other men to gawk at: her beauty was reserved for her husband. Strutting along in a fitted blue printed dress with knee-high boots, Temi located Adaora and gave her a massive smile.

'On time, Temi?' Adaora teased. 'Still kept me waiting!' She laughed, looking at her wrist. They both walked towards the college.

'Couldn't find anything to wear,' Temi said, smiling. 'You know how it is.'

'Ahhh, yes, when the possibilities are endless. I had the same problem this morning!'

'You look stunning, Ada. I love that dress on you, and your hair is so cute! How do you get that amazing curl definition?'

'I'm trying out this new technique. It's called the LOC method: liquid, oil and cream. My curls are really responding.'

They approached the imposing five-storey glass building with anticipation and nostalgia. Signing in at reception and being led into the main auditorium, they were overwhelmed by the hundreds of young faces peering expectantly at the various career and university stalls around the perimeter. Ten years had passed and now she had returned to take the role of speaker. Adaora stepped into the past, remembering her own journey as a student: sitting on the front row, overtly keen. The words of the speaker she had listened to had caused a ripple effect of inspiration and determination, and she wanted to have the same impact on the students in attendance. Temi looked over at Ada and noticed that she had frozen, a distant look on her face.

She nudged her softly. 'How are you feeling?'

'I am okay. I just get slightly nervous, speaking publicly. As soon as I am up there and into it, I will be fine.'

'You have nothing to worry about. They are going to love you!' Temi remarked, assuredly.

The principal gave a short address, welcoming the students, before introducing Adaora. She rose to a burst of applause, walking confidently onto the podium and placing her notes on the shiny black lectern. Full to capacity, the auditorium hummed with anticipation as she began to speak. Engaged and enthralled, the audience's applause kept coming, every time Adaora made a significant point. She was in full swing, making eye contact, telling humorous anecdotes, while keeping her message packed with words of wisdom and practical advice. Mid-swing, Adaora waited patiently for the applause to subside, taking a well-deserved sip of water before concluding.

'If you remember anything from today, I want it to be this. There are three agents of failure. One is self-doubt: that little voice in your head telling you why you should not do something. To be great, you need to drown that voice out with action. Second, procrastination is the killer disease of progress – putting things off till you find the perfect time to start. That perfect time will never arrive, so start today. Lastly, lack of consistency. If you are not consistent in taking action and following your goals, then you will fail and continue to fail. So, please. Go Ahead. Be Creative. Be Innovative and Dream Big. Thank you.'

Thunderous applause erupted, with a standing ovation from the motivated audience. She had completed her task successfully. After the closing remarks, Adaora made herself available, greeting students and answering questions as the crowd dispersed and Temi stood by, waiting. The organisers thanked Adaora for her impactful speech and gave her an open invitation to return. As Adaora and Temi collected their possessions to leave, two excited teenage girls ran over to them, slightly out of breath.

'Hi!' they both said simultaneously.

'Hey!' Adaora replied.

'My name is Rachel and this is Holly.'

'How can I help you both?'

'We are both applying for Uni this year and wanted to ask you more about your profession. Do you have five minutes for a quick chat?' Rachel asked. She was the confident one of the two.

'Yes, that's fine.'

Temi said, 'I need to make a few calls, plus, I need some coffee. Meet me in the Starbucks across the road.'

Adaora nodded in silent agreement before taking a seat with the two girls in the foyer.

'As soon as our teacher told us about you and said that you were coming to speak at the college, we looked into your background. After hearing you today, you are a role model to many girls our age, and we just want to know what path you took to becoming a psychotherapist.' Rachel said.

'Thank you so much for your kind words. It means a lot to me. Yes, I am a psychotherapist, and at the moment I use a method called cognitive behavioural therapy to treat my patients. I am sure you have come across it before.'

The girls looked at each other.

'Yes, we have heard of it, but not read into it,' Holly replied. 'Could you tell us a bit more about it, please?'

'CBT is a talking therapy that helps my patients change the way they think and behave. It is a way of reversing a negative thought process. CBT cannot stop peoples' problems but, rather, it helps them to deal with it in a positive way, rather than the problem being detrimental to their wellbeing. It is based on the notion that feeling, thoughts, physical sensation and action are all interlinked. So, negative thoughts patterns and feeling can have you trapped in a vicious cycle.' Adaora paused 'Are you still with me?'

'Yes,' they both replied, nodding.

'What type of problems are you talking about?' Rachel asked.

'Well, it differs. It is commonly used to treat anxiety and depression. CBT is also used for other mental and physical health problems. To be honest, there is so much to it, we could be here all day. With regard to my path, after studying at this college I went to University and did a three-year undergraduate Psychology degree at London Kings College. After that, I did a two-year MSc Postgraduate degree in Psychology and Neuroscience. While I was doing that, I got an internship as an Assistant Psychologist with the NHS for a year. To finish off, I did my three-year doctorate in Clinical Psychology at University College London, which I finished not too long ago.'

Rachel and Holly looked at each other, a bright twinkle in their eyes.

'Wow, that sounds like many years of hard work,' Rachel said.

'It was. You need to be very focused, because you will get tough moments when you will feel like giving up, but you have to keep pushing and remember why you started.'

'I know your friend is waiting for you. We don't want to keep you any longer, but thank you for being here today and sharing with us,' Holly said.

Adaora took out her business cards and handed one to each of the girls. 'Thank you. I am glad I could help. Feel free to call me if you have any other questions. I would be more than happy to help.'

Giving the girls a warm embrace, Adaora set off to meet Temi. She took her time crossing Islington High Street – just like when she was a student – walking towards Angel Station. Walking into Starbucks, she located Temi, sitting in a comfy armchair in the corner.

'You made it, then! I have already paid for your latte. Just tell them your name at the till and they will give it you.'

Young professionals were in the coffee shop, a few working on their laptops, others packed around a small table having a meeting, and some sitting in solitude. Adaora returned, carefully balancing her latte and a slice of carrot cake in her right hand.

'What an inspiring day!' Adaora stated, sliding into the seat beside Temi.

'It was indeed. Being back at the college again and watching you inspire all those young people was truly amazing.'

'I know. It is a moment I will never forget!' Adaora took a sip of the latte, too soon. Her tongue retracted at the heat and she quickly returned the latte to the table, taking a few forkfuls of cake to counteract the burn.

'So, what are you up to, the rest of the day?' Adaora asked.

'Well, Tony is back late today, so I want to make sure dinner is ready by the time he gets back from work.'

'Good old Tony, always working hard. What you cooking?'

'Not sure yet. I did some shopping the other day so I am sure I can figure something out when I get in… What are you doing? You should come over for dinner!' Temi insisted.

'I would, but not tonight. I have my swimming lesson today,' Adaora replied, tentatively returning the mug to her lips and blowing, before sipping again. The perfect temperature. She began gulping readily.

'How is that going?'

'Well, I'm six weeks in and I can honestly say that I am happy to be learning. My technique is getting slightly better, but my breathing is flawed.'

'You will get there. The main thing is – you found time to actually make it happen!'

'It's all thanks to you. You convinced me.'

'It's an important life lesson and besides, every time we have gone on holiday, you never get anywhere near the sea. At least next time, you will.'

'I will, indeed.'

'Yes, don't let that perfect beach body go to waste!' Temi winked, before gesturing at Adaora's mug. 'Are you finished? I think it's time we made a move.'

'Yes, I'm done, finally. Thank you for waiting. We should go, so you can cook up a storm for hubby.'

They parted ways outside the coffee shop, hugging and making plans to do dinner soon. Adaora was happy. Seeing Temi always put her in a good mood. It was a shame that work and other commitments had reduced their time together but she relished any moment they shared. When Adaora had moved out of the family home and away from the area, distance had been the main reason for not seeing one another so much, but Temi getting married had added another layer to the situation. They stayed in contact. Technology, social media and smart phones made that easy to do, but face to face contact reduced significantly. Added to that, Adaora's journey to becoming a qualified psychotherapist had been strewn with essays, reports and research. Other friendships hadn't survived these changes, but they were different: as close to sisters as you could get, they ensured that even in the midst of busyness, they made memories together. A lover of photography and snapshotting celebrations for her memoirs, Adaora found herself scrawling through the hundreds of pictures she had taken on Temi's wedding day. It was a beautiful occasion and Temi shone in a spectacular lace sweetheart-necked fishtail dress with a long train. She found a picture of them both pulling funny faces and laughed out loud. Even on the most formal of instances, they would revert to their playful ways.

Time had slipped away from Adaora again. She cursed herself for not leaving earlier as she attempted to navigate her car on the fastest route to the leisure centre in Harold Hill. Temporary lights and roadworks added more chaos than usual to the journey and she parked slightly haphazardly before rushing to the pool. Thankfully her all black one piece swimming costume was on under her clothes, so she peeled off the layers and stuffed them into the closest locker before entering the adult pool. Dipping her foot into the water to check the temperature, she entered the pool, swimming over to the others congregated at the far end. Adaora looked around. Not many people were in attendance for this week's lesson, she thought. Apologising for her tardiness, she received directions from the tutor and began practising. After a few laps, Adaora stopped in the middle of the pool, trying to catch her breath. Suddenly, her eyes caught a handsome man she had never seen before in the sessions. He looked bewildered, and walked over to the instructor. The instructor shook his head and the man sat down by the pool, adjusting his goggles. Adaora could not keep her eyes off him, trying her best to disguise it, but to no avail. Adaora thought he might be there to work on his fitness, since he was toned and looked more like a light heavyweight boxer, with a neatly trimmed beard and low level cut. Adaora carried on swimming, but wondered who he was. Her technique went out of the window, since she lost all concentration on what she was doing. The mystery man was in the beginners' section and was practising his kicks. He stopped, took off his goggles and in that moment caught Adaora looking at him. He smiled at her and carried on swimming. Adaora could not figure out why she found this man so attractive, wondering if it was his dark brown skin, or maybe it was the chiselled chest that had her lusting for him.

Mystery man ventured out away from the beginners' area, attempted to float on his back and quickly found himself submerged underwater. Adaora was the nearest to him and quickly swam towards him to help him reach the edge.

'Are you okay?' she asked.

He carried on coughing uncontrollably. 'I think so,' he replied, looking rather embarrassed.

'I take it that this is your first day of taking lessons.'

He continued coughing; the cough fused into laughter.

Adaora looked perplexed. 'What's so funny?' she asked.

'I remembered what a friend of mine told me, just before I came here. Not to drown myself on the first day.'

'Well, that was good advice on their part. You clearly didn't listen.'

He laughed sheepishly. 'Thanks for helping me out.'

'No worries,' she replied, moving to turn away.

'Wait… What is your name?' he asked.

'Adaora. And yours?'

'Charles.'

'Well, it was good meeting you, Charles. Try and stay above the water in the shallow end!' Adaora laughed as she swam away.

Charles sat on the side and watched her swim. He couldn't keep his eyes off her now, and Adaora could sense that he was watching her, so the smile on her face continued to grow, inch by inch. Adaora made sure she didn't look in his direction, while she practised her backstroke. Charles went back to the beginners' area and was handed a float, as the instructor told him that there was no need to feel ashamed there; this was a place where adults could learn to swim without judgement. But Charles was barely attentive, continuing to look in Adaora's direction.

After the swimming lesson, outside the leisure centre, Adaora stood looking in her bag for the key to her car. Charles crept up behind her.

'Where are you rushing off to?' he asked.

Adaora was startled and dropped her bag in the process. 'You scared me!' she said, relieved to know it was Charles.

Charles picked up her bag and handed it back to her. 'Apologies, I didn't mean to scare you. I just wanted to say thank you again for helping me out in the pool.'

'Don't mention it. Happy to help a fellow learner.'

Charles smiled at her, looking directly into her eyes. He was confident: a smooth operator. Adaora could barely keep his gaze – his eyes were mesmerising and she felt lost, looking deeper into them.

'Can I buy you a drink?' he asked.

'Right now?'

'Yes. Right now.'

'That's pretty brazen of you. What makes you think I would let you buy me a drink?' she probed.

Charles chuckled. 'Well, I saw how you were looking at me in the pool…'

He had an air of arrogance about him that intrigued Adaora. 'Only in case you drowned. Again,' she teased.

'And I'm sure you saw me looking at you!' Charles grinned. 'Besides, I need to officially thank you for practically saving my life.'

Adaora looked at him: an imposing figure; his deep voice made her feel weak at the knees. She could not resist. She had never felt like this for a guy so quickly. 'Yes, but only for one drink. It is a work night,' she said.

'No worries. I promise I will not keep you too late. Follow my car. There is a quiet little bar not too far from here.'

Charles got into his black Range Rover, and Adaora followed.

The bar was quiet: only five other people were there. They found a nice secluded section away from others.

'So, tell me – apart from learning to swim, what do you do with yourself?' Adaora asked.

'I used to work in the City as a financial consultant, but I gave up that life to start up my own business. I now run a chain of barbershops around London,' Charles replied.

'That is impressive. Why barbershops?'

'I was tired of waiting – generally in life – waiting on people when I was working in the City, then waiting for hours for barbers – that was one of the worst things. I decided I was going to create a chain of barbershops using new media to reduce waiting times, and create an atmosphere like no other. In my barbershops, I have pool tables, table tennis, games, and internet access. All in the bid to make sure people have an all-round great experience.'

Adaora looked at him intently as he spoke, naturally drawn to him. She believed in him and felt connected to his energy – a connection that she had never felt with anyone else. She could not understand what was happening but she did not want to give away too much.

'That's amazing – that you were able to follow your ideas through,' Adaora stated. 'Many people have things they would love to accomplish in life, but find reasons not to.'

'That is true,' Charles agreed.

'I spoke to some young people at my former college today and gave them that exact same message.'

'It is an important message and one I try to share with young people as well,' he said.

Time flew by. Both were engrossed in conversation with each

other. Then Adaora realised how late it was and told Charles she would have to leave.

Before they parted ways, Charles asked for her number. Adaora refused and told him that if he was lucky, he might get it next time he saw her.

Adaora walked to her car, smiling, thinking that she might have made a big mistake by playing hard to get. Well, only time would tell if she had made the right decision.

First week of April, and the clocks had just gone forward an hour. Losing that hour felt like an eternity to Nkechi. She had spent all night marking piles of assignments and the pile didn't seem to be getting any smaller.

Nkechi woke up that morning feeling as if she wanted to call in sick; but she knew she couldn't if she wanted to get all her work done and dusted before her trip to Nigeria. End of term was a mere touching distance away – only three days left with the students, one staff-training day, and then she would be off for two weeks.

Nkechi was often in a daydream state: mental pictures of her in Nigeria in the heat would fill her head, but she tried to keep those thoughts in check, especially when she was at work. Still, the countdown was in full effect. Monday was now done.

Nkechi strolled through the halls of the school, looking fatigued. When she got to her office, she looked at her to-do list. What she was dreading the most was writing her end of term reports for all her students – a task she knew she had to complete before she even started packing her bags for Nigeria. There was no time like the present, so Nkechi locked herself in the office and started the monumental task of marking and writing reports.

A few hours went by. The school was silent, since staff and students had called it a day long before. Nkechi looked at her watch: half past seven. She wondered why there was still so much light outside, standing up to stretch her legs and walking over to the window. She quickly remembered that the clocks had moved forward and they were now in the glorious British Summer Time.

Nkechi's phone started to vibrate. She rummaged through her bag, trying to find the phone, hoping she would not miss the call.

She found it just in time. 'Hello.'

'Where are you?' Patrick asked.

'I'm still at work, babe.'

'At this time? You need to take it easy before you burn yourself out!' Patrick sounded very concerned.

'I'm fine. I just have so much to do. If I wasn't travelling I could spread it out over the Easter break, but I need to do it before I leave,' she replied.

'Okay; no worries. Well, the main reason I called is because my family finally got a response from your parents. It looks like we are all set to get married! They have officially given their blessing for us to be man and wife!'

'That's good news,' she said, in a monotone voice.

'You don't sound very enthusiastic about it.'

'It's not that, babe. I am just so tired.'

'Then, just go home and rest!' Patrick insisted. 'You can carry on tomorrow. You sound so exhausted.'

'You are right. I'll just come in really early tomorrow.'

'That's good,' he said.

'Can I see you tomorrow evening?' she asked. 'I want to spend as much time with you as I can before I leave on Saturday.'

'I have a case at Chelmsford Crown Court tomorrow, but I should be back by seven,' Patrick said. 'You have a key. If I am not back, just wait for me at mine.'

'Okay. See you tomorrow. I love you.'

'I love you, too,' he replied.

The next evening, Nkechi walked into Patrick's apartment, picked up the letters from the floor and glanced at them. She stood there for a moment looking at his last name. *Mr and Mrs Eze*, she thought. Nkechi felt excited at the prospect of marrying a man she considered to be her soulmate.

She went to the kitchen and put away all the groceries she had bought for him. Then Nkechi sat down and pulled out her pile of assignments and started to mark. She was getting through them really quickly.

Nkechi could hear the keys in the door. That's when she looked at her watch and realised that it was eight pm. She had been sitting there marking for two hours and had forgotten to cook for Patrick! Nkechi ran over to the kitchen and looked through the cupboard where he kept all the take away menus.

'Hey, babe, I'm so sorry. I got caught up with my marking and lost track of time. What would you prefer, Indian or Chinese?' she asked, holding up both menus, pouting while trying to smile.

'It's all good. Sorry I'm late, anyway. Chinese is fine,' Patrick said as he walked over and gave her a kiss on the forehead. 'I'll have the king prawn fried rice with black bean sauce,'

Nkechi felt relieved; called the restaurant and made the order. They were both regular customers at Mr Wing's, and had built up a good relationship with them.

'How was your case?' Nkechi asked.

Patrick blew out his cheeks. 'It is intense. Manslaughter charge. My client was constantly bullied by a group of boys and one day he lost it and went for one of bullies. Unfortunately, the boy died from his head injuries. First day of the trial.'

'It's so sad when I hear about all these young people who lose their lives at such a young age,' she said.

'It is sad, but please let's not talk about work-related things tonight.' Patrick demanded, stroking her cheek.

Patrick and Nkechi sat in the bedroom after they finished their dinner. Patrick pulled Nkechi closer to him and gently started to run his hand down her thigh. She felt a tingling sensation. His touch felt warm to her, as he kissed her on the forehead and slowly made his way to her full, rounded lips. A gentle kiss at first; his lips felt soft on hers. She started to breathe heavily and he kissed the back on her neck, one of her sensual spots. He loved to tease her with that kiss. Nkechi felt weak. She rolled away from him and looked him in the eyes.

'Babe, stop,' she whispered.

Patrick could not hear her and decided to pull her closer again. She resisted.

'Is everything okay?' he panted.

'I want us to wait.'

'What do you mean?' he asked, looking perplexed.

'I want us to wait for when we get married,' she repeated.

Patrick could not understand why. 'But…' He sat up and moved to the edge of the bed. 'What?'

'I just want us to be celibate till we get married,' Nkechi explained. 'So we have something we can look for to on our wedding night. I want us to practise discipline.'

'Discipline? Well, school mistress, that was something I was looking forward to now!' he joked. 'Practice makes perfect.'

Nkechi was not in a laughing mood. 'Patrick, I am serious. This is important to me.'

'Okay...' Patrick frowned. 'I would understand if we had never had sex before and you wanted to save it till then, but I can't understand this. Besides... I am still hard.'

Nkechi took his hand and looked at him. 'I just need you to do this for me, please,' she said.

Patrick stared back, his eyes softening. He sighed. 'So – just for my understanding, which wedding are we talking about?' He raised one of his eyebrows, waiting for an answer.

'After the traditional wedding in August,' she replied.

Patrick blew a big sigh of relief. 'That's good. Because if you meant the white wedding next year, then we would have to really talk about this!' he mocked.

Nkechi pushed him off the bed, where he fell, arms flailing, onto the carpet. 'With regard to the traditional, I am only flying out Adaora and Gloria.'

Patrick slowly got himself back on the bed. 'You play too much,' he said. 'I will be flying over just Kola and Iyke. A few of the other guys will pay for their own tickets.'

'Can you believe it's only five months to go?' she said. 'I can't wait.'

'I know I definitely can't wait,' Patrick said, between gritted teeth.

That night, Patrick held Nkechi tightly as she fell asleep, looking peaceful and content. Patrick was still feeling deprived – and he now had a few months ahead to wait.

Saturday arrived and the sun was out in full force; Spring was in effect as the trees blossomed and children filled the park, all enjoying their Easter break.

Nkechi was excited about finally going back to Nigeria after such a long time. She and her dad had just finished checking in at Gatwick airport, which was very congested because scores of families were going away for the Easter holidays.

Nkechi took her mum aside. 'Mum, please… You need to clear the air with Adaora. How long will you both be acting like this?'

Mrs Edozie gave her a warm embrace. 'My daughter, do not worry about such things. We will reconcile.'

'Okay, mum.'

'*Ijeoma.* Safe journey.'

Patrick and Adaora both said their farewells. More hugs were exchanged before Nkechi and Mr Edozie headed through to the departure gates. Nkechi was relieved to be finally in the departure lounge, after the scare during checkout when her suitcase was nearly over the weight allowed – mainly filled with gift items her mum had packed in her bag for people in the village.

'Dad, how long will we be in Lagos?'

'I have some business to take care of, so I am planning for us to be there at least five days,' he replied.

'How long is the drive from Lagos to Nnewi?' she asked.

'It all depends on traffic. If the road is clear, seven hours. Worst case scenario, ten hours.'

'That's a long drive!' she said.

'Yes, it is, my dear.'

They were extra early for their flight, so they both shopped and looked around, trying to pass the time. Nkechi was already missing

Patrick and being in the fragrance shop only reminded her of him more. She picked up the Hugo Boss fragrance and sprayed it on her wrist, wanting to take his scent with her on the flight.

Nkechi met up with her dad again just before they boarded, her excitement continuing to grow. 'Dad, can I ask you something?'

'Yes, my dear, of course.'

'How much am I worth? What is the bride price, in essence?'

'My dear, it is a tradition that goes back many years. For me, personally, it is not about the money. Many people give a list and an amount, but never touch the money. There is no amount anyone could bring that would ever be enough, for my daughter.'

Nkechi hugged her dad. In that moment, she felt as if she was ten again: daddy's little princess.

The following week, Adaora was on her way to her swimming class, anxious and hopeful that Charles would be there again. All week, she had been thinking about that handsome stranger she had met in a pool. It was not a place she had ever thought she would meet someone.

Arriving at the leisure centre in good time, she looked around the car park but could not see his car. During the class, she started thinking that maybe she should just have exchanged numbers that day. This chain of thought did not last long, since she was optimistic that he would show up. Besides, helping people change their negative thought patterns was what she did for a living – so it was only natural that she started thinking positively about the situation she was in.

The hour was almost up and Charles was still nowhere to be seen when Adaora finished her last lap. She had now lost all hope that he would show up. She hopped out of the pool and wrapped herself with her towel, walking gingerly towards the changing room, disappointed.

As she made her way to her car, her phone started to ring. Looking at the phone, she could not recognise the number. It looked like an international call.

'Hello?'

'Ada, it's me!' Nkechi's familiar voice could be heard – but only slightly, on what was a poor connection.

'Nkechi! I can barely hear you,' Adaora said.

The line went quiet. Adaora looked at her phone to see if she was still connected, then heard Nkechi say 'hello' again.

'Is that better?' Nkechi asked.

'That's slight better,' Adaora confirmed, bleeping her car doors unlocked. 'So how is Nigeria treating you?'

'It's going really well. The weather is so hot. I'm in the shower, like, five times a day.' 'Yes, you must be enjoying it,' Adaora said, dumping her swimming bag into the boot and slamming the lid down. 'Same old grey skies and rain here. If we are lucky, the sun might make an appearance on the odd day.'

'Yeah, there was so much to do in Lagos, but we are on our way to the village right now. This journey is so tedious and the road and traffic are not helping at all.'

Adaora was now sitting in her car, seatbelt on. In her rear-view mirror, she noticed a dark car slowly making its way towards her. It parked right behind her, trapping her in her parking place.

'Hey!' she said involuntarily, peering into the mirror. 'Nkechi, can you call me back in about twenty minutes? Some idiot has just parked their car right behind me, blocking men in.'

'Alright, no worries. I'll call you later,' Nkechi said.

Adaora put down the phone, kissing her teeth. While she was trying to undo her seatbelt, there was knock on her car door. She glared through the door window, and there he was – fully suited and booted! Adaora's heart started to beat faster than normal. Charles stood there, smiling at her. There was something about him that made her slightly nervous. It must have been his piecing brown eyes: she could barely make eye contact. She felt naked as if he could see inside her. She lowered the window.

'Sorry for keeping you pegged in, but I couldn't let you leave without talking to you first.'

Adaora smiled at him while she fixed the head-wrap she normally had on after swimming. 'So, what did you want to talk to me about?'

'Well, since we met last week, I haven't stopped thinking about you…'

Adaora felt her heart race, but kept her composure, trying not to give away too much as he went on: 'The fact that I couldn't get in touch with you made it even harder. I had a late meeting today, hence I didn't make the lesson, but as soon as it finished, I had to make sure I came to see you.'

'Well, that's nice. And here I am,' Adaora said, sarcastically, hiding the fact that she was excited and elated that he had gone to such lengths to see her again.

'Here you are indeed. I came here to tell you that I will be taking you out this weekend,' he said, with a cheeky grin on his face.

'You seem pretty sure of yourself! What makes you think I would say yes?'

'Let's just call it a man's intuition.'

Adaora laughed. She took out her bag, pulled out one of her business cards and handed it to him. Charles looked at the card.

'Thanks, doctor,' he said, smiling at her. He went back to his car, shouting: 'I'll be in touch!' before driving off.

Thursday was always a busy day for Adaora, full of patients; although this particular Thursday was different, since during the Easter period, many of her patients were away. Adaora was in her office when the receptionist notified her that her 2pm appointment had arrived and Adaora instructed her to show them to her waiting area.

She quickly went through the notes of the new patient referred by her doctor: Paige Edwards, 13, who suffered from depression. Closing the file, Adaora opened the door and invited Paige, and the young woman who was with her, into the office.

'Hi, my name is Leanne Smith, Paige's social worker.'

'Hi, I am Dr Adaora Edozie.'

'Nice to meet you. I will be bringing Paige to the sessions every week until she feels comfortable coming on her own.'

'That is fine. I am sure you are aware that the session will be private between Paige and me,' Adaora replied.

'Yes, of course.' She looked over at Paige. 'I will be right outside.' She walked out and Adaora closed the door.

Paige had a blank stare, freckles sprinkled all over her pale face, and thick frizzy brown hair. Her hair was the only indication that she was mixed race: other than that, she just looked like a very pale Caucasian teenager.

'Would you like some orange juice?' Adaora asked. Paige ignored her.

Adaora poured some fresh orange juice and placed it on the table next to where Paige was sitting before she took her seat opposite her.

'Why do you think you are here today, Paige?' Paige sat still and made no attempt to answer Adaora's questions, so she went on: 'I understand that this might be overwhelming for you. You should know who I am before you feel the need to answer my questions. My name is Adaora, and I am psychotherapist who uses something called CBT as a method of treatment. I am here to help change any negative thought patterns you have and turn them positive. For that to work, we need to be able to talk to each other.'

Adaora waited patiently to see if Paige would respond, but Paige stayed silent. Adaora saw that the girl's attention was diverted towards the painting of the safari sunset. Adaora walked over to the painting, and put her hand on it, feeling its rough, thick brushstrokes of dry paint.

'This is one of my favourite paintings. Every time I look at it, it takes me to a happy place. I think about being there, under the orange sunset, looking over the glorious creatures we have on this planet,' Adaora stated.

Paige stood up and walked over to the painting.

'What do you see? Adaora asked.

Paige put her hands on the painting, too, slowly feeling the brushstrokes. She leaned over. 'I see…' Paige spoke softly. 'I see freedom.'

She looked at Adaora, and gave her a faint smile before sitting back on the sofa.

Saturday evening – and Shoreditch was thriving with partygoers. The night was still young and the binge-drinking had already started. Adaora, shaking her head in disappointment, saw people throwing up and urinating in the middle of the street.

She sat quietly for a few moments, gathering her thoughts while Charles was talking on the phone, having picked her up and now taking her to the City for dinner. Adaora was impressed at how clean he kept his car, which still had that new car scent to it.

They arrived at London Liverpool Street: one of the financial districts of London during the day that turned into a party district. Charles held Adaora's hand as they walked toward Heron Tower, entered the glass lift and headed to the thirty eighth floor. The view of London at night was spectacular.

'Beautiful view.' Charles stated.

'It most certainly is.'

Charles and Adaora stood hand in hand at the entrance of the restaurant waiting to be seen.

'Welcome to SushiSamba. Do you have a reservation?' the waitress asked.

'Yes, I do. Charles Udoji. It should be a table for two.'

'Yes. Right this way, please.' She ushered them to their table.

The restaurant ceiling was made up of bamboo sticks, diagonally interwoven, with single light bulbs that hung above each table. The lights were dimmed, and their table was right by the window overlooking the City.

Charles took Adaora's jacket and helped her with her seat before she sat down. She smiled at the gesture. Charles could not help but stare at her red dress; her make-up was subtle but the red lipstick matched the dress, which hugged her skin, showing enough cleavage to get his attention, but also saying she was a classy woman.

'You looked beautiful,' Charles said.

'Thank you. You look pretty good yourself.'

Charles wore a suede black blazer, trousers and loafers. It was his regular look and he always believed in looking as sharp as possible.

'I've always wanted to come to this restaurant,' she claimed, looking around.

'It is one of my favourite Japanese restaurants. Great food, great service and a great view. Can't go wrong.'

'Well, I'll be the judge of the quality of food. As for the service and view, so far so good.' Adaora said, folding her hands on the table. 'So. I have told you about my family and you are yet to tell me anything about yours.'

Charles' face went from one of smiles of delight to despondency.

'Sorry if that is a sensitive subject for you,' Adaora said in a sincere tone. 'Feel free to not answer.'

'No, it's fine,' Charles reassured her. He continued: 'I do not have any family. Both of my parents were killed in a road traffic accident in Nigeria when I was thirteen. I was brought back to the UK after a year and placed in foster care when no immediate family took me in.'

'So sorry to hear that.'

'It's fine. Life happens you just have to find a way to move past the tough times…' Then the food they had ordered started to arrive. 'Let's eat.' Charles said.

During the dinner, Adaora's phone rang. Looking at the phone, she saw it was her mother, but ignored the call and carried on eating.

A few minutes later, she called again. Although Adaora wondered why she was calling, they had not spoken on good terms for a while, and she was not in the mood to argue with her mum on what was turning out to be a perfect night. Then, Adaora's phone went off again – this time with a text message.

'Is everything okay?' Charles asked.

'I'm sorry,' Adaora said, staring at her phone. 'Something is up. My mum told me to call her, right now.'

'Please make the call if you want to,' Charles said.

Adaora walked to the entrance of the restaurant as she waited for her mum to pick up her call.

'Hello!' Mrs Edozie said, frantically. Her breathing was heavy and she could barely get her words out.

Adaora felt the panic in her voice. 'Mum, what is the matter?' she asked.

'*Ndi Nto*! *Ndi Nto* have your sister!' Mrs Edozie wailed.

'Mum, what do you mean *Ndi Nto*?'

'Kidnappers have taken your sister in Nnewi! Your daddy just called me.'

In that moment, Adaora's heart sank. She dropped her phone and sat on the floor.

Charles saw what happened and ran over to her. 'Adaora! Is everything okay?'

Adaora could barely get her words out. 'We need to go to my mum's house right now… please!' she shouted.

Charles ran back to get their jackets and paid for the dinner before they rushed out of the restaurant, while onlookers wondered what had happened.

Chapter Four

FOOT PRESSED ON THE ACCELERATOR, ITCHING TO GET TO HIS DESTINATION, Charles weaved through the traffic as best he could. Weekends populated the streets with black taxis, the large lumbering vehicles plaguing the roads – randomly stopping to collect or drop off a customer.

An eerie silence lingered in the car; the echo of anxiety was evidenced by Adaora constantly checking her phone, tapping the window and generally being agitated, impatient to get home. Her mind was full of conflicting thoughts: trying to stay calm, yet full of unanswered questions. With her shoulders tense, her left hand was gripping her right fingers until they turned white; the level of frustration continued to bubble and boil beneath the service.

As another taxi intercepted them, swerving diagonally across their path without signalling, Adaora screamed at the driver. The intense, shrill tone of her voice shocked Charles and he quickly responded, unsure if his gesture would be positively received but hoping she would not be offended.

Moving his hand from the gear stick to her thigh, he said gently, 'Try and stay calm.'

Taking a deep breath, Adaora rested her hand on top of his and squeezed it. She was highly strung and his touch reminded her that it was not helping the situation. Putting to good use the relaxation techniques she prescribed to her patients, she sat back, closed her eyes and focused on her breathing. The animosity that had hung over her relationship with her mother was forgotten; they were a strong family – when one was affected, they all felt the pain.

Replaying the conversation over in her mind, Adaora struggled to deal with the facts. Nkechi. Her beautiful sister. Kidnapped. Anything could be happening to her! The panic her mum had released deposited itself into her soul. It had been a long time since she had felt so overwhelmed and helpless: the last time this feeling had visited her was when Mr Edozie had suffered a silent heart attack. As a family, they'd had to band together to support each other during that difficult time; to survive and endure that season. Adaora gave herself an internal therapy session: negative thoughts were not in her nature and she knew the damage they had on behaviour and actions. She wanted to be in a calm state when she arrived at her mum's house.

Once the car was parked, Adaora flew out, running up the pathway. The door was flung open, revealing an atmosphere of chaos and confusion. In the living room, her mum was wearing out the carpet, pacing up and down and talking loudly – an open plea to the heavenly father for her daughter's safe return. Her eyes were red and puffy from the constant flow of salty tears.

Adaora ran over to her mum and gave her a huge hug. Mrs Edozie, finally able to share the burden of the news, crumpled onto her daughter in relief. Behind them, Charles had entered the house quietly. Unsure of his role in the situation, he stood awkwardly at the living room door, looking noticeably out of place. His manners, however, hadn't left him.

'Good evening, Aunty,' he greeted, feeling uneasy.

Adaora looked up, remembering his assistance and support and motioned for him to come closer. 'Mum, this is Charles, a friend of mine. He was with me when you called and drove me here.'

Ever the host, Mrs Edozie smiled warmly at Charles, through her distractedness. 'Good evening, Charles. Thank you for bringing her to me.'

Adaora was desperate to find out what had happened to Nkechi. She urged her mother to give her more details. 'So, mum, what did daddy say happened?'

The question set off a wave of anxiety and Mrs Edozie was visibly shaken by having to even recall the information. Lips quivering, the dam behind her eyes collapsed and the tears rolled down her cheeks.

Adaora pulled tissues from the box on the coffee table and gently wiped her mother's face as she looked off into the distance and began a wail that shook the foundations of the house.

'Ohhh! They have taken my daughter! They have taken my daughter!' The echo enveloped the room.

Placing her arm around her mother's shoulders, Adaora comforted her in silence, waiting for the grief to pass enough to allow her mother to speak.

A whisper arose from Mrs Edozie's lips: 'Earlier this evening, I was sewing some clothes for Mama Obi, when I received a call from your dad. The line was not clear but I could hear in his tone that something was not right. Since they set foot in Nigeria, my spirit has been concerned. When he told me *Ndi nto* had taken Nkechi I fell to the ground. The weight of the phone-call paralysed me. My worst fears have come true.'

Her eyes were welling up, but Adaora refused to cry; tapping her face with the tissue she sniffled, pulling the emotions back. Charles was still positioned by the door in an uneasy stance, shaking his head in disbelief.

'Charles, please have a seat,' Adaora's mum said.

Obeying her welcome, Charles sat tentatively on the armchair, unsure of what to say or do. The situation seemed inflammatory and he wanted to be present to support Adaora any way he could.

Mrs Edozie kept looking anxiously at her phone. 'I am waiting for your father to ring again. He told me not to spread the news yet, until he received more information. I have only told Patrick, and he is on his way here, now.'

'What about Chidi?' Adaora asked.

'I could not get through to him. You can try him again.'

Taking out her phone, Adaora attempted to call her brother, although she knew that if he answered, it would be out of character. Typically, there was no response. She called him again. No answer. As she was contemplating whether to text him instead, there was a knock on the door, so she got up to answer it.

Dishevelled, out of breath and worried, Patrick stood there. 'What happened?' he asked frantically as he entered the house. 'Any news?'

'Come in, Patrick,' Adaora said. 'No news yet.'

Patrick walked in and sat down opposite Adaora's mum. 'Good evening,' he greeted.

'Evening, my dear,' she responded.

Perplexed, Patrick looked over at the other male in the room and wondered who he was and why he was present at such a serious family moment. Adaora saw the look – almost dismissive – and quickly began introductions.

'Patrick, this is my friend, Charles. Charles, this is my sister's fiancé, Patrick.'

The two didn't exchange words but nodded at each other.

Patrick was still trying to catch his breath and turned his attention to Mrs Edozie. 'As soon as I got the call from you, I jumped on the train because my car is being serviced. There was too much traffic from Dalston station, so I started running. I still cannot believe this is actually happening.'

The phone on the table started ringing. Jumping out of her seat, Mrs Edozie picked it up. 'Hello... can you hear me?' Silence. 'Papa Ada, can you hear me?' she repeated. Adaora's mum put the phone on loudspeaker.

'Yes, I can hear you,' he replied.

'I am here with Ada and Patrick. *Kedu ihe na-eme ebe-ahụ?* What is happening there?'

Mr Edozie let out a huge sigh. 'Evening, Ada and Patrick. I am glad you are there to support Mama. It is a very difficult situation.' He paused. 'Early this morning, Nkechi and I had breakfast at a local food parlour. I had a few meetings throughout the day and she wanted to follow me, to make some contacts. We visited that land I bought last year in *Otolo*, and I needed to get some more money from the bank for the workers to finish fencing the land. We went to the Keystone branch on *Ezemewi* street.

'As soon as the car left the compound of the bank, three cars surrounded us – and at least nine men jumped out. Dressed in black, faces covered with red bandanas, hands full of guns and machetes…'

Here, Mrs Edozie whimpered, her hand flying to her mouth.

Her husband went on: '… threatening me. Telling me to give them the money. Nkechi grabbed my arm – I saw the fear in her eyes. I was worried about our safety – so I gave them the money happily, hoping they would be satisfied.'

Adaora could no longer hold her tears back. They fell angrily towards the floor as she tried to imagine Nkechi's emotional state.

'… They said it was nowhere near enough. They wouldn't let us go. Before I knew it, two of them had opened the passenger door and pulled Nkechi to the ground. I tried to pull her back in, but they were too strong. I got out of the car, shouting and screaming at them – demanding them to leave her alone. Nkechi was screaming as they stuffed her in their car.'

Patrick's face was set in a mask of fury, his hands in tight fists.

'… As I ran to save her, they put a knife to her throat and told me if I advanced, they would slit her throat.' Above Mrs Edozie's weeping, her husband's voice broke: 'I didn't know what to do. I stood still as they drove away, Nkechi screaming at me to save her.' His voice cracked. 'I collapsed in the street – my heart sank. It happened in broad daylight, so many people doing their business. And me. Broken. We have to get her back. I am doing everything I can. I have made reports of the kidnap and spoken to police commanders about what we do next.'

'Dad!' Adaora cried, desperately. 'What can we do from here? Can we call the police here?'

'My dear, just pray. The police there can do nothing, and would only liaise with the Nigerian force, which I am doing directly.

Mama – I will call you as soon as I can. Patrick – stay strong and look after my family.'

'Yes, sir,' he replied.

As the call ended, all eyes were lowered; sound muted.

The air was heavy. Adaora needed a moment to herself. She walked to the kitchen sobbing, wiping her chin with the back of her hand, her face wet with tears. She dialled Chidi again. After three rings, he picked up.

'Sis? You guys miss me that much, huh? Calls from you and mama today. What's up?'

Adaora didn't know how to form the words. They felt unfamiliar on her tongue. 'Something has happened in Nigeria. Dad just called – Nkechi has been taken. Kidnapped.'

Chidi laughed. 'You can't get me that easy, sis. April Fool's was a few days ago.'

'I'm serious, Chidi.'

'Oh, yeah, of course you are. I'm always the subject of pranks from you lot.' This was true. Nkechi and Adaora had made it their duty to tease Chidi, for his whole life. He was the youngest, and spoilt – not receiving the same hard discipline they had endured growing up. So, they had taken the mantle upon themselves.

'Chidi...' Adaora's voice broke. She wished it was a prank. That it wasn't really happening. The tears began to fall again and she sobbed into the phone.

Chidi asked his friends to leave his room. He sat on the edge of his single bed and tried to console his sister, still in shock, over the phone. Adaora didn't ever cry.

'Ada. How... I mean... when did this...? Nkechi... NO! This can't be happening. Where are you?'

'I'm at mum's.'

As Adaora was talking, Chidi was grabbing his keys, wallet and jacket. 'I'll be there as soon as I can.'

Back in the living room, the scene had not altered. Everyone sat, as static as when she had left. She walked over to Charles, and muttered, 'You really do not have to stay. I appreciate you sticking around this long.'

'It's totally fine. I want to be here.'

Adaora managed to muster a smile, glad he was there and willing to stay with her. Patrick stood frozen, his clenched fist repeatedly hitting his open palm. Then he started pacing up and down.

Mrs Edozie was shaking her head and mumbling things under her breath, then louder and louder until they erupted, grasping everyone's attention. '*Ike gwụla m!* I'm just so tired of that country. These people will not kill me,' she said.

Adaora walked over to her mother and hugged her tightly. They looked at each other. It had been months since they had experienced this amount of physical contact; but the situation was greater than their differences. They had the same aim. The same focus. To protect their family.

'Mum, why would anyone want to take Nkechi? It is not like she is known, back home, or has done anything to anyone back there.'

'*Nne*, kidnapping in Nigeria is not a new thing. It has been going on for years, but it had quietened down. It has nothing to do with Nkechi, personally. This is business and how some evil people make their living...'

Patrick interrupted: 'I remember when I was younger, my dad was talking about a family friend who was kidnapped in *Ozubulu*...'

'These bastards just want money!' Mrs Edozie continued. 'When kidnapping was rampant in Igbo land, many people who lived abroad – and even in Lagos – would refuse to travel back East. People were being taken and large amounts of money were always asked in exchange for the safe return of the person.'

'But it's not as if we're celebrities or millionaires!'

'Pah!' Mrs Edozie made an explosive noise. 'They think anyone who lives in Britain is wealthy!'

'How would they know who to target?' Adaora asked.

'It must be insiders,' Patrick replied.

'Exactly,' Mrs Edozie snapped. 'I am always wary when I go back, because you never know who you can trust. Even the people close to you can be capable of conspiring with *Ndi Nto*.'

'That is beyond belief!' Charles exclaimed. 'I just don't understand why people would do that to each other. It is not right.'

'It is because of greed. Some people have success – and animals like these bastards who have taken my...' Mrs Edozie could not continue. She could not bear to think about what could be happening to Nkechi. She got up from the sofa and made her way upstairs.

After staying a few hours, Charles departed. His kindness and compassion had not gone unnoticed by Adaora.

Sitting alongside Patrick, they attempted to discuss and comprehend the situation. Although they exchanged words, it all felt surreal; both waiting for the phone to ring with news that Nkechi was safe. That call didn't come.

Around 10pm, Chidi burst through the door, full of emotional energy. Dashing his bags to one side, he dissolved into Adaora's arms and hugged her tightly. As the only sibling Adaora could currently embrace, she held onto him, almost squeezing the air out of him.

'I'm so happy to see you,' she whispered in his ear.

'Where's mum?'

'She is upstairs, resting.'

Looking up and seeing Patrick, Chidi walked over to him and shook his hand, before pulling him into a bear hug. Hearing her son's voice from the bedroom, Mrs Edozie quickly made her way downstairs, her eyes red, her face tired. Overwhelmed with emotion, Chidi wrapped his soul around her; she was the backbone of the family but now she felt weak and Chidi wanted to give her whatever strength he had left.

They settled in the front room on opposite sofas. Full of questions and disbelief that such a thing could happen, Chidi heard the details from the rest of the family. When they had exhausted the available information, Chidi piped up: 'So what is dad saying? Are the police involved?'

At the mention of the police, frown lines manifested on his mum's forehead, in a tense ball of disapproval. 'We just have to put all our hopes in prayer, because that stupid corrupt organisation they call 'police' in Nigeria will not help matters.'

Chidi understood his mother's frustration but was still confused. 'So who is dad talking to, if the police are not useful?'

'We aren't sure,' Patrick offered gently, recognising the frustration in Chidi's eyes – the need to be doing something practical. 'He said he will call us back soon.'

'But what's happening?'

Having had more experience, Mrs Edozie attempted to fill in the gaps for a naive Chidi. 'When kidnappers have taken people, they will find a way to contact the family to give them a ransom amount.'

'So, if they make that contact…' Chidi started, the clogs in his brain ticking, 'can the police not trace who they are and apprehend them?'

His question was met with heightened sarcasm. 'Which police?' Mrs Edozie retorted. 'The same police that might be in bed with the kidnappers? The people who will all share, when the ransom is paid?'

'Mum, come on!' Adaora piped up. 'All these wild conspiracy theories! Surely that cannot be true?'

The reply came: 'Hmmmmm...' followed by a loud grunt in her direction.

Unsettled by the lack of information, Chidi abruptly stood up, his face a combination of pain and anger – his eyes squinting, his lips scrunched. He walked towards the door, his fingers fused into a fist and pulled back his right shoulder, releasing a massive thud into the opposing wall, before exiting. The unexpected noise caused everyone to jump and turn towards him, but he had already escaped.

Worried, Adaora ran after him. It was a position she had played often in their childhood. Chidi had a very short fuse and his inability to regulate his emotions had led to detentions, exclusions, fights in school. Adaora was always the one attempting to help him to manage his feelings; even now. In her career and education, she had started at home, desperate for Chidi to learn to channel his aggression into other areas, especially in sport. This had been working. The sound of that punch had transported Adaora back to the old, enraged Chidi.

She saw him sitting in the garden, nursing a swollen hand. Grabbing a packet of frozen vegetables, she went up next to him. 'Chidi are you okay?'

He remained silent.

'Just hold this against it, so the swelling can go down.'

He looked up and took the offering. 'Thanks.'

'I know you are angry, but hurting yourself will not help the situation. So, please, no more punches to the walls,' Chidi sighed.

'I just want her back.'

'She will be back. We just have to all stay positive.'

Adaora held her brother in her arms. They both stopped talking. She kept replaying, in her head, what she had just said to Chidi. Trying to believe it herself.

The leather sofa cushions screeched through the night, unable to soothe an unsettled Patrick. Sleep was cheating on him with someone else, and his eyes pierced, trying to make some sense of the darkness, as he listened to the constant ticking of the clock.

The sun rose and he was still conscious, unmoved by the birds chirping happily outside. His soul longed for Nkechi: to see her face, hold her in his arms. He couldn't bear the uncertainty.

Hearing the rhythmic footsteps he knew were Adaora's, Patrick sat up, rubbed the bags under his eyes and peered at the time. It was 9am. A few seconds later, as expected, Adaora walked into the living room.

'Morning,' she greeted.

'Morning.'

'Did you manage to get some sleep?'

'Not really. I couldn't stop thinking about her. My mind was constantly racing, trying not to think the worst.'

'I know exactly what you mean. I could not sleep at all.' She walked towards the kitchen. 'Would you like tea or coffee?' she called behind her.

'Nothing for me yet. I need to quickly buy a toothbrush.'

'We have a few spare, upstairs.'

'Ok, thanks.'

Shortly after, Chidi and his mother also rose from slumber and made their way downstairs, congregating in the living room. Sunday mornings usually began with the sweet melodies of worship songs projecting from Mrs Edozie's joy as she readied herself for church. Like clockwork. Without fail. Yet, this morning had brought a sorrow she couldn't escape. It sat on her back, weighing her down. Even her posture was downtrodden.

Despite her feelings, her faith remained. She summoned the household to her side.

'I want us all to go to church, so we can pray and let the pastor pray for Nkechi.'

The air echoed a deafening silence. Hearing the word 'church' Adaora flinched and refused to look at her mother.

Chidi, understanding the importance and also knowing that the suggestion was technically not a request, broke the silence. 'Okay,' he said.

Patrick nodded in agreement.

Mrs Edozie looked at her daughter and waited for the inclination of a response. 'Adaora, will you be joining us in church?'

'Yes,' she said between clenched teeth. She had her own reservations about religion, opinions she had debated before with her mum, but she knew this was not the time to resurrect old debates. She would do it, for Nkechi.

Adaora approached the PWC (Pentecostal Worship Centre) in Finchley, North London, with trepidation; it had been a long time since she had been inside a church building. She felt trapped inside the transformed bingo hall – now modernised and converted into a state of the art facility. As they were ushered to their red seats, Adaora considered the money that had been spent on the changes and pondered the question: at whose expense had they come? Her mother was a devoted Christian and had attended this fellowship for over a decade.

As a young girl, Adaora was sent to Sunday school along with her siblings and enjoyed being around people her age. However, as she grew, things about the church began to tug at her conscience and she began vocalising her doubts, asking questions that were always dismissed by her mother. The lack of attention to her inquiries left Adaora ambivalent; as soon as she was able, she left the church. Her mother regarded this decision negatively and they had often had heated discussions about her 'lack of faith'. Church was an important part of her mother's identity and culture; her attendance was flawless and she was well-known amongst the large congregation.

The worship team were in full swing, blending glorious harmonies over intertwined piano, bass and drum beats. Somewhere in the distance, a tambourine was being jingled enthusiastically. The lyrics were displayed on large screens over their heads and although the tune was catchy, Adaora could not bring her lips to utter the words. She shifted uncomfortably as the church swayed in a rhythm that didn't belong to her.

The atmosphere shifted as voices were raised to the heavens in powerful prayers. Adaora watched, with interest, the energetic display – all around, palms were upturned, necks bowed, eyes closed. Unidentifiable language rushed throughout the church as people began to speak in unknown tongues. Over the microphone, a plea for lost souls boomed; an invitation for anyone who wanted to accept Jesus as their personal saviour. Before long, the altar was full of people waiting for the pastor to lay hands on them. There was authority in his touch – people began to fall, as he anointed them. *Dominoes,* Adaora thought. As the pastor prayed, he began to declare words over certain members' situations and circumstances, walking along the aisles and stopping at various places. At one point, he stood directly in front of Adaora and her family.

His voice, intense and poignant, washed over them: 'There is a great burden on this family. Something has just happened that has brought you all to God today. Well, let me tell you that the spirit of the God is here.'

'Amen!' the congregation simultaneously said.

The pastor continued. 'I hear the Lord saying that the attack on this family is from the enemy, and it shall not prosper in Jesus' name. Anything that has been taken from you shall return to you, the way it was.'

'AMEN!' Mrs Edozie shouted victoriously, knowing that God had spoken directly to her.

The pastor continued to walk, decreeing and praying specific prayers over people. The core of Adaora's resentment had been shaken by his words. It was so relevant to their current state of affairs. She wondered if her mum had already informed the pastor. It niggled at her, the thought continuing to plague her mind throughout the service until they got home.

Later that evening, the call from Mr Edozie with an update finally came. He informed them that progress had been made. Contact with prominent members within the police had reassured him that Nkechi would be found. His voice came over the loudspeaker: clear, calm and succinct. He did his best to put everyone at ease, told them to continue praying and carry on as best they could.

On Monday, Adaora decided to stay at home. She had no patients and needed a day to recollect her thoughts. Emotionally, she needed time to process, herself, before being able to deal with others.

On Tuesday, she felt better; more relaxed, reflective and ready. There was nothing she could do to help Nkechi, except wait, and trust. At the appointed time, Paige and her social worker, Leanne, walked into Adaora's office.

Leanne smiled at Adaora. 'I'll just be outside if you need me.'

'Okay,' Adaora replied, offering Paige a seat. 'Would you like something to drink?' 'Water, please.'

Adaora smiled, pleasantly surprised at the progress – that Paige spoke to her straight away – given Paige's reluctance to communicate at their first session.

'I see you straightened your hair.'

'I was bored and was playing with my foster carer's hair straighteners,' Paige replied.

'Looks good either way,' Adaora said as she gave her the bottle of water. 'So, how have you been since I last saw you?'

'I'm okay.'

Adaora sat in an open posture; everything she did was to make Paige felt at ease. 'Tell me something you did this week, that you enjoyed.'

Paige sat there, her fingers interlocked, her left leg jiggling, her foot tapping the floor repeatedly.

'I did nothing I enjoyed this week,' she moaned.

'Okay. What do you like to do? What do you enjoy?'

'Look – I don't fucking enjoy doing anything!' she yelled. 'Why are you asking me these stupid questions?' A look of pure hatred bored into Adaora, burning her face.

Adaora paused. She had never doubted herself before but was starting to question herself now. She thought that maybe coming to work had not been the best idea, because deep down, all she could think about was Nkechi.

Adaora snapped out of her daze, and put down her note pad and pen. Adaora knew that Paige had a lot going on in her life – she could sense it. The problem was that she was now frustrated with her conventional methods of questioning. She needed to really connect with Paige so that she could help her.

'I know how hard this must be for you, to come in here and be asked questions that you do not want to be asked by a stranger, no less. So, here is what I want to do. I will let you ask me three questions, and I will be as open I as can be, so you can know me a little better before we concentrate on you again. Is that fair?'

Paige slowly looked up at Adaora and nodded her head slightly.

'Go ahead,' Adaora encouraged.

Paige stared out of the window, a blank look on her face. 'Why did you want to be a doctor?'

Adaora gave a silent sigh of relief. 'Right from when I was 13, a similar age to you, I was the type of person who wanted to help people in any way that I could. The older I got, the more I knew I wanted to be a doctor. The world is filled with terrible things and beautiful things. I wanted to be a person who helps people find the beauty in life.'

Paige looked up at the artwork. 'Have you been there?'

'Where?' Adaora asked.

'The place in that picture.'

'Oh, yes, once. It is one of the most beautiful places in the world. I hope to go back one day.'

'I hope I can go there one day…' A ghost of a smile started appearing on Paige's face as she sat back on the chair. She no longer appeared stiff.

'You have one more question,' Adaora said.

'Errrm… Do you have a sister?'

Adaora sat up with intent, her eyes widened. She was curious to know why Paige had asked her that question, poignant to her at the moment, but she tried to answer casually: 'Yes, I do have a sister.'

'Okay, what's it like?' She paused. '… Never mind. My three questions are up.'

'It's okay, feel free to ask,' Adaora insisted.

'Okay. Your sister. Tell me about her.' In that moment, Paige was unable to make eye contact with Adaora. Her eyes started to redden as they gradually filled with tears.

Adaora quickly grabbed some tissue from her desk and handed it to Paige, who wiped her tears. 'I miss my sister so much!' she wailed.

'What happened to your sister?' Adaora asked.

'When they took us away from our mum and put us in care, they separated us. I hate my mum so much. I haven't seen Emma in just over a year!' she yelled.

'How has it made you feel, being away from your sister for so long?' Adaora asked, her voice soft and sympathetic.

'I wake up pissed off, every fucking day!' snarled Paige. 'So much has happened in the last two years, but when they took Emma away from me, I felt like dying. And it's all because of that bitch and her fucking boyfriend!'

'I take it you are referring to your mum?'

'Yes!' she yelled. Paige's breathing got heavier, as the thought of her mum plagued her mind. 'You know what? I can't be here, right now. I'm sorry.'

Paige slammed the door on her way out. Worried, Paige's social worker popped her head in the office to make sure that all was well, and Adaora signalled that nothing had been damaged. Relieved, the social worker chased after Paige.

Adaora swivelled her chair towards the window and just sat there, looking out. The trees, a parsley green at this time of the year, lined up in perfect uniformity and gradually unfurling flowers of assorted colours had started to appear. A sweet scent slowly entered the window, left slightly open. Spring was finally here, Adaora thought, while her mind raced back to Nkechi.

Later on, that evening, Adaora made her way back to the family home. A series of distant explosions and spitting sounds rang out. Just as she was about to put in her key in the door, the noise continued, the sputter of what seemed like an engine that had finally died. Adaora walked into the house and greeted her mum, Patrick and Chidi.

'Any updates from dad?' she asked, as she had done by phone, periodically throughout the day.

'Not yet. We tried calling him,' Chidi replied, 'but he said he would call us back when he has an update.'

'Finally, some silence. Mr Jacobs really needs to replace that lawnmower,' Mrs Edozie moaned. 'That contraption has been disturbing everyone for over an hour.'

'I wondered what all that racket was, when I was outside,' Adaora added.

She made her way to the kitchen as her stomach alerted her that it was time to eat, with sweet hymns. She responded by dishing out some leftover pasta. She realised it was one of Chidi's dishes: tuna and sweetcorn pasta was one of his favourite and easiest things to make.

Just as she was about to tuck in, Adaora could hear her mum shouting her name. Adaora quickly ran back into the living room.

'Your father is on the line!'

'Oluchi, can you hear me?' Mr Edozie asked.

'*M na-anụ.* We can all hear you,' she replied.

'The kidnappers have reached out and have delivered a message. It is a ransom amount.'

'*Ego ole?*'

Mr Edozie hesitated. A brief silence followed, in which Adaora looked at her mum.

'25 million Naira.'

'WHAT?' Mrs Edozie shouted.

'How much is that in pounds?' Adaora asked.

'Roughly about 100,000 pounds,' Patrick replied, his voice quavering slightly. The seriousness of the situation had started to dawn on him. '100k...' he repeated. 'Where are we supposed to even find that kind of money?'

'And how do we know she is even safe and alive?' Mrs Edozie asked, stunned.

'It is a good thing they are asking so much,' her husband assured her. 'Think – she is a precious thing to them. They will keep her safe.'

'Dad, what about the police?'

'I am in contact with some of the highest-ranking officers, who have promised me they are doing all they can. We do not need to worry about finding the ransom amount. Hopefully, there will be a breakthrough. We just need to all stay positive and continue to pray for Nkechi's safe return.' Mr Edozie put the phone down.

Chidi stood up and walked out of the house. Adaora went after him but was told by her mum to 'leave him be for now'.

'Something doesn't feel right, and I can't put my finger on it,' Adaora stated.

Patrick could no longer hide the frustration in his voice. 'How can they be asking for that amount of money? Do they think everyone who lives abroad are millionaires?' His voice quavered, the more he spoke.

'They make assumptions, because we live abroad. Because we have business interests. They are informed by people close to this family,' Mrs Edozie said. 'Someone somewhere does not like the progress we are making. This an attack on your father's success.'

The others shook their heads sadly, in disbelief.

'Mum, I think it's time we let Gloria and the school know what is going on,' Adaora said. 'Nkechi is due to get back to work next week.'

'Yes, I agree. Can you please take care of that? When you leave, please tell Chidi to come inside. I need to talk to him.'

Each day that passed, when Adaora woke, she felt the weight of the world on her shoulders. Every morning, she hoped that this was all a bad dream, yet the harsh hand of reality slapped her in the face every time she called Nkechi's phone and she did not respond.

On Wednesday, Adaora sat on her bed and looked at the time: 7:29. She sat quietly looking down as she dialled Nkechi's phone again. She tried the number she was using in Nigeria, but no answer.

Adaora felt cold. The window was open slightly and a breeze crept its way towards her, raising the hairs on her arms.

Later that morning, Adaora had arranged to meet up with Nkechi's best friend, Gloria.

When Adaora broke the news to her, she was devastated and could not contain her emotions. They sat in Gloria's apartment, a short walk from their family home.

'How could this happen?' Gloria asked for the fifth time. It was, by now, a rhetorical question, put out there in the hope that the universe would respond. There were no answers to this question, just more questions. Gloria's voice was brittle. The more she spoke, the more she cried.

'What do we do now? Gloria asked.

'We wait for my dad to give us more news, but in the meantime, we need to tell the school what happened. I know it is still the holidays, but will any of the staff be there?' Adaora asked.

'Yes, human resources and some of the senior staff will be in, getting ready for next week.'

'Okay. I need to go there today, before I see one of my patients this afternoon.'

'I will come with you,' Gloria said, standing up, with determination. 'Just give me 10 minutes to get ready.'

Angel's Upper Street boasted many small independent businesses that thrived during the spring and summer periods. Coffee shops were busy with people having meetings and those casually catching up on some reading. Young people crowded the cinema complex, queuing up to watch the latest blockbuster that would have them talking for weeks. Besides, they only had a few days before it was back to school or college, and time for the serious work as they entered exam periods. It was a beautiful time to be a Londoner, people walked around with smiles on their faces. Adaora walked along the street thinking about her sister, thinking about Paige, and thinking about Kevin. She finally arrived at her destination, a small bookshop that made the most delicious coffee.

She often came to Mina's Books to read and to escape. It was a space where she could just be at peace with her own thoughts, without the distractions of the fast-paced outside world. Mina sold books from the African diaspora, and Adaora always felt welcomed here. Mina was a Kenyan, the same age as Adaora, who always wore her native Ankara and loved books and selling coffee. Adaora loved the unique smell of the freshly roasted coffee beans, imported straight from Kenya.

Near the exhibition of warriors in the far corner of the low-lit coffee shop, Adaora sat in solitude, staring at the images of ancient Kenyan warriors. Her phone vibrated and when she looked at it, a smile slowly blossomed on her face.

'Can I see you today?' the text read. It was from Charles.

She had not been able to give him much thought, owing to everything that was going on. She responded that if he was free he could come and see her briefly before she went back to her mum's, and she texted Charles the address of the bookshop.

Adaora never really shared her private space in this coffee shop with anyone, but when it came to Charles, she didn't mind sharing. Charles arrived an hour later, dressed casually in jeans and a denim shirt.

'Hey, how are you?' he asked, as he kissed her on the cheek. He looked over at Mina. 'Can I take this chair?'

'Yes, that's fine,' Mina replied.

'I'm okay, just needed some space and time alone to process,' Adaora said.

His handsome face showed concern. 'You should have told me. I would have left you alone.'

'No, it's fine. I've been here a while.'

'Any progress with your sister?'

'Nothing yet. My dad is still trying to reach out to some important people so they can help. The kidnappers gave us a random amount.'

'How much is that, then?' he questioned.

'100k.'

'SERIOUSLY?' his voice burst out. He looked around to see if people had heard him. 'Pounds?'

'Yes, it is absolutely ridiculous. I still can't believe this is happening.'

'How are the rest of your family holding up?'

'Not great. My brother has major anger issues and doesn't know where to channel that aggression at the moment, and my mum is just getting more despondent, day by day.'

'So sorry to hear that,' he said sympathetically.

'Thank you, I am just trying to stay positive and stay busy. Sitting around, I feel so helpless. That why I think it's taking a major toll on my mum. She works for herself and has no desire to do anything at the moment.'

'That is understandable.'

'How are things with you?' Adaora asked.

'I'm okay, business is going well. I'm more worried about you, to be honest.'

'That's so sweet, but don't be,' Adaora said, managing a smile. 'Nkechi will be fine and so will I.'

The two sat and talked for another hour. Adaora managed to convince Charles to try some Kenyan coffee, although he wasn't too keen on hot drinks. She insisted and he gave it a try. Much to his surprise, he liked it.

The bookshop was empty. Mina had already closed the shop, but allowed Adaora and Charles to relax. Mina and Adaora had a really good relationship, since Adaora had been a loyal customer ever since she had opened, 3 years before.

Adaora watched Charles while he was talking. She felt comfortable being around him: he made her feel safe. All these feelings rushing inside her did not make any sense at this point in time; it was not something she could emotionally process. A part of her felt guilty that she was here, possibly to have a good time, knowing that Nkechi was still abducted. In that moment, her face fell and she got up.

'I think I should go now. I need to get to my mum's.'

'Okay. Did you drive?'

'Yes, I did,' she replied.

Charles held her hand as they walked to the door, and he hugged Adaora. She stayed in his arms, and for a brief moment, it was where she wanted to stay. He looked at her and leaned in towards her. She felt her heart racing, knowing what was coming. All of a sudden, she felt like a teenage girl again. As his lips met hers, Adaora closed her eyes and put her arms around his neck. His mouth was soft and warm, and moved in sync with hers. Despite herself, she felt a tingle of excitement.

Adaora pulled away and smiled at him one last time, before she opened the door and walked to her car.

On Saturday evening, Adaora was at her family home with her mum, brother and Patrick. It had been exactly a week since

Nkechi was kidnapped, and their fears continued to grow, day by day. The all sat around the dining table. Patrick had just come back from visiting a client in prison. He normally has his facial hair trimmed to a neat goatee, but the last week had taken a toll on his appearance, and a stubbly beard was starting to take shape. Mrs Edozie moped around in her nightgown all day. She had tried to convince Chidi to head back to University and continue studying, but he refused and told her there was no way he could concentrate. Even at this point, Mrs Edozie was still thinking about her son's education.

The landline phone started to ring, and Mrs Edozie quickly picked it up. 'Good afternoon!' she greeted. She put the phone on loudspeaker.

'Afternoon,' her husband replied. His voice was slightly tremulous.

'Any progress?' she asked.

He hesitated, and the line went silent.

'Hello?' Mrs Edozie persisted.

His defeated voice murmured: 'I have lost all my hope in the police force in this country. All the high-ranking people who initially told me not to worry – saying that they would be doing their best to find Nkechi – have now said that they have no clear leads.'

'*Chineke!* These people want to kill me!' Mrs Edozie wailed.

'Daddy, it's Ada,' Adaora interrupted, urgently. 'What do we do now, if the police there are so inept?'

'They told me the best way to get Nkechi back safe and sound is to pay the amount the kidnappers requested.'

Mrs Edozie howled. Adaora covered her hands with her face and took in a deep breath before blowing it out.

'But dad – where will we find that type of…'

'Good day, sir, Patrick interrupted her. 'It is Patrick, here. That amount they are asking for is not realistic. I want to fly down to Nigeria. I feel helpless here. Doing nothing here is killing me!' Patrick walked towards the window onto the garden, and stood so he had his back to everyone. Slowly wiping the tears from his eyes, he managed to compose himself.

'Patrick, listen to me,' Mr Edozie said. 'Do not waste your money. You coming here will be the biggest waste of your time. Now we know that we have to raise some money, it is best for you to stay there and help to do so.'

'Yes, sir,' Patrick replied from a distance.

'Dad, my last payment of my student loan is coming soon,' Chidi cried. 'We can add that to the money needed. Look – we all just need to rally together now and get this money so that Nkechi can come home. No more feeling sorry for ourselves!' Chidi asserted.

'Yes, my son. That is the mentality we now need. I have to go. I have scheduled some meetings to see what assets and land I can sell to raise money. *Biko,* start putting your heads together so we can raise the money, since that is the only way we can get Nkechi home.'

'Bye!' they all said simultaneously.

Before Chidi had spoken, there had been an air of hopelessness in the room, and it was infecting everyone. Chidi's words were the propellant.

It was time to take action.

Chapter Five

EVERYTHING FELT STRANGE; THE ROOM CARRIED A WEIGHT OF EMPTINESS THAT penetrated the core of its soul, as if the walls were weeping for Nkechi. The creak of the bed echoed the creaking of Adaora's back as she arched herself upright. Sullenly, her fingers pressed her lower back, confused about where this pain had come from.

Something was off. She was in Nkechi's room, yet without her, it had lost its life; lost its beauty. Believing that the presence of her sister's things would comfort her, Adaora had wrapped herself in the sheets, inhaling Nkechi and exhaling pain.

Shuffling her way to the door, the sound of her mother's worship weaved into her thoughts. The normal sound of Sunday. Sameness within the difference.

The steam of the iron whirled around the green Ankara dress Mrs Edozie had selected for church. Between song verses, Mrs Edozie acknowledged her daughter with a nod.

Coffee was calling, and Adaora followed its call into the kitchen, setting the kettle to boil. Dragging herself to the bottom of the stairs she called up: 'Do you want some coffee?' No response followed, so she shouted up again. 'Chidi!'

'He went to the shop to buy some sugar.'

'Oh, okay.'

Her mum looked up at Adaora and then at the clock just above the television set. 'Look at the time! Will you not join us today at church?'

'Not today. I'll stay at home and start planning how to raise some money,' she retorted.

Mrs Edozie put the iron down, her hand on her waist. 'Adaora, Adaora – what is that supposed to mean?'

Not willing to get into an argument this early, especially without her morning coffee, Adaora shook her head and began walking towards the kitchen.

'*Bịa ebe!* I said "come here".'

She turned, reluctantly. 'Look, mum. Today is not the day for this – just go to your church and I will do what I need to do, here.'

'We must all devote our minds to God and pray for the safe return of your sister.'

Adaora looked up to the heavens. She hated repeating herself, but her mother continued to press this issue. As respectfully as she could, she gave her response. 'Mum, like I said, that is not a good use of my time. If praying to God is what you think will bring her back, then continue. As for *me...*' She pointed to her chest. '... I am going to raise the cash we were *told* to raise.'

'Adaora, why have you forsaken your God?' Mrs Edozie frowned. 'Please tell me – why are you like this? There is a spiritual battle against you and you are letting them in easily!'

Losing her patience, Adaora muttered under her breath before continuing. 'For one, he was never my God – *you* forced me into

106

the church. When I got older and started questioning things, you started despising my attitude. I was just seeking some answers! The more I learnt about our history and how the oppressors force-fed us Christianity, the more I rejected it. Mum, I have never forced my opinions on you, or anyone else, for that matter. So, please don't tell me any rubbish about spiritual battle.'

Watching from the corner of her eye, Adaora expected a backlash. Mrs Edozie clapped her hands once. '*Tufiakwa*. My daughter, I will pray for you.'

At this, Adaora returned to her coffee-making and Mrs Edozie her ironing, as Chidi walked into the house. Setting down the milk on the kitchen counter, he kept his distance, recognising the dissension in the air.

Adaora lay low upstairs until she heard them both depart. Finally alone, she grabbed a notebook and started scribbling ideas on how to raise more money. After a few minutes, the lack of writing began to infuriate her as her troubled mind blocked creativity from flowing. Ripping the page out and screwing it into a ball in her palm, she considered her impossible mission. A break was required. Tossing the paper into the bin, she grabbed her low boots and left the house.

She pounded the pavement with a determination that had no destination; her feet on autopilot, her mind consumed with racing thoughts. She could hear Nkechi's voice, her shrill scream and her imagination began to play moving pictures of her sister trapped, locked in a dungeon, her clothes torn, her face covered. Worse. As much as she attempted to gain control, these thoughts plunged up out of her subconscious.

Clissold Park. She walked into the huge green space, scanning for a perfect place of rest. Tranquillity. Finding solace under the shade of a large willow tree, Adaora sat on the freshly cut grass, sheltered from the beaming sun, enjoying the brief passage of a cool breeze. Exhaling, Adaora took out her phone, opened the calculator function and began tapping furiously at the numbered keys. The sums were not adding up to the answer she wanted.

Shaking her head, she whispered to the air 'It is not enough'.

A large congregation of sun worshippers lay prostrate, communing with nature, desiring to be blessed by glorious doses of Vitamin D. Two girls were chasing each other across the grass, their ponytails flapping against their cheeks, their mouths full of laughter, their eyes full of joy. Adaora watched them with a sad smile, her mind dredging memories of herself and Nkechi running with their friends. Carefree. Naive. Happy.

An explosion of engine-noises splintered her memories and Adaora turned, irritated. Three teenagers were poring over a small petrol car and remote that was making ear-splitting growls. Even when the engine calmed down and began a gentle hum, the peace had been destroyed. Adaora got up and left.

The evening brought a cool chill, the moon boasting its fullness against the darkened sky. In her apartment, Adaora sat listening to jazz instrumentals, a bottle of red wine on the table - her book in one hand, a glass in the other. Turning the page, after taking a sip, she realised she had lost the plot. Skim-reading the previous page, she sighed, annoyed at her lack of retention. She could not concentrate. Placing the book down, she closed her eyes. Then her phone began to ring. It had fallen between the sofa pillows and she rummaged to find it.

'Sis?'

'Hey, Chidi.'

'Is everything okay between you and mum?'

'Mmmm... Why?'

'Because every time I mentioned your name today, she kissed her teeth and started cursing in Igbo.'

Adaora laughed half-heartedly. 'Don't worry about that. We will sort out our differences one day.'

Chidi was upset, his voice started to crack. 'Look, I just want the whole family to be together and happy again. We need to be a unit right now and you and mum are at each other's throats – over what, exactly? Please, Ada, just try not to argue with her – please!' he pleaded.

Hearing the sincerity and pain in her younger brother's voice, Adaora was affected. She leant her head to the side, using one finger to wipe away an unwanted tear. 'Okay, Chidi. I promise.'

'Thanks, sis. I love you.'

'I love you, too.'

After a long morning of back-to-back appointments, Adaora decided to take the rest of the day off. As she walked along Chadwell Heath High Street, she was surprised at the high-energy buzz. It didn't resemble a Monday lunchtime, but felt more like a Saturday afternoon, as an unchoreographed flash-mob of people purposefully weaved in between the market stalls, moving in time with the traders' vocal anthems.

'Over here, love! Two bowls of bananas for a pound!' one trader bellowed.

Sidestepping the fruit and veg, Adaora focused on her way to Barclays bank. As was customary at lunchtime, the bank was full. She wavered.

A greeter approached her and once she knew that Adaora

wanted an appointment, directed her to the soft chairs. 'Please have a seat. Someone will be with you shortly,' she smiled.

A few moments later a tall, smartly dressed Indian man walked over to her. 'Miss Edozie?' he asked.

'Yes,' she replied, collecting her bag and standing.

'Good afternoon. Thank you for waiting. My name is Ashik. Please follow me.'

He was handsome. Almost too handsome to be a personal banker, Adaora thought. He deserved attention in Bollywood, on the big screen. Such beauty, hidden in Chadwell Heath! As she followed him upstairs, Adaora noticed that his voluminous, thick black mane was full of gel and slightly spiked in the front. They entered his quaint office with glass panels.

'Please have a seat,' he said, pointing, as he arranged himself behind the computer. 'How can I help you today?'

'I would like to arrange a withdrawal of all the money in my savings account, please.'

'Okay, that is not a problem. Can I have your card please?' He took her card and entered her details in the computer. He looked at the screen, squinting before putting on his glasses. 'Your total balance in your savings account is £8,795.'

'Yes. Could I please arrange for a cash withdrawal tomorrow?'

'Yes, that's fine. Can I suggest you leave something in the account, even if it is just 50 pounds?'

'But every pound counts!' Adaora exclaimed involuntarily. She hesitated at his look of surprise. 'Okay, but can I make it ten quid, just to keep the account open? Just make it £8,785.'

'I will personally make sure this is done for you, so you can pick it up tomorrow, any time from 11 am.'

'Thank you so much.'

Adaora felt some accomplishment, on leaving the bank; she had diligently put aside money every month into her savings account and although this was not how she had expected to use it, she was glad to have something to offer to save her sister. Walking back through the market, the smell of fish attacked her nostrils and Adaora was automatically repelled. She detested fish and quickened her pace, holding her breath past the fishmongers. Remembering that Patrick, Chidi and a few friends were coming over later that evening to discuss raising the money, Adaora stopped at a few stalls and purchased pasta, fresh vegetables, tangerines and pink lady apples.

When she got home, Adaora began making her famous fruit salad. She had been raised to always prepare something for guests and this was her favourite dish – she was known for it. At every social event Adaora would arrive, fruit salad in hand, and leave with an empty dish. It was a sure favourite amongst her family and friends. Food prepared, she turned her attention to the apartment, giving it a quick spruce and lighting a few scented vanilla candles. Her cleaning regime took barely five minutes; she hated mess and her apartment was always generally clean. Picking up her book, she reclined on the sofa awaiting her guests' arrival, trying to occupy her racing mind.

Patrick and Chidi arrived first, bringing smiles, hugs and greetings. Shortly behind, Temi and Gloria. Adaora burst out of her shell; the presence of close friends and family warming her heart. Her apartment was alive with conversation, voices, stories and people.

Temi walked to the kitchen to help bring out refreshments and noticed the book on the marble counter. 'Henry Louis Gates Jr is a brilliant writer!' Temi gushed. '"In Search of our Roots" is a great book. I remember when you bought that. Are you still reading it? How long has it been?'

'I know, it is a great book - so insightful, 'Adaora agreed. 'You know how my schedule is these days! Not enough hours in the day, unfortunately.'

'Well, whenever you finish that, you should read "Just Mercy" by Bryan Stevenson. It is a fantastic read.'

'What is it about?'

'Racial bias and injustice in the criminal justice system – against the disenfranchised in the States.'

'Sounds very interesting. I will add it to my reading list.'

This rapport between them was commonplace. Their mutual love of literature had brought them together in early adolescence and the love continued to grow. They used each other as libraries, sharing and borrowing from each other in their own personal reading group. They all congregated in the living room and there weren't enough seats for everyone, so Adaora brought in two plastic chairs from the kitchen and focused them all.

'Well,' she began, 'let's get straight to it. We all know the dire situation with Nkechi. After we spoke to my dad the other day, he said that the most realistic way to get her released from her captors is by paying the ransom. The police there seem to be no use and all we want is Nkechi back safe and sound.'

'What can we do?' Gloria asked.

'We need to raise money, as soon as possible. The total amount requested in pounds is 100k. My dad is working on covering the majority of that, but anything we can do to add to that will go a long way.'

Patrick seemed uneasy. His breathing was laboured and he kept shaking his head. 'I have already withdrawn 10k from my savings,' he said.

'I will be getting my last payment of student loan for the year next week,' Chidi added.' That should be just under two grand.'

Adaora smiled at them both, knowing they were both putting in all they had. 'Thank you, Patrick and Chidi.'

'Things are not easy at the moment, financially, but I should be able to contribute a thousand pounds,' Gloria admitted.

'Thank you so much, Gloria,' Adaora said. 'If you are sure...'

'Don't be silly, she is my sister also.'

Overwhelmed, Adaora began to sob silently. Embarrassed, she pulled some tissues out of her pocket and covered her face with her hands. Temi was the first to notice and stood supportively by her side, placing her hand gently around her shoulders.

'Stay strong, Ada. Nkechi will be home soon. I will also contribute a thousand pounds.'

Adaora got up and gave her a hug. 'Well, adding all that together, and the eight and half thousand I have, that should give us....'

'Roughly 22k,' Chidi jumped in, interrupting Adaora.

'I'll call my dad and tell him know how much we have put together so far, and hopefully, he is making headway over there,' Adaora said.

Patrick was still shaking his head, a distant look on his face. Noticing this, Adaora walked towards the door. 'Patrick, can I have a word, please?' she asked.

He followed her into her bedroom. Closing the door to give them privacy, Adaora turned to face him. She searched his face, picking up on his non-verbal signs. 'How are you coping?' she asked.

The weight suffocating Patrick – the burden he had tried to repress to appear strong, to keep the family together – disintegrated in that split second. His body collapsed into Adaora's arms, and she responded non-judgementally – allowing him to crumble. The extreme pain caused an outpouring of tears, since Patrick was vulnerable and he could no longer hide his emotions. The gates had opened. Adaora understood that Patrick was struggling to process the situation: his whole demeanour had changed since the incident; his liveliness, his joy had been sucked out and replaced with despair; a cloak of thorny discomfort.

'I miss her so much.'

Adaora had never seen Patrick cry before, but as a therapist, she knew that this moment was necessary, in order for him to regain strength. She held him tightly.

'I miss her, too,' she said gently.

Patrick wiped his tears away, looked at Adaora straight in the eye and thanked her before returning to the others.

One by one, they departed, until only Temi remained. Washing the dishes and reorganising the kitchen, Temi got to work as Adaora sat watching the news in the living room. Once the kitchen was spotless, Temi joined Adaora on the sofa.

'The news is filled with nothing but bad news. They were just talking about the Chibok girls. It has been a year since they were taken,' Adaora stated sadly.

'That is crazy! How time flies. Just yesterday it seems, the campaign for "Bring back our girls" was all over social media. Can you imagine how those poor girls are feeling?'

'Nigeria really needs a lot of work. Leadership in that country need transforming. When will they learn that putting the needs of the citizens comes first? Why must everyone line their pockets? It makes me sad.'

Temi nodded in agreement. 'Key infrastructure needs to be put in place. It's 2015, and reliable electricity is not even available in a country of over 170 million people!'

Adaora sipped some of the red wine next to her on the side table, picking up the remote for the television and switching it off. 'You know what? I don't even want to talk about the state of affairs in Nigeria any more. It is disheartening.'

'That's true. Anyway, how are things with you and your mum?'

'Not great, to be honest. We had a big bust-up when she asked me if I was going to church and I refused.'

Temi's eyes widened. 'I'm sure aunty wasn't too happy about that.'

'I just don't get it. Africans have bought into this whole Christianity euphoria more than any other people. We never want to take action. All we do is pray!' Adaora waved her hand dismissively. 'I am sure there is more prayer coming out of that continent than anywhere else, but how far have we come? I just told my mum my time is better spent trying to raise the money, rather than sitting in church.'

'I hear you,' Temi shrugged. 'But... it is not the time for division in your family. Try and make things better with your mum. You all need to stand strong together.'

'I will try,' Adaora replied. 'How is Tony?'

'He is fine. Working countless hours, trying to save up after we overspent on the wedding.'

'That's Tony for you – always going the extra mile.'

Temi picked up the bottle of wine, tilting it to one side. There was barely enough to fill half a glass.

'Should I crack open another bottle?'

'No way. Especially if you're not drinking any more. I have patients I need to see in the morning.'

'So how are things going with Charles?' Temi asked.

Suddenly, Adaora's mood perked up, her eyes sparkled and a huge grin appeared. 'Charles. Is. *Amazing!* she gushed. 'I haven't had the chance to spend as much time as I would like with him, because of the situation with Nkechi. But what makes him even more special is his patience and understanding.'

'I am so glad you have finally met someone you really connect with. He sounds like such an amazing guy, from what I've heard from you.'

'He really is, but it's still early days. Guess I'll just have to see how it goes.'

Noticing the time, Adaora called a taxi for Temi as they finished their glasses of wine and indulged in more girl chat. Waving Temi goodbye, Adaora locked her front door and smiled to herself. Not many could boast that they had such a great friend as she did in Temi. The years wreaked havoc with her friendship circle, the numbers dwindling with each passing season, but Temi was a sister. For life. Their bond only grew and their relationship gave Adaora great comfort, especially in dire situations such as this. Temi knew her moods, her flaws, her culture and all the occurrences that had built her. She didn't have to explain herself or pretend around Temi, and the freedom to be real was priceless.

The office had become her escape from reality. Delving into the private lives of her patients, problem-solving and probing, provided the perfect antidote for dealing with her own minefield. Busying herself with work was therapy. Adaora felt a lack of control over

Nkechi's situation, but the ability to be a catalyst for change in other people's lives kept her spirits up.

The long night with Temi was beginning to have an effect, since Adaora yawned repeatedly. She sat comfortably behind her desk, enjoying the brief break between clients and sipping on her latte, listening to the birds gossiping.

The mood changed significantly as gloom entered her office, emblazoned on Kevin's face: his countenance a storm brewing. Adaora quickly shifted back into work mode. All the signs indicated a negative incident, since Kevin usually displayed this particular look at the beginning of their sessions. A struggle commenced: Adaora began searching for answers but Kevin's barriers were firmly in place and open questions were met with shrugs and monosyllabic responses. Adaora, patient and persistent, continued more tactfully, but to no avail. The conversation danced in circles. Looking through his mood journal, Adaora was disappointed at the lack of content and gave Kevin a stern look.

'You didn't record anything, as I asked?'

Kevin's eyes found the floor, his lips still unwilling to part.

Once the session was over, Adaora let out a long sigh. Despite her efforts, the session had not progressed in the way she'd intended and she was frustrated. Lifting her cup, her face sank, since its lightness indicated the lack of substance within. Coffee emergency! Desperate for a pick-me-up, she grabbed her coat and marched to the local coffee shop. It wasn't her favourite, but it was effective.

Sitting at her desk, fresh brew in one hand, Paige's file in the other, Adaora immersed herself in the details. Lunchtime had passed and her growling stomach was pounding insults on its internal walls. Adaora ignored them. There wasn't time to attend to a proper meal, but she managed a few nibbles of Scottish shortbread she found stashed in her drawer.

Leanne and Paige arrived ten minutes late, apologetically blaming the road works. Greeting Adaora, Paige sat there as Leanne left the room. Holding a half-torn school exercise book in her hand, Paige waited for Adaora to sit, before thrusting it at her.

'What is this?' Adaora asked, unable to make out the words on the front cover.

'Just read the first few pages, please.'

As she opened the first page, she realised what it was and glanced up at Paige. 'Are you sure you want me to read this?'

'Yes.'

Monday 3rd February 2014,

So today was shit. What else is new? School sucks. All the boys are stupid and Megan is a total bitch. I hate her. Such a waste of my time. I don't want to go back there. Everyone is pain in the arse. Primary school was so much better. But to be honest, not going to school means staying at home and that ain't no walk in the park either. Sometimes I don't know which is worse.

I got home and Emma was all by herself again. There was nothing to eat again. Mum was nowhere to be seen. AGAIN. I don't understand how she can be such an idiot. Why does she keep leaving Emma by herself? She's only 7, for fucksake. Poor thing ran crying into my arms as soon as I opened the door. Thankfully, I had some change in my pocket to buy chips from Mickey's, so she didn't starve. Her eating is all that matters. I made sure she ate most of it. I didn't have time to do any homework. Had to sort Emma out, give her a bath and put her to bed. She wanted me to read her Cinderella. I think she hopes our life is some fairytale that we'll eventually get saved from. I can't break her heart and tell her there's no happily ever after in our future.

Adaora bit her lip, reading on.

Thought I had a few moments to myself but that prick showed up at the door, shouting and swearing like the jackass he is. I didn't want to open the door but he started pounding it down and I didn't want Emma to wake up, so I opened it. He shut the door and slapped me across the face. Not as hard as normal, but my cheek is still red. He wanted to know where mum is, like I've got a flipping clue - I'd like to know as well. But he got angrier every time I told him I didn't know. Angry at the truth.

Stupid bugger was hungry - we already don't have any food and he wanted to use the last of the milk for porridge. But I was saving it specially for Emma's breakfast tomorrow and so I told him. He ignored me, and I got mad. So I tried to take the milk off him and that's when it happened. He punched me all over. Proper heavy fist punches. My hands are still shaking as I write this. I've got marks on my face and my back is shades of purple and blue.

Today is the first time I am adding mum to the long list of people I hate. She came home drunk and when I told her what Curtis did to me she didn't believe me. I am tired of living here. I am tired of having no food, tired of that fucking shit school, tired of seeing

119

Emma cry all the time. I just want it all to stop. I am not looking forward to tomorrow, another morning of no breakfast, this time not even for Emma because of that prick. I guess I'll have to take her to school tomorrow as well because that drunk bitch can't.

I hope I have better things to write about tomorrow.

The weight of the passage hung between them: a thick, yawning silence. Adaora tried to gather her thoughts as she handed the book back to Paige, sitting with her arms folded and legs crossed.

Paige looked up at Adaora. 'Did you read the first 2 pages?'

'No just the first one,' Adaora admitted. 'That page alone gave me so much insight. Thank you for sharing that with me. It helps me to understand and put into context what you have been through. I remember in our last session you said that you get angry a lot. What do you think the triggers are, for that type of behaviour?'

Picking her nails, Paige shuffled in the chair, trying to find a comfortable position.

'When I remember Emma. Anything that reminds me of Emma makes me want to lash out there and then. Doesn't even matter where I am.'

'Okay. When you were with Emma, did you have that level of anger inside?'

'Yes…' Paige said sullenly, 'but I guess they were triggered by… other things.'

'Like your mum and her abusive boyfriend.'

'YES!' Paige shouted.

'Okay…'

Paige interjected. 'It's all my fault!' she wailed.

'What is your fault?'

Paige's tone softened. 'Why me and Emma are not together. When I'd had enough of Curtis hitting me and tired of having no food because Emma was starting to get really thin and ill, I told her teachers at school what was happening. And they called the fucking social services! I hate them, too, and all.'

'That was a very brave thing you did. Raising the alarm because you were worried about the safety of your sister. You wanted help, so why so much anger towards social services?'

'Because they separated me and Emma. The reason I called them was so they can help us. This is not helping us! Emma is the only person I care about in this world and I have not been able to see her in months!' Paige broke down in tears.

Adaora handed her some tissues and helped her to calm down. 'What do you think the consequences are, of your behaviour? Especially when it is set off by one of the triggers you have? For example – you thinking about Emma, triggering you to act out your anger. What are the consequences of that?'

Paige blew her nose. 'It will get me kicked out of school… and my relationship with my foster carer will not be so good.'

'So, how can you prevent the triggers taking you over the edge?'

Paige's eye contact drifted away as she thought about the question. 'I still want to think about Emma…'

'Of course!' Adaora said gently. 'It's how you think about her, and the situation… Remember what we said about you turning your thoughts around?'

Paige's brow creased in concentration. 'Hmmm. Rather than thinking about me missing Emma, I guess I could think about her being with people that can actually look after her.'

Adaora smiled, observing awareness start to manifest on Paige's face. The session finished on a positive note and Paige was in good spirits when she left.

After work, Adaora drove to her parents' house. Her mother and uncle were talking in the living room, her uncle working his way through a plateful of food, and she greeted them politely. Uncle Jonathan was her dad's youngest brother – affectionately called Uncle Jay. Although he was only a few years older than her, he demanded that she called him uncle. It was a matter of respect.

He stood up, to welcome her. He had good dress sense, wearing fitted jeans, a checked shirt and non-prescription glasses in a bid to look intelligent. She exchanged hugs with him, but he was a small man and could barely reach her shoulders.

'Your mother and I were just discussing the situation with Nkechi,' he said, resuming his eating.

'Yes, that is why I came – to update everyone on how much we have raised so far. I met with Patrick, Chidi, and a few of our friends. The total we have come up with is twenty-two thousand.'

A huge smiled appeared on her mother's face. 'My daughter, you people have tried!'

'That is very good,' Uncle Jay added. 'If you add my three thousand, that gives us 25k. Your dad will be calling us later this evening, to give us more instructions.'

'Mum, I tried to talk Chidi out of using his student loan money, but the more I tried, the angrier he got.'

'Ada, I know. I have tried the same thing but he insists he will use it to support us. My dear, what can we do? He wants to help.'

The tension between them had lifted. Mrs Edozie was proud of her daughter's efforts and they were both relaxed.

'Mum, where is Chidi now?'

'He went somewhere with Patrick. They said they will be back later on this evening.'

Adaora found her way into the kitchen, foraging. Food was guaranteed in the Edozie household; her mother prided herself on ensuring there was always plenty.

'Uncle Jay!' she shouted, sarcastically. 'Are you hungry?'

'I'm okay. Your mum has already filled my stomach. Didn't you see my belt undone?'

Adaora laughed, helping herself to the stew in the pot. Her phone began vibrating furiously, almost falling off the glass dining table. Catching it in time, Adaora swiped to answer and returned to the living room.

'Hello, daddy. Good evening.'

'Good evening, my dear; how are you?'

'I could be better.'

'Mmm. I understand. We are all trying our best. Are you with your mum?'

'Yes, she is here.'

'Okay, put me on loudspeaker.'

Adaora did as instructed and placed the phone in the centre so that everyone could hear what he had to say.

'So, we have received word from the kidnappers that we must have the money ready for them within a week. So, this time next week – Tuesday.'

'Where do these bastards think the money will fall from?' Mrs Edozie grumbled.

'Dad, we have raised 25 thousand here. What do we do next?'

'That is very good, Mama Ada.'

'Yes,' she replied.

'Withdraw all the funds from all our savings accounts. It should be just over 40 thousand. Hopefully the two areas of land I have put up for sale will go very soon. That should give us enough to complete the ransom. Is Jonathan there?'

'I am here.'

'Collect the money from Ada and Oluchi, and transfer the money to my normal account please.'

'No problem.'

'Okay. Keep me updated as soon as the money is transferred. *Ka chifoo.*'

The click of the ended call left an emptiness behind. They all sat, each reflecting on the situation, each attempting to process, each wanting it to end.

Uncle Jonathan gave them encouragement, made arrangements to contact them about the money transfers, and left for the evening. Adaora and Mrs Edozie sat quietly in the living room.

Adaora went to finish her food, but when she returned, she found her mum sobbing. Rushing over, she wrapped herself around her mother like a protective shield, wiping away her tears whilst choking her own back. Chidi was right. They needed to unite as a family.

'Mum, stay strong. Nkechi will be fine and she will be home soon. We have to stay positive.'

Adaora's words did not hold much weight on this occasion. The tears continued and Adaora struggled to console her mother. Thankfully, Chidi had not returned; his heart broke anytime he saw his mum in pain. Adaora wanted to bear the brunt of her mother's pain and give her strength, in return. Watching her mother crumble was a humbling and difficult experience; but there was no time to hold any contention. Her mother needed her. They all needed each other. To get Nkechi home safe.

The phone wouldn't stop ringing. Journalists. Pastors. Friends. Students. Chaos ensued while the community desperately tried to piece it all together. Since the school had been informed, the news they had tried to keep to themselves had leaked out. It was a hectic time, since Nkechi's kidnap had made the front page local news.

'Local Teacher Kidnapped in Nigeria' – the headline rang. People from all over wanted to share their concern and offer support. They were inundated with cards signed by teachers, students and their parents, all standing with them in hopes of her safe return. Some even made small contributions – five pounds, ten pounds, here and there. Although it was tiring repeating their thanks, reliving the situation and smiling bravely for the cameras, Adaora took small comfort from the words written in the cards. Reading through them, she felt hopeful and positive that Nkechi would be home soon.

Making her way to the car park after a tough day of one-to-one and group therapy sessions, Adaora felt drained. Her shoulders were aching from the weight of books and files in the numerous bags she carried. Throwing them all on the back seat, she felt her phone vibrate. It was a text message. From Charles. The weariness of the day appeared to melt and her face lit up in excitement.

'Am I still seeing you today? I will understand if you can't' – it read.

After quickly responding that she would still see him, Adaora put the key in the ignition and accelerated to her mother's house.

Flinging the door open, she was stunned by the crowd inside: a mixture of ages, mostly Aunties from Church. Slipping into respectful mode, Adaora greeted them before disappearing upstairs to drop off the letters and cards she had received.

She felt barricaded in by the intensity of prayer and intercession wafting through the house. The heat carried the uproarious sound of united voices in spiritual tongues, Igbo and English. Various languages, but the same message; the same prayer; the same faith. From experience, Adaora knew that this could take a while. All-night prayer meetings were commonplace, but Adaora was anxious to leave. Looking at her watch, she waited for signs of closing, fidgeting with her hair at the top of the stairs. Leaving in the middle of prayer would be considered rude and she did not want to cause any more strife between herself and her mother, especially not in front of guests. Full devotion mode ensued, and Adaora caught words and statements of hope as they drifted in her direction.

Eventually, the prayers subsided and the Pastor spoke. 'Oluchi, do not worry, God has told me your daughter will be fine. She will come home to tell a testimony.'

Mrs Edozie nodded and thanked the pastor and the members of the church for holding her family up, in prayer. Adaora waited for them to leave and came downstairs.

'Mum, I am leaving now. I will be back on Saturday.'

'Okay, dear. Drive safely.'

Her mother's plea for her to drive safely was necessary. Listening to her satnav while driving through small country lanes at 40 miles per hour made Adaora nervous. She felt unsure of herself as she arrived in Brentwood, surrounded by a panoramic view of large, green, open spaces and neatly divided farms. Eventually, she arrived at a row of semi-detached houses situated on a hill.

Parking was only possible near the bottom and when Adaora realised a climb was in order, she sighed heavily, looking down at her black patent heels. Taking her time, she walked up carefully, feeling the burn in her calves. Checking the door number was correct, mildly surprised at the size of the house, she straightened her afro, applied gloss to her lips and knocked confidently on the door.

Opening the door, Charles warmly welcomed Adaora inside, engulfing her in his large muscular arms. Her eyes widened in marvel at the vast house, which was beautifully decorated with mahogany walls, wide pegged wood flooring, a stone fireplace with antique light fixtures and huge windows with a view of the forest. Adaora almost missed the beautiful baby grand piano in the corner and wondered if he played. Charles watched her in delight as she took the room in, aware of its magnificence. This was the room that had sold the house for Charles.

'Wow!' Adaora stated, almost unable to find suitable words. 'This is very… impressive.'

'Thank you. I actually haven't done much to it.'

'I can tell. It feels empty,' she said, frankly, gazing around. 'Could still do with a woman's touch to really bring this house to life.'

He grinned. 'I agree.'

A loud beeping sounded out repeatedly.

'Dinner is now ready, I believe.' He had spent the day cooking for her: asparagus, salmon and potatoes with a sauce were on the menu.

'It smells delicious,' she said. 'Can I wash my hands, please?'

'Straight ahead, second door on your right.'

Although she needed to wash her hands, Adaora was more interested in the contents of his bathroom cupboard. Nothing adverse found and the cleanliness up to her standard, she dried her hands on a luxurious towel, and checked her face in the mirror before returning to the dining table.

Charles watched in anticipation as she put her forkful of food in her mouth. Knowing he was waiting for her reaction, she took her time, taking in the flavours; savouring the moment. She looked up at him and smiled mid-chew. Covering her mouth, she nodded her approval. 'That is really good.'

'I am glad you like it,' he replied, relieved.

During dinner, the conversation flowed naturally; the chemistry could be felt as they occasionally got lost in each other's gaze. Adaora especially loved the way he said her name. It made her tingle inside. The evening was perfect; full of intelligent conversation, laughter and good food. There was nothing she would change. She loved how he made her feel.

As promised, Adaora returned to her mother's house early on Saturday morning. Two weeks had passed since the kidnapping, and the ransom deadline was fast approaching. Her mother was cooking breakfast: Chidi's favourite – fried egg and sweet Agege bread, which was a family staple, although Chidi's love for it meant it often didn't last beyond a day – much to his mother's annoyance. After breakfast, Adaora could not settle her thoughts. She wanted an update. She needed to hear what was being done.

After asking her mum for a call card, she rang her dad.

'Hello dad, good morning,' she began, putting the phone on loudspeaker.

'Good morning, my dear. I was just about to dial your mother. By the grace of God, I have managed to sell the plots of land! With this 12 million naira, that should give us enough to pay the ransom.'

This was the news they had been waiting for. Despite the impossible task, they had raised the money as a family. Everything was in place.

'Thank Jehovah!' Mrs Edozie shouted, arms and eyes raised in praise to the heavens.

'Oluchi, call Jonathan and make sure that he has transferred the money. I want to make arrangements so we can pick up Nkechi on Tuesday.'

'I will call him now.' Mrs Edozie picked up the phone to call Jonathan and Adaora called Patrick to tell him the good news.

After arrangements were made, Mrs Edozie fell to her knees and began to utter a prayer of thanksgiving.

Hope had been restored. Soon, their beloved Nkechi would be home.

With the good news about the ransom keeping Adaora in good spirits, she was excited about her date with Charles that evening. Their relationship was flourishing. Since their date at Charles' house, their communications had increased and they wanted to spend more time together.

They met at Mina's bookshop. The venue was filled with people and conversations darted back and forth across the quaint place as more people arrived. That night was the book launch of a local poet. Her reputation preceded her and she was highly respected – people had come from all over, to hear her readings and get a signed copy of the collection. The available space was limited, but Mina had reserved a special table for Adaora and Charles.

Fola Nioanda, the poet, was a Pan-African and her supporters came out in full force. The room was full of black women with well-shaped afros or twists, Ankaras and ancient Kemet symbols. Adaora loved Nioanda's work and was excited to share the event with Charles.

'I absolutely love her poems. I read one particular poem, called

Freedom of the Mind, every week. It keeps me going. Her way of thinking and how she manipulates words is incredible!'

'Sounds like you really are a fan!' Charles grinned.

Adaora's eyes sparkled. 'Most definitely!'

The lights dimmed and the noise gradually subsided. A voice could be heard over the speakers but no one could see who it was.

'Freedom of the mind!' the voice echoed throughout the room.

Some people started applauding, and Adaora stood up, clapping delightedly. 'This is the poem I was telling you about. She is going to perform it first!'

Adaora had a wide grin on her face. Charles watched her, smiling, and took in a deep breath before standing up next to her.

'Freedom of the mind is subjective,' the voice started again, and this time Fola Nioanda came out from the back of the shop.

The audience started clicking their fingers in appreciation. Then, moans of complaint and tutting could be heard in the audience, as someone was walking through and blocking people's vantage points. The figure apologised as he continued picking his way through the seats. Adaora looked over in the direction of the complaints and she recognised the face of the man. It was Chidi, sweating and out of breath.

'Chidi! Chidi!' Adaora called.

The poet stopped in her tracks, staring, and the crowd began to boo this interruption. Chidi saw her and squeezed his way through, his face a mask of distress.

'What is the matter?' Adaora asked. It was a question to which she knew she did not want the answer.

'We've been trying to call you, but your phone is going straight to voicemail.'

'Yeah, the reception is poor in here. Chidi, you are scaring me. What is the matter?'

'Get out!' someone shouted, above the jeering.

It wasn't a conversation they could have in public. Adaora grabbed Chidi and directed him to the back of the shop. His eyes were wide and distant. He couldn't look his sister in the face.

'Dad just called and said that the kidnappers have taken the money but they have not released Nkechi,' he muttered urgently.

'WHAT? 'Adaora screamed. 'No, no! This can't be happening!'

Charles ran over and asked what was going on. There was no response.

Chapter Six

EMPTINESS FILLED HER INSIDES WITH DREAD, HEAVILY SEA-SONED WITH FEAR. Adaora struggled to stay calm as her foot floored the accelerator pedal. Dashing through the London roads with intent and purpose, her mood had dramatically altered from a few minutes before. The tightness of the air in the vehicle was affecting Chidi, who was hyperventilating in the passenger seat.

Scooping sorrow from her soul, she blamed herself for being love-struck and in the arms of Charles while Nkechi's safety was in question. Unwilling to involve Charles in the family's issues again, Adaora had pleaded with him to stay at the show. His face was a canvas of concern, but he respected her wishes, watching sombrely as she left with her brother.

Noticing that Chidi was having difficulty breathing, Adaora placed her left hand on his knee and squeezed gently before attempting to engage him in conversation. 'How did you know I was at Mina's?'

'I didn't. I remember you saying you were going out but I didn't know where. I checked your Facebook and the event came up.'

'Oh, that was good thinking, Chidi.' She glanced at his shocked face. 'I know you're scared. I am, too, but we have to be strong for Mum and each other, OK?'

'Yeah.' Chidi nodded, exhaling heavily as they arrived on their road.

The street was blocked with parked cars on both sides and Adaora began to get frustrated. Eventually, she spotted a space between a white van and a Mercedes A Class. It was tight, but there were no other options. On a good day, Adaora would have taken her time to fit the car in, but the urgency wouldn't allow for accuracy. She reversed too deeply, with no space to adjust and no patience to try again. In desperation, she left the car sticking out into the road and ran with Chidi into the house.

Gloom hovered over the house, engulfing each room in anguish and despondency. Chidi immersed himself in the depressive cloud as he searched for explanations.

With a tread of desperation, Patrick paced out a chaotic path across the living room floor. His face was a mass of throbbing veins and repressed rage, flooding emotions into his fist, rhythmically punching his cupped left hand. Reaching him first, Adaora's outstretched arms attempted to embrace him and pacify his pain, but there was no response to her gesture. His arms hung limply at his sides, while hers closed around him.

In the kitchen, Mrs Edozie sat immobile, with the countenance of a woman whose babies had been ripped from her womb. Adaora called her three times before she snapped out of her subconscious state and her eyes found the child still within cradling distance. Clutching at her daughter, Mrs Edozie poured herself into the embrace, wanting, by some miracle, for Nkechi to feel the warmth, too; for Adaora to transfer her feelings into Nkechi's veins. Silent tears fell. Hopelessness hit her; motherhood momentarily redundant. She had no words of comfort or strength for her children. No wisdom or encouragement; just the piercing wail from her core and the wetness of her tears.

'Mum, what happened?'

Looking into her daughter's eyes, Mrs Edozie sighed. She didn't want to repeat the news, didn't want to hear the words again. They were already wounding her inside.

She found the courage to speak; but even as the words fell from her mouth, her spirit prayed for it all to be untrue. 'Your father called earlier on this evening. As soon as I picked up the phone, I knew something had happened – just from the tone of his voice.' Mrs Edozie paused, shaking her head. '*Nwa m o!* My daughter! I just want my daughter home!' she wailed.

Adaora sat closer to her and held her hand. 'What did daddy say happened?'

'He said that the kidnapper took the money and…' She sobbed. 'And demanded more money for the safe release of Nkechi!'

'More MONEY?' Adaora shouted, her blood boiling, the stress beginning to combust within her. Every penny they could find, scrimp, borrow, had been used – and still her sister was no closer to home. Still, Nkechi's life sat in the greedy hands of evil men!

'That was my reaction, too,' Patrick said, gazing into the distance, trying to maintain his composure. His body did not feel like his anymore; it was a shell of brokenness, a jumble sale of aching, a tapestry of hurt. Nkechi was his future, and he couldn't be, without her.

'This can't be happening!' Adaora cried, her shoulders slumping under the weight of the news. 'We have literally used up all of our savings – plus more from those who contributed! And they are still asking for money!'

'Why can't the police help, now, since we know where they are?' Chidi asked, in his naivety.

'The police are useless animals!' Mrs Edozie retorted. 'They cannot be trusted. It is up to us.'

'How much more are they asking for?' Adaora asked, dreading the answer.

'I am waiting on your father to call again, to get more information on what happened. That is all he told me before he was rushed off the phone.' Mrs Edozie cupped one hand to her forehead. 'I honestly cannot take any more of this stress.'

Telling the others that he had some calls to make, Patrick opened the door to the garden. He was shaking and desperate for fresh air; he closed the door behind him, hoping to find clarity in solitude. Chidi, in a reflection of the same desire, also went to find space to be alone with his thoughts.

Watching the men leave, Adaora decided to stay with her mother in the kitchen. Knowing that stress was a major cause of illness, Adaora was worried about how her mother was coping; especially given the update that Nkechi was still with her kidnappers. They had all been holding their breath for a positive report and this had crushed them all. Adaora didn't want to let on how much it was affecting her, so she focused on keeping her mother at ease. Pouring cold water into a glass she handed it to her mother.

'Mum, Nkechi will be fine. We need to stay positive. Please take it easy – we do not need anything happening to you, also.'

Mrs Edozie put the glass on the table and smiled weakly at Adaora.

Devoid of the comforting smells of home, even the kitchen seemed foreign. There were no pots on the stove, no food ready, as was customary. Adaora knew there was no time or inclination for anyone to cook. Using her initiative, she ordered Jollof and fried rice from the local takeaway for everyone to share.

When the food arrived, Patrick and Chidi took their rumbling stomachs to the table and ate in silence while Mrs Edozie remained unmoving, refusing to eat. Trying her best to encourage her, Adaora fixed her a small plate, but her mother replied that she had no appetite. Mrs Edozie was sweating, Adaora noticed; even though it was chilly in the house. She knew her mum always complained about hot flushes but she sat silently, not mentioning it – her mind aggrieved by other thoughts. Everyone was unsettled; the usual laughter and conversation missing from the house. Sitting in the living room – together, yet apart.

The phone began to ring and Chidi jumped off the sofa to answer it, automatically placing it on loudspeaker. They congregated around the device, in a hush.

'Good evening,' Chidi greeted his father.

'Evening, Chidi. Are your mother and your sister there?'

'*Anọ m ebe.* What is the update on the situation?' Mrs Edozie cried.

'After I received the money that Jonathan transferred, we made arrangements with the kidnappers to deliver it. I was advised not to be part of the exchange. So, my good friend Nonso decided he would make the exchange.' Mr Edozie paused; each second felt like light-years. 'It was awful. They beat him almost to a pulp. He was bruised from head to toe. They collected the money and sent him away, saying they want an extra 5 million naira.'

Patrick interjected: 'Another 5 million – what is that? Roughly another 20k…'

'That is outrageous!' Adaora added. 'Where are we supposed to find that amount – again?'

Chidi, who had been the voice of encouragement and hope before, snatched himself away from the situation. He couldn't bear it. His fist made contact with the passage wall before he darted out of the house. Patrick got up to follow him.

'Leave him!' Mrs Edozie instructed. Patrick sat down obediently, and she addressed her husband again. 'How is Nonso? I hope he is not too bad.'

'It was a very bad beating. He was in hospital but has been discharged.'

'Thank God!'

'Nonso said there were about 6 of them when he went there, and they all had their faces covered. He said they were heavily armed. Many guns. He also said he saw Nkechi and she looked well and unharmed.'

With those words a cloud lifted.

'She's OK!' Adaora screamed.

'Praise Jehovah! They have not hurt my daughter!'

Patrick almost collapsed in relief. 'This is good news, at last.'

'The plan now is to find the rest of the money. The police are definitely not an option at this stage, especially now we know how heavily armed the kidnappers are. A confrontation might lead to Nkechi being harmed… or worse.'

'God forbid!' Mrs Edozie added.

'But daddy – how can we possibly get more money?'

'I will see what other assets I can sell. If not, I will have to see who I can borrow from. If there is anything you people can do from there, please do it. I will be in touch again soon.' Mr Edozie hung up the phone. The smouldering silence sat upon each of them. Concerned about her brother, Adaora grabbed her shoes and went outside to find him.

Perched tentatively on a low wall across the road, Chidi sat solemnly wiping his face with the inside of his sleeve. He heard his sister's steps, but refused to acknowledge her presence, preferring to keep his eyes raised to the heavens. Adaora called his name, but Chidi was unresponsive. He couldn't take a conversation; not now. Not after his heart had dropped and was in his shoes. Vulnerability had draped itself around him, cocooning him in weakness: a cloak of needles piercing his skin till he could see blood. But not his own – Nkechi's.

Adaora sensed that her presence was not welcome and gently touched her brother's shoulder before slowly crossing the road back to the house.

Shouting resounded from within. Suddenly, Patrick ran outside, frantically crying for someone to call an ambulance. Adaora reached for her phone, unsure of the emergency while Chidi flung himself off the wall and they bolted into the house, following Patrick into the kitchen.

The scene was tragic. Their mother lay unconscious on the cold floor, in the recovery position. Thrusting her phone into Chidi's hand, Adaora sank down beside her mother, holding her.

'Is she breathing?' asked Adaora desperately.

'Yes, so far. I checked,' Patrick reassured her.

The call connected as Chidi's tongue lost language, lost articulation, lost explanation. His painful cries were childlike. Taking charge, Patrick took the phone and explained that Mrs Edozie had collapsed and was unresponsive, giving their address.

'Wake up, Mum! Mum?' Chidi cried in desperation. 'Can you hear me? MUM!'

'Chidi, calm down. We need to wait for the paramedics,' Adaora said gently, aware that her brother had gone into shock.

The walls were closing in for Chidi. His chest felt tight and the room began to spin. He clutched his chest, struggling to gain control over his physiological responses.

Patrick grabbed his shoulder, looking directly at him. 'Chidi, help is on its way. Try to stay calm. It'll be OK,' he said, reassuringly.

'Patrick, what happened?' Adaora asked, stroking her mother's face.

'Your mum decided that she was finally going to get something to eat. I told her to relax, that I could serve her, but she insisted that she would do it herself. As soon as she walked into the kitchen, I heard a loud thump. I ran in and saw her lying there. Quickly checked her breathing and put her on her side, before rushing out to call you both.'

Time appeared to be in a hiatus as they waited for assistance. Then, moments passed in a whirr of flashing lights, hi-vis jackets, stretchers and sirens. While Patrick and Chidi followed behind in the car, Adaora sat in the ambulance, continuing to talk to her mother and holding her hand. She tried to stay positive, urging her mother to wake up. She put in a silent prayer to the God she wasn't sure existed, hoping her mother's faith would be enough to warrant a divine intervention. As they journeyed, the paramedics looked concerned, their voices suggesting unspoken worry, which began to unsettle Adaora.

After struggling to find accessible parking, Patrick and Chidi bounded into A&E, finding Adaora in the waiting area.

'Is she awake, yet? What happened? What's wrong with her?' Chidi asked.

Adaora patted the seat next to her and Chidi sank into its padding, looking anxiously at her for answers.

'I don't know yet, Chidi. The doctors are yet to say. As soon as we got her in, they rushed her away.'

Hours passed before a doctor finally attended to them. The lack of information ate away at them as they attempted to busy their minds with old wrinkled magazines and social media. Suddenly, he appeared beside them and cleared his throat violently, causing them all to look up, to see a stern look on his face.

'I am Doctor Harrison. Are you the family of Mrs Edozie?'

'Yes, we are. She is our mum,' Adaora replied, reaching for Chidi's hand. It was warm and clammy.

'Is she okay?' Chidi asked, his voice wavering.

'She is comfortable. Your mother suffered loss of consciousness. Blood flow to the brain was reduced.'

'Like a stroke?' Adaora asked.

'There are various reasons for a reduction in blood flow to the brain, but it's usually related to a temporary malfunction in the autonomic nervous system.'

'Auto... noma-ac? What? What's that? Is it serious? Is she going to be OK?' Chidi asked, confused.

'It's the part of your nervous system that regulates the body's automatic functions, including heartbeat and blood pressure. It is a type of fainting called 'neurally mediated syncope'. It can be triggered by emotional stress or pain. Has your mother undergone any pain or stressful occurrences recently?'

Adaora and Chidi exchanged knowing looks and both sighed. Dr Harrison looked at them, waiting for more information.

'My sister was kidnapped in Nigeria about two weeks ago, for a large ransom, and that is still ongoing.'

Dr Harrison looked shocked. 'I am so sorry to hear that,' he began, sympathetically. 'It is more than likely that that the emotional distress has taken its toll on your mother. Her blood pressure is very high. I know you thought her breathing was shallow, but her heart rate was just very faint. The blood flow to her brain has gone back to normal and she will be just fine. She just needs to rest. We will keep her in overnight, just to monitor her, but she should be fine to go home tomorrow.'

Adaora squeezed her brother's hand and smiled warmly. 'Thank you, doctor,' she said.

'Yes. Thank you, Dr Harrison,' Patrick reiterated, shaking his hand.

'Can we see her, now?' Chidi asked.

'She is sleeping, but will probably be awake within the hour. As soon as she is awake, you will be able to see her.'

With that, Doctor Harrison walked away to attend to more patients.

Chidi found himself experiencing joy, smiling widely. 'I am so glad she is alright,' he said, relieved.

'Me too,' Adaora and Patrick replied unanimously.

Around them, nurses were rushed off their feet as people kept filing into A&E with broken arms, sprained ankles, gashed heads, burnt toes. The three attempted to keep themselves entertained as

142

they waited. Chidi made a number of trips to the vending machine, his appetite returned, trying to appease his empty stomach with Snickers bars and fizzy drinks.

A nurse noticed them sitting there and approached them. 'Excuse me, have you been seen to?' She was young and pretty.

Chidi perked up. 'Yes thank you, we are just waiting to see our mother, Mrs Edozie. She was brought in a few hours ago. Dr Harrison said we could see her.'

'Oh. OK. Let me just check the handover notes. I've just come on shift.'

A few minutes later, she returned. 'I'm sorry. I've just been in, to check, and your mother is still fast asleep and visiting hours are now over. You're quite welcome to come back and see her tomorrow morning.'

Chidi put on his best charming smile. 'We have been waiting for a long time, is there no way you can sneak us in?'

The nurse smiled. 'Unfortunately, not. But if anything changes, we'll give you a call. I just checked her obs and she's doing well. The rest will be good for her.'

'Yes, Chidi,' Adaora agreed, poking Chidi in the side. 'We'll come back in the morning. Mum will be fine. Thank you, nurse.'

'Yes, thank you, nurse,' Chidi winked, before following Adaora and Patrick to the car park.

Bright and early the next morning, Adaora and Chidi planned to make their way to the hospital. Then Adaora's phone rang. It was Charles.

'I wanted to check in with you. I hope all is well. I tried to enjoy the show and I didn't want to disturb you, but I couldn't stop thinking about you.'

'A lot has happened in the last 24 hours. Just so much to deal with.'

'Do you want to talk about it, or no?'

'It's fine. You know the situation with my sister. Well, first off, the kidnappers took the money without releasing her – demanding 20k more. That is why I had to leave yesterday.'

'Oh, my goodness. That's dreadful. I'm so sorry to hear that.'

'That's not the end of it,' murmured Adaora. 'My mother then collapses and is rushed to hospital. It has just been an emotional rollercoaster.'

'Wow! Again, so sorry. Is she okay?'

'Yes, she is doing fine. She just need to rest.'

'Glad to hear it. Ada, listen – if there is anything I can do to help, please let me know.'

'I really appreciate that, Charles. Thanks, but we'll be fine.'

Gazing out of the front door, she saw Patrick approaching.

'Charles,' she said into the phone, 'sorry. I need to go; need to sort some things out. Thanks for calling. I really appreciate it. Talk soon!'

'Bye!' he said, but she had already put the phone down.

Patrick was a shadow of his former self. His appearance continued to deteriorate: his stubble had turned rough, his clothes wrinkled, his face tired.

'How is your mum doing?'

'She is okay. All the stress got too much for her.'

'It just feels like one big nightmare. I will come over to see her.'

'No worries. We're hoping she will be discharged later today.'

Adaora went up into her mother's room, quickly packing a bag of fresh clothes and toiletries. She checked her face in the mirror, noticed the bags under her eyes, and shook her head. She was worried about Patrick but realised that the stress was apparent on all their faces.

She returned to Patrick who was deep in thought. 'Even if we manage to raise the money again, how do we know that they will release Nkechi? They have already proved that they are not to be trusted!' Patrick ranted.

'It is true. But what other options do we have?'

'Surely the police can help, now? They must know where they are hiding.'

Adaora shook her head. 'No way. Even if they did know, I would not trust an operation led by the police. My dad's friend who was beaten said they were heavily armed. A confrontation with the police could lead to Nkechi being killed! That is a risk we definitely do not want to take.'

'That is a fair point.'

'We are heading back to the hospital now.'

'Okay, I need to sort a few things out. I'll make my way there, soon.'

'See you in a bit.'

The sun had come to play and told the wind to keep out; it was a beautiful day. In the air, birdsong harmonised with the hospital church bells as patients were led to morning mass.

Chidi looked around for the pretty nurse he had seen the night before. Locking eyes with her, he smiled as she walked over and directed them to their mother. There was a strong smell of iodoform lingering in the hallway.

Mrs Edozie was on the recovery ward with six beds in the room. Adaora pulled back the curtain. Her mother looked rough, in the white hospital gown, propped up on the bed, the table filled with cold toast and untouched soggy cornflakes.

Seeing her children, Mrs Edozie lit up, and pulled them into her bosom for an extended hug. Between them, thoughts of how differently yesterday could have ended hovered, but remained unspoken.

'Mum, how are you feeling?' Chidi asked, his voice full of concern.

'I am feeling better. I just have a slight headache.'

Chidi and Adaora sat down on the chairs next to the bed.

'Any update from your father?' Mrs Edozie asked.

'Nothing yet, but mum – you need to take it easy. We do not need anything happening to you,' Adaora warned. 'The doctors said part of the reason this happened is because of your high blood pressure and the emotional distress you have been going through.'

'Ada, I cannot help but be concerned! As soon as I woke up, all I could think about was Nkechi!' Mrs Edozie sobbed. Chidi picked up some tissue and handed it to her. 'My mind will not rest, regardless of what the doctors say.'

'Mum, please try. Nkechi will be home soon and we need her to see that you are well when she arrives.' Adaora held her mother's hand tightly, took some tissue from Chidi and wiped her tears.

'Okay, my daughter, I will try.'

Adaora lay her head on her mother's hand, resting on the side of the bed. She smiled at her mother and Chidi. 'Everything will be okay. We just need to stay positive.'

After spending a few hours at her mother's bedside, Adaora left to meet Temi and Gloria. After hearing the news, they were keen to show their support and visit. Over the years, Mrs Edozie had taken them both under her wing and treated them as extensions of her family. She had taken the time to nurture them and teach them the importance of sisterhood and true friendship. She had showered them with her precious nuggets of wisdom that they still lived by, now. Hearing that she had collapsed had caused them great upset.

In the hospital, Chidi was snoring in the armchair next to the bed and Mrs Edozie was barely awake; her eyelids extremely heavy. When she heard the curtain open, she sat up and, on seeing her adopted daughters, she managed a bright smile.

'Good afternoon, aunty!' they both greeted her.

'Good afternoon,' she replied very quietly.

Temi handed her the get-well-soon card they had bought for her.

'Thank you so much, Temi. How is your husband?'

'He is fine, thank you.'

'And how about your family Gloria? I hope all is well.'

'All is well, aunty.'

'We should be asking you how you are doing!' Temi said, smiling, yet concerned.

'My dear, I am okay, I just need to be in my own bed, now. This place is depressing me.'

Adaora cleared her throat really loudly and deliberately, next to Chidi. He woke in a fright, his arms flailing, almost knocking over the fruit bowl on the table next to him.

Adaora sharply jerked her head to signal him to follow her, but Chidi looked confused. She repeated the motion, her eyebrows raised. Chidi still looked bemused, and Adaora shook her head. Chidi could never take a hint. So she took direct action.

'Chidi, let me talk to you outside, please.'

Temi and Gloria both took seats and continued talking to Mrs Edozie as Chidi and Adaora disappeared into the foyer.

'How has she been?' Adaora asked.

'She has been fine. She keeps drifting in and out of sleep.'

'From what I saw, looks like you are the one drifting in and out of sleep! I do not get how you can fall asleep everywhere and anywhere, Chidi.'

Chidi laughed. 'Leave me alone, man.'

'I am glad mum is doing much better, though. Now, I can concentrate on how we will get the rest of this money for the ransom.'

Chidi rubbed his eyes. 'How are we going to do that?'

'I am not sure yet. Possibly loans, but the process might be too long. I need to speak to Patrick when he gets here later, so we can start thinking of ways to get the money.'

As they walked back to their mother's bedside, they heard laughter. Temi and Gloria had put their mother in great spirits. Adaora absorbed the scene, in contentment, knowing that this was exactly what her mother needed. Distraction. From stress.

Confident that her mother was safe in the arms of her companions, Adaora retreated to the waiting room area, using the hospital's free Wi-Fi to connect to the internet and complete a number of loan applications. She sifted through a number of sites, contemplating her credit score and the interest rates. As a sensible and responsible individual, Adaora had kept her credit score as spotless as possible, never missing a payment, with all her outgoings neatly organised in an Excel spreadsheet. Completing her details on her small touchscreen phone proved frustrating, and Adaora was thankful when she had completed three applications. This was the only option she had within her power, to collate the funds needed for Nkechi's release. It certainly would not cover the whole amount, but she had to do her part.

Patrick arrived at the hospital and saw Adaora sitting by herself. He had a huge smile on his face, so she wondered where this sudden burst of joy had come from. He came over and gave her a massive hug, almost lifting her feet off the ground.

She looked at him curiously. 'Not that I'm complaining, but you have some explaining to do, please. What happened? Why are you so happy?'

'I managed to get another 15 grand!'

'Wow!' Adaora looked at him, stunned. 'That is fantastic news! How did you manage that?'

'I put some money away for the house that I wanted to buy for Nkechi and I after we got married. Majority of our wedding money is gone.' He shrugged. 'As for the rest of the money, let's just say I owe someone.'

Adaora screwed up her face. Something seemed odd. 'Patrick, please do not get yourself into trouble.'

At this, Patrick turned to the opposite wall. He could not look Adaora in the face and did not want to get into a detailed explanation about what he had done. His childhood was full of friends whose destinies did not mesh with his; friends whose life choices had them on a fast-track to incarceration; whose autopilot was criminal activity. His area – Leyton, East London – was packed with people who gave it a negative reputation. He was an anomaly, breaking the statistics and the stereotype. Escaping the trap. This was one of the reasons he had been attracted to Nkechi – she represented the hope he wanted, for his future. He fell in love with her and she became his backbone, enabling him to turn away from all temptations and focus on building a life together. She was the positive voice encouraging him to continue when he wanted to give up on law school. Now, as a high-flying lawyer, he knew that he wouldn't have made it without her. He knew that he wasn't whole without her. He needed her back, so that life would continue to make sense.

Adaora was concerned that the past might have received a phone call from Patrick and he might be rekindling an acquaintance with unsavoury friends.

Reading her concern, Patrick attempted to nullify it. 'Ada, don't worry. I didn't do anything stupid to get the money. All that matters is that I have most of what we need to get Nkechi back here!'

Although his tone wasn't completely convincing, Adaora reluctantly nodded in agreement.

Discharged from the whitewashed enclosure of the hospital, Mrs Edozie was back in the comfort of her own surroundings. Although she was happy to be home, there was still a sense of loss. Her husband was far away and her daughter, missing. The house felt unfamiliar without them.

Chidi had taken the role of nurse, and was adamant that Mrs Edozie should follow the doctor's instructions to be on bed rest. He took pride in caring for his mother while the others were at work. It was something he could do properly, and feel that he was contributing to her wellbeing. He loved his mother immensely and the shock of the incident still hadn't left his sensitivities. His day was spent plumping pillows, making tea and generally keeping a smile on her face.

At work, Adaora was poring over the emails, awaiting responses from the loan companies. Finally, in the afternoon, she received confirmation that she had been accepted for a loan of two thousand pounds. Relieved and rejoicing, Adaora scanned over the minor details and realised that the balance could be in her account that same day, provided that she produced the necessary documents.

Finding a gap in her calendar, Adaora used it to rush home and sort out the paperwork. Fast and efficient, she made it back to the office in record time, with moments still to spare, before her next client. As she reclined in her chair, her phone rang. It was Charles.

As if he could see her, Adaora fixed her hair and wiped her mouth before answering the phone. 'Hi!' she responded, smiling sweetly.

'Hope you're Ok. Just wanted to call, to see how you were and how your mum was doing.'

His low voice stirred something within her, in spite of herself. 'Aww, that's so sweet. My mum is better. She is back at home and is recovering well. As for me, I am just trying to juggle things.'

'Oh, she's been discharged? That's great! I'm so glad!' He sounded genuinely relieved. 'It must be tough – so much happening all at the same time. For you to still be able to work and be there for your patients is a testament to your character. Amazing.'

'Thank you so much,' Adaora said, her face flushed red. Unexpected compliments caught her off guard, but she loved the fluttering feeling in her abdomen and the way her body responded to his voice. The phone calls were nice, but she longed to see him again, to be wooed by him, to nestle against his muscles as he wrapped his arms around her body. Her imagination was running away with her as he envisioned him.

'You're welcome. No need to thank me really; just commenting on the truth. So, how are you getting on, raising the ransom amount?'

'We have majority of the money, thanks to Nkechi's fiancé. And I managed to get a loan for two thousand, but we are still short by three thousand.'

'Well, in that case, let me help out. I can give you what you need to make up the balance.'

There was silence.

'Ada, are you still there?'

'Yes, I am.' Ada spoke resolutely. 'So – just the fact that you are willing to offer such an amount is amazing… but I cannot take your money.'

'Adaora, please don't insult me!' Charles exclaimed. 'I know the burden you and your family are going through. This is the least I can do to help. Rather than taking out more loans and paying interest, I am offering this to you now.' Charles's voice became huskier and more commanding. 'I am not even asking any more. You are going to take this money.'

The gesture was enormous and Adaora did not know how to respond. There was no way she would ever consider giving someone three thousand pounds without question, yet here he was – all authoritative and, she had to admit – sexy. All providing and generous. All humble and gorgeous.

'Ada! Ada?'

She snapped out of her daze. 'I promise I will pay you back.'

'You do not have to,' Charles said, 'but if that is what it takes for you to accept my money, then so be it. You can pay me back.'

'Thank you so much!'

'It is fine. I am more than happy to help. Tell me your account details and I will transfer the money now.'

Adaora gave him the information and while she was still talking to him, her bank texted her to inform her of her balance. Her joy was immeasurable.

She did not know how to adequately show her appreciation over the phone, so she said, 'I need to see you. Are you free later?'

'For you, of course! Let me know details.'

'Ok. I've got to go now. I've got a client in a few minutes. But I'll be in touch soon. Thank you sooo much!'

'No problem. Have a good day.'

Adaora sat daydreaming about Charles: what a godsend! As she conjured up images of them together, her body ached for his touch, her lips begging to be kissed. She shivered in excited anticipation of their date. But first, she had things to do. Quickly checking the time, she made a call to Patrick and informed him of the situation.

'Let me forward you my contribution, too,' he said.

Patrick transferred his money to Adaora and she sent it on to her Uncle Jonathon.

She called him to explain, and he promised to send it to her dad immediately.

Chidi had been doing an amazing job of keeping his mother in bed, and she was hating it. Boredom had taken over – she was going crazy, being left to her own thoughts. She needed to busy herself: that was her character. Lying around doing nothing was not her definition of resting – it was her definition of laziness.

When Chidi had to leave her, to call into the university, Mrs Edozie seized the opportunity to find her way into her sanctuary: the kitchen. To become herself again, she needed to engulf herself in normal activities. And cooking was her speciality. Nestled amongst her utensils and her heavy-duty pots, Mrs Edozie began to cook. This was her therapy – the process of creating delicious dishes from a few ingredients helped to take her mind off any external situation, as she filled each pot with love. Although her energy levels had plummeted and she needed to stop every few minutes to catch her breath, she was determined to make a home-cooked meal. Grabbing her chopping knife, a good handful of onions, spinach and Maggi cubes, Mrs Edozie got to work.

An hour later, the meal was ready. The kitchen was a maze of entwined fragrances and flavours – an incense of cultural celebration and worship. Food was the foundation of the family and Mrs Edozie was the catalyst to bring them all together. Hidden beneath the stainless-steel pot lid was a sea of yellow soup, infused with spinach, beef and oxtail meat. She smiled at her creation, inhaling strength from the sweet, peppery aroma. Feeling elevated and useful, she turned her attention to cleaning the kitchen.

When Adaora came home from work, she found her mum bent over the sink, washing dishes.

'Mum! What do you think you are doing?' she exclaimed.

Mrs Edozie kissed her teeth. 'My dear, I am tired of doing nothing. Sitting on that bed all day and night is not helping me. I needed to do something, so I decided to cook Egusi soup.'

Looking into the pot, Adaora smiled, attempting to steal a piece of meat without her mother seeing. 'I understand, but the doctors were adamant about the amount of rest you need.'

'Ada, don't worry. I will be fine'.

Adaora's eyes fixated on the soup her mother made. It was one of her favourites. In fact, the whole family loved the way she made Egusi. No one else could compete, with her particular method of making the soup.

'Okay, mum, but please go and sit down. I'll finish cleaning.'

Mrs Edozie slowly made her way to the living room, and sat down on the sofa. Adaora followed her.

'We managed to raise the other twenty thousand, and I have sent the money to Uncle Jonathan to send to daddy.'

Mouth opened wide in shock, Mrs Edozie felt a praise stretching from her spirit into her bones and she broke into song – an Igbo hymn. Adaora recognised the song and wanted to join in but was conscious that her mum's fluency made a mockery of her own language skills. The chorus reached a natural break, and her mother then spoke.

'So, Ada, how did you guys manage to raise the money?'

'I took out a small loan, Patrick raised most of it and my friend, Charles, also contributed.'

'My dear, well done. You people have tried. Let us hope that this nightmare will finally end and Nkechi will be home with us soon.'

Adaora went back to the kitchen and cleaned it all, while her mum lay down to rest on the sofa. Within a couple of minutes, she was summoned.

'ADA! ADA!' Mrs Edozie shouted.

Adaora ran into the living room, saw that the phone was ringing and that her mother could barely move from the position she was in to answer it.

She picked up the phone. 'Hello.'

'Adaora!' Mr Edozie replied.

'Good evening. Yes, it is me.'

'I wanted to call to let you know that I have received the money Jonathan sent this afternoon. *Nne,* you have tried. We are currently negotiating with the kidnappers.'

'Papa Ada, who will deliver the money this time?' Mrs Edozie asked.

'I will personally take the money myself. I can no longer put my daughter's life in another man's hands. I cannot take this anymore. I would rather die there, than not come back with Nkechi.'

Mrs Edozie immediately sat up, on hearing the seriousness in his tone of voice. Adaora and her mother made eye contact, stuck for words for a second.

'Papa Ada, please promise me you will be careful.'

'Yes, daddy, please be careful!' Adaora reiterated. She got up from her seated position, picked up the phone, took it off loudspeaker, and walked out into the hallway, speaking in a quiet voice to prevent her mother form hearing.

'Daddy, mummy didn't want me to add to your worries while you were there, but I wanted to let you know that mummy was hospitalised a couple of days ago. She collapsed.'

'WHAT?' Mr Edozie wailed.

'She is fine, now, daddy. The doctors just said that she needed rest,' Adaora reassured him.

'Ada please take care of your mother. I need to go. Hopefully, next time we speak, it will be good news.'

'Okay, bye, dad.'

Later on, that evening, Patrick and Chidi were both in the living room talking while Adaora was getting ready to go out.

There was a knock on the door. Patrick opened it and saw that it was Charles.

'Charles – right?' Patrick asked, as they both shook hands. 'I really appreciate your generosity. It is very kind of you to help us out, in the way you did.'

'Please don't mention it. I was more than happy to help. I just want the safe return of your loved one.'

Mrs Edozie walked into the room. 'Charles, how are you, my dear?

'I am fine, thank you. How are you doing?'

'I am feeling much better, thank the Lord.'

Adaora came bouncing down the stairs, beaming and dressed up for their date, as her mother continued, without taking a breath: 'I am sure everyone has already said this, Charles, but thank you for your contribution towards the ransom. You must stay and have dinner with us.'

Charles did not want to be rude and refuse the invitation – it did not sound like a request anyway. He looked over at Adaora to gauge what his response should be. She was visibly disappointed, but nodded to confirm that they should stay.

Charles took off his jacket and gave it to Adaora.

'I hope you like Swallow food,' Mrs Edozie said. 'Because we are having pounded yam and Egusi soup.'

'I love Egusi soup!' he replied with a huge grin on his face.

Adaora left Charles in the living room with Patrick and Chidi and went to finish preparing the meal, in an attempt to prevent her mother doing any more.

She was conscious that she had left Charles alone in a potentially awkward situation, hardly knowing anyone; so she kept popping her head in, to ensure that he was ok. She needn't have worried. Charles was in his element: the conversation was flowing between all of them, with laughter consistently arising.

Eventually, the food was ready and Adaora called them into the kitchen. As the youngest, the mantle fell on Chidi to bless the table. Immediately, he became introverted and embarrassed. Praying was not his forte, and they had company, too. As he struggled to begin, his mother abruptly came to his rescue and prayed over the food.

Although Charles was looking forward to the meal, he hadn't eaten with his hands in this fashion in a long time, and he appeared uncomfortable as he tried to wash his hands in the bowl provided.

Adaora smiled as she watched him struggle to roll the pounded yam in the dish. His lack of technique was endearing. Nudging him gently, she nodded towards her fingers and slowed down her actions, demonstrating how to roll, dipping her fingers into the centre and using it as a spoon to take the soup.

'So, the hollow is for the soup to stay,' he whispered.

Adaora chuckled to herself. 'Yes, that's the idea.' She whispered back.

Mrs Edozie found it quite amusing. 'Charles, where are you from?'

'I am Nigerian.'

'Then why are you acting like you have never eaten swallow food before?' laughed Mrs Edozie, puzzled. 'Didn't your parents feed you gari, ground rice or poundo?'

Adaora froze. A grey cloud hovered over Charles' expression and the mood changed. 'For the majority of my childhood, I was raised in foster care. My parents were killed in an accident in Nigeria, when I was young.'

'My dear, I am so sorry to hear that!' Mrs Edozie shook her head. 'That must have been tough, growing up without your parents.'

'Sorry to hear that, bro,' Patrick said.

'Yeah, man, sorry to hear that,' Chidi added.

'Thanks, but it's fine. I had to get strong-minded from a young age.'

'Well, you look to have done very well for yourself,' Mrs Edozie said.

Charles smiled as he practised putting the rolled pounded yam into his mouth. He was improving.

After dinner, Adaora and Chidi cleared the table together and Adaora then made the executive 'older sister' decision that Chidi needed to wash the dishes. It was the burden of being the youngest;

being spoilt by parents, but used as an errand-boy by siblings. He also didn't get choices. As the youngest, he had to wait for everyone else to choose their meat, leaving him with the measly leftovers. It was annoying, but it was his fate and he was used to it. So, he rolled up his sleeves and got to work.

Adaora wanted Charles' attention. Handing him the toothpick he had asked for, to worm out the beef stuck between his teeth, she signalled for them to go outside. Not wanting to stand in the doorway for inquisitive ears to hear, they went for a walk.

The street was half lit by adjacent lampposts, while the moon lazily beamed down from the sky. As they walked in the darkness, Charles' hand reached out for Adaora's. They found a quiet bench near the local park and sat close, enjoying each other's company, watching the skies, talking gently against the wind. The night was peaceful and romantic.

Sitting next to Charles, Adaora didn't want to move. She wanted him to embrace her tightly. Even as she thought it, he pulled her closer to him and cupped her face in his hands. They locked eyes, Adaora unconsciously biting her lip seductively and praying for him to kiss her. He made her wait, enjoying the beauty of her face, admiring the melanin in her smooth skin and the coils in her hair. He leaned in, closing his eyes as she moved in towards him. Their lips touched, and they caressed, embracing each other to express the emotions they hadn't had the courage to say. They communicated physically, as their tongues tied and their knees weakened.

Adaora pulled back first. The intensity was too much; although she wanted more.

Back in her office the following day, Adaora had a secret smile on her lips and a glint in her eye. Her womanly senses were tingling with the echoes of Charles all over her bottom lip.

She finished an early session with Paige and was happy that progress was being made. Paige had started to open up more, and their sessions were now constructive and productive. These days reignited in her a love for her job.

In between these thoughts, Adaora was waiting expectantly for her dad to update her about Nkechi. Experiencing all these feelings about Charles without having her sister to gossip with, over red wine, was horrible. She wanted her sister – she needed Nkechi back in one piece.

Charles sent her a text asking how she was doing and Adaora began to smile. As she was about to reply, a Nigerian number flashed across her screen. Her dad was calling. She stood and answered the call, looking hopefully out of the window. A despondent sky was looming over the city. Adaora was desperate for good news.

'Hello, Ada.'

'Yes dad?' she replied.

The connection was bad. The crackling was frustrating and she moved around the room, attempting to gain a better signal. She heard him saying 'hello' repeatedly. She managed to receive a better connection by standing awkwardly at the entrance to her office.

'Can you hear me, now?' he asked. Something had shifted, his tone was different. She held her breath.

'Yes.'

'Ada, we were finally able to make the exchange. They kidnappers have released Nkechi!'

The shrill scream of rejoicing that erupted from Adaora's lungs sent her receptionist running into her office. 'Is everything okay?'

'I am so sorry! Yes – everything is fine!'

Adaora could hear her dad laughing over the phone.

'How? When? What happened?' Adaora asked frantically. 'Is she OK?'

'Yes – yes. All fine. She is well. I took the money by myself to the location they told me. When I arrived, one of the young boys came and tried to take the money from me. I told him it was not possible until I saw Nkechi and she was in my arms.'

'Oh daddy!' exclaimed Adaora. 'That was dangerous, surely?'

Her father grunted. 'I felt like slapping the idiot. He looked no older than 20, but he was carrying a gun bigger than him, so I had to humble myself.' Adaora gave a yelp of fear, but her father continued. 'He went back to consult with the older member of their gang. They agreed to let Nkechi come to me, her wrists bound, so I quickly released her from the ropes they had her in…'

Tears leaked from Adaora's eyes, partly with relief, partly with the vision of her sister that she imagined, and the horrors she must have endured.

'I put her in the car,' her father was still explaining. 'They then took the bag of money from me. When they saw that all the money was there, they got into their cars. All I could hear from that point was laughter and chorus of "We are rich-o!" They drove off, and then we drove in the opposite direction. Nkechi hugged me tightly and she didn't want to let go.'

'Where is Nkechi, now?'

'She is fast asleep, safe and sound in our house. As soon as she wakes up, I will give you a call back.'

'When will you be coming back here?'

'We will be driving back to Lagos tomorrow and then we will book the next flight back to London.'

The news had sent shockwaves throughout her body. She began to dance in her office, in front of the large canvas hanging on the wall. Even Igbo hymns exploded from her mouth, tears falling down her cheeks.

She phoned her mum and they rejoiced together. Between songs, laughter, tears, prayers and praise, Mrs Edozie was elated. Her daughter – her daughter, finally! She was safe!

Chidi, hearing his mother scream, had rushed in to the living room. Hearing 'Nkechi' and 'safe' in the same sentence was emotional. He leaped for joy, punching the air in victory. They had done it! Together, they had got her back.

When Patrick received the call, he fell to his knees. He could barely hear Adaora over the sound of his own heartbeat, thumping with intensity. His better half was safe. That was all that mattered.

Later that evening, when Adaora, Patrick, Chidi and Mrs Edozie sat in the living room and Adaora called her dad, he picked up.

'Daddy, good evening. Is Nkechi awake? I am with everyone and we are all eager to speak to her!'

'Yes, she is. Hold on.' A faint low voice could be heard.

'Hello?' Adaora repeated.

'Hello, Ada, is that you?' Nkechi said softly.

A moment of silence followed. In that moment, Adaora's eyes filled with tears. It was the first time she had heard her sister's voice since the ordeal started.

'Hello, Nkechi. Yes, it's me – Ada.'

Chapter Seven

HUMIDITY, FRUSTRATION AND THE CONSTANT FLASHING OF BRAKE LIGHTS. Heavy traffic was rife. Roads were fit to burst, with extended queues of cars packed with passengers desperate to reach their destination. The hubbub was intensified by palms pounding steering wheels initiating an echo of horns blaring up and down the street.

Windows open, Nkechi hung out of the passenger side, willing the cars to move. The journey had been atrocious – a catalogue of broken down cars abandoned at roundabouts, clusters of carriages and lanes closed, causing backlogs – and the constant anguish of drivers. Even the vehicles were suffering – steam and smoke evident from overheating.

Nkechi watched a woman walk along the path, carrying a bundle on her head, her stride purposeful and determined, her back upright. She wished she, too, could use her legs to get to the airport. Despite her father's careful planning in booking the driver two hours early, they still were caught in the traffic. Overpopulation of the roads and the inability to get anywhere

163

fast caused locals to think twice about making arrangements to visit friends.

It was a time of reflection for Nkechi: to ponder, and long for home. She had felt at times that this day would never come; that her life was lost to evil. Shut down. Yet here she was, waiting to see the airport ahead. There had been little discussion between her and her father about what had happened; details spared as they focused on the present. She was safe and alive. That was the poignant point. That was all that mattered. And she reminded herself of this, as well as having assured her father – very pointedly, that they had not touched her. Finally, she was going home. Her trip to the motherland had been riddled with grief; she felt betrayed by the land and naïve in her expectations.

After a number of hours of snail-like movement, Nkechi saw the airport. It was a place of hope, another step in the journey home – where she belonged. After the car eased into a space and they got out, several young men surrounded them. Nkechi flinched unconsciously and stayed close to her father, clinging to his arm. The men filled their personal space, eager glints in their eyes – simply competing for a job: to carry the suitcases inside on the trolleys they held.

The intensity of their presence brought back terrible memories and she closed her eyes, trying to rid herself of negative thoughts. Until she was on the plane and in the sky, she would not feel safe, nor free from the grasp of her captors. They had released her body, but her mind still suffered.

Hands grabbed at their cases. '*Oga*, should I carry this one, also?'

Mr Edozie was not in the mood for pleasantries or assistance. Their game was obvious: each eager hand had a desire for monetary gain, and this trip had consumed enough.

Turning to the young slim man, whose worn slippers exposed his toes, Mr Edozie scowled. 'My friend, leave our bags! Did I ask you for your help? Stupid idiot!' he barked.

Having sent the driver to obtain a trolley, Mr Edozie fished in his pockets for cash. When the driver returned, he handed the notes to him. Looking at his palm expectantly, the driver's countenance soured once he counted the money. It was less than usual. Noticing his expression, Mr Edozie sighed to himself; he understood, but money was tight. Taking his daughter by the arm, he led her inside the newly refurbished airport to the check in desk.

A consistent pattern emerged. Wherever they turned – from the check-in, to being seated on the aircraft – an empty palm appeared, looking for a handout. As they walked through the airport, choruses of 'Anything for the boys?' followed them, hissed through the lips of police officers. The sense of entitlement annoyed Nkechi as she glared sideways at them. Her father's face was also displeased. They had been through too much to give attention to these opportunists.

Although he tried to ignore their comments, their weight began to accumulate, and his patience abandoned him. When the female worker at the luggage check attempted to confiscate an item from his suitcase under the false pretence of it being prohibited, she indicated that she would give it back to him – provided he filled her hand with cash. Mr Edozie could bear it no longer.

His voice amplified his irritation, reprimanding her in his best British accent. 'Listen to me very well! I will give you 10 seconds to give back my property. Do you know who are talking to?'

Flustered and embarrassed, the round woman's face visibly deflated as she hurriedly returned the item without comment.

A thunderous expression remained on Mr Edozie's face until he boarded the plane. Realising that their seats were at the rear of the plane, adjacent to the toilets, he summoned an air hostess and requested alternative seats. Fortunately, the flight was not full and the hostess obliged, moving them to a window seat towards the middle of the plane.

Fully buckled, seat upright, Nkechi waited anxiously for take-off. As the aircraft sped down the runway and leapt beautifully into the air, Nkechi watched her nightmare turn into a map of endless buildings neatly divided by dirt roads, blurred in the afternoon heat. Clenching her hands, Nkechi mouthed a little prayer to herself and smiled. Around her, a chorus of singing broke out, as a confident woman somewhere towards the front of the plane began to sing in joyous worship, thanks to God erupting from her soul in glorious melodies. The song rose in a crescendo of praise, as other passengers' voices avalanched forward, harmonising with hers in a mutual desire to worship God.

As the praise swirled around her, Nkechi felt light and uplifted, the weight that had been on her shoulders lying disregarded on the floor. Finally, she was going home, to safe spaces not shrouded in bad omens and dark thoughts. She was tired, and yet, sleep was cheating on her with someone else. Focusing on the clouds, she felt comforted by their peaceful nature and shape. Her mind took her back to previous flights, when the return to London meant disappointment – the end of holidays and sunshine. Adaora had always said that the UK was cursed with bad weather as punishment for the terrible atrocities it committed. Photographs of them in bikinis on the sandy beaches of Corfu – their favourite destination – littered their albums. They always travelled together, and on the plane home, Adaora would usually comment that she felt sick, going back to grey, cloud-infested London. Yet, this time, Nkechi could not find that feeling – engulfed by a sense of liberty and nostalgia. Even the air seemed to be infused with beauty when she stepped off the flight, closed her eyes and took a deep breath.

Mr Edozie watched her and smiled, happy that, despite the odds, he had done it. He had brought his daughter home.

Gatwick airport was swollen with passengers who stood in orderly lines around the slowly moving conveyor belt, waiting for their luggage. Behind her, the noise demonstrated that the airport was busy, but Nkechi stood patiently by the baggage claim conveyor, waiting for her case to arrive. The natural urge to check emails and get back in contact with everyone had come flooding back to Nkechi. But, her hand reaching for her jacket pocket, she suddenly remembered that the captors had taken her phone.

Noise burst from the family behind her as a mother attempted to control her four children, all aged under seven. Sweat dripped from the woman's brow sporadically as she twisted and turned, attempting to keep all four in her sight. On her hip, the youngest – a baby – was in hysterics, his face a mess of tears and mucus. Witnessing her plight, Nkechi gave her a warm smile before handing her a packet of tissues from her bag.

The mother was relieved. 'Thank you my daughter,' she began. 'Please can you help me with that pink…?' She was interrupted by the sight of her eldest, who had made a break for the luggage belt and was poised with one foot in the air, clutching the sides with both hands, ready to leap. Her tone switched from polite to stern. 'Jude! Get down from there! NOW!'

Jude was suffering from selective hearing – he did not even acknowledge his mother screeching his name and his eyes were focused on his escape route.

Mr Edozie was unimpressed by the child's behaviour and set into action. With purpose in his step, he strode over to the boy, picked him up and carried him to his mother. The boy would not escape her father's wrath. He was a stickler for obedience. Nkechi knew.

He set the boy down next to his mother, and bent his face to the six-year-old boy's level. 'Now, look here – when your mother asks you to do something, you must listen to her the first time. Do you hear me?'

Embarrassed Jude's eyes were fixed on his shoes as he hid behind his mother's legs.

She shook her head in disbelief before looking at Mr Edozie. 'Thank you, sir.'

'Why are you travelling with all these children, alone?' he asked.

'My husband had to stay back in Nigeria, as a family member fell ill suddenly.'

'Okay,' Mr Edozie's tone was strict, but kindly. 'Just make sure they listen to you. If not, you will struggle when they get older. Which is your bag?'

The young mother of four smiled at him and pointed at the red and black suitcases that were making their way around the carousel for the third time. After ensuring that the mother had all her items, Mr Edozie collected his own luggage and motioned to Nkechi. Smiling at the little boy and his mother, Nkechi waved before following her dad to the exit.

Home. It was time to go home.

Buckled up in the back of the Honda Civic cab, Nkechi sighed, thankful for familiarity. She inhaled the polluted air and settled into the back seat. The radio emitted soft R'n'B tunes while the driver chatted away to her dad. His thick East London accent and rhyming slang was hard to decipher, so Nkechi left the men to talk and turned her attention to the newspapers she had picked up. Her world had been consumed by her capture, but she was desperate to fill her mind with other thoughts than the recent memories she carried. She felt so far removed from current affairs. It would be good to turn her thoughts to the outside world, rather than the torment she had been though.

The black print declared the date '23rd May 2015' with bold headlines and accompanying photos. She learnt that Ireland had had a historic vote to legalise same sex marriages. On the following page, her heart softened to see a picture of an adorable baby girl in her daddy's arms. The Duchess of Cambridge had given birth to her second child. Nkechi noted how flawless Kate looked: hair tousled, make-up faultless – as if giving birth was like a day in the salon. Spotting the next article, about the earthquake in Nepal, Nkechi felt ill, however – she couldn't bring herself to read it, and neatly folded the paper in her lap.

The world had continued without her. It was as if she had never left; as if the reality of her situation had not existed – had simply vanished.

Looking out of the window, she realised that they were a few minutes from home. Perfectly rowed houses, shiny cars in driveways, dog walkers, couples holding hands. As she passed them, she held her truth deep in her stomach, yearning for her family.

The driver turned off the engine. Slowly unbuckling her seatbelt, Nkechi felt uncertain. She knew that behind her front

169

door, her family were waiting to embrace her – but she was suddenly conscious of her looks, and her lips and throat became dry as she began to panic. *What if it didn't feel the same?* she wondered. The trip had changed her, so how had it changed her family?

Taking deep, sharp breaths, Nkechi walked slowly up the familiar path. Before she had time to settle herself, the door was flung open and a whirlwind of emotions swooped her into the tightest embrace. Chidi had been the first to the door and had lifted his sister off the ground in his excitement, shouting her name.

The cab driver turned and watched the encounter in wonder. *What a glorious welcome!* he thought, as he struggled to lift the huge suitcases out of the boot.

Smiling, Nkechi hugged Chidi tightly and begged him to return her feet to the floor. The doorway was full of passion, individual emotions overflowing into Nkechi's presence. Adaora could not speak. Seeing her sister, her body became unresponsive: unable to scream, jump, shout or cry. As their souls connected in a hug, tears simultaneously fell down the sisters' cheeks. Impatiently waiting for her daughter, Mrs Edozie did a celebratory dance, her voice calling down the angels from heaven to praise with her. Her prodigal daughter had returned! Every bone in her body was directed by joyfulness, dancing around Nkechi before sweeping her into her bosom. Gloria stood behind the family, damp tissues hanging limply from her fingers, her eyes bloodshot red; glimpsing her closest friend. She wanted to run to Nkechi, but she knew it was more respectful to the family to wait in line. Her top lip was quivering and she struggled to compose herself.

'Gloria, please stop crying,' said Nkechi, throwing her arms around her. 'You are going to set me off again.'

170

'You know I can't help it,' Gloria replied, drying her eyes with the tissue.

Fidgeting and looking around, Nkechi was unsettled. Someone was missing.

Adaora noticed the look on her sister's face and smiled. 'Don't worry. He is here. He just went to put something in the garden for mum.'

Exhaling in relief, Nkechi's hand went to check her hair.

Patrick, too far inside the insulated shed to hear the initial screams, and unaware that Nkechi had arrived home at that moment, entered the living room, unaware. His eyes blinked: once, twice, three times. His future, his heart, his reason for being was sitting on the sofa! The thumping in his chest increased. Nkechi and he held each other's gaze for what seemed like an eternity – communicating in silent wonder. Paralysed, Patrick could not stop staring. It had been too long since he had seen her; his eyes took their time tracing her face into his heart again.

The room was silent. Nkechi walked gracefully towards Patrick and he opened his arms. Nkechi's head found the perfect spot on his chest and they embraced: long-lost lovers. Unable to restrain himself, Patrick gently lifted her chin and kissed her on the lips. Gloria began to weep again.

Mrs Edozie chuckled, breaking the atmosphere with her dry humour. 'My dear, you must save some tears for when you need them in the future.'

Needing privacy, Patrick led Nkechi through the kitchen and into the garden. Leaning against the wall, Patrick wrapped his arms around her again.

'Babe, I have missed you so much,' he whispered into her neck.

'I've missed you, too,' she replied, squeezing him tighter.

'Listen,' he said, earnestly looking into her eyes. 'Are you ok? Really? They didn't... harm you? Did they?'

'No,' Nkechi said, giving a firm smile. Then she buried herself in his chest again. 'No. Nothing like that.'

'I... It's been... I wouldn't have been able to...' Patrick stuttered, unable to articulate what was in his heart. 'I just... I'm glad you're back.'

'I know, baby,' she gazed into his eyes, her fingers playing with his beard and smiled. 'I can't even believe it's over. This feels like a dream. I just want my life back.'

'Yes, it's not going to be easy, but I am sure we will get by. The most important thing is that you are here.'

They shared a gentle kiss before returning inside.

In the kitchen, the blessed hands of Mrs Edozie and Adaora were busy preparing dinner.

Leaving Patrick in the living room, Nkechi made her first trip upstairs to her room, where more familiar sights greeted her. This was home – amongst her clothes, keepsakes, knick-knacks and organised paperwork. It felt great to finally be in an environment that she could control. She began to pick up various clothes around her room, refolding them into neat piles. The waft of fresh, exotic conditioner hit her nostrils and she smiled in recognition. Once the room was suitably rearranged to her standards, Nkechi sank into her mattress. The longing for the comfort of her own bed had tormented her for the past weeks and she closed her eyes momentarily, enjoying the moment. But feeling icky and unclean, she was unable to rest, and grabbed a clean towel from the top of her wardrobe, as well as her Veet hair-removal cream. Grooming was essential.

After steaming her skin in the scorching shower, Nkechi felt that she had removed all traces of Nigeria from her body. Feeling cleansed and refreshed, baptised into London culture again, she returned to the family who were seated at the dining table, waiting for her arrival.

The air was intense with rejoicing and smiles filled the room with love and gratitude. Finally, after all their efforts and sacrifices, Nkechi was where she belonged, in the safe haven of her family. Knowing the significance of prayer, Mrs Edozie decided to lead it herself, sparing her children the responsibility, on this occasion.

'Father, Lord, we thank you! We thank you for all you have done for us. We prayed and prayed that you would bring back our daughter and you have answered. We are thankful she is here, safe in our care. The bible says the devil is a liar. And any plans he has for this family shall never come to pass.'

'Amen!' they all shouted.

'We pray that you continue to protect and guide each and every one of us. Lastly, please bless this food we are about to eat in Jesus' name.'

'Amen!' they replied; all except Adaora.

The table was spread with a grand feast – all Nkechi's favourite cultural delicacies. A large pot of fried rice had caught Nkechi's attention and she watched, drooling for it to be passed in her direction. Without doubt, her mother's fried rice was the best – no other chef or restaurant could possibly compete with its immaculate texture and flavour. Many had tried; many had failed. Once she was handed the pot, she dealt a generous portion onto her plate, hoping no-one would call her greedy. Savouring the first spoonful, her taste buds danced and she chewed slowly and happily. It was the small things that were often taken for granted – Nkechi repeated this to her students often – and in that moment, she appreciated everything: the food, the company, her life. She looked around at the table full of people who loved her and realised that despite everything she had endured, she was blessed.

It was a work night and so, after dinner, Patrick and Gloria reluctantly left. Later, Adaora looked at the time and also decided to leave. She hugged her parents and Chidi and then went to find Nkechi, who was sitting in the garden.

Under the half-lit moon and clear skies with a slight breeze, Nkechi sat quietly.

'Hey, sis, I am getting ready to go.'

Hearing her sister's voice, Nkechi jolted out of her daydream and turned to face her. Even in the moonlight, Adaora could see the tears leaving trails down her sister's face.

'Sis?' Adaora questioned, sitting down beside her. 'What's the matter?' She looked into her face. 'Nkechi – is there something – did they… do anything bad to you?'

'No.' Nkechi shook her head, her eyes down. 'It's just…' She stopped. 'You know what? Forget it, I am just overly emotional. Plus – you have clients to see very early tomorrow.'

'Look at me,' Adaora insisted. 'I am here for you, no matter what. So, stop being a diva and talk to me.'

Nkechi smiled and turned away. 'It's just… being back home after all that has happened has made me feel so grateful for everything I have, especially my family. It was the only hope I had while I was with those bastards. I knew you lot would be doing everything you could, to make sure I got back home.'

'Of course, we were. But… you're sure that's all?' Adaora persisted.

Nkechi nodded, even summoning an embarrassed laugh. 'I guess just sitting here, thinking about getting on with life… and reminiscing… just got me slightly emotional, really.'

'It's always like that after a traumatic event. Don't feel that you need to rush into anything.'

'Yeah, I know. But I can't wait to get back to some sort of normality. And that will come when I am in my classroom again, with my students.'

Adaora giggled.

'What's funny?' Nkechi asked.

'I am just remembering your first week of teaching. You came home questioning all your life choices! All because of the traumatic experience you had, teaching teenagers for the first time!'

'Please do not remind me about that week!' Nkechi smiled, shaking her head. 'It was literally the worst experience I'd ever had, and I was ready to give up teaching then and there. The only reason I didn't, was because of you.'

'Was it really that bad? We both know you can be a bit of a drama queen!'

Nkechi sat and gave her sister a fierce look: the type of look a father would give his son if he tried to take the first piece of meat once the food was prepared. 'Really, Ada?'

'Look…' Adaora said, awkwardly. 'See, I know you have been through a great deal recently. I am not calling you out about that. But… what I'm saying is… normally. When I call you a drama queen just now, even your reaction is a tad overdramatic.'

Nkechi hid her smile from Adaora, enjoying the teasing, her nose in the air. 'Whatever.' Then she turned back round to face her. 'Yes, to answer your question. That first week of teaching *was* that bad. Those learners were possessed. They insulted me, they didn't acknowledge that I had authority over them, and some of them were aggressive and abusive.'

'That is no longer the case. You rule the classroom as if from an iron throne.'

'Oh, my God!' Nkechi screamed.

Adaora leapt up in fright. 'What is it?' Her face searched Nkechi's anxiously.

'That reminds me! Game of Thrones! The new season must have started!'

Adaora shook her head in disbelief. 'Is that why you are screaming?'

'You have no idea. I keep telling you to watch it.'

Adaora rolled her eyes, then looked at her watch. 'It is getting late. I'm going to head off.'

'Yeah, okay.' Nkechi got up to give Adaora a hug. 'Drive safely, okay?'

'Will do,' Adaora replied before making her way out.

Rushing back inside with an air of purpose, Nkechi's fingers found the Sky remote buried in the crack of the sofa. In the On-Demand menu, she found what she was craving: three new episodes of Game of Thrones. Gleefully, she skipped upstairs and pulled her quilt off the bed and carried it downstairs, wanting to be comfortable whilst devouring the new season. She was secretly grateful that she did not have her phone, sure that her Facebook timeline would be full of plot spoilers. Wrapped up like a tortilla, Nkechi pressed play.

Her intention was to only watch the first episode. That was wishful thinking. As each episode ended in a cliff-hanger, she eagerly clicked to start the next, and when the third episode ended, she felt at a loss. But it gave her a sense of normality again. Like the rest of the nation, she would now have to wait a week to continue her guilty pleasure. Plodding upstairs, she retreated to bed.

Nkechi sat up in a fright, sweat dripping from her brow. Half-conscious and unsure of her surroundings, panic set in. The glaring sunshine had found a gap in Nkechi's curtains and shone brightly into her room. As her vision cleared and the comforts of her bedroom came into focus, she exhaled deeply, instantly feeling more at ease. To avoid any further doubts, she pinched her arm, and the reality of the pain brought clarity and focus. The nightmare had passed. She was safe.

Later that morning, Nkechi enjoyed the full breakfast her mum had prepared especially for her. Between chews, they bonded again, talking, laughing and generally delighting in one another. Her mother's smile had found its way home as if in Nkechi's suitcase, and since her homecoming, it refused to budge, emphasising her high cheekbones. Mrs Edozie cherished every second, a reminder of her saviour's protection over her family and his unconditional love. Stomach full, soul satisfied, heart grinning, Nkechi was ready for the day.

House cleaning was a therapeutic escape and she turned her attention to the rooms around her while her mother sewed. As she wiped mirrors, dusted shelves and vacuumed floors, Nkechi felt reconnected to the house, solidifying her return. Before long, the house was gleaming and Nkechi felt accomplished. Now that the house was clean, she began organising the rest of her life. Signed into her email account, she began messaging the human resources department, informing them that she was ready to return to work. She needed to busy her mind and work was the perfect escape.

With the house sparkling and her affairs in order, Nkechi retreated to the living room to rest. Still needing to occupy her mind, she rummaged around to find the family albums. The five large, heavy books of memories lay around her as she worked her way through them all, reminiscing about her childhood, laughing at embarrassing pictures and questioning her parent's fashion choices; contentedly. During her memory session, Patrick called her and invited her out to dinner later that evening. The thought alone excited her: this was what she needed – time with her love. Her hair was a mess, though – and despite her mother's protests, she went out to get it braided.

Later, as she stood under the shower, Nkechi made a conscious decision to put everything behind her. She began to sing, the steam from the water enhancing her tone and vocal range. Baptising herself in newness, she emerged from the water redefined. It had been a while since she'd had the opportunity to get ready for a date and she was excited. She sat at the end of her bed, wrapped in a large charcoal bath sheet, recalling her outfit options and scanning her makeup collection. Examining her own face in the mirror, she delicately touched her cheeks, pouted at her reflection, smiled, and began to moisturise her skin.

After deciding on a lace purple body con dress and nude heels, Nkechi began her artistic magic on her face. The definition of an artist, her makeup skills were flawless; Nkechi smiled as she remembered the amazing transformations of her friends under her tutelage. She knew just the right amount of foundation and concealer to use to look natural, and the right hues to compliment any skin tone. Her attention to detail added to her talent.

Blasting a few afro-beats from her iPod, Nkechi began to dance and sing as she wrapped her newly-braided hair into a high bun. After spraying her favourite perfume and grabbing a clutch, Nkechi proceeded downstairs just as the doorbell rang. Rubbing her lips together to distribute the gloss, she opened the door with a smile.

She looked amazing, and she knew it. Patrick was shell-shocked. The distance between them during the incident had cause him to focus on her safety over her beauty. Now, in that moment, he was unable to speak. Beauty radiated from her pores.

'You look amazing!'

'Thank you,' Nkechi replied, smiling.

Giving him a quick kiss on the cheek, she said goodbye to her mum and closed the front door.

Lagging behind her so he could take in her curves, Patrick bit his bottom lip in anticipation. It had been so long, and he had missed her.

In attempts to meet the ransom, Patrick had sacrificed his beloved car, so Nkechi slid into the passenger seat of the Uber. Waiting for her to swing her legs inside, Patrick slammed the door shut behind her. Panicked, Nkechi let out a small cry and really jumped, looking around nervously, her breathing laboured.

The driver spun around anxiously. 'You alright there, love?'

Oblivious, Patrick got into the car on the opposite side, but realised that Nkechi looked uneasy. 'Babe, what's the matter?'

'It's nothing,' Nkechi insisted.

'Are we good to go, mate?'

'Yes,' Patrick responded, entwining his fingers with Nkechi's and holding her tightly, a concerned look on his face.

Dinner was strange. The food was good and the ambience of the popular Caribbean restaurant, Sweet and Jerk, was perfect. But between them, like an unwanted guest at the dinner table, sat an awkwardness as if their relationship had forgotten itself, in their being apart. Patrick was tearing his way through half a chicken as a waiter walked over to enquire how their meal was. Mouth full of flesh, hands greasy, Patrick nodded, unable to speak. Nkechi shook her head in amused disbelief at his barbarism.

'Babe, take your time!' she mocked, as she tenderly cut into her lamb.

Patrick was still unable to respond. He chewed his food rapidly, swallowing it before talking about his day. They continued eating and the inconsistent flow of conversation began to bother Patrick.

'So, Kechi, when are you planning on going back to work?'

Nkechi took a sip of her rosé, taking extra precautions not to spill it on her dress. 'I spoke to the HR department and they told me to take the rest of the week off. I can start on Monday.'

'That's good. I am sure you are itching to get back to some sort of normality.'

'I can't wait,' Nkechi replied, her voice aimed at Patrick, her eyes elsewhere.

Expecting her to continue, Patrick waited, but no elaboration came. The struggle to maintain a steady flow of conversation was irritating, but he did not know how to fix it. He kept catching her eye and smiling, even reaching out his hand to hold hers over the table, yet she continued to smile stiffly and hide behind her wine glass. She was acting nervously, as if this was her first date. After dinner, Patrick settled the bill and requested an Uber on his phone app.

As they exited, a black Mercedes pulled up, and a man asked, 'Did you call an Uber? What's your name please?'

'Patrick.'

'Okay. Thanks, please get in.'

180

Careful not to slam the door too hard, they sat in the back seat in relative silence for the duration of the journey.

Once inside Patrick's apartment, Nkechi kicked off her heels and reclined on the sofa with Patrick, leaning into his open arms, watching late night television. Patrick did not even know what channel it was on: his attention was glued to Nkechi. As he studied her averted face, he wanted to kiss her luscious lips, and more. Before her trauma, there would have been no hesitation, yet as he contemplated it, his heart began to race. Steadying his thoughts, he advanced towards her lips, but the movement caught Nkechi by surprise and she leant away initially, before hesitantly moving closer. Their lips met briefly before she pulled away.

'Is everything okay, babe?' he asked, concerned.

'I'm okay,' she replied very quickly before setting her eyes back on the television.

There was an issue. Patrick didn't know what it was, but it was obvious that Nkechi did not want to discuss it. Feeling slightly rejected, he put his arm back around her and decided not to investigate this distance any more that night.

The floor was a collage of items: leave-in conditioners, organic oils, hairbrushes, clips and hair bands. In the midst of it all, Adaora sat on the mat looking at her reflection, her right hand brandishing a hair dryer, left hand holding a section of hair taut. Over the noise, Adaora did not hear the knocking on the front door. But she saw her phone flash with a text and realised that Charles was outside.

Getting up quickly, she switched off the dryer, tied her robe around her waist and opened the door. She no longer cared about her appearance in front of Charles – their level of comfort with one another had grown and Adaora was confident in herself. Charles raised his eyebrows and smiled, not expecting to see her hair half blown out. Adaora giggled.

He hugged her and took off his shoes before entering.

'Don't mind all the mess, please. I really had to wash my hair today and as you can see – it is not an easy feat, dealing with black kinky hair.'

'It's fine.' Charles sat and watched as she finished blow drying the other side of her hair. 'Besides, you look cute, doing that.'

She looked up at him and smiled. 'How was swimming?'

'It was fine. I am finally getting my breathing right.'

'That's good, because you have been struggling with that for a while. Of course, it helps when you don't drown.'

Charles looked at her, wryly. 'I'll get there, one day.'

'I hope to join you again soon. I have missed quite a few lessons.'

Charles walked over to the kitchen. 'But you have a lot to deal with, so it's understandable why you have missed lessons. Do you want something to drink?'

'I'm okay, babe. Didn't you see my glass of rosé just sitting here?'

'Nope, I missed it, but I should have guessed you'd have some,' he teased.

The charm of watching Adaora painstakingly fix her hair had already worn off and Charles retreated to the living room, soon becoming engrossed in Sky Sports News. As a die-hard Arsenal supporter and passionate football lover, Charles was happy the season had ended with the Gunners winning the FA cup. However, he was enraged that Chelsea had claimed the Premier League title. He despised them.

Fixing her hair was a marathon task and forty-five minutes, later Adaora appeared sheepishly at the door. 'Babe I am almost done. If you like, put on the rest of that film that you haven't finished yet.'

'*The Notebook?*'

'Uh huh.'

'Okay. How is your sister?'

'To be honest, babe, I'm not sure,' she said from the bedroom. 'I think she is okay – she's determined to get back to normal, but we can't really fathom what she has been through and she's been pretty closed about it. We'll just have to give her time and see how she readjusts.'

'It must be tough for her mentally, being back, after that horrific incident,' he called from the other room. 'I'm hopeful, though, especially since she has you to talk to. Plus, your parents seem like wonderful people. Having that love and support from them is a strength in itself.'

A vision in pink silky lingerie skimming her knees, curves on display, Adaora appeared from the bedroom like a beautiful goddess, hair wrapped in a scarf. Gasping, Charles could barely contain himself.

'Yes, we are a close family and I believe that when one suffers, we all do,' Adaora replied, walking seductively over to Charles. In the half-light, her melanin tones glowed as she positioned herself next to him on the sofa and placed her head against his chest. Tracing delicate lines across her naked shoulder with his fingers, Charles inhaled her scent. Adaora's body reacted to his touch. Desperate to be closer to him, she wrapped her arms around him while he leant in, to whisper compliments into the side of her neck, in kisses. Unable to withstand the impact of his lips, Adaora curved her back, digging her fingers into his spine. His lips worked their way around the circumference of her neck, and Adaora's toes curled; her body twitching uncontrollably.

The magnetic pull of their lips connected in a passionate kiss, as Charles continued to caress her body. Adaora was breathing heavily, each touch rippling through her veins like silver shivers. His hands were made for her skin, and she was loving the gently patient way he appreciated her body. Her lips found his right ear, and as she exhaled into it, Charles flinched, groaning. Enjoying his reaction, and knowing she had found his weak spot, Adaora continued to tease him, running her tongue along the rim of his ear and nibbling on his lobe. The bulge from his crutch signalled to Adaora that he was ready for her and she stood up, arched her back, pulled him off the sofa and escorted him to her boudoir.

He put his hands on her waist, loving the movement in her hips as she walked slowly in front of him. Allured by the thickness of her thighs, her curvaceous behind and sexy legs, he couldn't help but bite his lips in anticipation. Closing the blinds and setting her iPod to an appropriate playlist, Adaora looked mischievous as she pushed Charles onto her bed.

Her eyes flickered open, a satisfied smile on her face as she realised that Charles had his arms around her waist. He looked so peaceful, she thought, watching his chest rise and fall in gentle breaths. After their workout, he deserved his rest, she thought to herself. Kissing him lightly on the cheek, she carefully manoeuvred around him to avoid stirring him. As if he subconsciously knew her intentions, Charles rolled over in his sleep.

Tip-toeing to the bathroom, Adaora checked her reflection before reaching for her toothbrush. She looked radiant. She replayed the intense passion of the previous night; each moment causing her smile to widen. After refreshing herself, she went to prepare a quick breakfast for herself and her sexy lover.

Both hands carrying plates of scrambled eggs and beans on toast, she gently roused Charles from sleep. The sight of her half-naked body holding food woke him up with a grin and as he dashed into the bathroom to freshen up, she noticed his morning glory and chuckled.

'How are you feeling this morning?' he growled on returning, squeezing her bum and kissing her lips.

'I am *really* good,' she gushed, a cheeky grin fixed on her face.

'Good. Because last night was really special.'

She blushed. 'It was for me, too.'

He looked seriously into her eyes. 'I have never connected with anyone the way I do with you... and that is, in all areas. And as for last night...' He blew out a breath. 'I have no words. My main thing is hoping that you were ready and comfortable around me.'

'I was definitely ready, and the whole night was just perfect. You definitely know your way around the woman's body!' she teased.

It was his turn to flush red in the face.

As they ate, Adaora found herself catching his gaze.

He was staring and laughed, blushing. 'What time is your first patient today?'

Glancing at the clock on the wall, Adaora checked the time. It was 9am.

'11. But today should be an easier day than yesterday. What about you? What are you up to today?'

Charles paused, wiping his mouth, before saying, 'I am going to see one of my old foster carers. She is really ill.'

'Oh, no. I am so sorry to hear that. Were you close, then?'

Charles removed himself from the bed, using the plates as a welcome distraction. He collected them and placed them on the side table, his back turned from Adaora, and she understood that this was a sensitive area. She waited, as the silence yawned between them.

Eventually, Charles cleared his throat and spoke softly, almost to himself in recollection. 'Mrs Morgan means everything to me. She cared, when my own family abandoned me, after my parents died. I remember being on that flight back to London from Lagos; the longest seven hours of my life. Only 13 and alone, I thought I was coming back to London to live with family, but when I got here, no-one would take me in,' he sighed, struggling to continue, the memories circling him. 'I ended up in foster care. I was moved around for a while before I was eventually placed with Mrs Morgan. I was in a really dark place and suffered from depression, but she changed the course of my life and made me who I am today. She brought light where I thought light could never shine…' his voice trailed off as emotions grabbed him.

Gently, Adaora rose, stood behind him and, wrapping her arms around his waist, held his hands.

He squeezed her hand gratefully. 'So, when I see you with your family, it brings joy to my heart and makes me wonder what it would have been like, growing up the way you did.'

'I am so sorry that you've had to go through all that,' Adaora murmured into the taut muscles of his back. 'Mrs Morgan sounds like an amazing woman. I really hope she is okay. Do they know what's wrong with her?'

'No, they don't,' he replied sadly. 'I really hope nothing happens to her. She is the only family I have. The more I think about it, I get angry because of those who abandoned me.'

Spinning Charles around to face her, Adaora tenderly wiped the single tear making its pilgrimage down his cheek.

'I would make sure I gave my family unconditional love and support, because I know the effects of their absence.'

Charles leant over and gave her a soft kiss. Adaora closed her eyes, feeling the fluttering of butterflies in her abdomen.

Charles picked his shirt up from the floor. 'Looking at your family and the love that surrounds it, it makes me want to model my family on that one day, when I have my own children.'

Time stopped. Adaora froze.

He pushed his arms through the sleeves. 'What about you? How many children do you ideally want to have?'

Her soul begged for the ground to swallow her up. She wanted to reboot her life; go back to last night, when lust and passion stripped her of inhibitions and she was freely exploring her own sexual desires. Anything but this, this source of tension – the deal-breaker. Her secret sin.

She attempted to camouflage herself in silence, praying that the subject would change, begging the heavens to cause temporary amnesia so she could return to the bliss of his lips on hers. Alas, her pleas fell on deaf ears.

Charles, halfway through buttoning his shirt, turned to face her. 'Babe, did you hear what I said?'

Adaora's mouth opened but her brain stopped responding. She heard herself say: 'Huh? Sorry, babe. I missed it'.

'I just said – how many children would you want, ideally?'

It was imperative not to raise suspicions. Part of her wanted to be honest, to confess the truth that the thought of growing life inside her – and childbirth – was close to repulsive. That every child-bearing bone in her body must have been removed. That she really didn't like kids and loved her career too much… Yet, as past failed relationships flashed before her, her tongue formed an alternative response.

'Two kids, ideally,' she lied, attempting to smile.

Charles' eyes lit up and he smiled back at her, nodding enthusiastically.

'I've always said two or three would be enough for me.'

'Mmmm. Two is enough for me.'

Two minus two, she thought, disgusted with herself. Her energy plummeted, her stomach sank and the butterflies she had believed to be permanent residents since she'd met Charles were served an eviction notice.

A fortnight had passed since Nkechi had returned to London, and she had submerged herself into the routine of work, busying herself with her students, planning lessons and marking assignments. She had barely stepped outside, apart from work.

Her friends had noticed and were pleading with her to join them that evening, to party in Central London. Nkechi refused profusely. The weather was humid, she felt sticky and she was dreaming of a relaxing bath, devoid of interruptions. Attempting to dance around drunk revellers was not in her to-do list. Eventually, her friends accepted defeat.

After dunking her aching muscles in a steamy bath, Nkechi relaxed in her room in her pyjamas, listening to jazz instrumentals. She was immersed in the melodious mix when there was a knock on her door. 'Come in.'

Chidi poked his head around the door. 'Are you going out tonight?'

'No, Patrick's working and… Why? What's up?'

'Do you want to play blackjack? I've missed beating you,' Chidi boasted.

Nkechi snorted. 'You have forgotten who you are talking to! I taught you how to play the game!' She hit him with a pillow. 'You know what? Give me five minutes and I'll come downstairs and teach you a lesson.'

Sitting in the living room, Nkechi and Chidi stared purposefully at their hands, studying their cards, watching the game, planning and scheming. On the sofa, Mrs Edozie sat on a nest of cushions, eating plantain chips and entertaining herself with *You've Been Framed*. Every so often, she would laugh out loud and throw insults at the people who had forgotten that common sense existed.

Nkechi's phone rang. She didn't pick it up the first time, assuming it was her friends again, trying to persuade her to go out. The phone rang again, so she glanced at the screen and saw that it was Patrick. He wanted her to come over to his place and told her he would pay for the cab to pick her up. She agreed.

She decided that she would beat Chidi one more time before she left, however. Chidi had no words. Nkechi kept her promise of victory, before changing into something less comfortable to go out.

She arrived at Patrick's flat within the hour, and after the usual pleasantries, hugs and short kisses, she sat with him on the sofa. An awkward silence kept interrupting them; the same atmosphere that had repeatedly tormented their interactions since Nkechi had returned. Patrick remembered the delight she'd had, planning their wedding, and thought that this subject would perhaps keep the flow of conversation going and the air positive. Pulling out their to-do list, he suggested they run through it and re-evaluate the plans.

189

Expecting excitement, Patrick was disappointed when Nkechi could barely look at him. Her eyes were vacant and cold, her face despondent, the beautiful dimples he loved replaced by sorrowful lines around her mouth.

'Kechi – is everything okay?'

'Yes,' she said quickly. 'I'm fine. Why do you keep asking me that?'

'Just… ever since you've come back, things have been different. I can't begin to know what you have been through, but… I feel like it's just me that you're different with. You are okay with everyone else.'

'Babe,' Nkechi muttered, her head down. 'I just need time to readjust. I need you to be patient, and just be here for me.'

Shuffling himself closer to her, Patrick cupped her chin and looked at her lovingly before closing his eyes and moving in for a gentle kiss. A warm sensation descended upon Nkechi as she began to relax and her body tingled with the increasing intensity of the kiss. It was the first time they had kissed so passionately since she had returned. Holding the back of his head, Nkechi pressed herself into him. His hands began to wander across her body, stopping to squeeze her inner thighs; travelling upwards, stroking her the edge of her panties – wanting her to feel as good as he did. She took hold of his wrist and kept it still, preventing his progress. He wanted more, and his hands became persistent, his lips tugging at her tongue. Without warning, Nkechi pulled away from him and distanced herself.

'I can't, just yet,' she said apologetically, walking towards the bathroom.

Disappointed, Patrick looked down at his erection and shook his head. *Maybe on her period.* He attempted to think other thoughts.

He wanted to rekindle the intimacy between them, but every opportunity seemed to be blocked by Nkechi and he couldn't fathom why. She wouldn't talk about it, either. He wanted to be one with her again, but the constant rejection was getting to him – it was like slamming the door on the face of an unwanted guest.

Appearing from the bathroom looking solemn, Nkechi announced that she needed to go home.

Patrick was puzzled. 'What's the matter? Are you okay?'

'I am fine. Nothing is wrong.'

Patrick wondered how many men in the world had heard that very same line, knowing full well that something was clearly wrong. Without pressing the issue, he called her a cab.

Sitting in the living room scrolling through her twitter feed, Adaora heard sobs. She jerked her head up, alert, and looked around, but no-one was there. Investigating, she left the room and realised that the sound was coming from outside the front door. Opening it, she found Nkechi sitting on the step, in floods of tears. was. Without a word but extremely concerned, Adaora reached out her hands, helped Nkechi up and led her to the sofa. Pulling a pile of tissues from the box on the coffee table, Adaora handed them to Nkechi before sitting down beside her.

'Sis? What is the matter?'

Mumbling a string of incoherent words, Nkechi attempted to vocalise her emotions. Adaora was unable to decipher the code, but didn't want to rush her. She hadn't seen her sister in this state before, but she knew that, in time, Nkechi would open up. She helped Nkechi take off her jacket, then she put her arms around her. They were like the yin-yang sign, with Nkechi in a black vest and Adaora in a white one, entwined.

Waiting for the sobs to subside, Adaora probed gently, 'Sis, what's wrong?'

'I just… can't…' Nkechi mumbled.

'Can't what?' Adaora asked. There was silence.

'Tell him?'

'Tell who, what?'

'Patrick,' she sniffed. 'Since I came back from Nigeria, I have been distant with Patrick. I could tell it has been eating him up inside, but I had no choice…'

Adaora squeezed Nkechi's shoulders in support as she continued. 'Today, I had to leave his house. Things were becoming heated. All I wanted to do was kiss him, but naturally, his juices started to flow and he made moves to have sex. That's when I had to leave.'

'I don't understand. Why was that a problem? Did he force you?'

Adaora waited for an answer, unsure what her sister was about to reveal to her. She loved Patrick, but if he had laid a hand on her sister in any way, she was ready to fight him like a man.

Nkechi sat, head bowed, eyes on the floor as tears dripped into her lap. Adaora held her. And waited.

'He touched me…' Nkechi whispered.

Adaora leant in closer to hear what she was saying.

'He kept touching me when no one was around. He said if I told the other kidnappers, he would kill me.'

The sudden realisation of what Nkechi was saying dawned on Adaora.

Nkechi continued, 'Every night he could, he would come to where they held me and touch me. I tried to scream. Then I realised that I was only screaming in my head. At first, it was just… grabbing me… stroking my skin… a fetish he used to get himself off…'

Nkechi choked down a sob. 'Till... one day, he actually took my clothes off and... went beyond just touching...' She stopped.

Unified in grief, Adaora buried herself in her sister's arms as their tears mingled in streams down their cheeks.

Chapter Eight

TEARS. DROPS OF MOTHERLY COMPASSION POOLED IN SADNESS, SPLASHED onto the floor. The eerie wail of a broken heart echoed around the room; a resounding hymn of pain, a melody of mourning that started in the depths of Mrs Edozie's soul, rising in a crescendo from her lips.

Her beautiful daughters had told a tale too horrific to process, and the shock ricocheted through her body. They had stolen her daughter's innocence – injected evil into the purity of her being and no one was being held accountable. All the nights she had spent on her knees – muttering desperate prayers, whispering and wailing, persisting and pleading with the almighty to wrap protection around her beloved offspring – had been no use. She was safe, yet she had been harmed. Irreparably.

Mrs Edozie wrapped herself around Nkechi's aching and would not release her, lulling her tears with love and four-ply tissues. Nkechi appeared shell-shocked. Once the words had left her tongue, she watched them cause sorrow in her mother's eyes and sighed in release. No longer a hostage to the secret, Nkechi was free of the burden.

Helplessly, Adaora struggled to know how best to react. She became restless – deep in thought, shaken and angry that her sister had been violated.

'Ada!' Mrs Edozie called. '*A chọrọ m mmiri, biko.*'

Almost robotically, Adaora walked out of the living room to fetch the water as she had been instructed. Hands clasping three chilled bottles, she returned, offering one to Nkechi, who refused, so she placed it down on the floor. Sitting on the opposite side from her mother, they sandwiched Nkechi like a protective barrier – pillars of support and understanding. They embraced her in the silence. Hand in hand, or arms around her, she was guarded. Too late.

Then Nkechi began to speak. 'The images are embedded in my memory. I cannot forget, even when I want to. The experience haunts me…'

Adaora squeezed her hand, and Mrs Edozie stifled a cry. She knew her daughter needed to talk. To release the pain.

Nkechi went on. Her eyes glazed as if in a trance. 'Clear-cut images. They just… repeat the trauma. Regurgitate the pain. No escape. I was so excited to be in Nigeria, desperate to soak up the culture, to find my roots and learn more about our heritage before the traditional wedding.' Nkechi's voice was almost back to normal – excited. 'Everything was a new experience. That day…' Her beautiful face went blank again, her gaze glassy. 'The day it happened, I was thinking about how best to use daddy's connections to network. I never would have thought…' She paused, looking at her feet. 'It was so sudden. A blur. Menacing faces. But in masks. Whirlwind. Chaos and panic. I screamed. I fought! I struggled, but they were too strong. They had guns! They bundled me into their car, pinning me down and I was hysterical…'

Mrs Edozie could no longer contain her weeping. She blew her nose quietly.

'... I couldn't breathe. My pulse was thumping in my throat. Terror washed over me. The car sped off and I saw daddy trying to chase. I couldn't stop shaking. I kept shouting at them to let me go. But one of the masked men became extremely impatient with me, demanding that I stay still and shut up. They just laughed and joked as we continued this long drive. I tried to locate myself but all I could see was hills of red dust mountains surrounded by cornfields...'

Adaora wiped away a tear of her own, and nodded encouragingly.

'They dragged me out of the car and pushed me inside my new prison. Eventually, they took off their masks. I was terrified. They say they kill victims who see their faces, don't they? I tried not to look. They were a cloud of dark skin, muscles and ugliness. Tribal marks and struggles scarred their faces. Three of them seemed to be in their thirties. The leader had tatty dreadlocks down his back and a horrible gold nose ring. He ordered a younger male to tie me up. He was different to the rest, youthful looking – mid-twenties, perhaps, and a few shades lighter than the midnight shades of the others. *Ocha* was his name. The main man went by the name 'Major' and the other two were known as *Ewu* and *Anu*. He tied my wrists with rope before taking me downstairs to a filthy, infested room.'

Adaora and her mother were listening intently, picturing the scene as Nkechi spoke, embedding themselves into her experience.

'I... I fully expected them to rape me... Why else had they taken me here? I had no concept of time. I sat there for hours with only the dripping of rain water through the plastic bags lining the ceiling as entertainment. My wrists were burning and I was thirsty. My lips were cracked, my shoulders aching. At some point, I heard the voices of Major and Ocha discussing struggles and I came to understand why I had been taken, as they discussed how much ransom they would demand for my release. I felt helpless. The amount rose higher and they laughed themselves into a frenzy. I knew it would be a strain on the family to raise that amount. I was worried I would never see any of you again.'

They all jumped. The door-chime of a visitor interrupted Nkechi's flow and Adaora reluctantly went to the door. She opened it, only to see a skinny black boy with large glasses and a geeky smile.

'Is Chidi at home?' he asked nervously.

'No, he's not. Try him a little later.'

Hurriedly closing the door, Adaora returned to her sister's side, looking apologetic for the disruption. 'Go on.'

Nkechi nodded before continuing. 'Sunrise to sunset, days blurred into one another. I couldn't keep up with what day it was. Slowly, they let me out of the dungeon and allowed me to see the outside, and walk around the compound. I tried to memorise my surroundings, desperate to escape, but we were enclosed in a forest. Just as I was getting used to the space, one day I was grabbed; they pounded on me, blindfolding me and tying my hands before throwing me in the back of the car. It was terrifying. Major began barking instructions in broken English. As we rumbled through the rough roads, the repulsive smell of their unwashed bodies made me heave. Hours passed. I felt disoriented and weak. I discovered that they were worried about being tracked by police – hence why we had left so hurriedly.

'When we finally arrived at the new location, they removed my blindfold and my eyes burnt. Another forest surrounded us, and in front an abandoned, miserable, half-finished house stood. Bamboo sticks lay everywhere, with heaps of bricks and unopened cement bags. The room they placed me in made me feel claustrophobic. It reeked of old urine, like a toilet bowl. I listened to their talk… attempting to piece together their motivations, hoping for clues that would help. Politics… they were always arguing about the newly-elected President Buhari; the impact his rule would have on the economy and their future. They spoke of kidnapping as a business venture that would secure their ticket out of poverty…'

Nkechi sighed, and went on: 'Although I appeared to be the centre of their plan, the older men ignored me, preferring to send Ocha to deal with me. I was glad at first – he wasn't as rough and intimidating as the others. At times, I caught him watching me but I didn't think anything of it. Until one night, he came into my room. I heard the shuffling of his feet outside before he entered, the heaviness of his breath; the stench in the atmosphere… He jeered, before placing his hands over my mouth…'

Her voice tapered off, cracking slightly. Adaora squeezed her hand tightly in support. The tears began to flow and Nkechi struggled to get her words out. Her mum wiped her tears away and held her other hand. They sat for a while in silence.

'You do not need to continue if it's too hard,' Adaora said.

Nkechi shook her head. 'No, it's fine. I have to tell someone. I have to… I need to… let it out, get it out… of my head.' She took a deep breath, closed her eyes momentarily and continued. 'I struggled. He kept trying to touch me. His slimy hands worming their way over my skin. Once, I kneed him in the groin and bit his wrist. At that moment, his whole attitude changed. He grabbed me around my throat and told me if I tried that again he would kill me instantly. Although I knew they needed me alive, the threat was real. I looked into his eyes and saw pure evil. His hands tightened around my throat. I didn't want to take any chances, so I kept still and bit my lip to stop from screaming.'

Adaora and her mother stroked her tightly clasped hands.

'A few days later, the news came that the money was ready. There were shouts of joy. The cackle of sinful hearts. That night, Ocha must have believed, like I did, that I would soon be back with my family. That night, touching was not enough. That night, he violated my soul; ripping my insides, sweating all over me, panting.'

A cry arose from Mrs Edozie, and a trembling hand fluttered to her throat.

Nkechi shook her head, eyes screwed shut. '... While I tried to picture myself on a beach. Tried to block out reality. Tried and failed. My tears – no use. My voice – no consequence. Screams swallowed by the walls.'

Mrs Edozie, holding her breath, stood up; the pain almost too much to bear. She walked to the window, her shoulders shaking with silent sobbing.

'I felt numb. Filthy. Disgusting. Yet, I held onto the hope that, shortly, I would never see them again. The money was there. I would be free. My hopes died when I watched them beat daddy's friend almost to death. They took me and the money back with them.' She gave a sob. 'And a part of my heart blackened in despair.

'They sat eating bushmeat and leaves. I refused it, preferring to take my chances of survival with fruits. I realised that Ocha would have another chance to come into my room that night, and who knew for how many more after. That thought threatened my sanity. I was determined not to be victimised again. Screaming was no deterrent. The other men hadn't even kept to the deal. They had no integrity. They would not care about my innocence.'

Mrs Edozie, eyes bloodshot, sat down again, holding Nkechi's hand.

'Finding a sharp stick on the ground, I smuggled it into my bra, determined that I would use it as a weapon against him. I wasn't afraid to die. I just didn't want that man inside me, ever again.'

Mrs Edozie shuddered, swallowing rising bile, but Nkechi pressed on. 'That night, I lay waiting for the shuffling of feet, the door to crack open, but it never did. I couldn't sleep, afraid he would catch me unawares. I guarded the door till morning. He couldn't look me in the eye after that, but he never entered my room again.'

'After days – weeks – of torture, of being held against my will by wicked men, my prayers were finally answered. I saw the outline of dad's face and my heart rejoiced. I would be safe. I would be free! I knew instantly that my incarceration was over. He had come to rescue me. Those bastards grabbed the money and went speeding away, laughing, having accomplished their plan. I collapsed into daddy's arms, sobbing. I just wanted to be back home.'

'It is okay, my dear. God was with you and he is still with you.'

Adaora rolled her eyes. This was not the time for a sermon.

Her mother continued: 'You have been through a very difficult time, my daughter. But God will not give you more than you can bear. He can mend your brokenness. Just believe, my dear. He can fix it for you. It is horrible, what has happened, but we have to trust in Him. I will keep praying for you...'

'Nkechi...' Adaora interrupted, desperate to change the subject. 'Sis, I am so sorry that you had to go through this. I can't even imagine the impact the trauma must have had. Whatever you need,

I am here. You know you can talk to me. But – seriously – have you been checked out, physically, since?'

The thought of her sister contracting AIDS… Or, possibly worse – being pregnant by her rapist, was too much to contemplate.

'Ada, please! What do you take me for? That is the first thing I did when I got back. Blood tests – the whole works – and everything came back negative.'

'We thank God!' Mrs Edozie shouted. Difficult conversations and topics were hard on their mother and she always reverted to her faith. 'Nkechi, you need to talk to Patrick and tell him everything. This is the man you are going to marry. Make sure you open up to your husband.'

'Yes, mummy,' Nkechi murmured. 'I will talk to him.'

Back at work, sitting at her desk, nursing a black coffee, Adaora stared intently into space. Her client was late and Adaora's mind was stumbling over the details Nkechi had revealed about her ordeal. She was in pain. Nkechi, her sister, was in pain and Adaora felt unable to concentrate. She wanted to make it better; to return to childhood when things were easier to deal with. When Nkechi had fallen from a tree, once, Adaora had rushed over to wipe Nkechi's tears on her t-shirt, to engulf her in love, rub her hurting places and soothe her wounds. It had taken a few minutes to console her, and when Nkechi attempted to limp home, Adaora was her shoulder to lean on. Nkechi's pain was her pain. But this time, Adaora had not been around to protect her.

Then, Paige and her social worker strolled into the office, fifteen minutes late. Adaora snapped back into professional mode, as the social worker apologised profusely before leaving the room.

Paige looked different: her outfit – light denim jeans, a white

202

vest top and denim jacket – looked brand new; her hair – freshly straightened – gently graced her shoulders.

'You look lovely!'

'Thank you,' Paige blushed. 'My foster carer gave me some of the money owed to me and I used it to buy a few bits and pieces.'

'Well, it really suits you. So, tell me what has been happening since you I last saw you? It's been almost three weeks, now.'

'Erm… Well, to be honest, I have been feeling a lot more positive. Anytime I think of something negative, I try to find a different way of thinking about it. But…'

'But – what?' Adaora enquired, knowing there was more that needed to be delved into.

'It's nothing,' Paige said quietly.

'Rest assured, whatever you say to me in here stays between us.'

Paige began fiddling with her hair, twirling the ends around her fingers. 'Can I get some water, please?' she asked politely.

'Sure.' Adaora walked over to her mini fridge and pulled out a chilled bottle of water.

She knew better than to push too hard. To rebuild rapport, Adaora revisited Paige's great fashion choices as she passed her the bottle. 'I love your jacket.'

'My mum is a fucking liar!' Paige burst out suddenly, standing up.

The intensity of the statement caught Adaora by surprise. 'Why do you say that?'

'Everything she has done and said has been a fucking lie! All just so she can be with that prick.'

Paige was enraged – she began pacing up and down the room, shouting and swearing. Adaora attempted to calm her down but Paige was fired up.

203

'Even after all the fucking abuse, leaving me and Emma in the house for days with no food – she still had to lie to me about my dad!'

Adaora urged her to have a seat. Once Paige had settled, Adaora handed her the water again and began to assess the situation. She needed the incident behind the rage.

'So, tell me what she lied about and how you found out?'

'I saw Sharon, who used to be a good friend of my mum, the other day at Ilford market. We talked for a while and then – she mentioned that my dad has been looking for me and Emma for a while! I couldn't believe it! I told her. My mum always said he never wanted anything to do with us! When I told Sharon that Emma and I are now in foster care, she screamed but then said she wasn't surprised. Got even more upset when I told her Emma and I were separated. She basically told me that it wasn't that my dad didn't want us. Mum made it impossible for him to be around, because he refused to feed her addiction.'

Adaora was sympathetic, knowing that the news must have been tough to hear and harder to process. However, she wanted Paige to apply the strategies she had learnt.

'Remember what we have been working on these past few weeks. From what you have told me, it seems that you have picked up on all the negatives from that conversation. What positive things could you take, from that conversation with Sharon?'

'Nothing!' Paige snapped.

'Now, Paige,' Adaora said. 'Think again. What is good about what Sharon said? How can you think differently about it?'

'Hmm.' Paige paused. 'I guess… instead of focusing on the lies… I could maybe think about my dad not being the prick I thought he was.'

'That's great. What else?'

'A possibility of actually seeing my dad.'

The session continued, just over the designated one-hour slot, as Paige began to open up and address some of her emotional needs and locate the factors that had caused them.

They had built a trusting relationship and Paige was utilising the sessions with Adaora well. She felt safe in her presence, able to articulate, and she felt listened to and understood, instead of judged.

The social worker popped her head around the door to see if they were ready. Paige gave Adaora a massive hug and thanked her before leaving. Knowing that she had helped to change Paige's outlook, and transform her from feeling angry to peaceful, made Adaora happy and proud.

A welcome breeze swirled around London, bringing the temperature of the evening to a bearable coolness. Summer had arrived in designer sunglasses and colourful shorts and the weatherman bore good news every day. The hope was that Summer would not be a fleeting guest.

Fanning herself on the train to London Bridge, Adaora couldn't wait to exit the sweltering carriage. It was rush hour and commuters had piled in, squashing themselves into tight spaces, all determined to secure a space on their journey home. Sticky, humid and unpleasant, the journey had been uncomfortable and Adaora needed fresh air.

Adaora met Temi on a nearby street and they made their way to the ice cream parlour. It was packed, but they had managed to arrive just as another couple left, taking their table near the back. After a while, the waitress brought over their orders. Adaora smiled when she saw her waffles topped with strawberry and vanilla ice cream. Temi's eyes also lit up at her custom order of random assorted flavours – a rainbow on the black plate. Adaora shook her head at the sight, laughing at Temi's indecisiveness: the display on her plate was evidence of that. Enjoying their welcome cold desserts, the two friends caught up on life, engaged in conversation amidst the buzz of the parlour and its background music.

'Tony and I are now trying for a baby,' Temi announced.

A wide smile appeared across Adaora's face. 'That is fantastic news, Temi!

'We have been married over a year now, and we are at a time when we can both commit to bringing child into this world.'

'You have always wanted a family, right from when we were in secondary school. I'm so glad you found the right man to make this commitment with. You'll be a great Mum!'

'Thanks Ada, that means so much to me.'

'I'm sure Tony is well happy that you guys are trying!' Adaora laughed, winking at her friend, 'Trying is fun!'

'Oh yes, he's doing a great job of trying!' Temi winked back.

'This is so exciting!' Adaora clapped her hands. 'Make sure you let me know when the bun is in the oven. I've got first dibs on godmother duties.'

'Of course, Ada. First choice for godmother… Guess I'll never get the same favour in return from you, will I?'

Awkwardly, Adaora turned her attention elsewhere, unable to maintain eye-contact with Temi. Pretending she was looking for someone, she scanned the pedestrians outside, attempting to avoid the conversation.

Temi had been her friend for too long to not notice her tactics. 'What's wrong?' Temi asked, wiping ice cream from the corner of her mouth.

It was evident that Adaora was hiding something, and Temi looked at her intently, waiting. Adaora knew she might as well open up, since Temi was a master at getting her to reveal herself. Still, Adaora hesitated.

'Come on… spit it out then.'

'It is about Charles,' Adaora said in a low monotone.

'Oh yes, Charles. The illustrious Mr Lover Man. I was going to ask, how are things in paradise?'

'Great, up until our last conversation.'

'What happened?'

'We were talking about his past. Then he brought up the fact that he wanted children.'

Temi winced, already understanding the look on her friend's face. They had been here before, discussing the reactions to Adaora's no children policy.

'That's when it happened. What I did not want to happen. The dreaded question: "How many kids do you want?"'

'What did you say?' Temi asked, already knowing the answer.

Adaora covered her face with both her hands. 'I said I wanted two kids.'

Shock shot across Temi's face: her mouth hung open, her eyes wide in surprise. 'Ada!' Temi began. 'Seriously? You lied to him? Why?'

This was the first time that Adaora had not been honest about her feelings around motherhood. It was a sensitive topic, always, and often resulted in the deterioration of relationships, but Adaora took it in her stride – always hoping she would meet a man who wouldn't mind. Temi's question weighed heavily between them.

'Ada… Ada? What is going on?'

'Temi... I literally have no words, right now,' Adaora quietly picked up her spoon and carried on eating her waffles. They tasted like cardboard now.

'So, what does this all mean?' Temi asked. 'Do you now want kids?'

'No.' Adaora shook her head. 'That hasn't changed. But the moment was so intense and so perfect that I didn't want to spoil it.'

Temi shook her head, her eyes wide.

Adaora tried to explain: 'I have so much history in the impact of that conversation. And with Charles – Oh, I really like him, Temi. I want it to work out and I was afraid! I'm still afraid, because I have never felt so strongly for anyone. Temi – please don't look at me like that. I know it was wrong. I know I have to tell him the truth...'

'It must be really difficult, because you have never lied about this before. You've always articulated your standpoint, even in the face of ridicule and rejection. I know you have feelings for him, Ada – your face lights up every time you talk about him!' Temi patted her hand. 'Even so, you can't continue this lie. If he is meant for you, he will love you for who you are – and not what he wants you to be. You are messing with the emotions of both of you – and it's dangerous. I understand why you did it, but please tell him the truth.'

Adaora looked at Temi and gave a tight smile. 'I will. I have to.'

Boxing was a passion for Mr Edozie: it was a sport he enjoyed discussing almost as much as he loved watching it. The intensity of the atmosphere in the ring, the different styles of fighters, the combat and competitiveness – all excited him. Mr Edozie knew boxing statistics like he knew his children's birthdays and was a wealth of knowledge on the sport. Whenever a bout was due, everyone knew that the remote and the television were strictly off-limits.

So it was, this particular Saturday evening, as Mr Edozie sat expectantly in the living room alongside Patrick and Charles. He had personally called and invited them over to watch the fight. Charles was pleasantly surprised: he relished the opportunity to spend time with Adaora's family and felt privileged to be personally invited. Patrick was happy to see Charles, too. Since he had contributed to Nkechi's ransom, they had started building a strong foundation for friendship.

The big fight was between welterweight rivals Timothy Bradley and Jesse Vargas. Mr Edozie had his money on Bradley, while Patrick and Charles were both backing Vargas.

It was a warm evening, and all the windows were open; yet still the heat was trapped in the house, especially in the kitchen where the Edozie women were hard at work.

Although Mr Edozie had attempted to share his passion with his children, Adaora and Nkechi had no interest in boxing. They were, however, passionate about their men and happy they were spending time with their father. Every so often, they would come into the living room and replenish the snack plates. Round, golden fried *puff puff*, *chin chin*, and meat pies were constantly being restocked as they ate and watched, enthralled by the intensity of the fight as the rounds went on.

Charles winked at Adaora when she walked into the sitting room again and she smiled before asking, 'Need anything else?'

'No, we are okay for now,' Mr Edozie replied without looking up, his eyes fixed on the fight, his hand blindly filling his mouth with food.

Adaora stood by the door and watched all three men, feeling warm. But then, her heart started to sink when the thought of her deception came crawling back into her mind. She knew she had to tell him the truth – but to what end? *What would it mean for their relationship?* she wondered anxiously, before returning to the kitchen.

Chidi got home half-way through the fight and quickly joined in with the snacks. 'Who is winning?' he asked, between bites.

'It's more of a slug-fest at the moment,' Patrick replied. 'Both men pretty much have no defences at all. They keep going at each other with clean shots.'

'They must have incredible chins. I am surprised that both men are still standing,' Charles added.

Mr Edozie did not even acknowledge his son, his face permanently fixed on the screen. He fluctuated between watching from over the top of his glasses to peering through his lenses when something impressive was about to happen. During the last round, all four men were on their feet as Vargas, the Mexican, came on strong, landing a clean right-hander to Bradley's chin. Bradley glazed over, his dark skin shining, and he stumbled across the ring but did not hit the deck. Charles and Patrick were screaming, looking at each other, waiting for Bradley to hit the canvas. There was some confusion in the ring when the fight was abruptly ended. In the house, too, the men looked at one another, open-mouthed in bewilderment. Mr Edozie looked anxious, removing his glasses from his face aa the ring announcer entered to read out the score.

'Ladies and gentlemen, your attention please. Referee Pat Russell signalled the end of the round, not the end of the fight. As a result, we will turn to the score cards to determine a winner.'

Mr Edozie held his breath.

'Judge Lucas scores it 116-112, Young scores it 117-111 and judge Bales scores it 116-112 for the winner – by unanimous decision – the WBO Welterweight World Champion… Desert Storm Bradley!'

At that, Mr Edozie jumped out of his seat. 'I told you small boys that Bradley would win this fight!' he said triumphantly, shaking his fist in victory.

Disappointed, Patrick and Charles could barely look at each other.

Charles picked up his bag. 'Sir, thank you for inviting me over. I really had a great time.'

'No problem, my son. You are welcome any time.'

'It's just a shame Vargas did not win,' Charles grinned, cheekily.

'Just listen to me next time, when I talk about boxing!' Mr Edozie laughed, and Patrick followed suit.

Charles went into the kitchen to let Mrs Edozie, Adaora and Nkechi know that he was leaving. Adaora told him to wait a moment, since she was holding one end of a length of cloth for her mum, who had piles of identical Ankara material. She was sewing traditional attire for a bride and her bridesmaids and Nkechi and Adaora had been helping her, while the men watched the boxing.

'Charles, would you mind giving Chidi a lift to his student accommodation?' asked Nkechi.

'No, of course not,' Charles said.

'Great!' Nkechi went into the living room to negotiate the deal with Chidi.

Adaora finished measuring the cloth she had in her hand before handing it to her mother. Adaora put on her slippers and headed to the front door with Charles.

'Bye!' Mrs Edozie and Nkechi said simultaneously.

Chidi was already standing in the front garden, waiting. 'Thanks for the lift, man,' he said. 'Although I wouldn't have bothered you myself. They seem to want me out!'

He held back and let them walk to the car by themselves, hoping to avoid witnessing any of that embarrassing romantic stuff at close quarters.

As they walked towards the car, Charles held Adaora's hand and Adaora's thoughts were racing, her palms sweaty and uncomfortable. She was flustered, unsure if this was the right moment to come clean. This had been her only opportunity tonight. But now, there was Chidi, too... But when should she say something?

Charles stopped and looked at her. 'Babe. Did you hear what I said?'

She hadn't. 'Sorry, babe, I was totally day-dreaming.'

'I said we should go back to Heron Tower, that restaurant we were at when you got the news about Nkechi. So that we can finally finish that date.'

'I'd love that.'

They arrived at his car, where he gave her a hug and a kiss on the lips. Adaora melted into it, before they broke off and he smiled, his dark eyes dancing.

Adaora opened her mouth but the words refused to come out. 'Goodnight' was all she could muster, before Chidi came sprinting up the path, threw himself into the passenger seat, and they drove off.

Adaora returned to the house, but something had changed, inside; sadness hung over them all. The room was held in a grasp they couldn't escape from.

'What is the matter?' Adaora asked.

Her words fell dead. No-one bothered to pick them up. Everyone was held in their own emotional bubble; all were solemn and silent. On the sofa, sat Nkechi: her eyes wet, her head against Patrick's chest. Patrick's face was a broken wall of pain. He did not know how to react, shaking his head while holding Nkechi close and blinking away tears. Mrs Edozie looked anxiously at her husband, who was pacing the room threateningly.

'If only I knew! I would have killed those bastards. I would have killed them all,' he chanted, in an anthem of regret and anguish.

'Ada, Nkechi finally told your dad and Patrick what happened in Nigeria,' Mrs Edozie explained.

Chidi had been deliberately left out of this conversation. Nkechi did not want him to use it as an excuse to do something irrational.

A vein in Patrick's forehead began to pulsate. He let go of Nkechi, punching his fist into his palm, repeatedly. 'I can't believe this happened to you!' he wailed.

'Nkechi,' her father said, seething. 'You could have told me in Nigeria what that animal did to you.'

Nkechi lifted her head slightly, disturbing the braids that hung in front of her face. 'Dad, if I'd told you, I know you would have reacted angrily, looking for justice, and what could you have done? They were heavily armed and I was not going to risk losing you, by telling you, there, when all I wanted was to come home. Even if I told you when they had gone, you would have wanted me to report it to the police. Imagine the delay? The tests? The interrogation? I just wanted to get out of there.'

Mr Edozie started ranting and shouting in Igbo. 'To think I gave those animals money! Not knowing they…'

Mrs Edozie walked over to try and calm him down. 'Papa Ada, please calm down, *biko*.'

Patrick took Nkechi to the garden and held her close. 'Baby, I am so sorry you had to go through this. Now I understand why you have been so distant.'

'I'm sorry,' Nkechi mumbled.

'No. Do not apologise for that. You should have just told me. I would have understood. To think you were processing this all by yourself is killing me inside!' He cupped her face gently. 'I love you with all my heart and I am here to protect you, so please open up to me so I can do what God put me on this earth to do – which is to protect, provide and make you happy.'

Nkechi smiled uneasily and stood on tiptoe to embrace Patrick. 'I know, babe. I'm sorry. I just couldn't find the words to start with…'

'And that you would tell me now, in front of your family – when we have been alone…' His hurt expression showed his incomprehension.

'I was afraid of your reaction,' Nkechi said, a tear rolling down her cheek.

Patrick rolled his eyes, sighed heavily and hugged her close. 'Never be afraid of me.'

Nkechi spoke again, her face pressed tight against her chest. 'Is it alright if we cancel the traditional marriage in Nigeria? I don't think I can go back there, for now.'

'Of course, babe. Absolutely. I was going to suggest the same thing, actually.'

'Good. So, that's sorted, then,' she sighed, relieved; hoping now that Patrick knew, that their relationship would improve.

214

Work was bothersome for Adaora: the sun was relentless and the lack of breeze caused her office to be stuffy and uncomfortable; the white plastic fan only circulating the hot air – not keeping Adaora cool at all. The pleas for warm weather had been received and London was baking in a heatwave and now, the same people were complaining that it was too hot.

Adaora fanned herself with some paperwork, sipping on an iced latte. She pondered how much the cost of air conditioning would be, since the heat was not pleasant for clients, either. Watching the clock, Adaora planned her evening. She was excited to have the opportunity to mentor the two college students she had met at the conference, who had taken her up on her offer to support them.

After work, Adaora made her way to Old Street, using the GPS on her phone to locate the youth club, whose address the girls had sent. The area had been a target for corporate investment; technology companies were moving in and even local names had changed. Adjacent to the red brick estate, was the project.

Texting the two girls to let them know she had arrived, they quickly came out to meet her.

'Hey, long time!' Adaora said, and the two girls smiled.

'Yes, it is,' Rachel replied. 'Thanks for coming.'

They hugged before escorting her inside, Adaora chatting: 'I hope you have both been well.'

'Yes, we are great,' Holly piped up. 'We are so glad you agreed to do this for us.'

'Please, don't mention it.'

The club was alive with the sound of youth: some competitively surrounding the pool table, others playing giant Jenga. They barely noticed Adaora enter, all engaged in their own activities. Holly led

215

them to a side room, where they all sat down, discussing their needs and questions. The two girls took notes and smiled at each other, attentively listening to every word that Adaora offered.

'It is important that you read and that you are thirsty for more knowledge, because in this profession – and in this world – you have to be ready for people to assume you are not capable. I have walked into clinics and people have assumed I am the nurse rather than the doctor. Especially as a black woman. There not many of us in this profession, and often it feels like I gate-crashed an exclusive party.'

Rachel nodded her head in agreement. She had often wondered about the realities of being a young black female doctor.

Adaora continued. 'My suggestion is, even before you both start university in October, that you are way ahead of the game. Read, read, read. What I would suggest you look into is person-centred theory. Next time we meet, we will discuss that.'

The girls both had a bright spark in their eyes and Adaora felt warm inside. She could see herself in them.

'Rachel, with regard to your problem with team work, I would suggest the Karpman drama triangle. It was really effective in how I perceived the notion of team work, especially when personalities clash.'

Rachel's facial expression was one of bewilderment, although she jotted down the name.

'Just to explain briefly, the model has three agents,' Adaora held up one finger after another, in turn. 'The hero, who is willing to do anything for everyone, but not looking at the root cause why they can't do it. The villain…' Here she counted off another finger. '… who likes to blame either themselves or everyone else. And finally, the victim… who is powerless. They can feel victimised by anything – like their boss, weather, and children.'

Holly gave a wry smile of recognition.

'So, the idea is to move from the drama format to the present format – where the victim becomes a creator, takes responsibility and stops complaining. The hero becomes a coach – whereby they stop fixing and empower others by supporting them, only. And finally, the villain becomes the challenger – who stops blaming, but creates a healthy pressure on other to support.'

'Wow! That's interesting!' Rachel said. She and Holly were busy writing away.

'Definitely going to look more into that,' Holly added.

'Yes, you should. It gave me a different perspective.' Distracted by a flash of light on her phone screen, Adaora looked at it.

It was a message from Charles: 'Are you ready?'

Adaora's thumbs speedily replied: '2 minutes.'

'Look, girls, it been a pleasure spending some time with you. I will see you in about two weeks or so,' Adaora said.

They exchanged hugs and smiles, the girls thanking her profusely.

In the darkness, thirty people were squeezed into Patrick's apartment, struggling to keep quiet, often bursting into fits of laughter; all waiting for confirmation. They were ready.

Before long, Adaora received the text message. She summoned for silence with her hands and informed the room: 'Alright, everyone – they are on their way up.'

A hush fell over the congregated guests, waiting with bated breath. Footsteps, murmuring, the sound of keys jangling and the opening of the door.

Patrick switched on the light and the room exploded in a joyous acclamation: 'SURPRISE!'

Nkechi was stunned. She smiled in bewilderment at the unexpected guests, before turning to Patrick and giving him a stern look.

As he leant over to hug her, she whispered a reprimand into his ear. 'I told you I just wanted a quiet night – with just you.'

Before she was able to continue her quiet scolding, she was inundated with hugs, welcomes, gifts and presents from well-wishers.

Patrick was unsure if she appreciated this – and the hard work that had gone into this get-together. He had spent the last three weeks planning and organising, while keeping it all a secret from Nkechi. He missed her sparkle, the way she lit up a room with her personality and wanted to make things normal again – give her an opportunity to socialise and regroup with her friends.

He watched her work the room and smiled. Since learning of her ordeal in Nigeria, they had been working on strengthening their relationship and steps had been made, but he sensed that something was still wrong. He couldn't quite put his finger on what it was.

Noticing him standing in the corner, Adaora walked over to him. 'Are you okay?'

'Not sure she is too impressed with the whole surprise thing,' Patrick replied.

'Don't worry about Kechi. She will be fine.'

'That's what I have been saying to myself, but as each day passes, I only see glimpses of the woman I was with, before this whole thing happened. Now, I just do not recognise some of the things she does and says.'

'These things will take time. An incident like that could have long-lasting psychological effects.'

'Can you talk to her, like you do with your patients?'

'No, I can't have a family member as a patient. It doesn't work like that. To get psychological help, she would have to be referred. That's if she wants it. She has to agree. I talked to her about speaking to a professional but she refused. All we can do is support her and make sure we get her talking and socialising.'

'Even while I was planning this party, she told me she wanted a quiet 28th birthday,' Patrick said, uneasily. 'I was getting nervous because it was too late – plans were already in motion. Then, at dinner tonight, we had a great time. She said it was perfect and we talked and talked. We haven't talked like that for a while. So, seeing her reaction when we came in, maybe this was a mistake. I should have quit while we were ahead.'

'Patrick, stop stressing yourself out. Go and enjoy the fruits of your labour.'

Following her conversation with Patrick, Adaora kept a close eye on Nkechi. Although she seemed to be engaged and enjoying herself, Adaora realised that Patrick had grounds to be concerned. It was a facade. Adaora could see right through it – her sister was appeasing her guests, but had no true desire to be in their presence. This was strange. After all, the room was full of Nkechi's closest friends and she loved to party. But her eyes were distant, her smile plastic. She entertained and mingled for a while, before quietly retreating to the bedroom.

One by one, the guests left and the 90s RNB classics faded out.

It was an evening steeped in romance and nostalgia. Back at the top of Heron Tower, Adaora and Charles sat across the table from one another, enjoying the ambience of the restaurant. Catching his eye, Adaora felt excited and giddy, aware of her growing feelings for him.

They consumed a three-course meal, expertly cooked and elegantly presented on each plate. Taste-buds tingling in appreciation, they both felt satisfied and content, and Adaora had found a new love for Japanese food. The waitress came over and cleared their plates.

Charles held Adaora's hands across the table and looked into her eyes, searching for answers. 'Babe, are you okay? You haven't said much. I am not sure if it's because your mouth was too busy with this food, or because something is on your mind.'

Adaora hesitated. She had hoped she could camouflage her thoughts, but it seemed that Charles had read her body language and knew something was up. As she attempted to find words, Charles' phone rang and he excused himself from the table. His absence gave Adaora time to compose herself and rehearse the difficult conversation she knew she needed to have. Charles returned looking despondent.

'What's wrong?'

'Business is not great,' he muttered. 'I am on the verge of losing another long-term contract. Plus, my cleaners are worried they will be out of a job – so I am just reassuring them.'

'Awww, babe, I am so sorry to hear that.'

'It's fine. Patrick sent a text I just picked up and that put me in a better mood. Says he has tickets for the first game of Arsenal's season, and he wants me to go with him.'

'It's nice you guys have this whole bromance thing going on!'

Charles laughed but refused to comment on that. 'So, babe, what were you going to say before I went on the phone?'

It was now or never. Her heart-rate sped up to the beat of a funky house track. With her palms wet with fear, she took a deep breath. 'Do you remember that conversation we had a couple of weeks ago, about children, and how many we both wanted?'

'Yes,' Charles said, eager to find out where this was heading.

'The truth is – I lied.' She stopped abruptly.

'Lied about what, exactly?' Charles looked at her, confused, scanning his memory to replay the conversation in his head. 'You really want eight kids?'

Struggling, Adaora hesitated before continuing. 'Wanting children.' She paused, but he still sat staring, uncomprehending. 'I do not want children. I have never wanted children.' Her voice grew quieter. 'I will never have children.'

Her statement stabbed the atmosphere, slicing it with the painful truth. She waited for a reaction, but Charles was still, his gaze secured on something on the wall behind Adaora. It was intense and the lack of response caused Adaora to wonder whether to interject or allow him space, for processing her words and their implications.

Finally, Charles spoke. 'Wait. I am confused. Why is this even something you would lie about?'

Adaora swallowed, pained. 'To be honest, this is the first time I have ever lied about it. Normally, I am upfront with my feelings about having children. But... after connecting with you on so many levels... and with me not expecting that conversation till much later...' She shrugged, helplessly. 'I just did not want to lose you. Especially after seeing your passion and desire for wanting children and having the perfect family.'

Charles shuffled uncomfortably in his seat, his face a collage of disappointment and confusion. He picked up his glass and took a sip of water, barely able to hold eye contact with Adaora.

Her confession had ruined their evening. She knew. All the beauty of what they had prior to her outburst had disappeared. All that was left was the bitter taste of dishonesty, grating the back of his throat. Adaora looked dismal, not knowing where to look or what to say; she began picking at her fingernails.

Charles cleared his throat, took another sip of water and addressed Adaora in a cold tone. 'Adaora. I can't believe what you are telling me. I just can't even process it, right now. I'm shocked. Shocked that you would lie about something so serious – and then keep it from me all this time.' He stood up, shocking her to the core. 'I can't continue this evening. I don't know what to say to you. I'm going to call you a cab. I need to be alone.'

Signalling to the waiter that he would like the bill, Charles paid and they left the restaurant in horrified silence. Usually, Charles would hold her hand or put his arm around her, but although he walked a step ahead of her, there was a far greater distance between them.

Out of courtesy, he waited for her cab to arrive – still silent – and then walked away, without a word.

Adaora got into the cab and burst into tears.

Summer continued to crank up the temperature, in the longest heat wave in recent years. It was mid-August and the media bore the sad news of an 87-year-old passing away due to the heat. Fears and warnings for babies and the elderly rose, as hospitals dealt with patients suffering from dehydration and sunstroke. The country was struggling to cope.

Fans were sold out everywhere, ice cold water lasted only a few minutes in shop fridges and the overarching mood was 'hot and bothered'.

It was Sunday and Mrs Edozie had persuaded everyone to attend church, as a family. Everyone except Adaora.

Attendance was high, thanks to the church's great investment in their air conditioning system and the room was a wave of colourful patterns, since people came dressed in traditional attire.

An usher led them to available seats. The musicians were uplifting the mood with worship songs melodiously arranged for the church choir. The Pastor urged everyone to stand for praise and worship.

Nkechi attempted to stand, but struggled to get on her feet. Patrick, next to her, offered his hand and Nkechi leant on him for support. As she stood, she felt dizzy and lightheaded and collapsed back into the seat.

'Babe, are you okay?' he whispered.

'I just feel tired. But… I think I need to go home.'

'Okay, let's go. I'll get an Uber.'

Patrick supported Nkechi along the row, signalling to Mrs Edozie that he was taking her home. Nkechi moved gingerly, looking faint and weak.

Mrs Edozie worried. She had hoped that church would have aided her daughter's mental and physical healing, and felt helpless watching her in pain. She closed her eyes and said a prayer of protection over her daughter as they left the sanctuary.

After the church service, Nkechi rested on the sofa in the living room, watching old episodes of *Boy Meets World*.

Mrs Edozie and Adaora were cooking, making Sunday dinner in the kitchen.

'I am worried about Nkechi,' Mrs Edozie said.

'Why?' Adaora asked.

'Can't you see she is not the same person? She doesn't talk as much. She has no energy and is putting on weight. And I know she has been called for a meeting with human resources at her school tomorrow. I asked her what the meeting is about, and she says she did not know.'

'Mum, don't stress yourself out. She is going through a depressive stage – which is hardly surprising – but as long as she has loving people around her and she is not left in her own thoughts for long, she will be fine, in time.'

Chapter Nine

THE PRESSURE OF LIFE HAD CAUSED A PERMANENT ACHE IN THE LOW HOLLOW of Adaora's back. She had decided it was time to get away for the weekend – to experience some tranquil beauty and immerse herself in the culture of another place, if only for a short while. A home away from home. She and her passport had yearned for the arms of her beloved – Barcelona – a city that had stamped its influence on her heart three times over.

Without a moment's hesitation and armed with her trusty worn suitcase, her journal and her longing, Adaora followed the draw of her soul. She told the family she wasn't paying roaming charges, so she wouldn't use her phone till she got back. It was a conscious decision to take a complete communications break – would be great to switch off for a while, now that Nkechi was safe. Even though she had been through a terrible ordeal, she was well-supported. Nothing worse could happen to her. Adaora felt able to relax.

She landed in the vibrant cosmopolitan capital of Catalonia, ready to regain ground, explore, revisit, reminisce. Immediately busying herself with the quirky architecture and art, she wandered, appreciating her surroundings. Using her basic Spanish, she conversed with locals, her accent and confidence growing, the more she spoke. The melanin in her skin recalled its sparkle; the ache in her back stretched itself into flexibility and she breathed peace. The gnawing in her abdomen took her to a small cosy tapas bar, where she relaxed with a book and ate slowly – enjoying the burst of flavours on her tongue.

Back home, the front door slammed shut as Nkechi ran in, crying hysterically.

Mrs Edozie was home alone and the sound of her daughter's suffering caused her to jump up from her sewing machine and run in the direction of the weeping. 'Nkechi, *ogini?* Why are you crying?'

Her face a mess: mascara running, nose leaking, red eyes clogged with tears, Nkechi could barely speak. 'M…mum!'

Her mother handed her a tissue. She wiped her distressed face, before falling onto a chair in defeat. 'Mum, I just came from the doctors, for another check-up. They made me do a pregnancy test… and… and…' her voice disintegrated into a squeal. 'It came out positive.'

'*Nne* – but that is great news!' Mrs Edozie screamed in joy. The thought of a grandchild causing praise and worship to spill over from her lips. Adaora would not give her any but she had done well with Nkechi – she would be a wonderful mother.

'Do not worry! You should be married before the baby comes!'

Nkechi's sobbing intensified with the mention of her upcoming marriage. Realising that her mother did not understand, she tried to vocalise the reason for her grief. 'The doctor says I am 12 weeks pregnant, Mummy. And Patrick and I have not been intimate for over five months!'

Realisation dawned on Mrs Edozie, as she started to piece the situation together. The baby was not Patrick's! Nkechi had returned from Nigeria about three months ago... The rape! This child was the seed of a rapist! Oh! More pain. More trauma.

Wrapping her arms around her daughter, she sang lullabies to her sorrow and held her as tightly as she could.

Adaora spent her weekend break engulfed in the rich history, gorgeous views and delicious restaurants. In a hiatus from connecting with the world, she was glad she had made a choice to remove herself from emails and social media updates.

On her final day, she visited one of her favourite places – the Boqueria – regarded as one of the best markets in the world. Her eyes scanned the vast assortment of fruits and vegetables on display in an array of colours: over 250 stalls in panoramic view – fishmongers, fruit-sellers and foodstuffs – plenty of options to exchange for hard earned cash.

Having bought hand-cream for her mum and sister, Adaora smiled as she pulled her suitcase behind her, sad to leave, but destined for home.

Stansted Airport greeted her with grey skies and threatening clouds. *Charming!* Adaora thought as she turned on her mobile data and checked her messages. She had a few work emails, fairly nondescript texts from family – things like 'Call me when you get home' – and a picture from Chidi. Nothing from the person she had hoped for. Disappointed, she chucked the phone back into her hand- luggage. He hadn't even tried to contact her! The weather reflected Adaora's mood as she wallowed in the misery of loneliness. Barcelona had provided her with a perfect companion – the ultimate distraction from reality. Yet, she was back. Back to the emptiness, the residue of hurt, another relationship failure.

She grabbed her phone again, scrolled through her gallery and found a 'couple selfie'. She was looking straight into the camera, smiling, while Charles was staring at her – a look of infatuation on his face. At the time, she had scolded him for not posing with her and grinning at the camera; but the genuinely adoring expression on his face was a realisation of what they'd had; what she had lost. Tracing her index finger over his face, she felt a pang in her stomach. She missed him. But her stubbornness would not allow her to call him. Dismissing the thought entirely, she made her way to her flat.

A hot shower later, Adaora decided that instead of ringing anyone as the texts had asked, she would go and give Nkechi and her Mum their presents. Having travelled alone, she was desperate to update them on the trip. Plus, the flat felt empty, reminding her that Charles would not be coming over to welcome her back with outstretched arms; wouldn't be wrapping his biceps around her and hugging her into his muscles, inhaling her skin or kissing her passionately.

Shaking off thoughts of him, Adaora got in the car, hoping the drive would help to adjust her thinking. Turning on the radio, she started singing along to '*Kisstory*,' listening to anthems from her childhood. Her head-bopping was interrupted by a traffic news announcement. Half listening, half waiting to get back to her music selection, she heard a report about an accident at the Redbridge roundabout. Since she had been heading in that direction, Adaora quickly reverted to her own navigation skills, and weaved through back streets to get to North London.

Parking a short distance from her mother's house, Adaora grabbed the presents from the boot of the car and strode purposefully towards the door. She was excited to share the pictures of her trip and remind Nkechi of some of the places they had visited together in the past. Balancing her bag and gifts on her hip, she turned the key and pushed the door open with her right foot.

'Hello!' she called. 'I'm back!'

There was no response to her entrance, which was unusual. Adaora wondered if they were all out. Placing her bag down in the passage and removing her shoes she heard rustling, and a deep sigh coming from the living room. Thinking it was Nkechi, Adaora rushed into the room, but instead, found her mother, surrounded by crumpled tissues, silently weeping on the sofa.

'Mum?' Unsure what had happened, Adaora sat down beside her, a querying look on her face. 'Mum? What's wrong?'

She placed her arm over her mother's shoulders and experienced prickly goosebumps – a result of the cold snap that had been present for the last few days.

'What's the matter?'

The sobs continued as Mrs Edozie folded over, her head continuing to shake in an attempt to erase the sadness from her mind. An inaudible mumbling fell from her lips.

Adaora sat for a moment, wondering how to assist. The temperature in the room was too low, and she went upstairs to get a blanket, returning and draping it over Mrs Edozie's shoulders.

Her mum suddenly looked up and noticed her daughter. 'The devil is a liar. The *Devil* is a liar. The devil *is* a liar. The devil is a *liar!*'

For her to blame Satan, Adaora knew something terrible must have occurred. 'Mum, please, talk to me. What's happened?'

'It's Nkechi.'

Terror washed over Adaora. 'What?' she urged. 'What's happened to Nkechi?'

'She is pregnant by that bastard! God will punish him, wherever he is.'

Adaora was confused. It was unlike her mother to use such abusive language towards Patrick. 'She's pregnant? But that's great, isn't it? Mum, you said you always wanted a grand ch....'

Even as the words left her mouth, her brain was connecting the dots, recalling information, piecing together the source of the anguish that hung so vibrantly in the room. Her face turned pale. She remembered Nkechi telling her that she couldn't yet face making love with Pat... not since...

'Mum – please don't tell me it's what I think.'

'My daughter, Nkechi is carrying the seed of a rapist! *Tufiakwa!*' The pain increased and her questions to the almighty followed. 'God, what have we done to deserve this?' As usual, her thoughts turned into prayers as she attempted to make sense of the turmoil. She was devout, a believer in God's sovereign will, yet this had rocked her soul.

The shock rumbled through Adaora's limbs, numbing muscles and emotions to a feeling of devastation. She could not speak. But – this could not be! *She said she had been checked out as soon as she got back! Surely they had tested her before now? What had happened?*

Her mother continued talking to herself and God.

Adaora asked urgently: 'Where is Nkechi?'

'She has finally gone to tell Patrick. She could not bear to speak to him till now. She has avoided him. I have had to field her calls.'

Adaora still couldn't believe her ears. 'What happened?'

'She came home two days ago, crying after coming back from the doctor. They suspected she was pregnant after her complaining

230

about sickness and headaches. She did the test and it came out positive.'

'But how can that be? She said she was ok… that she had been checked out…'

Mrs Edozie shrugged. 'A mistaken result – a faulty test – I don't know. All I know is this.'

The niggling feeling about Charles subsided as thoughts of Nkechi consumed her. As Adaora sat, head bowed, attempting to process this new level of pain, silence fell.

They sat still with their thoughts, when suddenly Mrs Edozie began to pray passionately, thundering questions into the atmosphere. The noise made Adaora jump. *What good will that do?* she thought. She looked at her mother with irritation, waiting for her to finish her spectacle.

'God is in control!' Mrs Edozie said triumphantly, before sitting down.

Adaora was shaking in disbelief. Emotions trapped in the back of her throat pushed their way to the roof of her mouth, and before she could think about the consequences, she unleashed them.

'God?' she mocked. 'Enlighten me! How, exactly, is God in control?' The words released their venom as she stood up and faced her shocked mother. 'You talk about protecting us with your prayers? Look what happened to Nkechi! Think about what we have been through! And please identify God's handiwork, so I know who to blame! Nkechi is still suffering the effects of this trauma – and all you can do is pray to your white Jesus!'

In one swoop, Mrs Edozie pulled back her hand and launched a ferocious slap across Adaora's face. The sound echoed in the room. Adaora clutched her cheek.

'How dare you talk to me that way! Am I your age? *Ewu!*'

The insult, being called a 'goat', was not as hurtful as her stinging face. It had been years since Adaora had been on the receiving end of physical discipline and like déjà vu, it brought back teenage memories. There had been a shift in their relationship ever since Adaora began questioning her faith, and this was not the first time she had been slapped because of it. Although it was, perhaps, her disrespectful tone and attitude that most deserved the slap.

Her mother also knew how to lash someone with words, and began throwing licks in Adaora's direction. 'Look at you! My daughter, you have spent years in education – you are a doctor, but you lack intelligence! Yes, Nkechi is suffering. Things happened outside of her control. But you. *Chai.* Everything is self-inflicted. You are an enemy of your own progress!'

Adaora's heart started to race, her face flushed in embarrassment. She hated this tradition of being put down by her own mother. It had done her confidence no favours as a child, and it still peeled away her external appearance of strength and attacked her inner core, even now.

Her mother was in full swing. 'Let's address your shortcomings. How is Charles? He is a good man, loving, kind, smart, strong. But we know it will not last. You will destroy this relationship, along with all the others because of your foolishness? Have you told him you don't want children, yet? Let's see what decent man will hang around, after hearing such rubbish!'

Adaora was stung badly. Stabbed by the truth of her mother's words. She began fidgeting, scratching her shoulder, unable to keep eye contact with her mother, her tear ducts welling up in preparation. Maybe her mother was right.

'You are my first daughter. Why can't you be more like Nkechi?'

The words tore Adaora's heart in two, bruising her deeply. She had always known she wasn't the favourite. But to hear these words spat at her with such disgust made her feel empty and numb.

'Here are all your mates your age, getting married, and you are sitting here questioning me about my God! That Charles is a good man, who deserves better from you – and here you are, talking nonsense.'

Adaora could take it no longer. 'JUST STOP IT!' she shouted, piercing her mother's stream of thought. 'You favour Nkechi! Fine! I always knew that, but why must you always cause issues between us? Nkechi is in a difficult place, and all you want to do is insult me!'

Removing herself from the room, Adaora slid her feet in her shoes, grabbed her bag from the passageway and made for the door, yelling behind her: 'All I want is to be there for her! Not argue with you about my life choices – which are frankly none of your business anymore!'

The door slammed shut. Adaora sat in her car and the tears began to fall heavily onto the steering wheel. She needed her sister. Her sister needed her. She dialled her number, but there was no response.

The usual sounds of pounding basslines and melodious tunes were missing from the apartment. A frantic atmosphere replaced the upbeat rhythms. A dozen freshly dry-cleaned suits were strewn haphazardly on the sofa, waiting to be returned to the wardrobe. There was no time for chores.

Amongst the clusters of plastic wrappings and metal hangers, Nkechi sat uncomfortably on the sofa. Around and above her, pacing the floor, Patrick tried to focus on the meaning of the words that had knocked his world apart, although he wanted to ignore the pain they carried with them.

'So, then, I made sure. I asked the doctor to do the test again. We even ended up doing it three times, because I didn't want it to be true.' The crack in her voice resonated. She was broken. The tracks of her tears were only the subtitles of her suffering.

The room seemed smaller, claustrophobic, crowded with messages, what ifs, confusion. Patrick felt trapped, but he continued walking up and down, seeking an exit, seeking escape, seeking air. His throat began to close up.

He turned and saw Nkechi – and in that moment, realised that his pain was nothing, compared with hers and knew that she needed him now, more than ever. He tried to comfort her, but the slithering plastic-covered suits repelled his attempts and he swept them onto the floor before sitting next to her.

'Baby, we will get through this. I know we will,' he said, unconvincingly.

Nkechi sensed the lack, concerned about their future. 'This was supposed to be the best year of my life and it is a nightmare. All I wanted was to marry you and to start our own family,' she sobbed.

The more Nkechi spoke, the more it felt like sharp arrows shot by archers were hitting Patrick. He lifted his head to face the ceiling, trying everything thing he could to keep the tears at bay.

Nkechi cried: 'I just want to wake up and realise this whole thing has just been a dream so we can get back to planning our wedding!'

Patrick nodded his head in agreement. 'Yes, babe, I wish it was a dream, too.'

Nkechi needed to be held by him, needed to hear his heart beat. He was sitting close, yet there was a distance between them.

'Can you hold me tight, like you normally do, please?' she asked, placing her head on his chest.

Patrick hesitated for a moment, but when Nkechi lifted her head from his chest and looked at him, so hurt, that's when he held her.

'What do we do, now?' Patrick asked softly.

'I don't know. I can't even bring myself to pray any more. All I am doing is questioning why God is allowing this to happen to me. I can't let thoughts like that plague my mind for too long.'

'It's totally normal to have those thoughts, but it's important to not let it consume you, 'he said, squeezing her tightly. 'Let's just try to relax. We don't have to talk right now.'

Buried in his chest, Nkechi felt safe and secure. She didn't want to be anywhere else. This is what she wanted – her man to love her and want her, despite the news. They could talk more later.

Seeking respite, they gazed across the room. Their attention was drawn to the TV: BBC 24-hour News.

'Oh! What's going on?' Patrick exclaimed.

The TV had been on mute while they had been talking, but reaching around Nkechi for the remote, Patrick turned the volume up. The scenes were distressing, and they both recoiled at the sight.

'Watching this puts things in perspective, really,' Nkechi began. 'Look at all these Syrian children – some having to go through barbed wire, just to escape the life over there. Just to think – many have drowned, trying to find a better life. Unbearable to see. So many lives lost…'

'It is just sad. The world is in a mess and it looks like it's going to get worse before it gets better,' Patrick said, before switching off the television.

There was a strange silence. Patrick bit his lip and scratched his head several times, agitated. He needed to say something. Against his chest, Nkechi's head moved with his erratic breathing, and she noticed that his heart rate had increased slightly. She waited patiently.

'There is only one solution to this problem,' Patrick stated.

Nkechi sat up and looked directly at him. 'What might that be?' she retorted, staring at him intensely.

The determined glare in her eyes made Patrick nervous, but he couldn't think of any alternative to fix the mess. He looked down at his hands. 'Abortion.'

The starkness of the word shook her. Not that it hadn't crossed her mind, but there were other options she wanted to discuss. This was not the 'one solution'. Disbelief took over Nkechi's body. She stared at the man she loved and shook her head.

'You act like you don't know me, sometimes,' she snapped, getting up from the sofa and grabbing her things from around the room – slipping on her shoes, picking up her bag. 'I can't deal with this right now. I have to go. I need to be alone.'

The abrupt ending to their conversation had Patrick's head in a spin. Did she really think he could bear her to give birth to a rapist's child? And what – did she expect him to bring it up as his own? Or watch her have it, then put it into care? A child that was half her own flesh and blood; half a monster's? It didn't bear thinking about.

When the opportunity came for him to meet up later that evening with Charles and one of his best friends, Kola, Patrick jumped at the chance. He needed male company, needed a distraction, needed to forget. Charles was quickly becoming a confidant and their relationship had continued to grow outside of the sisters' influence. They met up regularly, but Patrick didn't really want to discuss Nkechi's situation. Didn't want anyone to know. Hoped Nkechi would 'see reason' as he thought it. So he blocked off his emotions, for tonight, at least.

In Kings Cross, at a local pool hall, they sat waiting for a table to open up to start their game.

'What are you drinking?' Patrick asked.

'I'll have a Heineken, please,' Charles replied.

'Orange juice, please,' Kola replied.

Patrick looked at him and laughed. 'Are you being serious?'

'Yes, I am, fool. Just get me my orange juice,' Kola snapped.

'What? You don't want a man's drink? Mrs not letting you drink, anymore?' Patrick teased.

Charles smiled, trying not to laugh, aware that Kola was Patrick's friend and not his. But a cheeky grin appeared on Kola's round face, and he swivelled his chair to hide it from Patrick.

'I knew it!' Patrick laughed. 'Fola has put her foot down. This guy? You will forever be soft.'

'She just wants me to lose some weight and alcohol is not helping me with this belly.'

All three men were similar in height but Kola had the width advantage.

'Okay, I will get you your orange. I don't want Fola to say I influenced you, because I know how she can get.'

By the time Patrick came back, balancing the three drinks in his palms, Charles and Kola had secured a pool table and were racking up.

'Are you any good?' Charles asked.

'I'm okay,' Kola replied.

Charles took no prisoners. Breaking with a strong shot, he potted two balls early on and quickly cleaned up the table. Kola barely had a look in, only managing to pot one ball before Charles was lining up the black. It was a short game.

'Unlucky,' Charles said.

Kola laughed. 'Patrick, I think you might have met your match. This should be interesting.'

Patrick grinned, squaring up to start. 'Are you ready to lose, Charlie boy?'

'Stack them up. You know me – I don't say much. Just get it done,' Charles boasted.

They started the game. Charles was, at first, full of concentration. Then, further into the game, after missing a shot, he took a sip of cold beer and asked: 'Patrick – did you know that Adaora never wants children?'

Patrick was bent over the table, arm poised, measuring up his shot. He caught Kola's eye briefly. But he had the yellow striped ball in his sights, and he made it, with a delicate cut of the white ball.

'Yes, I did know,' Patrick said, standing up, stretching. 'And everyone connected to the family knows, because their mum is not best pleased, and she is very vocal about that. I take it you just found out.'

'Yes, she told me not too long ago,' admitted Charles, gazing uselessly at the balls on the table as Patrick knocked them up the table. 'And I just don't know how to take it, to be honest. I told her I needed time to think.'

'Do you want kids?' Kola asked.

'Yes, definitely.'

'Then what is there to think about?'

Patrick explained: 'I've known Ada for years, and at first, everyone thought it was a phase, but as she got older, her position on the matter got stronger. I couldn't tell you, as it was not my place to say. But at least everything is in the open now and you can decide what's best for you,' Patrick shrugged, hitting the ball. 'Damn it!' he added, after missing his winning shot. Talk of children was too close to home. He didn't want to think about it. Not until Nkechi had made a decision. Ideally, one he could live with.

It was now down to Charles to end the game. The black ball was perfectly placed near the corner pocket. All it needed was a gentle tap, which Charles executed to win the game.

Charles and Patrick looked at Kola, but with a dismissive wave of the hand, he signalled for them both to play again. Pool was not his game and he knew it.

'So, Charles, how did you react when she told you?' Kola asked.

'I was shocked because she had actually told me she wanted kids a couple of weeks before!' Patrick raised one eyebrow exaggeratedly, as Charles went on: 'Then she said, definitely, no way. And even when she said it, I thought it was some silly joke, but there were no laughing parts.'

Kola sucked his teeth. 'Man. No laughing matter.'

'When it hit me that she was serious, I had no words at the time. I mean, I feel cheated, that she allowed me to fall for her – and she held back this vital information about herself. Not just held back, but actually lied! If I had known at the start, I would never have gone there. I even asked her how many kids she wanted – so I was clear, anyway. Plus, I have never met a woman who doesn't want children! I didn't even know that was a thing.'

'You would be surprised!' Patrick said, wishing it were so with Nkechi, under the circumstances.

'I love her, but I want children, mate. I don't know what to do.'

'And – what if you had found out it was physically impossible for her to have children?' Kola queried. 'Would you have rejected her, then?'

'Hmmm… But…'

'Have you spoken to her about it?' Kola asked.

'Not since she told me.'

'What are you waiting for? One thing us men need to do more often is talk to our women. And most importantly, listen to our women, man.'

'Have you been reading *Cosmopolitan* again?' asked Patrick.

'It is important! I am now in a happier place with Fola,' Kola lectured, 'ever since I had a change in mind-set and I stopped being stubborn.'

Patrick could only smile to himself. He knew that when Kola got started with his lectures, he would never stop. Patrick, right from being young, would always seek advice from Kola. Even when Kola made wrong decisions in his own personal life, he always gave great advice to others.

Kola's words made Charles think. Maybe it was time he spoke to Adaora.

But first, he had to win this game, before Patrick claimed that the first win was a fluke.

'How are things with Nkechi?' Charles asked.

Patrick missed his shot. He could no longer concentrate on the game. 'To be honest, I don't want to discuss my life, today. Hence, why I am here, trying not to think about it.' The same lines of frustration he'd had when talking to Nkechi appeared on his face again.

'No worries, bro. I can respect that.' Then, Charles potted the black.

Kola stepped in. 'Have you two finished with pool, yet? How about we go somewhere else?'

'That's two in a row,' smiled Charles. 'I am happy to leave. Ask Patrick, though – he might want a rematch.'

'No, I am done for today. Another time – I would have you,' Patrick said, sounding defeated.

'If you say so, mate,' Charles replied, with a hint of sarcasm.

As they gradually made their way out of the pool hall, Charles turned back to look at Kola, who was gingerly strolling behind them, playing on his phone.

'Please explain to me why you support Manchester all the way – yet, you claim to have never even been to Manchester. How does that work?'

Kola rolled his eyes. 'I swear, you Arsenal fans get on my last nerves! Why do I have to justify why I support my team? All you need to know is – United for life.'

'Patrick, are you hearing this?' Charles said.

He repeated it, but Patrick was slightly ahead of them, and was in a trance-like state. Charles speeded his steps to catch up to him, and tapped Patrick on the shoulder.

'Are you okay?' Charles asked in concern.

'I don't think I am up to going to that bar, after all. I am going to head home.'

'Really?'

Patrick's leaving changed the dynamic of the whole evening. Charles and Kola also parted ways, understanding that they didn't really feel that they knew one another well enough, and that their meeting at all was only due to Patrick.

The loud vroom of the hoover signalled an attack on the dirt with military precision. Chidi brandished the stalk like a weapon, trying to distract himself by focusing on cleaning, making himself useful. Battling against grime, he felt as if the energy from the house had also been sucked out. Every room was occupied by dejection; an unnatural vibe hovering, as everyone attempted to deal with their understanding of what had happened to Nkechi.

Nkechi sat on her bed, willing her mind to escape to the locations in the book she was reading. Mrs Edozie had busied herself with metres of fabric, her foot on the pedal of the overworked sewing machine, and outside, Mr Edozie was getting his hands dirty, attempting to service the car single-handedly.

Adaora made her way upstairs and gently knocked on Nkechi's bedroom door.

'Come in.'

Pushing the door with her elbow, Adaora inched inside the half-lit room, with the curtains half-closed, and sat on the edge of Nkechi's bed. 'Can we talk?'

Propped to one side, her head resting on a bent arm, Nkechi did not bother turning around to look at her. 'Ada, to be honest, I am not in the mood for one of your sessions.'

'What do you mean by that?'

'You know what. Forget it.'

'How did the discussion with Patrick go?'

Nkechi licked her index finger and turned the page of her book.

'Nkechi, I am talking to you.'

Silence. Prolonged silence.

Adaora sighed. 'I am just trying to help.'

Nkechi closed the book and slammed it on the bed. 'Did I ask for your help? I specifically stated that I wanted to be alone; need my own space. But here you are, barging in! Desperate to fix things!' Her eyes bulged, the whites visible all around the dark irises. 'Why can't you just listen?' She jabbed towards her own ear, aggressively spitting out: 'I'm sure you were trained to do that. Concentrate on your patients. I'm not paying for your services and I don't want them! Stop psychoanalysing me!'

Taken aback by the sudden outburst, Adaora stood up and made her way to the door. 'Kechi, I can't say that I understand what you are going through...'

Nkechi interrupted: 'Argh! There you go again! You're not listening to me! Save your speeches – although you're a fine one to talk. It's not like your life is perfect! Solve your own problems! How about you start by telling Charles the truth and stop stringing him along – acting like you want a family in the future!'

'For your information, I have told Charles everything – and yes – it's over. And secondly, Nkechi, please have some respect, yourself, and mind how you are talking to me.'

Mimicking Adaora with a cruel 'Neh-neh-neh!' Nkechi's hand-gestures suggested someone talking too much. 'It is ironic, isn't it? You don't want children and here I am, pregnant with one I didn't ask for. Maybe mum was right, after all. Your problems are self-inflicted. You could easily be with the man of your dreams if you'd just open your mind. But oh, no – you've made your choice. Out of selfishness.' She waved her hand dismissively and made a sound of disgust. 'Whereas some of us have real problems and issues to deal with.'

Adaora was gobsmacked. Nkechi had always been in her corner, on her team. Now it seemed that her greatest ally had joined the opposition and was taking pleasure in shooting her down. 'I can't believe you!'

Frustrated, Nkechi swung herself off the bed and brushed past Adaora, walking outside. 'I need some air.'

Watching Nkechi leave, Adaora was stunned. She recalled the conversation, unpicking her actions and words; wondering how she had approached Nkechi to warrant such a response. As teenagers, sharing a room, they had often got into conflict, using words spitefully to wound the other; but they had left that in their adolescence. This was sudden, and uncalled for.

Adaora went to find her mother, telling her what happened – but conveniently leaving out the parts about Charles.

Mrs Edozie looked at her daughter sympathetically. 'It's mood swings, because of all the changes in hormones. It is bound to happen. Childbearing comes at a price. Some people lose their smile… and sometimes, themselves.'

Another reason why I shouldn't have children, thought Adaora.

There was less than a week left before the start of the new academic year, and Nkechi sat quietly in the waiting area of her local GP clinic. The short, blonde receptionist gave her a newspaper to read while she waited. Nkechi was grateful that there were not many people ahead of her. Surely the wait would not be long, she thought.

'Miss Edozie, Doctor Lee will see you now.'

'Thank you.'

She walked in Dr Lee's office, where he was glued to his computer screen. Nkechi coughed to get his attention, and he looked up and smiled at her. He was dressed in his usual casual, laid-back manner, in a shirt and trousers, with a pair of bright red Crocs on his feet. His office displayed artwork of dragons and decorated candles.

'How can I help you, Nkechi? I only saw you a few days ago. Is everything okay?' Dr Lee asked.

Nkechi shuffled in her seat. 'I am fine.' She paused, taking a deep breath. 'I just wanted to know my options, if I wanted to terminate this pregnancy.'

'Oh, I see.' Dr Lee nodded. 'Based on the circumstances in which this pregnancy occurred, I can totally understand. The process is quite simple. I can refer you to a specialist clinic where the procedure takes place. Two doctors sign the certificate for the procedure – one can be me, the other at the clinic.' He opened his drawer and pulled out several leaflets and handed them to Nkechi. 'These leaflets give the details and implications of a termination, and the other is for counselling afterwards, if need be.'

Nkechi could not look at the doctor, her eyes fixed on the legs of the table.

'I know this is an extremely tough period, and not one you should be going through alone,' Dr Lee said kindly. 'My advice is – if you are thinking about it, you should come to a conclusion as soon as possible. Although the procedure can be done even up to twenty-four weeks, it is advised to be done as soon as possible. Ideally, within 13 weeks of conception.'

Nkechi looked up at the doctor. 'When can you book me in to see the specialist?'

'No referral needed, initially. You can just ask for an initial consultation yourself.'

'Thank you, doctor,' Nkechi said as she slowly got up from her seat. 'Oh, yes, doctor,' she suddenly thought. 'While I am here, I have been feeling so lethargic all the time, and I'm constantly feeling dizzy. Also, my breasts have become super sensitive and tender. Is this normal?'

'Yes, what you've described are typical symptoms for women in their first trimester. I would suggest plenty of water to rehydrate you – which may alleviate the fatigue and dizziness. And for the breast symptoms – you could try possibly changing the type of bra you wear, to add more comfort.'

'Okay, thank you.'

Watching Nkechi slowly walk out of the office, Dr Lee sighed. Having been her doctor since she was a little girl, it pained him to watch her go through such hardship.

The journey back home was rife with questions, sitting in the crease of her neck, poking her with possibilities.

Back home, working her way through the leaflets, Nkechi read up on the procedure in secret, hiding them in the pages of another book, fearful of other people seeing and judging her. Guilt in the back of her throat made it difficult for her to swallow: her mouth dry and extremely thirsty. The word 'hypocrite' sat in her mind as she contemplated abortion. Her religious belief was strong, but she wasn't sure how strong any more. And Patrick seemed so lost to her – so fixed on what should happen. She couldn't discuss it with him. In many ways, she didn't even recognise her own actions or thoughts – and such a decision was difficult to make. The thought of termination filled her with terror and despair, yet the consequences of carrying this child to full term and raising a reminder of her abuse was also terrifying. As was losing Patrick. Although, if he wouldn't support her own decision – whatever that might be, perhaps he wasn't the man for her. She was so confused!

Nkechi was desperate for a drink. Going straight for the fridge, she poured herself a glass of juice, drank it one go and poured another. Outside, Chidi sat in the garden in nothing but a white string vest and faded boxers, texting any girl that would give him attention. Nkechi was suddenly taken by a mischievous thought, a welcome distraction from her worries. Slowly creeping up behind him, Nkechi tried to approach him to give him a fright, tiptoeing as light as a feather.

'Nkechi, I know you're there,' he laughed, mocking at her attempt to scare him. 'It's okay. Maybe next time.'

She flung herself down next to him. 'What have you been up to all day?'

'This is it. This is me, until October, when I have to go back to uni.'

'Surely there are better ways of spending your time off, rather than sitting here doing nothing?' She leant against him with her shoulder, pushing him playfully. 'Why don't you do something constructive?'

'Like what?'

'Hmm, that is a question – for later. But for now, how about we catch a movie and you can buy *me* some ice cream for a change?' Nkechi suggested. 'Only, not in your underwear.'

Excited about the prospect of spending some quality time with his sister, Chidi got up straight away to get ready. Nkechi watched him depart, shaking her head at his bony frame and non-existent butt-cheeks.

'While you're up there,' she added. 'Do you mind shaving off that fluff you are calling a beard…'

'Really Kechi,' Chidi turned, walking backwards to face her. 'That is a low blow. You know how long I have been waiting to grow something! And now you want me to – What? No way!'

A typical Chidi took his time getting ready, much to Nkechi's frustration. The end result was worth it, however, as he appeared at the top of the stairs wearing a pair of fitted chinos, a new t-shirt and his favourite boat shoes. Looking him up and down, Nkechi nodded her approval before they left.

They talked all the way to the cinema. It was a time of sibling bonding; Chidi pointing out girls he liked the look of, and Nkechi telling him what he needed to do to improve his prospects of securing one of those fine ladies. Chidi, being the provider paying for the movie, chose the film: a new horror. Arms full of popcorn, sweets, drinks and nachos, they sat in the leather premium seats and relaxed.

This relaxation did not last long for Nkechi, who was easily frightened and kept jumping out of her seat – at one point, spilling popcorn all over the floor. Chidi couldn't control his laughter. After an hour and a half, they emerged blinking from the darkness, into the street.

'So how did you find it?' Nkechi asked.

'I think the first *Sinister* was much scarier than that. But obviously, anything scares you – so you must have thought it was really good.'

'You know what? This is the last time I watch a horror movie with you!'

They sat in the ice cream parlour for over an hour, Chidi keeping Nkechi's spirits up with his general loveable nature and humorous anecdotes. He took his sister down memory lane, recalling the embarrassing things that had happened to Adaora and Nkechi – diverting the attention away from his own mishaps.

'Okay, enough about me and Ada. How was your first year of uni?'

His countenance resembled grey clouds as he fiddled with his spoon and avoided Nkechi's gaze.

'Chidi, don't ignore me. How was it?'

He grimaced. 'I do not want to talk about it, to be honest.'

'Why? What happened?'

Tapping his foot anxiously under the table, Chidi made circles with his spoon in the melted pool of ice cream in his plate. Unable to answer. Unable to form the words he knew would change the mood. He didn't want to witness disappointment take over his sister's face. Couldn't bear it.

'Chidi, stop being silly and spit it out. It's me you are talking to – not mum.' Nkechi leaned in towards him and gave him a reassuring smile. 'It can't be that bad.'

'I failed my first year!' Chidi exclaimed.

Nkechi's face barely moved. 'Is that all? Chidi, believe me it is not the end of the world. You are more than capable. Why do you think you failed?'

'With everything that was going on with you, I just couldn't get my head around doing what needed to be done.'

Nkechi manoeuvred herself in the booth, so she could sit closer to him. She put her arms around him and gave him a massive hug. 'I am back and I am not going anywhere. In October, you will redo the first year and any support you need – I will be here to make sure you get this degree. Don't worry about mum and dad. We can tell them together. I am sure they will understand.'

The relief on his face was obvious. 'Thanks, sis.'

'Don't need to thank me.'

'Can I ask you one favour, please?'

'Yeah. What is it?'

'Can you make up with Ada? I don't like it when you fight.'

Nkechi kissed her teeth. 'I would hardly call that a fight; but I hear you.' She gently punched his arm. 'OK. I might have overreacted. I will talk to her.'

'Cool.' he grinned. 'Thank you.'

When they arrived back home, Chidi ran upstairs while Nkechi went to the kitchen. She took a cold bottle of water out of the fridge and drank several cups in quick succession. A temporary brain freeze ensured Nkechi stopped at three cups, and she sat at the dining room table, holding her head.

'Mummy good evening.' Nkechi said, wincing as Mrs Edozie walked in.

'Are you okay?'

'I am fine. The water was just too cold and it gave me a brain freeze.'

'Yes, that fridge is something else. It is not even set to the highest. Anyway, these papers slipped out of the book you left on the table...'

To Nkechi's horror, her mother was holding some of the leaflet the doctors had given her. Nkechi recoiled. Her face painted a picture a thousand words could not describe, and she was unable to make eye contact with her mum.

'I believe you are doing the right thing, my daughter.'

Nkechi was taken aback. This was her deeply religious mother – advocating that she kill a baby. Puzzled and confused, she answered: 'Mum, I have not made up my mind yet. I am not sure if I want to terminate it, as it goes against everything I believe in!' she lamented.

'Nkechi, listen to me. I know you have strong beliefs – as I do – but this situation can be an exception. My daughter – please listen to me. How can you enter marriage with this burden? Please, for the sake of your marriage.'

Nkechi flushed red. 'I just wanted to know what my options were. That is why I got all the leaflets from the doctors.'

'*Nne*, I understand.' Mrs Edozie patted her hand. 'Just keep in mind what I said.'

Nkechi took the leaflets from her mother and put them in her pocket. She was not ready to continue the conversation. She had been on such a high after spending the evening with Chidi that this was like crashing from a great height, cancelling out all the good that had been done. Her mother had returned her to reality. She was pregnant. She was pregnant by her rapist. Her fiancé wanted her to have an abortion. Her mother wanted her to have an abortion. She did not know what she wanted. As she sank back into her own miserable situation, the words of her mother replayed in her ears.

Resting after patients, Adaora lay on the sofa in her office, getting her thoughts together, when there was a loud knock on the door. Briefly checking the time, Adaora called out for them to enter.

Strolling in, wearing a red, form-fitting dress, Nkechi smiled widely. Seeing her sister, Adaora kissed her teeth and returned to watching the ceiling tiles. The silent treatment was Adoara's usual game plan – it always had been – so Nkechi knew what to expect. Still, they had come through the other side of a vast number of squabbles and Nkechi also knew how to break her resolve.

'Hey, sis!' Nkechi said brightly, not expecting an answer. She didn't receive one. 'Ada, I am sorry for lashing out at you the other day. My head is just in a place where I can't think straight. My mood keeps changing, my body is changing and I do not know what to do. You are the only person I can really talk to about this.'

Looking at her sister from the corner of her eye, Adaora caught Nkechi giving her puppy-dog eyes. It was the look she had perfected. A look of neediness. One that could change Adaora's mind; one that had stopped her telling her mother when Nkechi broke the plates or lost something special. It had worked before and it was working now.

Adaora rolled her eyes, sat up and addressed her sister. 'I am not mad at you. I am just upset that you have to go through all this.'

'Good, because we all know that you can't stay mad at me anyway,' Nkechi chirped.

'Don't push your luck,' Adaora said as she walked to the fridge to get some bottles of water.

'I went to see Dr Lee, and he gave me some leaflets about abortion. I swear I can't even look at them anymore.'

Adaora handed Nkechi the bottle of water, listening.

'Patrick has hinted he wants me to have an abortion. And even mum is saying the same thing.' She mimicked her mother's voice. '"How will you go into marriage with a rapist's baby? It would never be fruitful. It will never work." You know how she goes on and on,' Adaora sighed, rubbing her face from side to side.

'What do you feel?' Adaora asked.

'I know how I feel about abortion, regardless of the situation. I advocated against it as a pro-life campaigner for many years at uni. Ada, you know this – you were at the heated debates.'

Adaora nodded, remembering a young passionate Nkechi, taking on a room full of abortion supporters with zeal and conviction.

Nkechi went on, sadly: 'So, for me to now be even considering termination… It shows that I am all talk and should never have spoken for women who have been in this situation.'

'Have your views changed on abortion?'

'Of course, not. I still believe that every child conceived and starting to form in the womb of a woman deserves a chance of life! Abortion only happens because of the circumstances of the people, outside of the miracle taking place. All they think about is their own situation – and it is selfish! Which is exactly where I am. I am thinking about how my husband will feel… will my marriage work? What about the unborn, the seed, who had nothing to do with why he or she is now here?'

Adaora explained, 'For me, the argument is futile. Like I have always said, life is precious, but ultimately, it has to be the choice of the woman. I think we are all pro-life to some degree, but forcing people to keep unwanted or even severely damaged babies is not the way. And making abortion illegal will make it more dangerous for women.'

'I agree. I am more pro-life in terms of morality than using the law to force people. Making informed decisions to protect life… but this experience of being um… r…rape…' Nkechi spluttered. She lay her head on Adaora's shoulder.

Adaora put her arm around her. 'You don't have to say it or relive it. Whatever you decide, I will be here to support you, no matter what.'

'Thanks, sis. This is why I love you. Now, is that you vibrating, or is it me?' Adaora tapped the sides of her trousers and pulled out her Samsung. 'It's mine.' Instinctively clicking on a message, she gasped in surprise. 'It's a text from Charles… He wants to see me around 6.'

Nkechi smiled, grateful for distraction. 'How are things with you and Mr Charmer?'

'Not great. I told him about not having children and we haven't really spoken, since.'

'Hmmm… that's not great. Why did you not tell him at the start?'

'Before I knew it, I was falling too deep and didn't want the feeling to end.' Adaora shook her head, looking down, her lip trembling. 'Now, I don't even think I deserve to be with anyone. Maybe I am not good enough the way I am.'

Nkechi was shocked. This stance was totally foreign to Adaora's personality – usually very self-aware, confident and positive. It was unnerving to hear the opposite. As sisters, they supported each other and it was now Nkechi's turn to listen. Pouring out her soul, Adaora went into depth about her feelings for Charles, saying things she would never tell another person. The questions she had concerning their future were apparent. Adaora was scared of the relationship ending. Reassuring her, Nkechi reminded her sister why she was of value, why she was worthy of love, why she deserved a partner who wanted more from life than offspring – and had more to give her.

'And if he wants to talk – maybe he has reconsidered,' Nkechi suggested. 'And you will find a way forward. Together.'

As Nkechi spoke to her, Adaora's spirits lifted, and she began to feel more hopeful about the meeting with Charles.

'So, go, meet him – and knock him dead with your beauty!' laughed Nkechi.

'In my business suit?' Adaora said in dismay. 'I have no time to go home…'

'No. In my dress,' laughed Nkechi, reaching behind her and unzipping. 'Swap. It's just like when we were teenagers.'

Adaora laughed, unbuttoning her blouse. They handed over one another's clothes and after re-dressing, they stood appraising one another.

'Besides, that dress was getting a bit tight for me, anyway,' Nkechi said ruefully. 'Looks amazing on you.'

Adaora let Nkechi fix her hair and makeup, before making her way to her favourite coffee shop.

Standing in the hazy atmosphere of coffee steam and dusky sunlight, Charles was deeply fascinated by a book on Queen Nzinga. He turned the book over and read the blurb before flicking through the pages on the famous Congolese warrior.

He turned around and saw Adaora, looking breathtakingly beautiful in a red dress that caressed her curves the way he loved.

Adaora knew she looked good. It had been a long time since she had seen Charles and her stomach began to roll. She wanted to melt into his arms and instantly connect her lips with his, but the uncertainty between them was written on his face and the status of their relationship was unclear.

Standing up, Charles leant over and gave her a hug. It was quick and very Christian, the type of hugs she would receive from members of her mother's congregation. A respectable, sisterly hug – all shoulders and not much else. Adaora was disappointed. Visibly. The lack of intimacy and connection in the embrace worried her.

'Are you okay?' he asked.

'Yes, I am good, thanks.'

There was an air of awkward silence. Adaora hoped he would rectify that by looking into her eyes and giving her a kiss on the lips. *A girl can only hope*, she thought.

'Do you want something to drink?'

'Don't worry. Mina is already bringing me my special.'

'Okay. Let's have a seat here.' Charles opened up his posture so she could pass by, and she took her time, her hips seductively grazing his crotch. Charles' body murmured in response, reminded of what he had been missing. Charles coughed and tried to focus.

'I will just get straight to the point, really. I have been thinking a lot about our last discussion and I just have a few questions.'

Adaora was fiddling with her nails. She hoped that he would understand, that he would not judge her, that they could get past this. 'Okay, what are they?'

'Why don't you want children?'

Wow. He certainly was getting straight to the point. Although she knew the question must have been brewing, it still hit her like a blow to the face, and she had not prepared a response.

He persisted. 'Please help me understand.'

Mina placed Adaora's drink in front of her, smiling at the couple. It had been a while since she had seen them, and she asked after their health before sidling away. Thankful for the interruption, focusing on the steam waving hallelujahs in the air, Adaora picked up the mug and blew gently, taking a hesitant sip before looking at Charles. He was looking directly at her, waiting, his face unreadable.

'It's hard to fully know when it began…' she explained. 'But I've never felt that nudge, that urge. Even when I was younger I wasn't like other girls. I didn't play with baby dolls and dream of being a mother. I was moved by the conditions of the world. The hatred. The devastation. Pain and suffering. With each generation, it seems to get worse and I don't want to bring a child into that.' She noticed Charles shift in his seat, but she continued. 'As I reached adolescence and adulthood, that feeling grew stronger and I made up my mind not to. I can't bring an innocent child into this polluted, corrupt existence and be responsible for explaining why there is so much destruction and hate.' Adaora returned the mug to her lips and took a long sip, waiting for a response.

Charles was looking at his hands. 'Hmmm,' he said, tentatively.

Adaora continued to wait. There had to be more. Yet Charles's mouth did not open. She probed: 'Is that all you have to say?'

'Sorry. Still processing,' he said, frowning. 'I respect everything you have said, but I do not understand it.' He rubbed his face with his hand, not looking at her. 'We are perfect for each other in every other aspect – apart from this.'

Something was brewing and Adaora felt the atmosphere shift. Sitting up straight, she began to breathe heavily, trying to calm her nerves.

Charles went on: 'You have your beliefs, and they look like they are set in stone.'

There was a gap that began to widen between them as Charles straightened himself at the table. He was struggling to find the words, his hesitation apparent, heavy on his lips.

'Charles, please just get to it. What are you saying?'

He looked across the table at Adaora, her gorgeous face assaulted by worry lines across her forehead. He cleared his throat. 'I want to have a family and that is something I cannot compromise on. I think we need to put an end to this relationship, as we both have different visions of our futures.'

Finally.

The gasp of dread had wormed itself into their space.

Adaora picked up her purse and without looking at him, whispered, 'Goodbye, Charles.'

Chapter Ten

DAYS AT THE BEACH, HOLIDAY ADVENTURES, ICE CREAM, SHORTS AND STRING VESTS all disappeared as the summer period yawned its way into autumn. 'Back to School' slogans filled shop windows with 'every student needs' at discounted prices, as parents stocked up for the new term. There was a readiness for change in the air, the disappointment of summer ending blended with the excitement of newness: new uniforms, new books, new teachers and new friends.

The postman delivered a weighty letter addressed to Mr Edozie, his name written in scrawling script. It signalled importance, and was stamped with 'East London University'. Using his beloved letter-opener, he revealed his own season of change. Offered a promotion to become head of department for Business, Mr Edozie could not contain his elation as his feet lifted him into the air and his right fist pumped the air in rejoicing. The title carried prestige, recognition and responsibility. As an academic with a strong work ethic, the job offer was greatly appreciated, showing he was valued in his field. It was also welcome news financially, to help the family.

Busying herself in her favourite place, Mrs Edozie was hard at work in the kitchen in a flurry of catering magic; her hands whizzing – chopping onions, yam, scotch bonnet peppers. A whirlwind of spices surrounded her as she prepared her husband's favourite soup: *ofe nsala*. She knew it was guaranteed to put him in a good mood.

Mr Edozie was a believer in multiple streams of income for security: a concept he had drilled into his daughters and practised himself. Despite their father's constant preaching, the mantle of entrepreneurship, of building for you, using your inherent God-given gifts to create a residual income had only fallen on Adaora. Nkechi was content in her 9-5 teaching job. Or with marking and preparation, it was more like 8am-9pm. But Mr Edozie had always had business interests and investments, and despite the large pay-out they had made to pay Nkechi's ransom, Mr Edozie was busy building up his empire again.

Beginning to pound the boiled yams, Mrs Edozie heard the sound of frustration spilling from her husband's lips, and she knew that God had placed this recipe in her mind and spirit to calm him.

From the living room, speaking on the phone, Mr Edozie's raised voice thundered through the walls as he paced up and down, his hands dramatically waving in the air. 'Kelechi, listen to me very well! I am tired of repeating myself! Do not leave that port until you have identified my container! I have many goods coming from Japan and I need you to make sure that all the right processes are carried out.'

There was silence as Mr Edozie waited for the response. It was not to his liking. 'MY FRIEND!' he said. 'SHUT UP your dirty mouth!'

Dropping the pestle and mortar on the kitchen counter, Mrs Edozie rushed into the living room. 'Papa Ada, *Ogini?*

'This stupid boy is trying to give me a migraine!' Mr Edozie raised one finger at his wife. 'Oluchi, hold on,' he said, speaking back into the phone. 'Kelechi, just do what I have asked you and call me back when it is done.'

Putting the phone in his back pocket, he turned to his wife, rubbing his temples with both index fingers and shaking his head solemnly. His voice was troubled. 'Oluchi, we are in serious financial trouble. Some of the money we borrowed... I am now being chased down for repayment.'

'My dear, from who?' Mrs Edozie gasped.

'Paulinus.'

'Eh?' came the shocked reply. 'Paulinus from the past? Look at all the things you have done for him – and he is already hounding you down for payment?'

'Can you imagine?' Mr Edozie sighed. 'Even the land I had to sell at a discounted rate is now increasing in value, just in a short space of time.'

As the provider, Mr Edozie was aware of the repercussions of their circumstances. The burden began to show in the worry lines on his forehead.

Mrs Edozie understood his concern and placed her hand on his cheek, looking at him intently and smiling. 'God will find a way for us. He always has and always will. My husband, do what you can, please,' she reassured, before rushing back to her boiling fish.

Mr Edozie sat bewildered on the sofa. This was all too much. These past few months had been impossible. He looked at his house, the luxurious items, and the purchases they had made. The family had a reputation of being good, responsible stewards, enjoying

261

the finer things, but with a good financial plan. This situation was unfamiliar territory and stress began to seep under the front door. Cutbacks had already been made, the most sacrificial being the sports package on their television subscription.

As he contemplated the next steps, awaiting a call back from Kelechi, Mr Edozie smelt the tantalising meal his wife was cooking and his mouth began to water. He loved how she took care of him and silently thanked God for the support network he had.

When she called that it was ready, Mr Edozie sprang from his seat in anticipation. Sitting at the table, he closed his eyes and allowed his senses to appreciate the aroma. The soup reminded him of family. The tastes brought peace to his troubled soul and he put all other thoughts aside as he began to feast on the fish and spinach masterpiece.

Chidi bounded into the house, ravenous, and headed straight for the kitchen. Knowing her son, Mrs Edozie offered him a plate of soup. After realising which soup it was –his father's favourite – Chidi kindly refused, opting for leftover coconut rice. The closer they got to finishing their food, the more withdrawn he became, although Mr and Mrs Edozie didn't notice. The couple retreated to the living room in good spirits and sat together, watching the news and conversing in Igbo.

Outside in the hallway, a nervous Chidi stood awkwardly, palms sweaty, taking deep breaths and counting to ten; a bundle of anxiety and hesitancy. He needed to take the first steps to honesty, yet his feet were nailed to the floor.

Nkechi came down the stairs and saw him standing there. She paused for a moment, watching his lack of confidence, before approaching him gently. 'Chidi, are you okay?'

Chidi tried to smile but he was too busy concentrating on the potential repercussions of what was coming. 'Kechi, I don't think I can do this,' he muttered, more to himself than to her.

'What? Tell mum and dad?'

He nodded. 'I need to tell them. I can't keep it to myself, but I'm scared. Education is everything to dad – you know that.'

Seeing the look of fear in her brother's eyes, Nkechi softened. Less intellectual than the girls, Chidi had never experienced the expectations that she and Adoara had. He was the baby, and the only boy; a blessing to the household and the apple of their mother's eye. Nkechi remembered having to break bad news to her parents when she was young – things she had done, or not done, that she might be punished for. Their look of disappointment was always worse than their disciplining her.

She grabbed his hand. 'Don't worry. I'll be right with you,' she stated, matter-of-factly, looking him straight in the eye.

At that moment, Chidi's soul was encouraged; the warmth of his sister's hand in his and the knowledge of her support comforted him. He smiled. He could always count on his sisters to have his back. They had stood with him when he admitted to going through a pregnancy scare with a girl he barely knew. As his elders, they had done a great job steering him in the right direction, even if it meant a stern word or long lecture. He loved them for it.

Chidi squeezed Nkechi's hand, took a deep breath and walked into the living room; Nkechi following behind, like a bodyguard. He sat opposite his parents and cleared his throat to get their attention. They looked up.

'Mum, dad. I need to talk to you. There's something I have to get off my chest.'

Mr Edozie put the television on mute and looked at his son. *A handsome boy; respectful, educated. A son to be proud of,* Mr Edozie thought, as he wondered what could be so important. This very formal approach was unusual for Chidi, who was laid back and jokey.

Mrs Edozie was also searching her son's face for clues. He was troubled; she could tell by the way his left foot was tapping the floor. Seeing their expectant faces, Chidi lost his tongue. He looked at Nkechi for support and she smiled and nodded encouragingly.

'My son, what is the matter?' Mrs Edozie probed. 'Are you not feeling well?'

'No Mum, I'm fine. It's something else.' He swallowed, and seconds went by.

'Nkechi, do you know what this is all about?' Mr Edozie asked, impatiently.

'Please, dad, just let Chidi speak.'

Chidi was fidgeting with his hands. 'It's about university,' he offered.

'Is it school fees? Have they gone up again?' Mr Edozie began. 'All these money issues! When will it end? How much is it, now?'

'No, dad, it's not the fees.'

'So, then, what? Talk now.'

Chidi took a deep breath. 'I've been having a very tough time. The work has been relentless and I was struggling to cope. I managed to come up with a system to help, but when all the stress happened with you and Nkechi in Nigeria, I couldn't focus. Dad, I'm sorry.'

Nkechi felt guilty. She was the reason behind this conversation, albeit out of her control.

'Sorry for what?' Mr Edozie asked.

'My results came in. They weren't good enough. I failed the first year...' Chidi could not continue the sentence. He covered his face with his hands.

Mr Edozie was enraged; not even able to look at his son, the pulse in his veins throbbing an angry beat. He turned to his wife, motioning in Chidi's direction. 'Mama Ada, talk to your son! What do you mean, you failed the first year of university?'

Standing up, infuriated, Mr Edozie began shouting in Igbo, a thunderous expression on his face. Sitting still, watching her son, Mrs Edozie was calm. She was not surprised by the news; she had witnessed the effect the incident had had on Chidi. He was not himself during that period.

'All this money I've thrown at you, to support your education! And you fail! My own son! An Edozie. Failure. Others do not have the opportunities you have – the support, the finances. Many would kill for your chances and you ruin them! DISGRACE!'

Chidi had curled into his spine, unable to deal with the relentless attack from his father, his self-esteem disintegrating; demoralised with every sentence.

Nkechi rushed to Chidi's aid. 'Dad, please stop! It is not all Chidi's fault. He told me how things were, when I was taken, and it had a great impact on his mental state. '

Listening to his daughter, Mr Edozie remembered that they had all had a trying time.

She elaborated. 'It would be hard for anyone to retain information in uni while knowing there was a problem back at home. Plain and simple – that would have an adverse effect on most people! So, it is important to put things into perspective and move forward.'

It had been difficult for them all. His wife gave him a warning look.

Slouching back down into the sofa, he put his glasses back on his head and addressed her. 'My daughter, I have heard what you had to say. I agree that it played a part, but it still should never have happened. We are Edozies and we must all excel.'

Chidi was quivering in his seat. He had always been fearful of his dad's temper and could not bear to upset him.

Nkechi continued advocating for her brother. 'We spoke. Chidi will repeat the year and has agreed that he will pay his way through it, so you do not need to provide him with one penny until he has moved to his second year.'

Looking over at his son's curled-up frame, Mr Edozie's heart softened as he realised that his son had gone to lengths to accept responsibility and take action. He stood, walked over to him and put his arm over his shoulders.

'C-Boy,' he called him. It was a term of endearment that held memories of son and father bonding. Hearing his dad use the nickname he had given him at four years old, Chidi immediately responded by straightening his back, looking up at his dad and smiling uncertainly.

'Look, I am sorry for shouting at you. It came to me as a shock,' he explained, patting his son's shoulder. 'Don't worry too much. Next year you will pass. Just prioritise and complete all the work. Have you heard me?' Mr Edozie asked, pulling Chidi's ear lobe: the infamous trademark gesture of most African parents.

Soul restored, Chidi nodded and smiled widely. The weight of keeping this secret close to his chest had been released and he felt free.

Mrs Edozie also embraced her son. 'It is well, my son.'

Safe in the arms of his parents, enveloped in their unconditional love, Chidi exhaled relief.

A collage of tears, wrapped in crumpled Kleenex, lay scattered across the bedroom floor. A trail of emotions; internal turmoil displayed in soaked tissues.

Unable to hold day-to-day contents, her mind had relinquished control to her heart's pulsating hurts. Wandering around her apartment aimlessly, Adaora began to get irritated with herself, stuck in a valley of regret and disappointment.

She caught her reflection in the mirror and realised that her eyes were red and puffy; cheeks stained with salty residue. She sighed. *Enough.*

She approached her neatly organised wardrobe, looking for something to wear. The pristine condition and order did not reflect her feelings. Her hands found the dress she had worn on their first date and she recalled the butterflies she felt; the way a look from him would leave her breathless. She began to pull clothes out in rapid succession, throwing them all over her mattress and floor.

Her knees gave way and she crumbled into the floor, sobbing uncontrollably. The mess represented her turmoil. By her reaction, she realised how deeply she wanted this relationship to work.

Loneliness was a rod upon her back, reminding her that she had thrown it away. Her decisions had created this emptiness, a gaping hole in her ability to be ok. She tried to shake it off, but the feeling persisted.

Lost in a mass of flashbacks and remorse, Adaora's phone vibrating on the table shuddered her senses back to reality. She picked it up reluctantly.

'Hey, Ada, guess what just happened to me?' Temi greeted her excitedly.

'Hey...' Adaora said, her voice flat. Although she would usually love to hear the latest from Temi, she was not in the emotional space to deal with or respond to issues outside her own.

'What is wrong? You sound terrible.'

Not willing to talk about it, Adaora lied. 'I think I am coming down with something.'

'Aww, babe, you just need to rest up and maybe I can bring you some soup later. Hopefully that would make you feel better.'

'No need to go out of your way. I will be fine. Can we talk later on, and you can give me your gossip then? I am just feeling really tired.'

'Okay... Make sure you call me, later on.'

'Will do.'

The clothes were still strewn about the floor, and Adaora didn't have the strength to deal with them yet. Shoving stuff aside to create a space on her bed, she lay down and looked at the ceiling, still consumed by her thoughts. This was stupid. She should practise what she preached, she knew. Thinking, imagining, and dreaming – before long, she was sound asleep.

She woke twenty minutes later and shook herself into action. *It doesn't have to be like this,* she thought, determined to remove herself from her feelings and into the presence of other people.

Jumping in the shower, she allowed the steaming hot water to wash away the negativity she was carrying. Fresh and alert, Adaora opened her bathroom cupboard. She noticed that, to her surprise, there were no sanitary towels left. This was abnormal for Adaora, who was always on top of things. Scrambling around in her wardrobe, she looked through her work bags before finding a spare pad. Making a mental note to hit the shops, she got ready to see her sister.

The Edozie household was back in the general swing of things; everyone at peace involved in their individual activities. Having sacrificed his beloved sports package Mr Edozie was glued to Sky News, watching the highlights. Foot on the pedal of her well-used sewing machine, Mrs Edozie was bent over, working the stitches in the colourful strips of Ankara.

Adaora greeted them both before going to the kitchen, where she found Nkechi looking frantic.

'What are you looking for?'

Nkechi jumped and hit her head on the cupboard door, wincing. 'Ada! How many times have I told you to not to startle me?'

'Sorry.' Adaora walked over to her. 'Are you okay? Do you want some frozen vegetables to put on it?'

'No, I am okay,' Nkechi said, rubbing her head with her hands. 'It's just the initial impact pain, that's all.'

'What were you looking for, anyway?'

'The peeler. I want to make some apple crumble.'

Adaora's eyes lit up; she loved apple crumble, especially when Nkechi made it. It had been a long time since her teeth had sunk into the gorgeous combination of apple and cinnamon sprinkled with sugar, topped with a rich oat crumble and served with fresh vanilla ice cream. Her attempts to reproduce it had consistently failed, so she left it to the expert.

Walking to an inappropriate cupboard, Adaora rummaged for a few seconds before revealing the peeler. She smiled apologetically.

Nkechi frowned. 'Why is it in there?'

'It's my fault. Last time I was here, I used it to peel some potatoes.'

'Ada, can you please put things back where you found them? This is no longer your house,' she mocked.

It was not the first time Adaora had been told off about not putting things in the right place and it surely wouldn't be the last.

'So, Ada, are you going to just stand there or are you going to help me peel these apples?'

Adaora washed her hands and picked up her apron.

Nkechi went to help her tie it. 'Why do you even need an apron?'

'Well, after we peel the apples, we will need to make the crumble – right? So, I do not want any flour on my clothes.'

Nkechi rolled her eyes. 'Only peel eight of the golden apples, please.'

Adaora started peeling. 'Guess what?'

'What?'

'Charles broke up with me.'

Nkechi looked at her sister sympathetically. 'Aww, Ada, I am so sorry!'

'It's okay,' Adaora muttered. 'But when it is all said and done, it comes back to the fact that I do not want children. It was a deal breaker for him, and that's that.'

'When did this happen?' Nkechi asked.

'A few days ago,' she sighed, unable to make eye contact, focusing on the apple skins.

They did not notice their mother standing in the doorway behind them, eavesdropping.

'How do you feel, Ada?' Nkechi asked, while she poured and measured the quantity of flour needed.

'It's painful… All I can do is think about him…'

'Why shouldn't it be painful?' Mrs Edozie interrupted.

At the sound of her mother's voice, Adaora spun around and looked at her, aggravated by her presence. Adaora rolled her eyes, before turning her attention back to the apples. She wasn't in the mood for a confrontation. Vulnerable and emotionally exhausted, all Adaora wanted was to share her feelings with her sister. As she tried to zone out on her mother's lashing tongue, Mrs Edozie walked into the kitchen, her voice full of detestation.

'It was only a matter of time before the truth would be out. You are here, talking about painful... How exactly do you think Charles is feeling?'

The sisters, used to their mother's lectures, hoped that ignoring her would end it. They silently continued preparing the crumble.

Unfortunately, their lack of response did nothing to quell Mrs Edozie's passion. 'Adaora, it seems like all the education you received did not give you an ounce of common sense! You do not need a PhD to know that every man would like to have a family. You are here, doing *shakara* because you went school.'

Clenching her teeth, Adaora struggled to compose herself. Feeling her sister stiffen beside her, Nkechi held her hand and shook her head.

Ever the peacemaker, Nkechi turned to face her mother. 'Mum, please. It's enough.'

Ignoring her daughter's pleas Mrs Edozie retied her wrapper, falling from her waist. 'Adaora, Adaora, Adaora! How many times did I call your name? *Ogini?*'

Refusing to be goaded into an argument, Adaora washed her hands and dried them on her apron before removing it. She turned to face her sister. 'Nkechi, I am just going to leave. Save me some apple crumble, please.'

271

She attempted to walk to the door but her mother stood defiantly in her path.

'*Ebee ka į na-aga!*' Mrs Edozie shouted, but still no response or acknowledgement from Adaora. 'Adaora, is it not you I am talking to? I said, where are you going?'

'Mum, please, I am not in the mood.'

'In fact – just go!' She flapped her hands dismissively. 'You need God and serious prayer in your life.' Mrs Edozie stepped aside to let her pass.

But Adaora did not move, and in one swift motion, threw her purse to the floor. 'What do you mean by that? All this, because I do not want to worship a God that our oppressors gave us while they enslaved us? Or because I do not have maternal hormones running through my blood? That's why you must devalue me and everything I have accomplished?'

'The devil is a liar!' Mrs Edozie tapped her foot and shook her head. 'The devil is a liar!' she shouted over and over.

'This is part of the problem. No one ever takes responsibility. Everything is always because of the devil.' Adaora retorted.

'That young man did the best thing for his future, leaving you.'

The words cut into Adaora's soul and her face turned to stone. Nkechi knew her sister was about to explode, and she tried to signal for her to leave, but Adaora was unrepentant.

'LISTEN!' Adaora yelled. 'Keep your prayers and your God! I will be just fine. I do not need children to complete me.'

Mrs Edozie raised her hand as if she was going to slap Adaora. '*Kpuchie ọnụ!* Shut up your dirty mouth and remember who you are talking to!'

'STOP IT!' Nkechi shouted. 'I have decided that I will keep the baby!'

A hush fell. Nkechi had used her news deliberately, attempting to defuse the situation that was brewing. It had worked. Both women looked at each other and realised that there was more to discuss than their disagreement. Bewildered, Mrs Edozie reached for one of the kitchen stools, sitting in an attempt to process the information. Adoara was also in shock. Walking over to her sister she embraced her tightly.

'You are the strongest woman I know. Everyday you find a new way to inspire me,' Adaora said softly to her sister. 'I am here to support you, no matter what.'

'*Chineke*. Nkechi, are you sure of what you are saying?' Mrs Edozie said bitterly. 'This is a big decision that will change the course of your life.'

'Yes, mum, I know; but I also have morals that I cannot alter. God wants me to have this baby.'

Adaora smiled to herself, glad that the tables had turned; desperate to see how her mother would respond to God being used to make this argument. Although they had different views on Christianity, Adaora respected her sister's faith; mostly because she didn't try to choke her with scripture and condemn her to hell on any given occasion. Adaora sat smugly waiting for the backlash, for her mother to bring reproach upon herself.

For once, Mrs Edozie was silent. This was an incident she did not have an answer for. She could not justifiably encourage her daughter to have an abortion, knowing that the good book was against killing. The emotions were too much for her, as she sat between two daughters. Both of them acting against her wishes bothered her intensely. She got up to leave the kitchen, shaking her head in disbelief. This was not the future she had pictured for her children. That her first grandchild would be fathered by a rapist did not sit comfortably with her spirit.

'God is in control,' she muttered to herself.

Standing uncomfortably outside the locked door, Nkechi shuddered in fear. There was no going back, she thought, her stomach churning. Nausea began to overwhelm her and she leant against the wall, taking a few deep breaths and waiting for it to pass. As she regained her composure, she heard voices approaching the door: laughter and chatter. Before she could knock, the door opened.

In the doorway, a beast of a man stood: sturdy, muscular, intimidating; his skin ruptured with nasty-looking tattoos, his eyes a portal for evil. Blinking, Nkechi looked at him, recognising his aura from years before.

Patrick looked over his friend's shoulder, wondering why he had stopped short, and was surprised to see Nkechi. He motioned in her direction. 'Chemist, you remember Nkechi – my long-time girlfriend and, now, fiancee?'

'Yeah, I remember her,' he drawled, looking her up and down mischievously. 'Can never forget a pretty face. Congrats on dropping the ring. Sign of a real man,' he said, winking at her.

Reluctantly forming a smile, Nkechi manoeuvred between them to get into the apartment.

Patrick's friend raised a hand. 'P – we will link up soon. Take it easy.'

'No worries. Blessings,' Patrick said, before he closed the door. He walked into the living room and gave Nkechi a hug. 'Babe, I wasn't expecting you.'

Arms limp, Nkechi stared at him intently. 'What was Chemist doing in your apartment?'

Patrick loosened the tie from his three-piece grey Armani fitted suit, and walked towards the bedroom. 'Kechi, I know what you are thinking, but it is not like that.'

Following him, Nkechi tutted. 'Patrick, please tell me, then – what is it like? He is known as 'Chemist' and we both know he didn't study Pharmacy.'

Patrick was undressing, his back to Nkechi, desperate to get into comfortable clothes. 'Listen, don't stress. He was just collecting something that I owed him, that is all. You know I can't go backwards in life.'

She persisted. 'What was he collecting?'

Patrick hesitated, and gently placed his suit on a separate hanger, trying his best not to make eye contact with Nkechi.

'Patrick?' She walked around to face him directly.

He pressed his lips together, staring at her. Then, admitted: 'When we were looking for money for your release, he was willing to lend me a bulk amount, when no one else could.'

Hearing his response, Nkechi's features softened. Her fears that Patrick had got caught up into the wrong crowd again diminished. Chemist was only back in Patrick's life because of her, because Patrick loved her and had wanted to get her back. Moneylending was not as bad as drugs. And they had been desperate.

Grabbing a pair of charcoal tracksuit bottoms, Patrick continued. 'So, now I have a payment plan with him, he collects every now and again. Babe, trust me – I am far removed from being on the streets with Chemist and company. Meeting you and being with you is why I am now working for a top law firm and can look back on all that with disdain. Without you, I wouldn't be here. So, you see, you have nothing to worry about.'

Nkechi walked into Patrick's arms and she held him tight. 'Okay, baby, just be careful,' she said softly. 'How was work?'

'Well, it's the last day of the trial today and it is all down to the jury now. So, we will just have to wait and see what happens.'

'How are you feeling?'

'Pretty confident. We put together a strong case and the CPS had some flaws in their evidence, so we are really hopeful.'

'That is good to hear,' she smiled, cupping his cheek.

'How was your day?'

'Hmmm, my day was okay...' Nkechi sat down on his bed. '... until Adaora and my mum got into it, again.'

'Surprise, surprise! What else is new?'

Motioning for Patrick to sit next to her, when he did so, she grabbed his hand and held it on her lap. Patrick realised she wanted to talk, her manner showing that there was something on her mind. She hadn't turned up unannounced for no reason. He became attentive.

'Patrick, I wanted to talk about what happened. I know we have avoided discussing it, but you made a comment that I was not happy with at all. I want us to talk about it.'

Shifting in his seat, Patrick became concerned. He also had been thinking about their last interaction. All he wanted was them to be a couple again. Strong, in love, on the same page. Something about her tone made him feel that their reality was about to change. Slowly placing his hands on her stomach, Nkechi held them in place. Patrick tried to move them away, but Nkechi kept them steady. Their hearts were both racing.

'Can you feel that?'

Patrick wanted to leave; wanted to rewind the last few minutes – in fact, the last six months; wanted to be not having this conversation. He closed his eyes, half listening, half struggling to breathe.

'There is life inside me, Patrick. Life. Even though I still cry at night, even though I still wake up in cold sweats, thinking that animal will appear, to touch me again.'

Reliving the pain, remembering that he wasn't able to protect his princess, that a monster had penetrated her and impregnated her, weighed heavily on Patrick. He couldn't look at Nkechi.

'Even after all that has happened, I cannot go against my beliefs,' she stated. 'So, I have decided. I will keep the baby.'

The words were bullets, shot through Patrick's heart. Attacked, his body was automatically in fight or flight mode. Standing up, full of adrenaline and agony, he paced up and down, breathing heavily. Feeling trapped and claustrophobic, unable to put his feelings into words, he spoke to the wall, with his fists. Punching – self-harming, till his knuckles were as bruised as his heart.

'How can we start a family like this, Nkechi?' he cried. 'This makes no sense.'

The force of his words and the anger in his actions worried Nkechi. It had been years since she had seen this side of him. 'I have made up my mind, Patrick.'

'How can you?' he yelled. 'This is just selfish! How can you sit there and make such a huge decision, as if it doesn't affect both of us?'

He was losing control and Nkechi was not comfortable being in the apartment. He picked up the remote control and threw it across the room. Not willing to get caught in the crossfire, Nkechi collected her bag and headed for the front door.

'Where are you going?'

'When you can control your anger, maybe we can have an adult conversation,'she said over her shoulder, before gently closing the door behind her.

All the way home, Nkechi could not stop shaking. It was not the response she had wanted or expected from Patrick. Their relationship had suffered serious damage and the cracks were showing. Holding her tears, she longed for the privacy of her room, to release them into her pillow.

Opening the front door after 11 pm, she was surprised to see her parents still up, sitting in the living room. It seemed that she had interrupted a serious affair. Both wore anxious looks on their faces. Her father summoned her with his hand.

'What is the matter?' she asked, concerned.

There was hesitation as her parents exchanged looks, trying to decide who would be the deliverer of the news. Nkechi was dealing with her own emotions and the suspense was frustrating.

'The kidnappers who took you have been caught,' Mr Edozie said. Nkechi did not react. Mr Edozie continued. 'I received a call today and a picture of the three that were captured was sent to me, to help identify them.'

'Only three were caught?'

'Yes, one of their men was killed during the shootout with the police,' her father replied, scanning her face for any hint of emotion. There was none.

'Which one was killed?' Mr Edozie was just about to answer when Nkechi interrupted: 'To be honest, I do not care. Nor do I want to know.' Nkechi stood up. 'Goodnight.'

'Goodnight' Mr and Mrs Edozie replied, bewildered.

Dashing up the stairs, Nkechi bounded into the bedroom. As soon as she closed the door, the tears fell. She was a jumble sale of emotions. She couldn't process them, or deal with them.

Needing refuge, Nkechi removed her clothes and crawled into bed. With the light off, she attempted to find peace, yet the actions of the day plagued her. The argument with Adaora and their mum, Patrick reuniting with Chemist and showing signs of his old self. And now, learning that the father of her unborn baby could be dead. Her body rested, but her mind would not let her have that same privilege.

Work had become a struggle for Adaora. She turned up every day, punctual but without her usual sparkle. Even the receptionist realised that something was not quite right: Adaora's greetings had become flat and emotionless. Her brain was on autopilot as far as her role was concerned; still willing to put in the work with her patients, however, she saved her energy for one-to-one sessions. In between clients, she could barely find the motivation to complete her administrative tasks, producing the bare minimum. It was hard to focus; she would often find herself staring out of the office window, considering the eventualities of her relationships. Using the time to analyse all her previous boyfriends, she tried to identify when each had discarded her. Although all the endings had been difficult, the current situation with Charles was the only one that had affected her life this intently. All she wanted was him. Being without his smile, not being able to share her day with him, missing his voice, the way he said her name, the way he touched her – it was almost too much to bear. Charles was different from the rest. They had a connection that was special – almost perfect. But he was gone.

When work was over, Adaora recoiled into her shell, back at home. With no motivation to cook proper dinners, she feasted on the typical comfort foods of a broken heart: chocolate, ice-cream and red wine. The mood in the apartment was one of intoxicating grief as she mourned her loss; even the songs she played were a soundtrack of her temperament. Reclining on her sofa, she listened to the words of *'The Script - Breakeven'* and as the lyrics squatted in the pit of her stomach, she felt even more miserable.

"Still alive but I'm barely breathing,
just prayed to a God that I don't believe in,
cause I got time while she got freedom,
cause when a heart breaks, no, it don't break even."

The tune inflicted damage to her psyche. She needed Charles. Grabbing her phone, she scrolled to his number, but her thumb refused to press the call button. She weighed up her options; she didn't want to sound or act desperate. Sighing, she scrolled past his name and called Temi instead.

Hearing the brokenness in her friend's voice, Temi told Adaora to come over. Pulling herself up from the couch and snatching an unopened bottle from the table, she made her way over.

Temi had the wine glasses in hand, as she opened the door for Adaora. She knew the drill: her friend needed to vent, needed the company of a trusted confidante. But first, Adaora would catch up with Temi's news.

'How are the baby-making sessions going?' Adaora asked, summoning up a cheeky grin and handing Temi the bottle.

'Tiring,' Temi replied, using the corkscrew and unleashing the alcohol. 'We are even having *marathon* sessions on the weekend.'

Adaora's jaw dropped as she held the glass for Temi to pour into. 'What does that even mean? Marathon sessions?'

'Yes, girl!' Temi said, laughing at her friend's expression. 'Tony is a like a machine these days. Once the first batch has been dispatched inside me, all he needs is 10 minutes to rejuvenate, and we are at it again.'

'Urgh! That may be too much information!' Adaora sipped at her wine, smiling. 'Well, by the sounds of it, that baby will be in your belly soon enough.'

'I hope so. I can't wait to be a mum. Just the thought of growing a human inside my womb – it's so exciting!'

Adaora's face changed. She sat silently; not agreeing or disagreeing. Not wanting to stamp all over Temi's excitement with her own unhappiness.

Temi was not insensitive. 'I know you miss Charles,' she said quietly. 'It is written all over your face. Would you ever sacrifice your ideals for a shot at being happy?'

Adaora sighed. 'I have thought about it, Temi. It's one of the reasons I lied about it initially, but after a lot of heart-searching, I had to own the fact that nothing has changed. I still don't want children. I told him the truth.' She drained her glass.

Temi nodded, trying to appreciate her stance, but not quite understanding. For herself, having a family was the most amazing gift. She respected Adaora's decision, though.

'Fair enough, girl. Then you are going to have to just let him go. It was not meant to be, then.'

'I know,' Adaora reluctantly agreed. Temi always had a way of speaking some sense into Adaora. It was subtle but it was what she needed to hear.

Adaora poured herself another generous glass, then hovered the tipped bottle above Temi's glass. Temi shook her head. 'Just in case I'm pregnant! I'm sticking to one glass while we're trying.'

'And ironically, I am drinking for two,' said Adaora, taking a sip. 'Having your share.'

Deciding that that was enough moping, Temi tactfully changed the subject. 'By the way, did you go on the Reparations March a few weeks ago? I have been meaning to ask you.'

'No, I didn't get to go,' she said, swallowing down some more wine. 'To be honest, all this marching is only clocking up foot mileage; they do not actually care about us and our history. How can David Cameron, the Prime Minister, say we basically need to get over slavery? He would never say that about the holocaust! And do you know why?'

'Why?'

'Because, as black people, we have no economic power anywhere in the world.' She took another mouthful of wine, shaking her head. 'The one place where you would think we have power would be the mother continent – but that is where it is worst! Africa has been, and will continue to be, raped of its natural resources. Most of our ancient artefacts are sitting in European museums. Temi, please do not get me started. The whole situation saddens me.'

'What you said is the key. Economic power. But we are too divided to even formulate a plan that would push us in the right direction.'

'Exactly! And on that note, I need to be pointed in the direction of more red wine.' Adaora said, and Temi laughed as she got up and pulled another bottle of wine from the cupboard.

September, back to school. Usually one of Nkechi's favourite times of the year. The opportunity for a fresh start; new students always looking smart and anxious in their freshly ironed uniforms; new connections to make and new young people to inspire. This year was different.

As Nkechi redecorated her classroom, brightening the boards with motivational statements and schemes of work, she felt deflated. She would not have the opportunity to support the new intake: in a few months, she would be on maternity leave. Being pregnant was also having an effect on her moods: often tired and lethargic, she struggled to keep up the same pace and energy in her lessons as she had in the past.

After school, Nkechi sat in her class and pondered on the ways in which this pregnancy would change the course of her life, her aspirations and ambitions. Previously, she had been determined to set up her own businesses, write her own books and make changes to the curriculum, through research and policy. Now, as she sat rubbing her stomach and imagining the baby respond, she realised that her passion for those things had departed. She had changed. Closing her eyes to take a well-needed rest, she heard a knock on her door.

Expecting a staff member or a lost student, she shouted: 'Come in!', her eyes still half-closed.

As the person entered, she straightened herself in the chair and opened her eyes. To her surprise, it was Patrick, standing solemnly above her, a visitor's badge on a lanyard draped around his neck.

'What are you doing here?'

'We need to talk,' he said, his tone urgent.

'And you think this is the appropriate place for us to talk?' Nkechi exclaimed, raising her arms into the air in disbelief. 'Here? Now? Really, Patrick?'

Patrick took a few steps back, looking around anxiously, and rubbed his hands together. 'I know it is not, but I just had to see you. I've got to talk to you. Please hear me out.'

Nkechi crossed her legs, resting her elbow on her thigh and her chin in her hand. She waited, one eyebrow raised.

Seeing that she had calmed, Patrick took a deep breath. 'Firstly, I want to apologise for my temper last time. It was unnecessary. I'm sorry.' He paused, struggling to find words. 'Nkechi, I was wrong to respond like that. I accept that. But the bottom line is that I do not want you to have this baby, and I need you to reconsider. You don't know how hard this is for me.'

'Hard for you?' Nkechi interrupted, scornfully. 'Patrick, you have no idea what it feels like to be in my shoes.'

Patrick attempted to respond but Nkechi stood up and pointed at him, her hand dangerously close to his face.

'Hard for you?' she repeated, poking the air with her finger. 'And what about me, Patrick? You think I'm okay? You think you're the only one struggling?'

Her words came thick and fast, hurled into his face. Patrick looked dismal, unsure what to say. He moved away from her, but her voice followed him.

'Do you think I want to be in this position? You have no idea what I'm going through, because you haven't even bothered to ask! All you care about is how this baby will affect you, when I am the one who is carrying it. I'm the one who will have a child kicking me when I want to sleep! The constant reminder of a baby conceived by a rapist!' Nkechi was almost screeching at him, her face red. 'I have thought about abortion, many times! I have battled with it. I wanted it all to go away. Wanted it to never have happened. But this baby did not ask to be born; didn't have a choice in how it was conceived. Unlike you, I am not so selfish as to only consider myself in this situation. There is a life inside me. And I will not become a murderer! I could never live with myself. So there. I. Am. Keeping. This baby.' She paused, looking over at Patrick.

His fists were clenched, his body tense, his chest heaving as he tried to control his breathing. He walked back over to where she stood. He looked at her, remembering how she had made his life complete; such a fighter.

'Nkechi,' he began, his voice torn. 'You know I love you. I always have. My life would not be what it is without you. The day I met you, I wanted you to be my wife; dreamt of us being together forever, starting our own family...' His voice trailed off as his eyes went down to her definite bump. He hesitated. 'It's just... The way things have worked out... I mean... I love you... that hasn't changed... but...'

'But?'

Patrick paused; his eyes found the floor.

'But what?' Nkechi demanded, fear fuelling her tongue. Her breathing became laboured. 'Patrick, are you leaving me?'

Silence.

Nkechi looked down at her stomach then up at Patrick. He had not answered, and that was answer enough. The well of emotion in her lungs escaped into a scream, and she punched Patrick repeatedly in the chest, her face a mess of tears. Patrick attempted to hold her, but she pushed his arms away. In a wave of wrath, she pulled her engagement ring off and threw it onto the floor. It bounced before rolling under a table.

'GET OUT!'

Bending down to pick up the ring, Patrick put it into his pocket. 'Nkechi, listen – I didn't ….'

'GET OUT, PATRICK!' she screamed, punching and pushing him towards the door.

He left, turning back to see Nkechi slumped over her desk, sobbing.

The sun rose each morning and greeted a hollow heart. Each fresh day brought the revelation that nothing had changed. Struggling to emerge from the refuge of her mattress, Nkechi didn't want to get up. There was nothing to get up for. She longed to be able to press 'system restore' on her life and erase this whole year.

Eyes clamped shut, teeth sinking into her bottom lip, she rolled onto her stomach and thought about praying. It seemed useless; the words she had uttered every night before bed had done little to prevent her from this pain. This suffering. It had been days since Patrick had obliterated her future, and nothing held meaning. Work was unbearable; every little thing her students did irritated her, and Nkechi was often in a bad mood. Home was no solace either.

Speaking would only aggravate her emotions, so she decided to simply stop. She stopped talking to her family, to her friends. She talked only at work when she had to. Her body operated, but her mind was distant, and her spirit seemed to desist. Appetite gone, her room became her sanctuary, her place of asylum. Away from the noise, the expectations; away from life.

Concern grew amongst the family as Nkechi became more

reclusive. Chidi tried his best to cheer her up, but his attempts amounted to nothing; he walked away defeated. Adaora, understanding the psychological roots of behaviour, knew that Nkechi actions were related to her thought processes and she tried to get Nkechi to talk – but despite her training and education, Adaora was unable to get a response.

Mrs Edozie felt that her daughter was being irresponsible and although Nkechi had chosen to be mute, Mrs Edozie did not struggle to fill every silence with her own voice and opinion. The constant nagging was griping at Nkechi's nerves, especially since it was repetitive. All her mother focused on was her lack of appetite; lecturing her about the effect it would have on the baby.

Mr Edozie watched his family attempt to prise Nkechi out of her solitude and realised that their methods were ineffective. His approach was different: respecting her decisions and giving her the space she required, he showed his love and care for her by coming home from work early to buy or cook tempting treats especially for her; leaving trays of food in her room each night. He said nothing as he brought them, allowing Nkechi to respond in her own way. After a few nights, Nkechi began to eat his food and would take the empty plates to the kitchen to wash them, walking over to her dad and bowing as a sign of gratitude.

Nkechi had finished a long day at work. She wanted to rest and hoped no-one was home. To her disappointment, her mother was in the kitchen and although she tried to sneak up the stairs inconspicuously, Mrs Edozie heard her come in and approached her before she could get up the stairs.

'Ahh, so you are home! When are you going to stop this nonsense, Nkechi? You are bringing the whole family down!' she cried. 'Every day, you don't talk, you don't eat. I have cooked every meal especially for you – and you refuse. How many times do I need to tell you that you will make the baby suffer? Why plan to keep a baby, just to let it starve?'

Nkechi was furious. All the emotions piled on top of her over the last few weeks were bubbling over, and she could no longer stand the sight of her mother. Marching up the stairs, she stormed into her room, grabbed a weekend bag and began packing. She had no definitive plan on where she would go, but another day under this roof would be the end of her.

Downstairs, Mr Edozie, exasperated with his wife, was reprimanding her for driving Nkechi further away. He was. Worried about Nkechi, he went to her room and knocked on the door. Hesitantly, he opened it, but Nkechi continued packing, barely looking up.

Mr Edozie sat on Nkechi's bed, upset that she was considering leaving the house. Ever since Nigeria, he wanted to keep her close; he already felt he had failed as a father by not being able to protect her. Now, he wanted even more to keep a watchful eye over his princess.

'My daughter, please. Come and sit here.'

Nkechi stopped packing. Looking up at her dad, she saw that his eyes were filled with sorrow, and it pained her. She sat next to him on the bed.

Mr Edozie smiled, and patted her hand. 'I don't know if I have ever told you this story, Kechi, but I believe that, today, you need to hear it,' Mr Edozie began. Nkechi was attentive, so he started: 'A firstborn son is the wish of many African men. And in fact, that wish is not just specific to us. Other cultures, too. But as an Igbo man, it calls for great celebration. Ada was first. A girl. When she was born, I cried tears of joy. I didn't care that she wasn't a boy – I was so overwhelmed with the beautiful gift God had given. And then your mother got pregnant with you…' Mr Edozie smiled, squeezing Nkechi's hand. 'There were people spreading fear, telling us that you would die in the womb. These naysayers! We knew we serve a God that can do much more than we can ask or think, so we prayed, every day. I had my hand on your mother's stomach and we committed our second child to Him. This was the season when your mother's faith bloomed. We believed our prayers would be answered.'

Nkechi nodded, transfixed by the story, her free hand resting on her bump. Mr Edozie was emotional, his voice breaking in places, as he reminisced on their testimony. His wife had been so strong during that trying time.

'So, when the hospital informed us that there were issues with the pregnancy and you could be born two months early, it ripped us apart. So many nights, your mother cried, thinking that the curses would come to pass…' Mr Edozie's eyes welled up.

Nkechi grabbed tissues from her dressing table and pressed one into his hand.

'They had to do an emergency caesarean. You were in an incubator in the special care unit for weeks. Tubes all over your body, unable to breathe by yourself. So premature that they were worried you wouldn't make it. We came to see you every day. Prayed over you, continued to trust in God, and you began to improve. Every day, the nurses would tell us about your progress and then one day you started breathing independently. And look at you, now! A beautiful, intelligent, inspirational woman.'

Tears began to flow down Nkechi's cheeks. It was not often that her dad was this open about his feelings with her. The moment

289

was a special one; that bound them even closer together. One that would not be forgotten. Nkechi put her head on her dad's shoulder, wiping her eyes on his shirt.

'Kechi, my children are blessings from God. I didn't care about carrying on my family name, but rather, doing my best for all of you. You came into this world a fighter, with the heart of a lion! I was so proud of you. I still am.' He stared directly into Nkechi's eyes, and she felt his warmth touch her heart. 'You have overcome so much to get here, and today you are showing me how much of a fighter you are. It has been tough – we cannot diminish that, but I believe God is using you for a bigger picture, for his purposes. I almost lost you once, but I will not, again. So, my daughter, unpack your clothes and stay with your family. We shall overcome, together.'

Nkechi grabbed her dad, her arms around his neck, and hugged him tight.

'Thank you,' she whispered.

It was the first time she had spoken in a week.

The time was passing quickly. Nkechi's bump grew bigger and bigger until she could barely see her toes. Nkechi had a distinct waddle to her walk, was tired of not being able to fit into any of her clothes and needed a break from the responsibility of other people's children. Strangers seemed to gravitate to her pregnancy bump and it felt odd when they commented, and congratulated her. With no engagement ring, and no sign of Patrick, the reality of her decision began to weigh on her mind. Thankfully, as Mr Edozie had said, the family had rallied around to support her – especially Adaora.

Adaora had made sure she had cleared her calendar to allow her to attend all Nkechi's scans and appointments. She even spent her weekend at an antenatal class, learning all about the different stages of labour, what to expect, and how to support Nkechi through it. They had already decided that Adaora was best placed to be her birthing partner, since there was no way that Nkechi could endure labour with her mother fussing around her and praying up a storm in the hospital wing. The pregnancy had brought them closer together. Adaora was in charge of ensuring that she was taking her antenatal vitamins, drinking lots of water, and convincing her she wasn't fat.

Firmly in the third trimester – in December – Nkechi was struggling to feel attractive.

'Wear the red and black maxi dress, Kechi. It looks gorgeous on you.'

'Don't lie to me, sis. I've had enough of people telling me I'm 'glowing' when I just feel like an ugly beached whale.'

'You're pregnant! You're meant to put on weight.'

'That's alright for you to say, Ada. You look stunning in that white and gold dress.'

Adaora smiled, checking herself out in the mirror. Nkechi was right. 'Well, sis, it is a special day!'

'Exactly! Your birthday! The big 30! Can't believe it's here already,' Nkechi said, still looking for the maxi dress Adaora had mentioned.

There was a knock on the bedroom door and Chidi peeped his head around the corner, his eyes closed. 'Are you decent?'

'Yes, Chidi, come in,' Adaora laughed, excited about the celebration.

'Ada, you look great! Kechi, come on! Mum and dad are ready. You always take forever!'

Nkechi threw a pillow at Chidi's head. 'I do not!' she exclaimed, finally finding the dress she'd been looking for. 'You look good though, Chidi. I see the barber hooked you up nicely.'

'You know... You know... Gotta look good for Ada's big day.'

'Mmmm... Ok, can you leave now? I gotta get dressed.'

They arrived at the Turkish restaurant, all looking prestigious: Mr and Mrs Edozie matching in traditional attire with the siblings right behind: flawless. Nkechi had booked out a small section of the restaurant and a few close friends were already seated there when they arrived. A number of people complimented Adaora on her outfit, and her scent. It was a pleasant surprise that Charles had remembered her birthday and sent her some Chanel perfume, which she was wearing. It reminded her of his attention to detail: it was the one she had always wanted. She looked around the table, saddened that Charles and Patrick were missing. Their absence was felt by Nkechi, too.

It was a night of good food and great company. Adaora was exalted by everyone who had come out to help her celebrate, and at one point after the meal, they all made toasts in her honour. Soon, it was Nkechi's turn to make a speech. Hormones all over the place, she had already teared up. Taking her time, she stood up, her bump covered beautifully in the dress, hovering over the table.

'Thank you all so much for coming. I'm trying to keep my composure, but my sister means so much to me. I don't know what I would do without her. She is truly the most wonderful sister in the world and I love her so much.' She turned to face Adaora. 'Adaora, you are my inspiration. Ever since you were young, you would determine something in your heart and make it happen. I am astonished by you. This beautiful woman that sits before me is amazing. Dr Edozie – can you believe it?'

The room erupted in applause. Adaora blushed, smiling intently at her sister.

'Words can't describe how much love and respect I have for you. You are dedicated to making sure other people's problems are solved and your compassion and care is there for all to see. You know what I think. I will stop there, before I start crying, but yeah – happy birthday, sis. I love you.'

'I love you, too,' Adaora mouthed, beneath the applause.

With Nkechi's due date fast approaching, Adaora had blocked off time from work and was keeping Nkechi company as they waited for nature to take its course. As the due date came and went, Nkechi was getting impatient, feeling sluggish and uncomfortable, especially when the baby's head pressing against her bladder or bowel kept her rushing to the toilet. Adaora was trying her best to keep her calm, and since long trips were out of the question, they spent days at home, watching old films.

On one occasion, Adaora went into the kitchen to prepare a snack for them both and heard a squeal from the living room. A pool of water was at Nkechi's feet. It had started! Springing into action, Adaora grabbed the maternity bag that they had packed previously, found Nkechi's pregnancy notes and escorted her carefully to the car, before driving off.

She parked up at the hospital in record time and rushed Nkechi to the maternity ward. After handing her notes in at the desk, Nkechi sat and waited for her name to be called. The ward was full. Everywhere they looked, women were bursting with the fullness of birth and screams echoed from behind closed doors. Nkechi's contractions had begun and the tightening pain she was experiencing felt alien and irregular. Adaora reminded her of what they had learnt at the antenatal class and held her hand, reminding her to take deep breaths and remain calm. Having her sister beside her would help Nkechi – she hoped, anyway – to deal with the increasingly strenuous event she expected labour to be.

Before long, Nkechi was admitted and placed on the ward. A friendly-looking midwife, seeing the look of anxiety on her face, spent extra time informing her what to expect, while she examined her. Already 3 centimetres dilated and in escalating pain, Nkechi spoke about her birth plan and asked for gas and air.

Adaora had already put on the playlist they had prepared in advance and soft instrumental music filled the air. Counting the frequency of contractions, Adaora did not leave Nkechi's side, often rubbing her lower back to help with the pain.

Nkechi was tired, and with her face a twisted mess of agony, she asked to be re-examined. Although hours had passed, she was still not in active labour and she panted her way through the pain, inhaling the gas deeply whenever the contractions erupted.

Seven hours later, the midwife announced that Nkechi's cervix was fully dilated and the baby was ready to make a grand entrance. Adaora, meanwhile, had stolen a moment to call her mum and dad and let them know what was happening.

The horrific screams that spilled from Nkechi's mouth caused Adaora's hairs to stand on end. She hated seeing her sister in so much pain. The nurse indicated to Nkechi that she needed to keep pushing, but Nkechi felt drained.

'I can't do this!' she cried.

'Yes, you can Kechi,' Adaora encouraged. 'You're almost there! Keep fighting.'

Hearing those words reminded Nkechi of what her dad had said to her, and she felt a surge of strength work its way through her body. Gritting her teeth, she continued to push as hard as she could, as the waves of pain continued to wash over her.

'You're almost there, hun,' the midwife encouraged. 'I can see the head! Pant for me, now. Short pushes. One – two – three – four.'

Nkechi gave a mighty roar, and the midwife yelled, 'That's it! Yes! Well done!'

Standing at Nkechi's side, her eyes on stalks, Adaora saw the miracle of birth. And then, the baby's lungs opened and screamed loudly, announcing its arrival on earth.

Adaora squeezed Nkechi's hand. 'You did it, sis!'

'Congratulations! It's a baby girl!' the midwife said, holding up the baby.

Nkechi turned her face away.

Adaora was stunned. She looked at Nkechi, sagged, slouched and exhausted. 'Kechi, it's a beautiful baby girl' Adaora said.

There was no reaction from Nkechi, although she was clearly conscious.

The nurse attempted to hand Nkechi the baby. 'Time for some skin to skin with mummy, little one.'

Nkechi did not look at the baby or the nurse; but remained expressionless, almost in a trance-like state. The nurse tried again, but Nkechi refused to take the baby and rolled over, away from them. The nurse looked to Adaora, questioningly, for help.

'Nkechi?' Adaora called.

Silence.

Shrugging, the nurse walked over to Adaora and motioned

for her to hold out her hands. She did so, instinctively. The nurse carefully placed the baby in her arms.

Adaora looked down at the tiny, beautiful baby, wrapped in a pink blanket and something strange stirred within her. Sitting on the chair next to the hospital bed, Adaora peered at the newborn in wonder, and smiled.

Chapter Eleven

TWENTY-FOUR HOURS LATER, NKECHI HAD NOT RECOVERED. APART FROM HER ASSAULT, giving birth to her child was the most traumatic day of her life.

The room was filled with flowers, cards, and teddy bears: a colourful backdrop to the weeping of her soul. Her eyes vacant, her mind throbbing, her mouth silent. Her parents visited, happy, then anxious and concerned, but Nkechi barely noticed them.

Throughout the labour, the same feeling of hopelessness – lack of choice and control – had arrested her as the rape. Flashbacks of the perpetrator and the event repeatedly played behind her eyelids.

All around her, unfamiliar eyes had stared at her nakedness, examining her vagina – a place that had been cruelly bruised with sexual violence now had had medical equipment shoved inside. Contractions had taken control of her body and strangers had been constantly touching her without consent. She felt violated. Exposed. Raped again.

Now, she was too scared to bond with a baby that had caused her to relive her suffering; not even wanting to look at it: afraid that the rapist's face would greet her.

'The Edozie baby,' the staff muttered. 'Mum is rejecting her.'

The whispering and judgements amongst the young nurses had soon reached Adaora's ears and she had made it her mission to inform them of the trauma that her sister had endured.

A change occurred. More helpful, empathetic and supportive, the nurses took turns to check on Nkechi and schedule the night feeds between them.

Concerned that Nkechi should not be left alone, Adaora ensured that Mrs Edozie and herself worked as a tag-team, doing shifts at the hospital. Most of the time, Nkechi did not even acknowledge their presence; locked in her own world, unable to cope with reality. Adaora spent every minute she could at her sister's side; watching her retreat to some internal refuge, unable to verbally express herself. Adaora kept a close eye on her body language, willing her to smile.

Sitting in the armchair next to the unresponsive Nkechi's bed, Mrs Edozie peered down at her grandchild, wriggling in her arms. She was precious. Thinking back to when she had given birth to Adaora, Mrs Edozie's heart was overwhelmed with joy. The innocence! The perfect features and cute yawn! The utter dependence on other people. Her heart longed to protect this gift, wrapped tightly in a hand-made blanket. Face to face with her legacy, Mrs Edozie was filled with guilt that she had wanted this life to be terminated before meeting the world. Repenting in her heart, she kissed the baby's forehead. The baby responded by opening and closing her mouth, her face turned inward, nuzzling towards her breasts, bobbing her head looking for milk. An advocate of breastfeeding, Mrs Edozie looked up at the hospital bed, defeated, knowing it was not the time to lecture Nkechi on the goodness of natural milk. Her daughter had not even held her baby, so there was no use attempting to persuade her to feed her. Reaching for a ready-made bottle, Mrs Edozie began to hum a lullaby, putting the teat in the baby's open mouth.

Arms full of toiletries and essentials, Adaora took the lift up to the recovery ward, hoping that Nkechi had improved since the previous day. She weaved through the hospital, smiling at the nurses before reaching her sister's bedside. Seeing her mother cradling the infant, Adaora reached over to stroke the baby's cheek, before handing her sister the bag. Desperate to connect with her new niece, but feeling a sense of divided loyalties, with Nkechi being so detached, Adaora sat on the edge of the bed, waiting for her mother to finish feeding the baby. Ignoring them all, Nkechi silently took the toiletries and slipped away to shower.

'Adaora, would you like to burp her?'

Adaora jumped off the bed, grinning from ear to ear. Her mother almost chuckled at the excitement on her face, relieved that one daughter was taking some interest.

'Oh yes, please!' Adaora gushed, holding out her hands in expectation.

'Be gentle. Get a muslin, and put it over your shoulder,' Mrs Edozie began, stepping up out of the chair so Adaora could sit comfortably. Once Adaora was seated, Mrs Edozie handed her the baby. 'Support her head. That's it; lean her on your shoulder.'

'I have done it before! Well, tried to,' she laughed, too glad to even feel insulted. She was actually grateful to follow her mother's instructions, aware that her arms were full of an innocent life; she did not want to anything to harm her.

'Now, leaning back so she is supported, rub her back slowly, in circles.'

'Is this right?' Adaora asked.

'That's perfect, my dear,' Mrs Edozie replied, sitting down on the hospital bed.

The baby began to squirm, so Adaora changed positions slightly and began to hum *Twinkle Twinkle* as she continued to rub her back. After a few minutes, the baby burped, spewing some milk out onto the cloth. Smiling, Adaora placed the baby on her lap and wiped her mouth.

Mrs Edozie was ecstatic. Seeing her daughter take on such a maternal role with ease and comfort over the last day had been a welcome change.

In the bathroom, Nkechi struggled to recognise herself in the mirror. Her womb now empty, a weird, swollen pouch sat in its place, covered with livid stretch marks the baby had left behind.

Struggling to do basic things, Nkechi took her time, her limbs crying out in agony as she bent over to remove her underwear. Sighing, she climbed carefully into the shower and allowed the steaming hot water to cleanse her bruised skin. Standing under the heat, Nkechi watched her tears freefall down the plug hole. She still felt dirty. Reaching for the soap, she began to scrub hard, attempting to remove all the stains of her experiences, to take the invisible tattoos off her skin. Although she was clean, she still felt dirty on the inside.

Sighing, she traced the dark circles under her eyes with her index finger and wondered if she would ever be the same. She had forgotten the old Nkechi. Something had changed within her and she wasn't sure how to get it back. Knowing visitors would arrive soon, she put on the new nightdress Adaora had packed for her, looked in the mirror again and tried to force herself to smile. Her rebellious muscles resisted.

Her delight walked into the ward, grinning from ear to ear, almost running to see his baby niece. Chidi could not wait to meet her! He had left Mr Edozie and Gloria talking as he raced to the bedside. Hugging and rattling off his greetings to Nkechi, who said nothing, Chidi was not offended – he had been warned that she seemed to be suffering from post-natal depression. And in fact, her behaviour was hardly different from how it had been for the last few weeks. He had grown used to it.

With all of them around the bed, it began to feel cramped and Nkechi felt claustrophobic and uncomfortable. She peered out from the covers, not willing to talk and watching them interact with a new life she had overlooked.

Mrs Edozie began to teach Chidi the correct way to hold the baby. Gloria held Nkechi's hand, while Mr Edozie stood awkwardly at the foot of the bed. Adaora decided to let them all have some time with the baby.

'Nkechi,' Adaora announced, 'I'm just going to the shops. Can I get you anything?'

Shaking her head, Nkechi did not even bother to look in Adaora's direction. Adaora left.

Gloria squeezed Nkechi's hand, noting the distant expression on her friend's face. 'Kech, that baby girl seems to have taken your genes.'

Gloria looked expectantly at Nkechi, who impassively removed her hand from Gloria's grasp and lay quietly gazing into the distance. Saddened, Gloria went over to greet the baby, while Nkechi became bored of the circus and rolled over, turning her back on everyone.

301

Outside, Adaora's feet paced the gentrified streets. Homerton hospital, a beacon in the heart of Hackney, had become surrounded by new businesses as investors set their sights on the area. Seeking food to nourish her, Adaora reached a number of shop doors, but the scent of meat – greasy and fried – wafted in her path and insulted Adaora's sensibilities. Desperate for a healthy option, she carried on searching; but only fast food and oily options greeted her.

Irritated, she made her way back to the hospital, deciding to utilise the Costa coffee shop inside. Taking her place in the queue, she peered into the open fridge, analysing the sandwiches and fruit pots available. Nothing excited her. Deciding on a latte, she gave her order to the barista and waited to be served.

'Yeah, can you direct me to maternity, please? Cheers.'

Hearing a familiar voice somewhere behind her, Adaora turned around, unsure who it was. Standing at reception, looking devilishly handsome, carrying a beautiful bouquet and pink teddy, stood Charles – unaware of her presence.

Spinning around quickly, averting her face, Adaora struggled to get her money together, unable to concentrate, her heart pounding in her chest. It had been a long time since she had seen him, and the unexpected sight was causing panic throughout her nervous system. Touching her hair and pressing her lips together, Adaora wished she had a spot more makeup on. Determined not to catch his eye, she kept her gaze on the counter.

But as Charles walked past the coffee shop he noticed her and stopped. 'Adaora?' he called.

Taking her time, Adaora pocketed her change before slowly turning around to face him. She smiled sweetly, and walked towards, him maintaining eye contact. Watching her, his eyes scanning up and down her gorgeous physique, Charles subconsciously licked his lips, appreciating her devastating looks. Standing within touching distance from him, Adaora's heart and body sang a melody of longing and she tried to maintain her composure as he reached around her and kissed both of her cheeks. She wanted to embrace him, place her hips against his and feel his manhood press her lower belly, yet she couldn't.

Around them, people weaved in and out, looking for different wards, leaving the building to smoke and reuniting with loved ones – a whirlwind of action that seemed to accentuate their own stillness. Adaora and Charles only had eyes for each other. Their bodies desiring a lingering touch, they attempted to keep their composure. Things were different between them. Civil. Polite.

'How have you been?' he asked.

'I've been good, just trying to live. What about you?'

'Can't complain to be honest. Just still pushing hard on all fronts.'

'That's good to hear.'

The small-talk died a painful death, leaving awkwardness resting between them.

'So… how is Nkechi?' Charles began, 'Chidi told me she'd had the baby, so I thought I would come and see them both.'

'And you came with gifts! So sweet of you,' Adaora smiled, remembering how caring and compassionate Charles was. 'To be honest, it is quite difficult. Although physically the birth was ok, Nkechi has not spoken to anyone and is refusing to even hold the baby.'

'Wow. That sounds tough.' Charles looked saddened. 'It sounds like postnatal depression…'

'I agree. She has been offered support but won't engage. So, we are doing our best to keep her comfortable and… just hope that, eventually she will let us support her better.'

'I'm so sorry to hear that. Is it still okay if I see her?'

'Yeah, sure. I am going back up now.'

Adaora made her way to the lift with Charles. He kept a step behind so he could take in the voluptuous frame she had squeezed into skin-tight jeans. Simple, yet perfect. She was a vision. His feelings began to rise as he remembered her nakedness between his sheets. Sighing, he tried to suppress the thoughts, knowing that all they had were only memories, now.

They reached the ward and Charles greeted Mr and Mrs Edozie before turning to Nkechi. Unsure how to react, he presented the flowers and soft toy, leaning them on the side of the bed.

'Hi Nkechi, I hope you don't mind my visiting. I just wanted to see how you and baby were doing.'

With her face turned to the wall, Nkechi did not acknowledge Charles at all.

Mr and Mrs Edozie attempted to make conversation with Charles but after a few minutes, he could not stand the awkwardness. Making his excuses, he left.

The following day, Nkechi was discharged from the hospital. Placing the baby in the removable car seat, Mrs Edozie proceeded to wrap her in a number of blankets, commenting that the cold spell had continued and she didn't want the baby to catch a cold. They carried her out, leading Nkechi by the arm, too.

Struggling to secure the car seat into the car, Mr Edozie complained about new technology and how much easier it had been when Nkechi was younger. Finally, all strapped in, they continued the journey home.

Inside the house, Chidi had been working hard, blowing up balloons, putting up banners and making the place welcoming for his sister and niece's arrival.

As he heard the door open, standing on his chair, reaching up to stick the last corner of the banner to the ceiling, he turned around. 'Welcome home!' he proclaimed, grinning as they walked in.

Unmoved, Nkechi walked past him without a word and made her way upstairs.

Defeated, Chidi let the banner fall to the floor with a heavy heart. His parents exchanged uneasy looks.

Given Nkechi's lack of interest in the baby, Mrs Edozie had got her husband to retrieve the cot from the loft and set it up in their own room, next to the bed. They were uncertain what the future would hold.

The household began to readjust to having a baby in the house. As the main carer, Mrs Edozie was often tired, having to wake with the baby every couple of hours or so to feed her. She spent most of the day resembling a zombie, but was so in love with her granddaughter that she barely noticed – and persevered. At times, Mrs Edozie would try to give Nkechi the baby, but each attempt caused Nkechi to retreat more into her seclusion: barely eating, spending most of the day in her bed.

Adaora shared the responsibility with her mother, choosing to spend as much time as possible supporting her sister and getting to know her niece. Now an expert in all things to do with newborns, Adaora was in the swing of things. She knew her niece's routine by heart and could feed, change, bathe and burp her without assistance. Growing in confidence and – oddly – in her maternal instincts, she found that she enjoyed bonding with the newest member of the family.

It was time for a nap. However, the newborn was fighting sleep. Determined, Adaora was walking up and down the passageway, singing lullabies and rocking the baby gently.

Unexpectedly, Nkechi came downstairs. As usual, she looked distant – her eyes vacant.

'Kechi, we really need to name this beautiful girl,' Adaora began. 'I think we are all tired of calling her "baby".' No response from Nkechi. 'What about…'

Taking flight, Nkechi turned and walked back up the stairs into her room without a word.

Juggling work and home, Adaora was always busy. Sitting at her desk, she looked at the time, wondering where her next client was. Half an hour late was very unusual. Picking up the phone, she attempted to contact them, but there was no response on any of the numbers she had. The slot passed and she continued seeing other clients until 5pm.

As she was packing up to go back to her mother's house, the phone rang.

'Is that Dr Edozie?'

'Yes, it is.'

'My name is Pamela Wright, from Havering Social Services. I just wanted to inform you that one of your patients, Paige Edwards, tried to commit suicide last night.'

A coldness worked its way down Adaora's spine.

'Oh, my goodness! That is dreadful news. Is she okay?' Adaora exclaimed. 'When she didn't show up for her appointment, I knew something was wrong, but couldn't get through to anyone. What happened?'

'We are not sure yet. All we know, at this point, is that the foster carer found her on the floor this morning. She was rushed to the hospital and her stomach was pumped, as she had swallowed a number of pills. She is now in a stable condition, but when she is able to talk, we were hoping you could find out exactly what happened, for her to take such actions.'

'Yes, of course. What hospital is she in?'

'Queens Hospital in Romford.'

'Okay. Thanks for letting me know, I will head over there now.'

Frantically clearing her desk, Adaora rushed to her car and made her way to the hospital. As she drove, she replayed their last session in her mind and wondered what could have happened for Paige to take such drastic action.

In the Edozie household, Mrs Edozie was filling the air with the sweet melodious tunes of her ancestors as she walked through the house, lulling the baby to sleep with classic Igbo rhymes. Closing her eyelids softly, swayed by the rhythm and rocking, the baby began to drift off. Feeling accomplished, Mrs Edozie walked back into the living room and sat down.

Across from her, Nkechi sat clothed only in a dressing gown, her hair a tangled mess, her skin ashy, her complexion grey. The sight of her daughter caused worry lines to appear on Mrs Edozie's brow. She had tried to communicate with Nkechi, yearned for her to resurrect from the gloom that surrounded her, but nothing was working.

She tried again. 'Nkechi *biko*, I need you to talk to me. Please say something. Anything.'

Eyes glued to the television screen but without interest, Nkechi made no attempts to respond. Still holding her granddaughter, Mrs Edozie was at a loss. Nkechi's appearance and mental state seemed to be deteriorating before her eyes. Mentally, Mrs Edozie repeated to herself: 'God has not brought us this far to leave us'. Her faith remained strong, even in the midst of a storm. She needed support and prayer, consistently calling on the saints to help her daughter overcome this battle.

'Nkechi, Pastor Onyeka and a few people from the congregation will be coming soon to see you and the baby.'

Upon arrival at Crane Ward, Adaora felt anxious about seeing Paige. That familiar iron-metallic smell exuding from most hospitals captured her nostrils. At the desk, she was informed that visiting hours were almost up, before being pointed in the direction of Paige's room.

Outside, the foster carer stood, in the middle of taking a phone call. They exchanged sorrowful looks before Adaora gently opened the door. A collage of tubes and wires connected to beeping machines covered a peaceful Paige, her eyes firmly closed.

In the chair beside the bed, the social worker sat. Lifting her head to acknowledge Adaora, she managed to muster a small smile. 'Doctor said they pumped all the tablets from her system, and she just needs to rest, now.'

'Okay,' said Adaora. 'I was worried when you both didn't show up today. I just sensed that something was wrong.'

'The past 24 hours have been crazy. I am just so glad that she made it and we are past the worst.'

Walking around the bed, Adaora peered over at Paige's still body, reaching to touch her hand. Adaora squeezed it gently before releasing a sigh. It was devastating to see one of her clients in such a position.

Although Adaora would have loved to stay, noticing the time, she realised she needed to return to look after her niece. Explaining to Leanne that she would visit again the next day, Adaora left quietly.

Her journey home was mudded with contradictory and condemnatory thoughts, as Adaora queried if she had missed any signs with Paige. As her therapist, she felt most qualified to have foreseen such an attempt, and the situation had rocked her confidence. She felt responsible. Guilty. Examining herself, she reflected on all the time she had spent mulling over her relationship with Charles and wondered if she had been distracted; if this had had an adverse effect on the quality of care she was giving to her patients. Coupled with the last few months of taking time off to deal with family emergencies, the inconsistency in appointments could also have had a negative effect. As she drove, she attempted to shake off the pessimistic thoughts before they consumed her.

Pastor Onyeka stood 6 foot 6 tall, and smartly dressed in a sharp three-piece suit; armed with a bible in hand and accompanied by two deacons. Leaving the sleeping baby in the cot, Mrs Edozie came downstairs to greet her guests, inviting them into the living room before attending to their thirst.

Nkechi remained in the same position, looking beyond everyone at the television, desperate for escapism, not willing to be the centre of attention not retaining any of the information. Patiently Pastor Onyeka sat beside her, attempting to engage her in conversation. The deacons, sitting opposite, sipped on bottled water and waited.

After fifteen minutes of one-way conversation, the pastor decided to change techniques.

'Oluchi, can you please go and bring the baby, so I can pray for them both?'

A few minutes later, Mrs Edozie returned, baby in her hands.

'Can we all, please, bow our heads in prayer?'

As Mrs Edozie bent to sit in the sofa, the front door opened and Adaora walked in, startled by the unfamiliar faces, but switching quickly into respectful mode.

'Good evening,' she greeted.

'My daughter, you are welcome.' Pastor Onyeka said, gesturing with his hands for her to enter the room. Adaora bridled slightly at this. *Does he own the place now?*

He continued: 'Please join us – we are about to pray.'

Mrs Edozie waited to see how she was going to react and their eyes met. Walking into the corner nearest to Nkechi, Adaora closed her eyes, but did not bow her head.

'Father, Lord, we are gathered here today to thank you for delivering another miracle unto this world,' the pastor declared. 'You have brought this child to this house for a reason. There is a reason why your love is everlasting. We ask you, Lord, to be with this mother and daughter in Jesus' name.'

'Amen!' Mrs Edozie shouted.

'Father, we know that there are active agents trying to destroy this family. We know there are unknown forces trying to penetrate the happiness of this family, but they shall never succeed – in the name of Jesus. They shall never have the satisfaction of knowing their evil plans have come to fruition. In Jesus' name.'

'Amen!' they all said, except Adaora and Nkechi, who was staring blankly at the muted television screen.

'Father, Lord, we know you have a plan because what God has written, no man shall erase or take away. Be with this family always and forever.'

'Amen!' they replied.

Putting his hands on Nkechi's shoulders, the pastor assured her that everything would be okay, smiling at the baby before making his way to the door. The deacons followed. Mrs Edozie passed the baby to Adaora before heading outside to talk to the pastor.

Adaora smiled at the baby and sat down with her, right next to Nkechi. Ever so slightly, barely noticeably, Nkechi turned her head to glance down at her offspring. Acknowledging the movement, Adaora smiled but did not comment. It was the first time Nkechi had shown any sort of inclination towards the baby.

The baby began to cry, just as Mrs Edozie walked back in saying, 'Give her to me, Adaora. She needs feeding.'

Adaora did as instructed, slightly saddened that her bonding time with her niece had been cut short. Slumping back into the sofa beside Nkechi, she began to fiddle with her hair.

'How are you feeling today?' Adaora asked. She was now used to talking to Nkechi without getting a response. 'I hope you've had a better day than me. Remember my patient I always talk about, Paige? She tried to kill herself yesterday.'

Flinching, Nkechi looked directly at Adaora.

'Yes, it is so sad,' Adaora translated her sister's response. 'I am just coming from the hospital, now. But she is going to be okay, so I am thankful.'

Adaora sat in silence with Nkechi for a moment; then she spontaneously hugged Nkechi and squeezed her tightly.

Adaora continued. 'Today just put things into perspective for me. Paige is just a young girl who wants to be with her sister. She has been separated from her for such a long time – I am guessing she'd had enough and wanted to just end it!' She clasped her forehead, briefly. 'Social Services? I despair. So, I've decided… I now want to reunite her with her sister… if it is the last thing I do. This whole system is stupid and flawed. How can they do that?' Adaora asked, knowing full well she wouldn't get a response. She looked at her sister. 'But no matter what we go through, we will always have each other. Family matters so much. I love you, Kechi, and I am here for you.'

Adaora went to hug her again, but this time, Nkechi held Adaora back. For a moment, staring into one another's eyes, Adaora felt their connection reignite. Taking advantage of the situation, Adaora stood up, held Nkechi's hand and led her to the kitchen. They both stood in the doorway, watching the baby eat as their mother fed her a bottle. A faint smile appeared on Nkechi's face. It was the hope that Adaora wanted to see.

Charles hadn't been able to get Nkechi out of his mind: her lifelessness, the look of devastation pulsing from her eyes; he needed to talk to someone about it. Standing in the foyer pressing the lift button, looking up at the numbers to ascertain when to expect the lift, he began to tap his foot. After a few minutes of waiting, he became impatient and turned to the stairs. Halfway up, he questioned his fitness levels as his breathing became heavy and laboured. Finally reaching the door, Charles took a minute to compose himself before knocking loudly.

'Yes, brother,' Patrick said, opening the door. 'Come in.'

Walking into the apartment, Charles automatically began to remove his shoes, aware that cream carpet did not wear well under grubby soles.

'How have you been?' Charles asked. 'It's been a few weeks.'

'I have been okay,' Patrick replied unconvincingly. 'Just trying to readjust while I find new meaning and motivation to wake up in the mornings.'

'I hear that, bro,' Charles responded, noticing that framed snapshots of a happy couple – the memories of a loving relationship – filled the space, no matter where he looked. Nkechi's arms around

Patrick's neck as they posed at the Eiffel Tower; early pictures of them dating, and right in the centre of the room – an enlarged canvas of them both at the Northern lights, kissing against an illuminated greenish skyline. Patrick caught Charles' eye appraising that picture.

'That is my favourite moment and picture with her,' Patrick said, a beaming smile on his face.

'I can see why,' Charles nodded, rubbing his chin in thought. 'To be honest, that is why I came here today to see you.'

Patrick looked at him, trying to keep a straight face. 'You want to take me to the Northern lights.' He burst into laughter.

Charles rolled his eyes. 'You are never serious.'

Patrick could not stop laughing, but when he realised that Charles was still straight-faced, he stopped. 'Tough crowd.'

Charles still looked serious. 'Patrick, I came here to tell you something important.'

'What is it?'

'It's Nkechi.' Charles paused and looked solemn. 'She's had the baby.'

Stunned, Patrick's face morphed into darkness, the laughter long-evaporated. He suddenly looked very uncomfortable. On one hand, he was upset that Charles knew before him, upset that no one in the family had bothered to let him know. Yet, at the same time, he appreciated Charles coming to inform him.

'Is she okay?' he asked tentatively.

'No, she is far from fine. Physically, she is well and the baby is healthy, but Nkechi… it's so strange, bruv. I went to see her and she didn't even acknowledge me. Or anyone. Adaora said she hasn't even touched the baby at all and won't speak to anyone.'

Patrick's heart began to flutter. He was feeling pain for Nkechi; wishing things were different – that she had made a different decision, or that it had never happened at all.

'I don't even know what to say. I just knew… her having this baby would not be good for her, mentally.'

'She is in a dark place, and she needs all the support she can get. Losing you and then having to go through this part of the trauma alone is too much. She is hardly eating, mate. She is depressed.'

Patrick's body became very heavy, suddenly, and he sat down, rubbing his hands over his face several times.

'I know it is a hard pill to swallow, but you need to go and talk to her. You loved her. Actually – you still love her. You need to man up and go and see her. Sitting here, knowing she is in need, is selfish.'

Patrick muttered, 'I do love her, and hearing that she's in this state is breaking me in pieces. But I can't just up and go get her. Things didn't end well and maybe I'm the last person she wants to see. What if it makes her worse?'

'Well, I don't see how things could get much worse to be honest – but there's only one way to find out. You have to do something.' Charles placed his hands on Patrick's shoulders. 'I am here if you need support, but I want you to understand that she needs you.'

There was no response and Charles was unsure that Patrick had been motivated into action. 'So, are you going to see her?'

Patrick hesitated with his response. 'To be honest, I am not sure. Don't think I can go back, after the way things ended.'

Shaking his head, Charles decided there was no more he could do to convince Patrick. Leaving him to his own conscience, he made his way to the door.

'That is really sad to hear,' he said, before leaving. 'I hope you do the right thing.'

Something had stirred and shifted within Nkechi. Within the household, she was slowly growing more attentive to how her mother handled and fed her child.

Hearing the splashing sounds of her mother bathing the baby, Nkechi reclined in the living room with a newspaper. January 15th 2016 – the headlines declared a progression in the case of a big heist that had occurred in Hatton Gardens in 2015. The case was now in court. Her eyes scanning the words, Nkechi attempted to stay focused on the page but her concentration was wavering.

In her mind, the same phrase kept repeating: 'What God has written.'

It didn't have any relevance to her and she tried to ignore it. However, the phrase kept niggling at her, until she grabbed a pen and paper and scribbled the words down, over and over again.

Walking into the living room with the baby wrapped in a soft white towel, Mrs Edozie was pleasantly surprised to see that her daughter had brought out the Pampers and the powder. Noticing the small shifts in her daughter's behaviour made her heart glad. She praised Jesus in her heart as she began to oil the baby's skin.

Nkechi sat watching closely, until Mrs Edozie gestured for her to help. She hesitated. Then, anxiously, Nkechi took a nappy and tried to put it under the baby's bum. The baby was wriggling around, kicking her legs frantically and Nkechi lost confidence. Her hands started to shake and she took a step back.

Mrs Edozie reassured her. 'Don't worry, my daughter, soon you will be able to do it without any fear,' she said, finishing the task for her.

Once the child was clothed and swaddled in a pink blanket, Mrs Edozie walked towards her daughter and gestured to her to take the baby. Nkechi stretched out her arms tentatively, her heart beating fast, her bottom lip quivering in anticipation.

Mrs Edozie gently placed the baby into Nkechi's arms, helping her to support her head and neck. Nkechi looked at her mum, silently wanting assurance that she was doing the right thing. The baby was warm against her body, and the perfectly round face began to settle as she recognised the scent of her long-lost mother. Nkechi's womb leaped as she bonded with her daughter, staring at her preciousness. So consumed was she by the new connection, she did not even notice that her mother stepped out of the room.

Walking back into the room, Mrs Edozie was armed with a baby bottle. 'Nkechi, you know we cannot keep calling this child "baby". You are yet to name her.'

Nkechi said nothing. It was too much to ask.

Helping to position Nkechi and the baby comfortably, Mrs Edozie instructed Nkechi before handing over the bottle to her.

As the baby fed, taking huge gulps, Mrs Edozie noticed the paper that Nkechi had been scribbling the phrase on. 'Nkechi, did you write this?'

Nkechi nodded, embarrassed.

'Why did you write it so many times?'

Nkechi shrugged. She didn't know why she had written it so obsessively, nor did she know why those words had come into her mind.

'Pastor Onyeka says that phrase all the time, when he prays.'

Nkechi was relieved to realise that the phrase must have come from her memory, although she'd had no recollection of this at the time.

Her mother went on: 'He says it because he believes that when God has a plan for you and it is written, nothing can take that away.' Mrs Edozie paused, and after some consideration, added quietly, 'You know, the Igbo translation of "what God has written" is "Chidera"… That is actually a beautiful name.'

Nkechi gazed down. The bottle was almost finished and she continued looking at the baby. 'Chidera…' Nkechi said softly.

Leaping into the air at the sound of her daughter's voice, and startling Nkechi, Mrs Edozie let forth a mighty 'Praise to God!' and began singing and dancing all over the living room. The burden had been lifted! Her daughter was holding her own daughter and finally the baby had a name!

'It must be God's grace and mercy!' Mrs Edozie sang at the top of her lungs.

'I love the name,' Nkechi said, as she leant down and kissed baby Chidera on the cheek.

Adaora was determined to not be just another professional. She cared about her patients – especially Paige. She had chosen a gorgeous bouquet of flowers, a box of chocolates and a teddy at the local gift shop and walked into the hospital with her hands full. She struggled to push Paige's door open, using her elbow and knee.

Walking in, she saw Paige sitting up in bed, watching the television. Adaora smiled, happy to see her awake. 'So what are we watching then?'

Turning her head, Paige gave her a huge grin and switched off the television with the remote that lay next to her. 'Just earlier episodes of *Friends.*'

Adaora handed her the bunch of pink tulips, which she knew she would love. 'How are you feeling?'

'I am okay, just tired and feeling dizzy.'

'Okay. Doctors say you will be just fine.'

'I am trying to tell them I'm fine, so they can send me home,' Paige said doubtfully. 'But I can't leave just yet.'

'Yes, there are a few protocols they need to follow before that judgement is made.'

Paige emphatically crossed her arms and feet, giving a 'huff' sound in frustration.

'Paige, is it okay if I ask you a few questions?'

'Okay.'

Adaora sat on the chair next to the bed, pulling it closer. 'Why did you try to end it?'

Paige looked down on her bed, hesitating. While she was deep in thought, Adaora, to break the intensity and take the pressure off Paige, took the flowers and put them in a jar of water.

'I was tired of crying myself to sleep every day,' Paige said, to Adaora's busy back. 'I was tired of not being able to see my sister again. And for me, that was the hardest part.'

Adaora sat down again, listening.

'So… ending it all…' Paige swallowed, '… seemed like the only answer… and I thought I was successful until I woke in the hospital.'

'So, being away from Emma was your main factor?'

'Yes,' Paige whispered. 'No matter how many sessions you do with me, as long as Emma and I are apart, I will always have negative thoughts. All I could think about was just being in a peaceful place. I didn't want to deal with it anymore.'

Adaora leant forward. 'I understand totally what you mean by feeling deflated and low because your sister is away and there is nothing you can do to bring her back. I have also had a traumatic time, recently. My sister was kidnapped in Nigeria a few months ago. It was the most difficult time in my life and like you, all that plagued my mind were the negative things that could happen to her. Gradually, I had to start believing that she would be fine. And that is what I want you to do for me. One thing you need to remember is that if you had been successful in ending your pain, you would only be creating a fresh pain for Emma whenever she found out.'

Paige kept her head down, and she picked at her fingernails.

'Paige, look at me,' Adaora said, and the girl's head slowly tilted up. 'I want you to know that I will do all I can to help to reunite you and your sister, because I know what it is like. As children, you both deserve to be happy.'

Paige jerked her head up in surprise and beckoned for Adaora to come closer, then hugged her. 'Thank you!'

'No need to thank me. Sisterhood is important and you and your sister are important. They made a mistake separating you, and I promise to help fix that mistake.'

It was not within her professional capacity or protocol for Adaora to make such promises to a client, and she knew she had crossed professional boundaries, but she was operating from a place of love and empathy. She was determined to reconcile the two sisters.

Chidera was developing, growing chubby, and thriving in the Edozie household. At one month old, her eyes could track her teddy as they danced it across her field of vision, she had discovered her hands and feet, and loved people singing to her. She was a joy, forever smiling and cooing contently. Everyone loved her, and Nkechi was amazed at how much she was changing.

Adaora was so happy that Nkechi was operating as a mother to Chidera now, thankful that the storm seemed to have passed.

She was still conscious of the long-term effects of trauma and depression, so was keeping a close eye on her sister, checking in on her daily. Being an aunt was an amazing experience. Adaora felt an almost unexplainable overwhelming sense of love for her niece and Nkechi loved watching the two bonding. Chidera lit up when her aunty was around, clinging onto her.

Nkechi was thinking more positively and enjoying life again. Being supported by her mum and sister was allowing her the opportunity to get back to her health-conscious goals. Her pre-pregnancy jeans still did not fit and she had no intention of buying a whole new wardrobe, so she actively scheduled short gym sessions when she could, throughout the week. Nkechi was in a happy place, having accepted the blessing she had received, and her faith had also been restored. Chidera was hers, and she brought a level of happiness that she had never experienced before, which no one could take away from her.

The lovers' festival had come and gone. The red roses, hearts and constant reminders to single people that they were alone, were finally over. Adaora sat in her office between clients, pondering on Charles. She kept flicking through his Facebook page, his pictures causing her to miss him even more. They hadn't had any contact since the hospital, but Adaora had been unable to get him off her mind since that day. It had revived all the feelings she had tried to suppress. Sipping her coffee and flicking through her phone, she fantasised about what she would say if she did call. Mid-daydream, her thumb distractedly pressed the call button and before she was even aware of it, she heard the phone ringing and scrabbled to see what she had done. It was too late. His name shone from the screen and he answered.

Alarmed, she put the phone to her ear and took a deep breath. 'Hey, Charles! How are you?'

'I'm good,' he said, his voice puzzled. 'How are you? Is everything okay?'

'Yes, all is well,' she blustered, her face burning. 'Just thought I'd say hi.'

'That's nice of you,' he said, even more bewildered. 'Hey, I would love to talk, but I am actually about to step into a meeting. I'll speak to you another time. Take care.'

She froze in horror and humiliation. The call disconnected and an immediate cloud of regret descended over her head and refused to budge all day.

Most of Patrick's days were spent in the company of criminals. He had seen them all – old, young, male, female. In holding cells and interview rooms, he had a show-reel of information about behaviours, similarities and differences. But one thing was consistent. Guilty people wore their regret like sunglasses. It darkened their facial features, clouded their moods. And after reflection, he would see it hover on the end of their noses as they shook their heads in dismay.

One afternoon, as Patrick was ending a long day in court, he looked at his reflection and immediately recognised that he, also, was wearing regret. And it weighed heavy. Ever since Charles had given him the news about Nkechi, weeks before, he had battled with whether to make contact or not. What would it achieve? Could he live with Nkechi having that child? Could he live without her? Had she changed so much? Would she ever forgive him, anyway? His fear of rejection had won. Up to now. But, recalling the specific young man he had represented, whose regret was so strong that he had accepted responsibility and pleaded guilty, even though he could have been easily acquitted, Patrick also was determined to follow his example, and right a wrong. Grabbing his keys, he made his way to the Edozie household.

Fear arrested him, his heart beating a grim instrumental. Plucking up all the courage he could, he knocked on the door.

A few moments later, seeing Patrick outside the open door, Chidi scowled. 'What do you want?'

'Is Nkechi here?'

'Yes, but I don't think she would want to see you.'

'Chidi, can you please call her for me?'

Leaving the door slightly ajar, Chidi walked to the kitchen, his face a mess of anger, his hands curled into fists. Nkechi, Adaora and Gloria looked up and saw his expression.

Nkechi spoke first. 'Who is at the door?'

Chidi could not bear to cause his sister pain. He opened and closed his fists, unsure how to respond.

'Chidi,' Nkechi repeated impatiently. 'Who is at the door?'

Under his breath, Chidi muttered, 'Patrick.'

'Who?'

'Patrick!'

'TELL HIM TO GET LOST!' Nkechi shouted, getting up from her chair in blind rage. Obscenities began to flow from her lips like rivers; her voice becoming increasingly louder with every sentence. 'Of all the times! Now! He chooses now. After I've found peace, he comes to disturb my stillness.'

Patrick could hear the commotion, and shifted uneasily on the doorstep. Chidi came back, his face stern as flint. 'I told you… Go away,' he said, slamming the door shut.

In the kitchen, while Gloria looked on in horror, Adaora was attempting to calm Nkechi down. 'Sis, sis – listen to me…'

'The audacity of that low-life prick! Turning up here, after all this time! What the…'

'Nkechi! Please, you're going to wake Chidera. Sit down.' Adaora stood up to go to the front door.

Nkechi's face was strained; small veins pulsating on her forehead. 'Don't you dare go out there and talk to him, Ada! He doesn't deserve it.' After a few minutes of ranting, Nkechi had tired herself out and sat back down. 'I still can't believe he thought he could come here and I'd just walk out to see him,' she murmured, her chest heaving lightly.

'Maybe you should have just heard what he had to say,' Adaora said. 'That's just my opinion.'

'Well, I personally think you did the right thing,' Gloria added. 'What is there to say? We all know what he did. It's simple. Get lost.'

'Exactly!' Nkechi exclaimed, raising her hands. 'I have nothing to say to him and I do not want to hear anything from him, so let's just leave that conversation there. Thanks.'

Adaora was stunned at Nkechi's reaction. It had been years since she had shown such anger. In her teenage years, Adaora had had to step in a few times, in school, to stop Nkechi fighting other girls, but she had thought those days were behind her. For Patrick to cause her this much pain and anguish showed Adaora just how hurt Nkechi was.

Cries came from the baby monitor.

'Ada, could you please get her…' Nkechi said, trying to calm down. '… while I clean up before I feed her?'

'Sure,' Adaora said, jumping at the chance.

After a few minutes, Adaora brought Chidera downstairs. The baby was rubbing her eyes and whingeing for food. Sitting in the living room, back propped up with a few cushions, Nkechi reached for her breastfeeding pillow and placed Chidera on it. Unclipping one cup of her nursing bra, Nkechi guided Chidera to the nipple. It had been a real struggle introducing breast milk to Chidera after she had adapted to the bottle, and Nkechi had wanted to give up a number of times, but looking down at her daughter, she was thankful she had persevered. The bond was beautiful.

Eyes rich with pride, Nkechi stood outside St Monica's Catholic Church a couple of days later, on a fine June day, holding Chidera and smiling while the photographer snapped pictures of them. It was a special day. After the mother and daughter pictures, the rest of the family and friends were asked to gather for a photo. Nkechi looked around, pleased that her child was surrounded by so much love, culture and faith. Gurgling, babbling and playing with her mother's bracelets, Chidera looked adorable in a long white lace dress, enjoying being the centre of attention. Mrs Edozie motioned to the priest to join them for the pictures. After baptising Chidera, he was happy to oblige. Once she had bonded with the baby, Nkechi had always planned to baptise Chidera, believing in the significance of demonstrating her commitment to raising Chidera up to know God and be strong in her faith.

Now six months old, Chidera was already loving time on her tummy, making motions to crawl. A gem in the family, she continued to bring joy to everyone around her. Mrs Edozie had always told Nkechi that Chidera's complexion would get darker; that babies had various shades of black to their ear and would always end up the same tone of black as at the top of the ear. Sure enough, she now matched Nkechi's skin-tone.

After church, the Edozie family and a few friends went back to the house to eat and drink to continue the celebration. There was double the reason to celebrate: the results for Chidi's repeated first year had shown that he had passed with flying colours.

Later on that evening, when everyone had left, Nkechi and Adaora spent time in the garden under a bright full moon. A slight breeze was much welcome after the humidity that had made the day sticky. Chidera was in Adaora's arms, slowly drifting to sleep.

Adaora looked at her fondly, and then up at Nkechi. 'Kechi, what you have done is truly beautiful. Not many women would have the strength to do what you have done.'

Nkechi seemed a little confused. 'What do you mean?'

'Everything that has happened in the last year... to now love a baby that was conceived in the most horrible way. I know, at the start, it wasn't easy to get to this point, but the fact that you have is a testament of your strength.'

'I could not have done it without the support of our family and friends. Especially you, Ada.'

'Every time I look at Chidera, my heart warms,' Adaora smiled. 'She has brought this family closer together.'

'She is surrounded by people who love her, and that's all I can really ask for. I am thankful for her life and for the love and support we both have. Not many women in my position have that same luxury, so it is never good for us to judge another person's circumstances.'

'That is very true.'

'Ada, I have seen the way you look at Chidera,' Nkechi began, gently. 'And you have a bigger connection with her than anyone else. I think she is even fonder of you than me. From day one, you have carried her and held her as if she was your own. Is there any possib…'

'I know what you are going to say,' Adaora stopped Nkechi in her tracks. 'And if I am totally honest, this thought has been running through my head non-stop… and I still do not fully understand. I now think about what it would be like to be a mother myself. It's not just because I have looked after Chidera: many of my friends in the past have had children and I have carried them and been around them. For some reason, this feels different.'

Nkechi's eyes lit up. 'Ada – what are you saying?'

'I don't know what I am saying.'

'Well, I will say it for you. I AM GOING TO BE AN AUNT!'

'Kechi, you are so silly.' Adaora looked down at Chidera. 'Be quiet, before you wake her.'

Chapter Twelve

A CHORUS OF BLACK MEN — COMMUNICATING, DEBATING, AND DISAGREEING. The noise was like family; comfort in a community of men, of all ages, experiences, and a plethora of opinions. Reclining in black leather chairs they sat, peering at their reflections in the mirror opposite, awaiting transformation by skilled hands. It was a relationship built on trust; of understanding of hairlines, and mutual respect. The barbers were attentive; not just to haircuts and styles, but to their customers. They listened as clippers buzzed; shaping foreheads and shaping lives. There was no rush: each customer was permitted a counselling session. A personal experience, a one-to-one connection.

Smooth Cuts was a hub in the community, cutting hair for generations. Patrick had found solace in its sanctuary for over a decade and was loyal to his barber; even introducing Charles to him. Realising that regrowth was attempting to make a comeback and his neck hairs were grisly, Patrick was due a shave. Sitting in the corner of the shop, he waited for Charles to arrive. It was packed, at least 6 people in front of Patrick.

Two barbers stood, equipment in hand, like skilled hair surgeons in theatre. Scales, Patrick's barber, was 6ft tall, with a belly laugh and a wise tongue. His weight, carried around his midsection, had led to his nickname.

Charles walked in, weaving between the conversations, to where Patrick was sitting, looking distant. Charles sat down next to him.

'P. What's going on? Are you okay?'

Patrick sighed a long exhalation of regret. He placed his right hand over his face and cringed. 'Charles, I messed up big time.'

'What happened?'

'I took your advice and I went to see Nkechi…'

'And?'

'Full shut-down, bro. She was not having it at all.'

Charles shook his head empathetically, unsure what to say.

Scanning his customers, Scales looked over and saw Patrick looking unusually despondent. 'Bruv – what's happening? You're looking mighty stressed over there.'

Realising that his face must be giving him away Patrick tried to find a smile. 'Long story,' he replied, flatly.

'P, I know that look. There is only one type of problem that would give a man that look – and that is a woman.' Scales pointed with his clippers. 'As men, we have many stressful looks: the look when your car fucks up, the look when your money is low, and the family-causing-stress look. But that look, there, is women trouble.'

As Scales analysed his life, Patrick couldn't help but smile genuinely. Known as 'the therapist', Scales could discern people's emotions in an instant, and he was definitely a master of all things women-related.

'So, what is the problem?' Scales asked.

'Long story short, I messed up and now I am trying to get her back, but she shut me down.' Patrick shuffled in his seat, knowing that ears were open, and he didn't want to share all his personal information with strangers.

Scales nodded, focusing on his customer's hair. 'Classic problem. As men, we all fuck up on a regular basis, but trying to get back in the good books is an art-form. Many men don't think before they act, even when they mean well. From what you have said, and I don't know the nitty gritty details, but... you have to ask yourself this: Do you know what you want, after your apology? Are you in a position to fulfil what you have said? If not, you are wasting your time and hers.' Scales carried on cutting.

'I hear you, Scales. Trust me, I hear you.' Patrick faced Charles. 'What do you think? Obviously, you know all the details. What do I do?'

Charles looked at his friend, seeing the worry in his eyes; desperately seeking answers. 'Well, P, Scales has given some good advice already. It really resonated with regards to this situation. So, the question is for you to answer. What is your long-term plan? You want to apologise, I get that, but then what? The baby is here now and is a major part of her life. Are you ready to accept the baby? This is deeper than just you and her.'

Listening to Charles' response, Patrick's brain started ticking. The consequences of trying to reconcile with Nkechi had been illuminated. 'I guess I haven't really thought about it like that. All I wanted was to just speak to her.'

Charles put his hand on Patrick's shoulder. 'You have to know for sure before you try to see her again. But don't give up; keep trying till you make things right.'

'I will do. Thanks, man. I appreciate the advice.'

Although being a mother was a beautiful thing, all Nkechi's time was consumed with the daily tasks of being a parent: night feeds, schedules, bath-times. Nkechi often looked at her reflection in the mirror and wondered how her body was able to adjust to sleep deprivation overnight. When the opportunity arose for some baby-free time, Nkechi jumped at the chance – even monotonous chores like food shopping. With her mum watching Chidera, Nkechi and Adaora drove to Tesco to do the weekly shop. It was a welcome change of scenery for Nkechi and some much-appreciated 'sister time' for them both.

Pushing the trolley, Nkechi strode through the aisles with purpose, directing Adaora to the various items they needed for the house. Scanning the shelves for the beer their dad had ordered, they loaded a few into the trolley. He was adamant about having enough cold beer to drink now that the football was back on. They continued shopping, then suddenly Nkechi stopped abruptly.

'What's the matter?' asked Adaora.

'I'm not too sure about that beer we bought. I'm sure he said Stella; not Becks.'

'Just text him, in case. You know how dad is.'

Nkechi took her phone out of her pocket and typed a quick message. A few moments later the phone buzzed. Mr Edozie confirmed it was Stella he wanted, and the girls went back to change the beer over.

'Just as well you checked. Our lives wouldn't be worth living!' laughed Adaora.

Crossing things off their list, they continued to shop.

'Nkechi, look how many vegan products are now available.'

'Yeah, there is quite a range now, but the prices are no joke.'

'Yes, living clean is expensive. Charles was actually thinking about trying it for 6 months. I wonder if he did...' Mentioning his name, Adaora's thoughts began to spin. She stood awkwardly in the middle of the aisle, picturing his features, his muscular tone, his voice...

Nkechi tapped her on the shoulder. 'So... Ada, guess what I have been looking up?' Nkechi asked, steering the trolley widely around a five-year-old who was running in circles.

'What might that be?' Adaora queried, smiling at the toddler's antics.

'There is a community online of women who have previously said they do not want children, but are now thinking about it – or have actually had children and were glad they'd made that decision.'

'Sounds interesting...' Adaora smiled, knowing that Nkechi had conducted the online search in her favour. 'What did you find out?'

'I was reading this woman's story, and she reminded me so much of you. Never wanted children, very career-driven, unable to sustain relationships.'

'Whaaat?' Adaora exploded, coughing.

'You know what I mean,' Nkechi laughed. 'She was very successful but even with all the success and money, there was an emptiness inside she couldn't place. It took a near-death experience to change her perspective. She realised she wanted to leave a legacy, through her offspring. She became a mother at 41!'

'Mmmm,' Adaora replied, thoughtfully. 'What a turnaround. I guess everyone's purpose is different. Sometimes what we think we want is not actually what we desire. People can change their minds.'

With the trolley overflowing with goods, they made their way to the checkout, carefully placing the food items in categories on the belt. Adaora seemed deep in thought.

Nkechi whispered to her: 'What are you thinking?'

'The fact that I never felt like this before. I am wondering what happened to the strong opposition I felt.'

'Well, something's changed in you. I guess like you said, maybe what you thought you wanted is no longer what you want. I'm just excited at the mere possibility, Ada. You're such a natural with Chidera,' she said, placing items into her shopping bag as they were rung through the till. 'And I've always wanted you to be happy. Every failed relationship you've had has been hard for me to endure. Especially with Charles. I could tell you loved him. And… now the barrier that stopped you has gone…'

Adaora looked at her. 'What am I supposed to do now?'

'Find Charles. Talk to him. Do not worry about all that chasing a man bullshit – pardon my French. Sometimes, in life, our inaction damages and limits opportunity. My advice is to talk to Charles and have a conversation.'

Adaora smiled and gave Nkechi a hug.

Nkechi tutted. 'Ada, save your hug for later. The lady is waiting for us to pay.'

Fuelled with hope after the conversation with her sister, Adaora's thoughts continued to whirl as they made their way home. With Nkechi singing out loud to the radio, Adaora sat silently next to her, deep in thought about Charles. Since his name was inscribed on her brain, she began to allow herself to open up to a potential future. But, as she pictured being back in his arms, negativity began to creep in her daydreams. Because with her fantasies, she remembered the last time she had tried to reach out to him – when he never called back.

Stomach growling, Adaora looked up from her computer at the clock and realised that it was time for lunch. Collecting her bag and coat, she walked along the main road, ever aware of the fast-food outlets and lack of healthy options for lunch. She had a craving for a gorgeous Caesar salad, since the thought of greasy burgers and fatty chips sitting in her abdomen for the remainder of the day made her want to vomit. Contemplating going into Marks and Spencer's for a decent sandwich, she noticed the great number of people spilling into pubs on both sides of the road. Curious, she popped her head into the doorway of one of the pubs and saw a tremendous crowd of football lovers glaring at high-definition televisions, hands full of cold pints, in anticipation. Adaora shook her head, wondering how she could have forgotten – after buying all the beer for her dad – it was England versus Wales; the group stages of the European cup. The fans had deserted their jobs for the privilege of watching twenty-two men chase a ball around a pitch. Amazed at their excitement, Adaora continued walking until she found a quiet, cosy Mediterranean restaurant.

Sitting in a comfortable booth, Adaora ordered her salad and a small glass of red wine, before turning her attention to the decor. A lover of art, she appreciated the attention to detail: the canvases on the walls, the candles, all adding to the overall feel. Her stomach started to growl. Aware that the restaurant wasn't busy, she hoped her food would be quickly prepared.

Without a book to read, Adaora began to use the time to consider her affection towards Charles. An internal conflict began, over whether to call him or not, and she battled her indecisiveness throughout her meal. Hunger gone, head clear, plate empty, Adaora reached for her phone and dialled his number. She heard his voicemail kick in and hung up.

The waiter walked over. He was tall with a stubbled beard and eyes the same colour as the ocean – and Adaora was caught off-guard by how clean-cut and handsome he looked. She could easily see him on the front cover of a men's fashion magazine.

'I hope everything was to your satisfaction, madam,' he said, meaningfully, looking into her eyes. If she wasn't mistaken, he was flirting with her.

'Yes, the food was amazing and I will definitely be back.'

'Fantastic.' He asked, 'Would you like some dessert?'

'No, thank you,' she said primly. 'Just the bill, please.'

Leaving the restaurant, Adaora's eager fingers dialled Charles again: same outcome. Disappointed, Adaora walked back to the office.

With only a few clients to see, she was finished early. She sat reclined in the office chair, replaying the conversation she had with Nkechi and letting her imagination run wild. Charles had to be the one for her, she thought. She had never felt this kind of intense emotion about anyone. And now her feelings had shifted about motherhood, the need to call him, to hear his voice, and communicate her heart, deepened. Hearing his voicemail again, she became anxious to go around and see him, urgently.

Before she knew it, she was in the driver's seat, key in the ignition, driving to his workplace. She had no plan. No strategy. Hoping that when their eyes met, all anger would melt and he would embrace her with longing.

Parked up, she applied lip balm, checking herself out in the sunscreen mirror; briefly fixed her hair and took a deep breath.

Walking towards the foyer, she was overcome with expectations; her heart thundering in the back of her throat. Attempting to keep her composure, she walked towards the receptionist, who smiled at her in recognition. As far as she knew, Adaora was still Charles's partner.

'Hi. I was just wondering if Charles is here at the moment.'

'Yes, he is,' the receptionist replied, scanning the calendar on her screen. 'Is he expecting you?'

'No, it's just a quick visit. I couldn't reach him on the phone.'

'Ok, well, he has no meetings booked in, so I'm sure it will be fine. Please go straight through.'

First hurdle overcome. She had made it – and he was in.

Surging in her chest, there was an overwhelming tightness that Adaora tried to shake off. She ignored urges to run back to the parking lot, and prepared her mind to see the man she was in love with. She was ready – to apologise, to explain, to be vulnerable in front of him. All her walls had collapsed; her heart was wide open. She needed him. But first, she needed to catch her breath and steady herself.

As she stood in the foyer, about 15 metres away, the lift door opened and Charles stepped out. Adaora's stomach was in knots, her knees weak, her mouth dry. Pressing her lips together, she waited excitedly for him to turn and see her. But Charles's attention was back in the lift - he reached in his hand and drew out a beautiful, tall, caramel-skinned woman by her hand. She was giggling and Charles leaned in towards her, his hand around her waist, to give her a kiss.

As if she had been slapped, Adaora backed out of the foyer quickly, before he could see her and left, asking the receptionist not to mention her visit.

Her face flushed, her eyes stinging, Adaora was a mass of emotional confusion. Embarrassed, she scolded herself for being so stupid, as she tried to drive through salty tears that blurred her vision.

Finally home, she slumped onto her sofa, a fresh carton of Ben and Jerry's Cookie Dough on her lap, and dialled Nkechi.

'I went to see Charles.' Adaora stopped. Silence lingered for a few seconds.

'What happened?' Nkechi asked, tentatively.

'Nkechi, all I wanted was to just be with him. I was willing to do whatever it took to be with him!' Adaora wailed.

'What happened?'

'I wasted too much time. Mum was right, this whole time. I met the man of my dreams and I let him slip through my fingers. Mum was right!'

'Ada, calm down and tell me what happened.'

'I tried calling him but I think he must have changed his number, so I went to his office and… he was there, but… argh. I saw him kissing another woman!'

On the other end of the phone, Nkechi covered her face with her hand. It was a shock to hear and Nkechi wished she could be with Adaora to comfort her. She had come through such a journey to get to this point for Charles, and Nkechi could only imagine what it felt like to have it all ripped away.

'Oh, Ada. I'm so sorry. I really thought you two were made for each other. It seems he has moved on. In any other situation, I would say "keep fighting" but… having another woman involved – it gets complicated.'

'I know…' Adaora said miserably. 'They looked happy together.'

'Did they see you?'

'I don't think so. I managed to sneak out quickly. I was so embarrassed.'

'Oh, hun. You poor thing. It must be so difficult. I know how much you care for him. But there are plenty of fine men out there who would love a chance to be with you. But... I think you might just have to let Charles go.'

Adaora swallowed. All her fears confirmed. 'Mmmm. I agree. This is not healthy. Look at me, for Christ's sake! I am acting like a schoolgirl.'

'Love will do that to you. You tried your best and did everything you could. Now, you have to focus on yourself.'

'Part of me feels so stupid. I could have had it all. Now I've lost it. I guess it's time to move on.' Adaora had been saying this over and over to herself. She desperately wanted to believe what she was saying, but her mouth and heart were not in sync. 'How is Chichi?'

'She is fine. She is asleep, having her nap.'

'That is too cute. Well, Kechi, let me leave you. I know you must have a lot to get through for work. Thanks for listening, sis.'

'Yeah, if you need to stay busy, feel free to help me with all this marking!' Nkechi joked, trying to lighten the mood.

'You know I don't need your help to stay busy, Kechi. But thanks for the offer. Give Chidera a kiss from aunty when she wakes up.'

'I will. Love you.'

'Love you, too. Bye.'

Nkechi put the phone down and decided to fold some laundry while Chidera was asleep; but before she could finish the task, she heard the telling groans of a hungry baby. Leaving the clothes, she went upstairs to soothe Chidera. The peaceful sounds of a sleeping baby were long gone and Chidera was in full-blown meltdown mode. Needing her hands to prepare the bottle, Nkechi attempted to wrap Chidera with some Ankara material tied around her back. Despite her efforts, the wriggling Chidera was making it difficult to secure her and after a few attempts Nkechi gave up, took Chidera downstairs and placed her in her play pen. Waiting for the kettle to boil, Nkechi tapped her foot impatiently, aware that Chidera was restless. The wails from the other room continued as she scooped formula into a freshly sterilised bottle. Whilst counting scoops, Nkechi heard the door bell, completely throwing off her counting. There was no one else home and Chidera's wail had escalated; so Nkechi screwed the lid on, shook the bottle and in a 'supermum' movement, picked up Chidera and, balancing her on her right hip, walked towards the door. Thankful to be near her mother, Chidera quieted, playing with her mother's clothes.

'Who is it?' Nkechi queried, before opening the door a fraction.

On the other side, Patrick stood solemnly, nervous. Seeing him, Nkechi was irritated and attempted to close the door; but Patrick caught it.

'Nkechi, please hear me out,' he pleaded.

Chidera looked at the stranger at the door and began to babble, smile and reach out for him. Witnessing such innocence, Patrick felt guilt strangle him, and he was unable to speak. Locking eyes with Chidera, Patrick's heart melted, his legs felt weak.

The hesitation began to irritate Nkechi. 'Patrick, say what you have to say. As you can see, I am busy.' She continued shaking the bottle to mix the formula.

Eyes still glued to Chidera, who was playfully attempting to grab his royal blue tie, Patrick did not respond to Nkechi. Taking a step back, Nkechi removed Chidera from its temptation.

'Patrick, I don't have time for this. Move from the door and don't let me see you here again. Or I will not be as calm.'

This time, Patrick made no attempt to stop the door from closing and Nkechi slammed it shut, kissing her teeth. She juggled Chidera on her hip as she checked the temperature of the milk on her hand, and retreated to the living room.

Seeing his face had dampened her mood.

Sitting behind her desk, Adaora sat looking at Paige's file. She tried to focus on the words but they all became merged as she drifted into a daydream. She couldn't stop thinking about Charles; all the special moments would come flooding back to her in a show-reel of remembrance before ending in the image of his lips on another woman.

Frustrated that he was still affecting her thought processes, Adaora snapped out of her daze, sat up straighter in her chair and gave herself a pep talk. There was no time to live in the past. He had moved on. She would, too.

Readjusting her focus, Adaora looked at the screen of her phone and dialled the number she had looked up. 'Hi, my name is Dr Adaora Edozie. I am looking for a Mr Christopher Edwards.'

'Sorry, he no longer works here. He left a few months ago.'

'Do you know where he went?'

'I'm sorry. I don't.'

'Ok. Thank you,' Adaora replied, before hanging up the phone.

Adaora was determined to make this right. She had promised Paige, and she was a woman of integrity. Shaking off the distractions of Charles, she worked on her strategies to find Mr Edwards – making lists, searching the internet, looking through the file for any clues. Concerned that this was the key piece to Paige's well-being, and understanding that no-one else was going out of their way to locate Mr Edwards motivated Adaora more.

An hour later, with no solid leads, frustration set in.

Hesitating on the front step of the house, Patrick took a deep breath. The detached house with oak windows, a freshly cut lawn and beautiful, arching trees held his childhood memories between its bricks. After a few moments, he took out the front door key and opened it.

His parents were sitting together on the sofa, watching a Nollywood film. Surprised by his presence, they exchanged looks before acknowledging him.

'Good evening,' Patrick greeted, shifting from one leg to the other, standing awkwardly in the doorway.

His mum turned to look at him. 'So, Patrick. You managed to find your way back here. Look how many months have passed since you have graced our door.'

Her tone held a mass of disappointment, which weighed Patrick down. Shame immediately sat upon his shoulders. There were no words. No defence. He had neglected his family, without warning, without explanation. The bitterness hung in the air.

His father cut the silence. 'Patrick, how can we help you?'

Neck bowed, eyes firmly on the floor, Patrick struggled to articulate. He began to mumble.

'Speak up, Patrick,' his dad said.

Patrick looked up and cleared his throat. 'Mum, Dad – I am sorry that I haven't been in contact for months. I let many people down and I just needed be alone.'

340

'*Onye nzuzu!* Patrick – you are a new type of fool!' Mrs Eze yelled.

'*Wetuo Obi biko.* Calm down – let him finish,' Mr Eze said calmly, patting his wife's arm gently. He nodded at Patrick to continue.

'I know I have disappointed you. I know that the way things ended between me and Nkechi hurt you. I was selfish. I made mistakes. But I am ready to make things right. I have had time to really think, and ponder over everything, and it has been eating me up inside. I want to make it better, but I don't know how.'

'Patrick, your behaviour has brought real shame to this family,' his father said. 'How can you act so irresponsibly? Things were happening, and you did not once come here to seek advice from me, your mother or any of your uncles. Why?' Mr Eze paused and looked at Patrick, but no reply followed.

'When was the last time you saw Nkechi?' Mrs Eze asked.

'I went to see her yesterday, but she refused to see me.'

'Why wouldn't she refuse?' she replied, sarcastically. 'How about the baby? What is the situation?'

'She ended up having a baby girl, and they are both doing fine, from what I saw.' An involuntary smile teased his lips at the thought of Chidera's chubby fingers squeezing his tie.

'That is good to hear. Nkechi is such a strong girl!' Mrs Eze replied. 'So, Patrick, it is not until things have reached rock bottom that you remembered you have a family to help?' his mother scolded.

'*Biko, nyere m aka?*' Patrick pleaded.

His Igbo was rusty, but he needed to soften his parents up. It worked on his mother, who stood up and embraced him. Patrick was teary-eyed but managed to keep the tears firmly in their docks.

'It will be well, my son,' Mrs Eze said.

'Patrick, we have heard what you have to say but I am not sure how we can help you at this stage,' Mr Eze said. 'It takes a man to know when he has done wrong. Even though it has taken you time, well done for coming home, my son.'

Back in the arms of his parents, Patrick felt a sense of relief.

After spending a few hours with them, Patrick went to Shoreditch to meet up with a few friends for a game of five-a-side football.

When he arrived, he saw that only Charles and Kola were there, in the distance, ready. Shin pads on, yellow socks pulled up, Patrick walked over and greeted them both with a firm handshake.

'How are you both doing?' Patrick asked, as they walked to the pitch.

'I'm good, brother. Can't wait to kick ball,' Kola replied.

'Yes, it's been a while. Hope my lungs are still in good order.' Patrick looked around. They were still covered in darkness. 'No floodlights? I can barely see my own hands.'

As they approached the dark green carpet, the floodlights came on. 'That's more like it,' Charles said, rubbing his hands together.

'What have you been up to all day?' Kola enquired.

'Work, then I went to see my parents.' He added, 'Yeah. I needed to see them. To speak about Nkechi.' Charles lifted his eyebrow and Patrick explained: 'I had to ask for help. I have been really struggling with it all. It was hard, going back to my parents, but it had to be done.' Removing his trousers, Patrick exposed his hairy legs. In his shorts, he felt ready to play. Grabbing the ball, he began practising some footwork.

'Did you try and talk to Nkechi again?' Charles asked.

'Yeah, I went over to the house, but she wasn't interested in anything I had to say. She wasn't shouting this time, but she made herself very clear. I could have done more, to be honest, but I completely froze.' Patrick passed the ball to Charles who kicked it to Kola, who was busying himself with his stretches.

'What do you mean, you froze?'

'Like, literally. She came to the door and everything I had planned to say disappeared. She was there, holding the baby, and I just froze...' Patrick shook his head. 'I fucked up big time, Charles. When you first told me Nkechi'd had the baby, a sinking feeling in the pit of my stomach appeared and it hasn't gone. It was worse when I saw her and the baby.'

Charles signalled for Kola to come over. He put his hands on Patrick's shoulders. 'What's done is done. There is no way we can change the past. We can only work on changing the course of the future.'

'P, listen. As Charles said, focus on what you can do now – and just do it. Let the past be. If not, that sinking feeling you have will consume you.'

'Thanks, boys. I really appreciate the support. I love her so much. I am willing to do whatever it takes to get her back,' Patrick said, with a little more bass and zest to his tone.

Kola kicked the ball at Patrick, who managed to control it and keep the ball close to him.

'Enough of all this soppy shit. Can we man up and kick some ball?' Kola said, mockingly.

'We still have to wait for the rest of the lads to show up, first,' Charles replied.

Patrick kicked the ball as far as he could and Kola was eager to retrieve it. 'So, Charles, how are things with you?'

'I'm good. I met someone else.'

'Seriously?' Patrick felt stung – he didn't know if it was on Adaora's behalf, or his own tiny pang of envy.

'Yeah. Had to move on.'

Kola came running back with the ball. 'What are you two talking about, now, looking so serious? Aren't you going to warm up?'

'Hold on. Charles was just telling me he has a new woman in his life. So, details, bro.'

Kola rolled his eyes and stood fidgeting with the ball, uninterested in the conversation.

'Her name is Felicity. She's 30 and works as a financial analyst in the city.' Patrick nodded, impressed. Charles went on: 'She is cool, I like her.'

'So, you are happy, then?' Kola stated.

'Yes, I am,' Charles replied, with a smile on his face.

'Wonderful,' Kola said sarcastically, before dragging them both to the centre of the pitch.

Not long afterwards, the rest of the players arrived and Kola finally got to play the game of football he was so desperate for.

Finally, progress had been made. After all the hours spent on the end of the phone, and the relentless emails over several months, the search was over. Adaora made her way to meet Paige's dad, feeling a huge sense of achievement and relief. There had been moments when it had felt like an impossible task, but her perseverance had served her well.

Driving through central London traffic, in an effort to get to South Croydon, Adaora glanced at the time, hoping she would not be late, since Mr Edwards had already informed her of his busy work schedule. With a few minutes to spare, Adaora found a parking space and walked briskly into the small cafe they had agreed to meet in. The lunch hour rush was in full effect and the walls were sweating with local builders ordering huge plates of food. Finding a free table, Adaora slid into the seat and ordered an orange juice. Eyes firmly on the door, she waited for Mr Edwards.

A short man with a light complexion and an abundance of freckles walked in. Initially, Adaora disregarded him, but as he walked towards her with some purpose, she realised that he must be Paige's dad.

'Good afternoon – Mr Edwards?' Adaora greeted.

'Yes. Afternoon, Dr Edo…' He paused.

'It's fine. Just call me Adaora.'

'Okay,' Mr Edwards sat down, looking around nervously, his hands twitching. Sweat had broken out on his forehead.

'Are you okay?' Adaora asked.

'I'm fine. I just have a condition that makes me very uncomfortable in crowded places.'

'Would you like to go elsewhere?'

'It's fine.' Paige's dad looked sideways at the builders. 'These lads will soon leave.'

'Can I get you anything?'

'A glass of water would be great, thank you.'

Adaora signalled to the waiter, who took the order and quickly brought over both of their drinks. Adaora took a sip of the orange juice, which tasted cheap and bitter.

She put down the glass and smiled. 'Well, firstly, I would like to thank you for meeting with me. As I said on the phone, I have been working with Paige for a while and I am very fond of her. I know there are many unanswered questions she has about her upbringing and I hope we can clear some of those up between us.'

'Thank you for getting in touch,' Mr Edwards said, his trembling hands making his water shake in its glass. 'It was a shock when I got the call. I have missed my girls every day for years, so this opportunity means so much to me.'

'Could you please tell me what happened?' Adaora asked. 'And why you lost contact with the girls and their mother?'

At the mention of their mother, Mr Edwards got very tense and took anxious sips of his water.

'I realise this must be difficult, Mr Edwards. Please take your time.'

After a few moments, Mr Edwards looked over Adaora's head, as if gazing into the past, and began to explain. 'Well, it is a long story, and I don't think I can get it to all of it, but I'll give you the short version. I am an old-school grafter. I make an honest living and I looked after my girls. Always did. But their mother, she wanted more. Wanted to be spoilt with expensive items that I couldn't afford and it was a real source of tension between us. She cheated on me, got herself a richer fella and wanted me gone. She started making wild accusations to the police about me, until one day I came home and… the girls… her… they were all gone. I tried to call the police, tried to get help, but no one cared. No one believed me. I tried, but I am not very well and get very weak quite quickly. I couldn't afford to pay anyone to help, so eventually, I had to stop looking.'

'How terrible! I'm so sorry you had to go through this Mr Edwards. Hopefully, we can right some wrongs.'

'I just want my girls back. Emma was just a baby. You said you have been working with Paige. How is my little angel?'

The cafe had emptied. Adaora looked empathetically at Mr Edwards who was attempting to hide his shaky hands.

'Well, she is very emotional, sir. Things have not been going too well and she was struggling to cope… Unfortunately, she ended up in hospital.'

'Hospital?' He looked up, concerned. 'Is she okay?'

'She's getting better. I don't really want to get in to it, here,' Adaora said, looking around, 'but I have brought you the contact numbers and forms to get in touch with social services. I'm hopeful that you will get access to her. It should help to answer a lot of the gaps in her memory.'

'Thank you so much,' Mr Edwards said, squeezing Adaora's hand, his eyes full of tears.

The months were melting into each other. Calendar pages fell and summer was buried for another year, paving the way for grey skies and crying clouds. Adaora marvelled at how quickly time was passing. Every time she looked at Chidera, she had grown, learnt a new skill, got heavier, or was making new sounds. She was a constant reminder of the passage of time. Adaora loved babysitting her, since spending time with her niece gave them an opportunity to develop a unique bond. She sat on her parents' sofa, watching, with awe, Chidera's agility in crawling around the room. She was on a mission to collect all the scattered balls and return them to the play pen, but without a firm grip, they kept escaping and rolling around the carpet, with her following closely behind.

On the armchair, Mr Edozie sat watching the television, focused on the summer sports summary in the news. A lot had happened. From the Euros, to Andy Murray's victory, and Zika virus in Rio – the news anchors commented on all the achievements and disappointments. As the Olympic footage was shown, Adaora took her eyes off Chidera and was glued to the screen. She relived Usain

Bolt's three gold medals, appreciating Team GB's best Olympics in modern times: coming home with 67 medals.

Chidera bumped into Adaora's leg. Smiling, Adaora looked down and redirected her path. Her phone began to ring. Hearing it, but unable to locate it, Adaora scrambled around, finally seeing it down the side of the sofa. It was not a number she recognised.

'Hello?'

'Hey, Ada.' She could barely hear the voice. It sounded familiar, but the line wasn't clear and the voice was cracking.

'Sorry, I can't hear you. Who is this?'

'It's Charles.'

Adaora's heart stopped. After hours spent daydreaming about him, suddenly he was on the other end of the line! He sounded broken. Adaora knew something was wrong.

'Hey, is everything alright?' she asked.

'Not really. Can I please see you today, if you are not busy?' There was an urgency in his tone.

Squinting, Adaora wondered what could have caused him to sound so distraught. 'I am babysitting Chidera till Nkechi gets back from her meeting in a couple hours. Is 7 o'clock fine?'

'Yes. I can meet you at Mina's, if that's okay.'

Hanging up the phone, Adaora was in a daze. The whole conversation seemed surreal. Something was definitely wrong; but the fact that, out of all people, he had called her – *it must mean something*. She scanned her memory, trying to piece together any information he had shared that would warrant such a reaction. She was completely stumped, but also happy that he wanted to see her.

Chidera crashed into her legs again, looking up at Adaora, her arms outstretched. Adaora bent over and picked her up, tickling her under the chin. Chidera was laughing, and fascinated by Adaora's hair clip, kept reaching to pull it out. Moving her head sharply, Adaora laughed. Trying to distract her, Adaora began singing nursery rhymes, helping Chidera do the actions to her favourite song; head, shoulders, knees and toes. They played until Nkechi returned and Chidera was due to have a nap. Saying nothing to her sister, but rushing to get ready, Adaora redid her hair, sprayed her favourite perfume and left.

When Adaora arrived, Charles was already sitting in their usual corner.

Adaora walked over to Mina and gave her a hug, whispering, 'How long has he been here?'

'He came in about half an hour ago. He looks distressed.'

'Okay. Thanks. Let me go and find out what happened. Usual, please.'

Standing up tall, Adaora walked over to Charles, slowly taking in the image of him. *He looks so handsome*, she thought, remembering what he looked like underneath his clothes, what his touch felt like, the sensations he made her feel. Her heart began to pound as she got closer to him; all her emotions rising to the surface. Noticing his distress, Adaora urged herself to focus.

Charles stood, and gave her a hug. Adaora inhaled his aftershave, and fell in love all over again. Letting go of her too soon, Charles pulled out her chair. As he sat down, Adaora saw the stress lines on his forehead and the trails of tears down his cheeks. Putting her feelings to one side, she became increasingly concerned. 'Charles what's going on? Is everything okay?'

He hesitated as Mina brought Adaora's tea over. 'Careful – it's really hot.'

'Thanks,' she replied, distracted.

Charles looked over at Adaora. 'Thank you for coming. I really need to talk to you.'

'Yes – you had me worried on the phone. Even more so, now I can see you. What has happened?' she asked, slowly tilting the teacup onto on the tip of her tongue. *Mina was right!* she thought, feeling her tongue recoil at the heat.

'Ada, do you remember my foster carer I told you about?'

'Yes, vaguely. Mrs Morgan?'

'Yes, her,' Charles replied, his voice breaking. His eyes closed momentarily. He let out a small whisper: 'She passed away a few days ago.'

Adaora's face saddened. She wanted to reach out and hold him, but didn't know if it was appropriate. 'Oh, my goodness! Charles, I'm so sorry to hear that. I know how much she meant to you. What happened?'

Charles bit his bottom lip, attempting to stop it from quivering. 'She had a stroke a few weeks ago, but never really recovered from it and her body eventually gave up.'

'That is so sad. I'm so sorry.'

'I just needed to talk to you. I haven't told anyone else about my past and you are the only person I trust.'

The words swirled around Adaora's abdomen, making her feel special. It had meant something, that he had called her. She was special. In the back of her mind, she wondered why he hadn't confided in his own girlfriend, but she shoved that thought away.

'Charles, I am glad you still feel like you can talk to me.'

'Yeah, it has been hard trying to deal with it all by myself. I find myself telling everyone I am alright, while I plaster this fake smile on, to stop them from asking.'

'One of the hardest things while grieving can be loneliness and solitude. Wanting to be away from everyone is not the best way to move forward. Find people who you can talk to, release some of your frustrations, and do not be afraid to cry.' As she was speaking, Adaora suddenly had a horrible thought that he might only want to talk to her because she was a therapist.

'I understand,' Charles murmured. 'But it is easier said than done. I have no one else in my life at this point. All the people who have ever mattered have passed away.'

What happened to the woman she had seen him with? Adaora pushed away her curiosity. 'Yes, I can't even begin to imagine. But what I will say is that I am always here for you, if you need to talk.'

'Thanks, Ada, I really appreciate that.'

Charles signalled for Mina to come over. He ordered some more coffee and made sure to ask her to use the Rio beans that brought out the flavour. Charles smiled.

'What is it?' Adaora asked.

'I was never much of a coffee person until you introduced me to this place. Now all other coffee places are obsolete, in comparison.'

'I told you Mina had the best coffee in London,' Adaora said, boastfully.

'You did, indeed.'

There was silence as they both looked at each other. Adaora was the first to shift her eyes elsewhere.

Charles cleared his throat, gazing into the mid-distance. 'I was with Mrs Morgan when she passed away. It was a moment I enjoyed, just before her flame finally blew out. We spoke. Her speech was severely impaired, but I was able to understand what she was saying. One thing she said… has had me thinking. It was about regret. She told me things she'd regretted in her life. And it was sad, because those regrets made her depressed, even on her deathbed. I tried to comfort her, but all she was interested in was telling me to make sure I had no regrets.' He looked down at his hands, slowly flexing his fingers in wonder.

'Do you have any regrets?'

'When she told me that, only one thing kept coming into my mind.'

Adaora dared herself to imagine that this was the moment she had been waiting for. Her mouth felt dry, and she looked up at him shyly. 'What was that?'

Charles was staring intensely into Adaora's eyes, taking all of her in, replaying all she had meant to him. His heart felt secure in her presence. He smiled at her. 'It was you.'

Pounding chest, shock and awe overwhelmed Adaora in that moment. Butterflies in her stomach did gymnastic flips. She didn't realise that she had been holding her breath. She tried to appear unmoved, while inside, her emotions were in uproar.

Before Adaora could say a word, Charles continued. 'A few months ago, I met someone else and we were dating for a while. But... I had no connection with her. Well, maybe I did, but I was comparing her with you. I tried and waited to see if I would feel something for her, but... I didn't. She was a nice person, but she deserved to be with someone who could reciprocate the love she was showing me.'

Adaora could barely breathe, again. The obstacle, the woman who had stopped her pursuing the love of her life, was no longer in the picture. Waves of joy began to wash over her soul. Adaora was the reason he had broken up with her, because she wasn't Adaora.

Her tongue was dry. She could only ask something banal. 'How did she take it?'

'She was grateful that I was honest with her, and we ended it amicably. But... the more I thought about what Mrs Morgan said, the more I've thought about you and why it didn't work out for us. My desire for wanting children has not changed, but I had to look at regret on a scale. What would I regret more, later down the line? Not having children? Or knowing that I let you go?'

Adaora stared, wondering if this was just one of her daydreams. Across the table, Charles' hand reached out and found Adaora's, placing it over hers, and his thumb began to trace circles over it. Adaora felt the warmth inside her increase with every touch, tingles running up and down her arm.

Charles continued. 'I have lived thus far without children, but these past few months without you have been painful. You are the best thing that has happened to me, and I need you in my life.'

Shock ricocheted through her body, drumming silence into her spine. Charles had now interlocked his fingers into hers. Adaora closed her eyes, and opened them again. It wasn't a dream.

'Charles... the joy I am feeling right now... words cannot do it justice. But I have to come clean about something.'

'What is it?' Charles looked stricken, suddenly expecting rejection.

Adaora paused. 'Two months ago, I tried calling you several times, but your line was dead. So I just went to your office to tell you something, but I never made it because I saw you with the woman you just spoke about. Seeing you kiss her deflated me, and that was the end for me. That was when I finally decided to let you go.'

Charles straightened his back, unsure how to react. Knowing that he had missed out on seeing her when she had wanted to talk, because of a woman he had no connection with, bothered him. 'Ada,' he began, squeezing her hand gently, 'what were you going to tell me that day?'

Adaora took a deep breath. 'I had been thinking, about you. About us. I couldn't get you off my mind. I was distracted all the time, even at work. I came to your office because I needed to talk to you, face to face.' She squeezed his hand, feeling her palms sweating. 'Things have changed in me. I always thought I had no maternal bone in my body. I was so sure that motherhood wasn't for me. Yet, since my niece was born, something is different. I don't feel the same, anymore. Love conquers all. Despite all the hate in the world and the horrendous way she was conceived, she brings in so much love.'

Charles's face exploded into a grin. His countenance had completely changed and he was sitting at the edge of the chair, anticipating, but he still needed to hear her explanation. 'So, Ada, what exactly are you saying?'

Adaora looked at him and smiled. 'I guess I am saying – I am never ruling out kids.'

Leaping out of his chair, Charles hugged her so tightly that he lifted her feet off the ground, before looking deep into her eyes and kissing her intimately. Mina and the only other customer in the shop smiled at each other.

'Ada, I love you and I never want to lose you again.'

Ada gasped, still amazed. 'The fact that you were ready to compromise on having children – to be with me – means so much to me, I don't think you understand! I love you, too, Charles,' she said softly, burying her head into his chest.

In Adaora's office, Paige sat comfortably. Her face was flushed, she looked healthy and Adaora was pleased with the progress she had been making since her suicide attempt. Her sister Emma came up often during their sessions, and their relationship was a pivotal part of their discussions.

'Can I ask you something?' Paige asked.

'Yeah, sure. Go ahead.'

'What does sisterhood mean to you?'

'What a question! Let me think. Well, sisterhood... is... erm.' Struck by the question, Adaora paused, looking upwards. 'That is a really good question and I have never actually had to answer it before. Hold on – let me gather my thoughts.'

Paige sat patiently, twirling the ends of her hair around her fingers.

Adaora considered, and spoke. 'I guess, for me, sisterhood has a lot to do with unity. Unity – as well as friendship, love and trust. It involves a special bond. Sometimes, it's biological; other times, it's just having a special friend who's earned that place in your heart.' Paige was listening intently as Adaora continued: 'It is knowing that there are others ready to fight your corner, ready to support you, encourage you and lift you up when you fall. An unconditional love, so that, no matter what happens, they will be there for you. Even when you make mistakes. Someone you can tell your secrets to. A person you trust.'

While Adaora shared her thoughts, Paige smiled and nodded knowingly in agreement. 'Yes, I agree with you. Thank you for sharing. It means a lot to me.'

'You're welcome, Paige. Thanks for the great question. Really made me think. You know, there is something I have been waiting to tell you.'

'Really?' Paige had no idea what it could be. 'What is it?'

Adaora shuffled the papers on her table, trying to keep a straight face. She was excited to share the news and see Paige's reaction.

'I know how much family means to you, and the questions you have about your younger years. So, I decided to take matters into my own hands, put on my detective glasses and go on a search to find your dad…' Adaora paused.

Paige's face was a maze of wonderment. 'And… what happened?' she asked eagerly.

'I found him.'

Those three words penetrated to Paige's core and the force lifted her out of her seat, with a huge grin. 'How? Where? When?' she asked frantically.

'A few months ago. But I couldn't tell you. Social services have just cleared it for him to visit you and Emma.'

Paige's knees lost all strength and she kneeled on the floor, her face a mess of tears. Her sobs were heartfelt; an outpouring of appreciation for everything Adaora had done. She couldn't find words. Adaora knelt beside her, handed her a tissue and smiled.

Through her tears, Paige managed an earnest 'Thank you! Thank you so much.'

'You're so welcome, Paige. I'm sure that this is just the beginning of your story. I'm hopeful that you and Emma will be reunited and that you will have the opportunity to gain clarity and understanding about your childhood. Seeing you happy, especially after everything you've been through, is such a joy.'

The new season of the Premier League had begun, and, sitting with a cold beer in his hand, Mr Edozie was fixated on the football: West Ham vs Chelsea. After much badgering from his wife about her precious Nollywood films, he had extended the Sky system to the bedroom and kitchen, so they were both happy – and he could watch the football in peace.

His phone rang as Chelsea were about to take a shot at goal, so he ignored it. After the ball went out for a corner, Mr Edozie reluctantly answered.

As the person on the line began to talk, Mr Edozie's countenance changed, becoming solemn and serious. Putting his beer down, he looked around for the remote. Unable to locate it, he walked over and physically put the television on mute. An eerie silence filled the space as Mr Edozie listened intently, nodding his head every so often. There wasn't much vocal input from Mr Edozie, since the other person had much to say.

Ten minutes later, a break occurred, enabling Mr Edozie to respond. 'Okay, my brother, I have heard what you have said. I will make arrangements on my side, and from there, we will see what happens, *Jisike.*'

Mr Edozie put the phone down and immediately called his wife. His bellow had Mrs Edozie running out from the kitchen.

'*Ogini,* why are you shouting my name like that?' she scolded, waiting for an answer.

'Patrick's father just called me. Their family want to come and make peace, but we need Nkechi to cooperate. I need you to talk to your daughter, *biko.* They plan on coming this weekend. He was very apologetic for Patrick's behaviour and insisted that they must come and make things right, the proper way. Even if this relationship is to be finished, we must conduct ourselves properly.'

'Okay, I have heard, but you know your daughter can be as stubborn as you! Let's hope she will listen to me.'

Mr Edozie returned his attention to the football.

Before the match had ended, Mrs Edozie appeared at the door, shaking her head. 'I told you that girl would not listen to me. She has refused.'

'Call Nkechi.'

Moments later Nkechi came downstairs after receiving the summons from her mother. She looked wary. 'Yes, dad?'

'The Eze family have made contact and would like to make things right with our family...'

'Yes. But daddy...'

'Nkechi!' he said loudly. 'Let me finish.' Huffing, Nkechi waited for her father to continue. 'We are very peaceful people in this family. We must honour our traditions. The Eze family – not just Patrick, but his kinsmen – will be here this weekend. At least both families can then go their separate ways and have closure.'

Unhappy with the situation, but unable to object to her dad's wishes, Nkechi reluctantly accepted the news.

Saturday evening, expectation filled the house: an atmosphere of unknowing, mixed with the cultural smells of a well-attended kitchen. The women of the house – with baby Chidera – were sitting in the kitchen, tending to food and watching a Nollywood film chosen by Mrs Edozie. They knew that, at any minute, the doorbell would ring.

Nkechi was in a strange mood, barely talking to anyone, willing the night to be over. Adaora had Chidera on her lap, playing a game of peekaboo.

In the living room, Mr Edozie, his brother, and Chidi sat waiting. Although Saturday night football was on, Mr Edozie had sacrificed it, knowing that he wouldn't be able to watch it with guests. Chidi shifted in the sofa. He was very protective of his sister and did not want anything to happen that would cause her upset. He was fidgeting, not making eye contact with anyone, trying to distract himself with his phone. A girl was texting him, but he was uninterested and unable to keep up the conversation.

The doorbell rang and Chidi sprang up from his chair. He opened the door and greeted all who stood behind it, surprised to see Charles as part of the entourage.

Patrick looked defeated, his shoulders slouched, unable to maintain eye contact as he entered the living room.

'*Nnọọ,*' Mr Edozie and his brother greeted them.

'*Dalu,*' Patrick's father replied. 'Thank you for welcoming us again to your lovely home. Unfortunately, this time the circumstances are not as joyful.'

'Please – have a seat.'

Before sitting, Patrick's father handed two bottles of Remy Martins to Mr Edozie. He accepted the gift and called for the kola nut to be brought into the sitting room. After the prayer over the kola nut, each person was given a piece to eat.

'Chidi, go and call your sisters and your mother.'

When Chidi entered the kitchen, the women knew it was their time to join the gathering. Irritated, Nkechi took Chidera from Adaora, rolling her eyes, and then she walked slowly behind the others.

Peering into the living room, flashbacks of her traditional introduction interrupted her thoughts. The same people were gathered, but this time for the ending of their beginning. She shook her head, wishing she were anywhere else, almost willing Chidera to cry so she could take her upstairs. Adaora's and Charles's eyes met and smiled at each other. Nkechi was still standing in the door frame, until her father motioned for her to come closer and to sit opposite Patrick and his kinsmen. She sat. Patrick briefly met her eyes as she glanced upwards and tried to offer a smile, but Nkechi looked away, jiggling Chidera on her knee. The baby beamed at them all, making it impossible not to smile back.

With them both in front of him, Patrick began to feel overwhelmed with emotion, his heart thumping, his hands clammy. As Chidera wriggled in her mother's lap, unwilling to sit still, Patrick could not take his eyes off her.

Patrick's dad cleared his throat and addressed the room. 'We are here today to right a wrong, a wrong caused to this family by Patrick Eze: my son. They say a wise man will learn from his mistakes, but a wiser man will learn from other people's mistakes. Patrick came to me because he wanted to make amends, but it came to nothing when the young lady refused to hear him out. Even if she had accepted, this meeting would still have had to happen.'

All the elder men in the room nodded their heads in agreement.

'Nkechi, our daughter, we are so sorry for what happened to you and for our son abandoning you when you needed him the most. Please accept our apology.'

Licking her finger and wiping a smudge of food off Chidera's chin, Nkechi remained silent.

Mr Edozie was about to speak, when Patrick's father interrupted him. 'Sorry – before you speak, Patrick has something he would like to say.'

Patrick straightened his posture, and looked directly at Nkechi. 'Words cannot describe how low I feel right now, knowing the pain that I caused you.' He paused, his voice cracking, his eyes heavy with tears. Tears were not a man's behaviour he had been taught, and he tried to fight them. Nkechi was unmoved. 'Nkechi, there are not enough words to make right my wrongs. I abandoned you when you needed me the most. I was selfish. I know that now. I have spent every day thinking about you, wishing you were with me. Sorry is not enough. Words are not enough. I understand that.'

She looked up at him and noticed the pain in his eyes, the seriousness in his tone, the love in his voice. Nkechi face softened. The bitterness she had held against him began to leak out of her heart as she listened to him speak.

Seeing her looking into his eyes, he gained confidence. 'Nkechi. I love you. With everything that is in me. Without you, I have suffered much and I realise and understand better now the difference you make in my life. I am not me, without you. When you were in Nigeria, my heart was broken. I did everything in my power to get you back. I needed you. I felt like less of a man for not being able to protect you. Knowing that your life was in the hands of evil men consumed my every thought.' His face had twisted in distress, lines furrowing his forehead at the recollection. But his eyes softened, looking at her. 'When God brought you back to me, I just wanted our love story to continue, to be yours forever. But you being pregnant. It rocked me. I couldn't fathom how to love a child that was not mine. I retreated. I chickened out. But... I made a mistake. I thought I couldn't do it.' He paused. 'I was wrong. I can. And if you let me, I will. I want you back and I am ready to raise Chidera as my own.'

Gasps filled the room. Adaora had her hand over her mouth, covering a silent scream. Shock flitted across all the kinsmen's faces.

'If you would allow me,' Patrick said, uncertainly.

Nkechi was overcome. Each sentence had poured healing into her wounds. As his declaration settled in her soul, tears sprang from her eyes and flooded down her face. She nodded.

Patrick knelt before her and reached out his arms to receive Chidera. Nkechi hesitated, looking over at Adaora, who smiled and nodded.

Chidera playfully giggled and reached out to Patrick, and Nkechi followed her lead, slowly handing her over. Taking a deep breath, Patrick smiled, Chidera's presence in his arms causing the tears to unleash.

Chidera's chubby hands patted his face, dabbing away the tears. Patrick's father handed him a tissue, but Patrick used it instead to wipe Nkechi's eyes.

The room was full of happiness at the reparation. Even Chidi was content with what was happening.

Walking over to Adaora, Charles embraced her tightly and then greeted Mrs Edozie warmly. Overjoyed at her daughter's reuniting with their partners Mrs Edozie, reflecting on how far they had come, lifted her eyes to the heavens in silent thanks.

'My dear daughter.' Mr Edozie put his arm around Nkechi's shoulder and squeezed her tightly. The embrace made Nkechi cry even more.

'Adaora,' Patrick said. 'Could you take Chidera for me, please?'

Adaora retrieved her niece, throwing her playfully into the air before tickling her under her chin. Charles, watching Adaora so involved and happy with Chidera, smiled knowingly to himself.

Still on his knees, Patrick pulled out a ring from his pocket. 'Kechi, I want everyone here to bear witness to what I am saying, here, today. I want you to be my wife and I want to protect and provide for you and Chidera until the day that I die. You make me a better man and I would not want to spend the rest of my life with anyone else. I love you. Will you marry me?'

Falling to her knees, too, Nkechi gasped. 'Yes,' she said softly, handing her left hand to Patrick. 'Yes, yes, and yes! I love you too.'

As Patrick placed the ring on her finger, Nkechi threw her arms around his neck and they held a long embrace. Patrick kissed her neck gently, whispering his love into her skin.

After a few moments, Patrick pulled out a set of keys from his back pocket.

'Do you remember that house we went to visit, just before everything happened? Well, these are the keys to our new home!' he exclaimed, jangling them.

Screaming, Nkechi almost knocked him over as she buried herself into his arms once more. 'All I ever wanted was to be with you. You are my soul mate and I truly believe this experience will only make us stronger. I love you, Patrick.'

'I love you, too.'

Against the wall, Adaora looked at Charles adoringly, as they whispered the same words to each other.

The atmosphere had lifted. Mrs Edozie rushed to get celebratory drinks from the kitchen. Chidera wriggled herself onto the floor, crawling around; the only one blissfully unaware of what had happened. Joy and happiness cloaked the families.

Mr Edozie looked down at his granddaughter and smiled.

'What God has written, no man can destroy.'

Acknowledgments

Before I even began to write this book, I spoke to one of my editors, Jemilea. She not only gave me the confidence to go ahead with the story, but through the writing process, she helped me bring the story to life as she had done with my previous book. Thank you for all your hard work, and I know we have more books to work on together in years to come. I would also like thank you, Linda Innes: a fantastic editor who cleaned up and polished the book. I love and appreciate all your input and hope we can continue to work together for future projects.

My many thanks to Alexis Watts, who gave me deep insight to what it is like to be a psychotherapist. The knowledge and information you shared helped me immensely.

To all the women I interviewed to get an insight of what it is to be a woman, much love and gratidude. There are too many to name, but I truly appreciate your time and your patience.

Special thanks to Chinelo Oganya – you have been incredible throughout this journey. Writing the book was the easy part, but finding ways to share it with the world is hard. When I doubted myself, you were there to support and picked me back up. I appreciate your input and guidance and will forever be grateful.

To everyone at The Crib youth project – thanks for the continued support.

To my family, your love and support is what keeps me going. Love you all.

Concern about gang culture is on the rise. Gangs lead young people into danger and create community division, fear and deep distrust. However, the friendship, support, security and sense of belonging they give young people is a powerful draw. Through his Consequences Programme, Emeka Egbuonu aims to give young people a real sense of the consequences of their actions.

Taking a group of young people from London to Los Angeles, he looks at how gang membership has ruined lives in the 'gang capital of the world'. Emeka examines the pain of families who have lost young people to knife crime on the streets of London and tries to identify what drives young people into the vicious cycle of gang culture.

Starting from the slave trade, Emeka's insightful look at the breakdown of the family unit, peer pressure, stereotyping and racism gives an uncompromising message to us all. With interviews and powerful accounts of knife crime on both sides of the Atlantic, this book pulls no punches.

Ambitions of the Deprived chronicles the lives of four teenage friends as they experience life through a lens of contradiction, conflicts and struggles for space and identity. Refusing to be limited by the stereotypical expectations of society due to their race, age 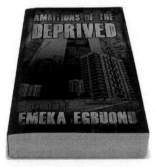 and social status, they pledge to rise above their circumstances and succeed against the odds. At the brink of adulthood, they have high aspirations and great motivation for careers in teaching, law and the Olympics.

In their destitute area, violent gang members and a local murder uproot the boys' plans when one of them, Junior, becomes unwittingly caught up in the crime. His innocence is of little importance when the trial tarnishes him with the same brush as the perpetrators. Family in disbelief, friends in uproar, community in protest – the effect is devastating. As the pressure mounts, ambitions are put on hold, friendships are tested and loyalties broken. Unless the trial can be overturned, labels will continue to criminalise them.